THE

NPC

# THE NPC

SASHA -
A WISE MAN ONCE SAID:
" SHITHEADS GONNA SHITHEAD."

THAT MAN? ABRAHAM LINCOLN.

NAW, JUST KIDDING. IT WAS ME.

— Tim

# TIMOTHY DAVID

Copyright © 2021 by Timothy David

All rights reserved.

ISBN:  978-0-9882278-1-1 (print)
          978-0-9882278-2-8 (ebook)

Cover design by Jeff Brown *(www.jeffbrowngraphics.com)*
Book design by Wordzworth *(www.wordzworth.com)*
Editing by Nerine Dorman and Nancy Osa
Bullshit detection and correction services by David Petrini

*For Shawna, my favorite quest giver.*

# DAY
# 1

# Southend – Deodin

The door of the library opened with a strained, rusty groan. Several shouts sounded from the entry foyer as six men poured into the room. Deodin couldn't make out every excited shout and cry, but the general message involved "finding him" and "killing him."

As usual, Deodin was the "him" in question.

He sighed. He wanted to read the entire book, but he had run out of time. The book was far too heavy and cumbersome to take with him. He ripped out a single page and clumsily stuffed it into his pocket. As he returned the book to its shelf, he glanced over the second-floor railing to see his attackers. They were clad in red pants and tunics.

Red mages.

As they spread out to cover more ground, Deodin felt a small touch of relief. It was late and the library was otherwise empty. Whatever idiocy came next, it wouldn't involve any of the innocent people from Southend.

Certainly, red mages were dangerous and prone to violence. Members of this sect of wizards abused magic to pursue their own selfish, personal goals. For most of his adult life, Deodin had found himself on the wrong side of their sinister plots and self-serving schemes. Fortunately, Deodin's enemies were color coded. Any mage wearing a red costume would try to kill him on sight.

Deodin heard more noises from the murderous search party on the floor below him. They were shouting instructions about surrounding him and destroying him with deadly magic.

While any reasonable person would fear for his life, Deodin did not feel threatened or concerned. Instead, he was annoyed at the timing of it all. This whole encounter was trite and inconvenient.

The interruptions to Deodin's agenda were normal, for he was *sheyaktu*, a word humanity had borrowed from the ancient orcs. The term described his almost transcendent mastery of magical power. He wielded supernatural abilities that far outstripped the likes of the red mages. From time dilation to the changing of inertial laws, Deodin's toolbox rendered him a blend of man, magic, and weapon.

Being *sheyaktu*, "adventurer" became his unavoidable career path. With this vocation came a danger that always found him, regardless of context, circumstance, or plausibility. Whether his adversaries be monsters or men, Deodin would slay more enemies on a given Thursday afternoon than a soldier might encounter in an entire tour of duty.

A sensation of obligation took hold in Deodin's mind, conveniently arranged as a bulleted checklist:

*Escape Southend:*
- ☑ *Recover the orc poem*
- ☐ *Survive the red mages' assault*
- ☐ *Escape the burning library*
- ☐ *Flee to the docks*

He paused for a moment.
*Burning library? The library isn't on fire—*

On cue, one of the mages attacked with a fireball spell, hurling a blazing sphere through the air toward Deodin. The attack missed and the incendiary burst landed at the center of the bookshelves behind him, setting them ablaze. The flames would soon spread and consume the entire second story and the wooden support pillars that framed the stone blocks of the library.

*Ah. That fire.*

Despite the frequency of these kill-or-be-killed encounters and random acts of arson, Deodin was paradoxically at peace. After all, being a so-called "god killer," he rarely felt as if he was in actual danger. Run-ins with mages, monsters, and murderers threatened his punctuality, but seldom his well-being. Eventually, he had come to regard these battles as necessary chores in his life, much like shaving his face or trimming his toenails.

The far greater challenge, he had learned, was his singular, ongoing struggle with the world. Deodin didn't feel unlucky so much as a target: it seemed as though life itself conspired against him.

He came to refer to this conflict as his battle with "the Universe." While other people enjoyed a simple daily routine, the Universe dragged Deodin through a life of perpetual action, adventure, and danger.

*Like this bullshit.* Deodin frowned as the red mages climbed the stairs toward him en masse. The fire had spread to the heavy timbers of the library's frame and now burned steadily. The room filled with a thick, choking smoke. The mages should be fleeing for their lives, not pressing their foolish attack.

Yet, he didn't blame them. The Universe had brought both parties here, to Southend and this library. A series of quests had driven Deodin to explore a mystery that threatened the Crown, the region of the world a hundred miles to the north. This confrontation at the library was merely a piece of the puzzle he was compelled to solve.

From what he had learned during his adventures, the Crown was in great peril. The orcs of the region had begun to unify and prepare for war. Within weeks, a horde would march on one of the Crown's major cities. The death toll of such an attack would be measured in the tens of thousands.

Deodin, *sheyaktu* and professional hero, was the only one who could stop the threat that promised to exterminate every man, woman, and child of the Crown.

Deodin felt an ominous tremor in the floor. The fire had reached the support pillars of the library's domed ceiling. Mortar between the ceiling's heavy stones had started to flake away and the burning support timber began to yield. In just a few more moments, the ceiling would collapse and crush him under tons of flaming debris and rubble. Deodin ran from the mages toward a stained-glass window at the end of a hallway lined with flaming bookcases.

He dove, shattering the second-story window, just as the ceiling gave way. As he fell, Deodin channeled a magical spell to momentarily slow the passage of time. He landed softly and silently, with enough clearance to safely witness the total collapse of the library. Flames shot upward while tons of stone brick and burning rubble fell inward, destroying whatever, and whoever, was unfortunate enough to remain inside.

Deodin raised his eyebrows. The timing of his escape and the total ruin of the library felt a bit much. Nearly every milestone in his adventuring portfolio included an overly dramatic spectacle such as this. He sighed again and reached into his pocket to make sure that the clue had survived the ordeal. He unfolded the page he'd torn from the book, satisfied that it would serve his purposes.

*Escape Southend:*

- ☑ *Recover the orc poem*
- ☑ *Survive the red mages' assault*
- ☑ *Escape the burning library*
- ☐ *Flee to the docks*

Whether it made sense or not, he would travel to the Crown, stop the orc horde, and save humanity. Adventure, drama, and heroics came with the territory—the fate that Deodin had accepted for most of his adult life.

Of course he'd do it. Of course he'd investigate the plot that imperiled the Crown. But he wanted something in return. For the first time, he added something to his mental to-do list. If he had to save the world, Deodin would first learn why the Universe demanded it.

# DAY
# 2

# Ruby (The Docks) – Pel

Pelium Stillwater stood on the Ruby pier, waiting for the crew to deploy the gangway. Onboard, Bartlett, the ship's captain, waved to her with both hands. She waved back, relieved that he had arrived and eagerly awaiting the colorful, vulgar explanation for his tardiness.

His ship was hours behind schedule. Even with a stop in Bayhold, a trip from Southend should have put the craft in Ruby by late afternoon. Instead, it had arrived two hours past sunset. With calm seas and a cloudless sky, Pel was concerned about the cause of the delay.

"You're late! I missed an evening *opportunity*," she called, stressing the last word to suggest that her lost appointment was personal.

Pel tucked a tress of her hair behind her ear before withdrawing into her cloak, pulling it over her shoulders and arms. She backed away from the edge of the pier to give the captain enough space to come ashore.

"Well. Sorry to disappoint ya. When you get to be my age, most of your late-night 'opportunities' end in disappointment," the man replied with a playful amount of scorn. His raspy voice had enough weight to carry over the rest of the noise of the dock.

Captain Bartlett skittered down the wet gangplank to greet Pel. He was a surprisingly nimble man for one of his bulky stature and the amount of alcohol in his blood. He strode right past the boundaries of normal personal space and clutched the woman in an embrace.

Once released from his grasp, Pel could recognize him properly: dark hair, tanned skin, intense eyes, and a sincere grin buried under his mottled beard.

"It's good to see you too," she replied with a gasp.

"The brightest facet of Ruby!" he exclaimed, his hands on her shoulders. He looked her over with an almost paternal pride.

"I was worried," she confessed. "You're never late and the seas were calm. The Crown has been so dangerous of late, I had feared the worst."

"Is it that bad up here?" he asked with a sidelong glance. "I hear all kinds of whispers. They can't all be true."

"I don't like what I see," she said.

"With … ah … your actual eyes or your instincts?" he asked delicately. "Because your eyesight is right shitty."

"Instincts," she replied with a smile.

Bartlett sighed.

"Well. We don't pay you to be wrong, do we? What do your instincts tell you? What do I need to know?"

Pel paused, weighing the best way to share the bad news. Even though they were business partners, Bartlett was a dear friend. She had known him for many years and their meetings were normally the highlight of her day. And his as well. She would much rather catch up on his personal life than frighten him with the alarming news of the Crown.

"Nearly every story I hear is related to orcs," she explained. "Nothing within Ruby's walls, but the Crown is alive with scares and sightings. I feared that something happened to you in Bayhold, or even Southend."

Bartlett scoffed. "We never even made it to Bayhold. We were so far behind schedule that we had to come straight here.

There was some sort of fire at Southend's great library. The dockhands weren't available until the fire was contained."

"What caused the fire?" Pel asked.

"They didn't exactly say." Bartlett's tone and the look on his face expressed insincerity. He deliberately turned away to glance at the white, three-spired tower that dominated the city skyline. Bartlett didn't need to say it, but he attributed the fire to the red mages of Southend.

"Total pricks," Bartlett added with a scowl. "Whether in Ruby's Tower, Southend, or anywhere else." After a moment, he spoke with less venom. "Sorry. You were telling me about different savages. What about the orcs of the Crown?"

"Visible, for the first time in a long time. And not just inland, in the mountains. Eight merchant shipments have been lost in the past few weeks, to and from the northern villages. There have been orc sightings and whispers of an Encroachment. Plans are in the works to arm the militia and most of the merchant caravans travel under armed escort."

Bartlett squinted. "Encroachment? Ya, right. The orcs woulda learned their lesson from the last time."

Pel decided that it would be impolite to pick a fight with Bartlett over the nature of orcs, Encroachments, and anything else related to the Crown. The man had never been more than two miles from an ocean or river. He was certainly unqualified to remark about dealings deep within the heart of the Thick, the heavy forest that carpeted most of the region. Instead, she offered a playfully condescending bow of her head.

"If I am wrong, you are welcome to a refund." The captain was a good friend, but he was also a client. He didn't have to like, or even believe, the information she provided as her service.

Deep down, she hoped she was wrong. However, in all her years as Ruby's primary information broker, she had honed her acumen and analytical skills. She was the living library of Ruby's intricate machine of commerce, culture, and politics. Everything about the recent orc activity was atypical and alarming. It was a topic few people wanted to address, but similar reports had come in from every source she had.

Bartlett was astute enough to pick up on her tone and her body language.

"You're serious? Encroachment? It's not just rumors an' whispers?" He was clearly reluctant to fully commit to the grim reality she described.

"I wish I could say otherwise." She sighed.

"Gods, Pel, if anyone else were to tell me that Skycrash was coming again, I'd laugh in their face. You're the only one who would make me look up."

She smiled at Bartlett's flattery. "My reputation is my lifeblood. Fortunately, my bad news is about the possibility of an orc invasion, not another worldwide apocalypse."

"Small comfort." Bartlett snorted. "Unless you have any more terrifying news, can we change the subject? I have other business." He gestured to the ship behind him. *The Maiden's Tears* rested well below her normal water line.

"Late and laden," Pel commented. "What did you intend to offload in Bayhold?"

"Cloth from Southend."

"Let me recommend a man named Winston. He operates a modest shop two blocks east of the Evertorch. He has a huge order and an impending deadline. If you deliver tonight, his workers can get an extra half day of work."

Bartlett nodded. He paused for a moment before clearly being struck by a different thought.

"Oh! Speaking of surplus cloth, I have something for you." He reached into his backpack and produced a crumpled, black ball of cloth. With a flick of his wrist, he revealed the cloth for what it was: a scandalously small woman's undergarment.

A sudden inferno of embarrassment overtook Pel. The only thing brighter than the chagrin on her face was the idiotic grin on his. Bartlett savored her uncomfortable squirm for a moment longer before continuing.

"I kid, Pel!" He crumpled up the underwear and stuffed it into his shirt pocket. "*This* is for you."

From his pack he retrieved a larger garment that promised to cover much more than the one he'd displayed a moment ago. He held it up for her to examine, as it was almost long enough to drag on the ground. Bartlett's gift took shape.

A cloak.

By Ruby standards, it was exotic, something from the southern coast or the East. The garment felt luxurious to the touch, unlike anything Pel had seen in Ruby. A variety of silks made up the inner layer, stitched under a more durable fabric. Its dark, thick leather exterior promised to be sturdy yet was also uncannily supple. The cloak's craftsmanship seemed other-worldly: it was more delicate than her bed linens but was as tough a sail.

Bartlett's gift made an immense improvement over the ragged, dilapidated wrap she currently wore. Bartlett never drew attention to it, but Pel had noticed that he always managed to overbuy stock that would coincidentally replace her most tattered clothes.

"Thank you, Bartlett. It is beautiful."

"You're quite welcome, my dear. The East continues to come to life. The cloak is from a small trade settlement, out past Tomorrow's Gate."

This came as news. Tomorrow's Gate was the very edge of human lands, nearly 250 miles southeast of Ruby. The outpost was the last chance for people to turn back before they ventured into the dangerous, monster-filled region known simply as "the East." Pel had always believed the world beyond Tomorrow's Gate was too dangerous for human settlement. Yet, Bartlett claimed such a community was stable and developed enough to produce a garment like the one she held.

Aside from treasure-seeking expeditions, humankind had avoided the East since the Skycrash event, nearly 350 years before. Any successful colonization of that region could dramatically change the course of human history, to include the Crown and Ruby. This information would be valuable to Pel's local clients.

"This is profound news," she said.

"I spoke to the merchant who sold me the cloak. She said that it was crafted from the hide from one of the murderous mobs of the East." Bartlett chuckled.

Pel paused her exploration of the garment's stitching at Bartlett's mention of "mobs." The word was the Crown's shorthand for the nightmarish creatures found in the Thick. Now, after all these years, what had started as a local colloquialism had made its way to the far south and to foreigners like Bartlett.

"Really," she replied with a polite but obvious skepticism.

"Well. The woman who sold the cloak also said it was imbued with powerful magic of the East. You tell me. How magical is it?"

Pel exhaled with a scoff. "It's not magical in the slightest," she said without hesitation and with total certainty. "But nevertheless, it is beautiful. This must be worth far more than all of our business dealings, past and future."

Her remark was not a polite overstatement. Pel would describe her living as an information broker as "modest." Others would describe it as "impoverished." As he usually did, Bartlett downplayed his generosity.

"Hardly! I bought the entire stock for a handful of copper. Sold out of the rest of them in Southend for a huge margin!"

Pel slipped out of her cloak, exchanging it for the one Bartlett held. Even if it was leftover stock from the merchant's business dealings, it was as lovely as his gesture. She nodded her thanks again.

"Any suggestions about the rest? Or for my trip back south?" Bartlett gestured back to his ship. Their social encounter had run its course and Bartlett still had business to conclude. It was late in the evening, after all.

"For anything else you carry, take it to the Evertorch market. Demand is high. Prices are high. As I said, much of the inland trade has been disrupted. Goods are more scarce than normal. This shipment will sell much better than usual, but I will ask you to be reasonable about your margins. These are my people."

Bartlett scolded her with a dour expression for implying that he might profiteer from the circumstances. She smiled to herself, reminded that he was as noble a man as she had ever met. She trusted him enough to make a wise decision about the next bit of information she would share.

"As for your return here, your holds should be filled with arms and arrows, weapons that can be used by commoners and archers."

"Weapons? You've never suggested anything like that before," Bartlett said quietly. "You really think Encroachment…?"

"I don't know for sure. We can only be certain once we see the orcs on the march. By then, it will be too late. All I can say is that within the next few weeks, I suspect that any weapons you bring here will be purchased. And put to use."

"Well, this is a first-class moral dilemma. Thanks."

"Maybe we'll be lucky. Perhaps the orcs will fight among themselves and Ruby can address other monsters." She glanced at the ominous Tower long enough to make her point. "Regardless, leave as soon as you can. You will have a head start. There are other captains with whom I share the same good-faith arrangement. They will pick up my letters when they arrive. They will know what you know, but they don't dock until tomorrow."

"I expect nothing less, my friend," Bartlett said with a smile and a nod.

Pel's empire of information was founded on a reputation of honesty and fairness, but she still had her favorites. Bartlett's ship was fast enough to reach Southend first and large enough to stop by Bayhold on the way back. Her tip would help him, as it always did.

He reached into his pocket and pulled out a coin purse. She brought her hand out from beneath her new cloak, gesturing for him to put it away.

"Wait until you return."

He looked up with mild surprise.

"Eh? You don't want a share in the guilt in becoming an arms dealer?"

"Not at all. But you will be more generous when your pockets are filled with gold, not silver," she said with a quick waggle of her eyebrow.

"That's more like it," he said with a playful, respectful nod.

He paused momentarily before reaching for something in his shirt pocket. He retrieved the familiar black ball of cloth. Saying nothing, he tucked it into her cloak's outer pocket with a wink and smirk that seemed to say *just in case*. He tapped her heartily on the shoulder, turned back around, and marched up the gangway to the deck of *The Maiden*.

Pel smiled. Bartlett was a noble man and a good friend. She was glad she had waited for him. Her information would help him, she'd see a percentage of his sales, and any weapons he brought would ultimately serve the people of Ruby. It was a satisfying and productive night for everyone.

Business concluded, she decided to head to the Burning Boar, one of Ruby's taverns. Perhaps she could line up business for tomorrow. And, hopefully, Garret would still be there, even after she had backed out of their evening plans.

Her plans changed, though, when she saw something impossible emerge on the far side of the docks.

# THE DISCOURSE ON MAGIC (CHAPTER 1): FOUR AXIOMS

*Excerpted with permission from The Discourse on Magic, by Thierren Dowdy, the noted Grand Mage of the Western Isles (from Chapter 1, Section 1: The Four Axioms)*

The question asked most frequently is, "How does magic work?"

Perhaps I'll spare the reader the time it takes to read this narrative and merely answer the question outright: *we're not entirely sure.*

We can start the conversation with the obvious: Skycrash. However, most of our history focuses on the thousands of giant stones that rained from the sky and the devastation the event created. History tends to focus on the collapse of the eastern empires, the conflicts, and humankind's brush with extinction. If history considers magic at all, it is almost always in the form of the monsters that Skycrash brought with it.

We often forget that magic, and our understanding of it, began about 350 years ago, in the ruins of a fallen world. Only now, as humanity has begun to fully recover, can we begin to study and harness magic.

For those of us who have dedicated ourselves to a discipline that is equally fascinating and frustrating, we can best describe magic as a means by which we can bend certain natural laws, yet we must obey another, different set of practical laws. That is, by use of magic, we can bend or break the known and tested laws of the world, but only with certain limitations.

This brings us to the first axiomatic rule of magic, summarized by a charming metaphor:

- You can borrow from the bank of reality, but only in small amounts, and for only a short time

17

A *spell* is simply an effect that changes the rules of how the world works. Casting that spell is the means by which a magic practitioner shapes that change.

Perhaps the clever reader will wonder the following questions: Why are there these limitations? What's to prevent a mage from doing anything and everything he wants?

This is the excellent transition to the second axiomatic rule of magic that we've been able to learn, throughout our studies:

• The greater the scale of natural law you wish to break, the more difficult that spell is to research and cast

Think of magic as a minor way to cheat natural laws. Perhaps you have forgotten your flint and steel and need to light a fire. You could use magic for this and certainly remain within the first two axiomatic laws. It is a relatively minor thing you wish to accomplish, so it complies with the first law. And it is a very simple spell to cast, so it complies with the second law.

This brings us to the third axiomatic rule of magic we've learned:

• The larger the natural law you wish to break, the more likely you will kill yourself as you try to cast the spell

As far as our research has concluded, this is a truism that lends itself to any practice of any magic, regardless of the goal.

And finally, along the lines of scale, other questions remain: Why isn't magic more widespread? Why aren't there so many mages that everyone can enjoy the fruits that magic can bear? Why can't everyone use magic all the time, for all our problems, forever?

Those of us who study and research magic would like to be able to answer that question in the fourth axiomatic law, but we haven't really been able to agree on how to word it. If the decision were left to me, I'd simply say:

• Magic is not for everyone

# DAY
# 2

# Ruby (The Docks) – Pel

Pel could see magical effects. Nearly three years prior, a permanent version of a magical detection spell had been cast on her. In her eyes, supernatural energy glowed with a blue light and its brightness and shade correlated to the power behind it.

The modification to her vision came at a heavy cost, however. The process had left her nearsighted. Beyond a few paces, the mundane world was blurry, indistinct, and monochromatic. Worse yet, she seldom "enjoyed" the benefits conveyed by her augmented eyesight. Even in Ruby, the most magical place in the civilized world, magical auras were rare.

Nevertheless, she had become an expert in reading and interpreting them. The man on the far side of the dock glowed with magic in a way unlike anything she had seen before. It wasn't just strange or unusual; in her experience, what she saw shouldn't even be possible.

The stranger faced away from her, slinking from the ship toward the buildings along the pier. Contextual clues suggested he had disembarked from *The Maiden*, but because he hadn't descended the gangway, the logical conclusion was that he was a stowaway. It was the only explanation for why Pel hadn't seen him earlier.

Were the circumstances different, she would have called out to Bartlett. Instead, she studied the man with equal parts of curiosity and amazement. The magical aura that surrounded him was beautiful and complex, yet also strange and foreign.

It was powerful as well, considering its brightness. The stowaway was veiled in a glow so intense that she could see him from across the pier.

Finally, whereas magic was almost always a function of concentration and will, every aspect of this man was unusually casual. Even in practiced mages, Pel could see the changes in the glow as their concentration waxed and waned. Such a fluctuation was normally rhythmic or cyclical, like a heartbeat or breathing. The stowaway's aura had no such rhythm or fluctuation. It shone without interruption.

The supernatural energy about the stowaway was not the result of a spell. He did not wear any enchanted items. He was no mere practitioner of spellcraft, like any of the mages of the Tower. The man himself was magical.

Pel assembled the clues. She had spent her entire adult life as an analyst, consuming unrelated sources of information and identifying their commonalities. Looking at the man, she saw something that she had believed to be a myth: *sheyaktu*.

# Ruby (The Evertorch) – Deodin

Known throughout the Crown, Ruby's famous "Evertorch District" was lit by enchanted torches that produced no heat and required no fuel. The lighting was an extravagance intended to symbolize how the mages from the Tower helped improve Ruby's quality of life.

*The lights of a place called "Ruby" should be red*, Deodin thought.

Instead, they glowed a sickly green that was underpowered, unflattering, unpleasant, and gave the entire area an unhealthy feel. The market's mood reflected its lighting: dismal, depressing, and miserable.

Deodin stood at the edge of a deserted alley, peering into the giant courtyard where merchants and vendors had aligned nearly two hundred tents and canopies in neat rows, surrounded by simple one- and two-story buildings. This hub of commerce may not have been attractive, but it was convenient. Deodin experienced a mild, familiar sensation as he overlooked the quad. The Universe had compelled him with a task.

*Gather equipment for your journey:*
- [ ] *Tunic*
- [ ] *Boots*
- [ ] *Tools and equipment pack*

The Crown was a vast region, a sprawling world that covered hundreds of square miles that were greatly diverse in topography and climate. From the fog layer of the coast to the temperate rolling hills of the interior, the dense forest of the Thick, and the ice-peaked points of the mountains, one might encounter all types of conditions. It was foolish to travel unprepared.

Deodin stopped at a merchant tent, his gaze landing on a magnificent leather corselet that was outrageously superior to every other item in the store. The basic piece of body armor was matte black and its stylings were stealthy, sexy, and dangerous. It embodied everything he wanted to look like. While holding its glorious sleeve, Deodin imagined himself lurking in the shadows, invisibly stalking his enemies, striking from a blind spot, and dealing instant death.

"I want this," Deodin said with wide eyes, mostly to himself. For the first time in a great while, he desired something sold by a vendor. Most of the adventuring gear he encountered in the world was decidedly mundane or poorly made. Only occasionally did he feel that an item was truly exceptional in craftsmanship and quality.

Yet, whenever he found such an item, he seldom wanted it. Those who designed and crafted fine, magically imbued gear seemed to categorically suffer from an impairment of style and good taste. Nearly everything Deodin encountered in his travels was a complete eyesore. Often, patterns or hues would horribly clash with everything else. And should an item pass the color challenge, it would likely be outfitted with decorations or accents that conflicted with Deodin's modest, modern sensibilities. Horns and tusks? You got it. Feathers and beads? Of course. Skulls? Here, have a dozen.

Finally, if the garment was color appropriate and free from horns, hooves, and heads, it would likely feature other design choices that hindered Deodin's adventurous lifestyle. Many of the armor pieces were decorated with hard edges that would collect water or snag on vegetation. And in some instances, a suit of armor would be fitted with spikes that posed significant, ironic safety hazards to the wearer.

The lesson he had learned over time was that if a garment promised to make his adventuring life easier by augmenting his powers, it would almost certainly look ridiculous. Yet what he saw in front of him was just a sensible, handsome, hard-leather corselet. Simply designed, reasonably color-neutral, and excellently crafted.

*No ridiculous shoulder pads!* He smiled.

The first two words out of the merchant's mouth, however, crushed his hopes.

"Greetings, adventurer."

Deodin sighed and gazed at the leather armor again. Deep down, he knew he wouldn't be walking away with it.

The merchant's phrasing was wrong for this situation. The man should have used nearly any label other than "adventurer" when greeting a potential customer. Deodin carried no weapons or equipment and was completely underdressed for adventure. His need for such gear was the reason for being in the market in the first place.

Rather than a neutral greeting to a customer, the merchant's words were a clumsy segue to something else.

"I see that you wish to upgrade your armor to the Corselet of Impenetrable Darkness." The merchant gestured to the garment that Deodin had been eyeing.

"I wish to *buy* the armor," Deodin clarified.

He retrieved a bag of coins he had hidden in his breeches, more wealth than the entire Evertorch market would see in a month. Deodin shook the pouch to emphasize just how much money it represented. Surely, a tiny fraction of this bag would be payment enough.

The merchant didn't flinch.

"This is a reward for those who serve my organization, the Trade Cabal. To acquire it, you must complete a series of tasks. First, to summon the spirit of Longkwestchaen, you will need to light the fires of eternal vision," the merchant narrated. "Deep within the bowels of Blackheart Mountain, you will find the Prince of Ashes, an evil monster born of both man and fire. Slay him and return with his heart."

Blackheart Mountain, its bowels, and every other part of it were located northeast of Stoneheart Point, hundreds of miles away—well past the Thick and deeply into the monster-dominated ruins of the East. A journey there was a preposterous detour from Deodin's plans, never mind the fact that something called the "Prince of Ashes" dwelled in its depths.

"This is money," Deodin explained, opening the bag to show the merchant what was inside. "I can exchange the money for goods and services. This is how commerce works."

"With the heart in hand, you can begin the ritual to summon the spirit," the merchant replied stubbornly.

"After I summon the thing, I can have, or buy, the corselet?"

"No," replied the merchant. He continued, much more interested in his explanation of the tasks than in closing a sale. "Then you must slay the spirit and collect its protoplasm. The protoplasm serves as fuel for the Beacon of Awakening, which must then be taken to the icy tips of the Crystal Spire."

Naturally, the Crystal Spire was practically on the other side of the continent.

"Once in the Crystal Spire, The Beacon of Awakening—"

"Do you have anything for sale that doesn't involve multiple journeys to the furthest reaches of the world?" Deodin asked with a sigh. He cast a longing, regretful gaze at the Corselet of Never-Going-To-Happen.

The merchant nodded at a garment that could only be described as a cylinder of cloth attached perpendicularly to two other cylinders of cloth. It resembled a jacket, but it seemed more like a child's drawing had come to life, rather than something intentionally crafted by a professional. It was also orange and purple, bold color choices in the best of circumstances.

"Can I pay for the black one and subcontract these chores to locals?" Deodin asked, jiggling and jingling the positively enormous amount of coin he held. The gesture was a final, pleading effort to remind the merchant of how sales traditionally worked.

The merchant hardly paused, certainly not long enough to pay serious attention to Deodin's question.

"Once in the Crystal Spire, The Beacon of Awakening—"

"I'll take the hideous one," Deodin said.

\* \* \*

Deodin surveyed the market and evaluated his current set of objectives.

*Gather equipment for your journey:*
- ☑ *Tunic*
- ☐ *Boots*
- ☐ *Tools and equipment pack*

Fortunately, the boot merchant was not a gatekeeping questgiver. In fact, there was nothing interesting or exotic in the inventory. As boot vendors went, he was appropriately pedestrian. Deodin began the transaction by nodding to the boots on the far side of the table, implicitly asking their price.

"Fifty curdains, then," the merchant said.

Deodin had no idea what that meant.

Even before Skycrash, Ruby had a history of isolationism. It seemed completely within the city's character to use a proprietary, local currency when everyone else used the standard of gold, silver, and copper.

"How many silver is that?" Deodin asked.

The merchant seemed unprepared for that question. He glanced over his shoulder conspicuously, his face running flush with color. He displayed all the behaviors of someone trying to be sneaky, yet none of the characteristics to suggest he was any good at it. After an eternity of deliberation, he reached an answer.

"Two hundred."

It was an outrageous price, for certain, perhaps ten times the cost of similar boots elsewhere.

"Do you also demand a series of chores, each of which requires the internal organs of a monster?" Deodin asked, briefly wondering how sustainable such an economy could be.

"Costs more if ya spendin' silver," the shoemaker explained, even though the man's body language suggested that the actual reason was much more complex.

Deodin paused. He could pay the price, but the scam was all wrong. The man's demeanor was wrong. The merchant was preoccupied about someone or something else, not the customer he was currently fleecing.

"A hundred," Deodin replied.

The merchant agreed and made no additional counter-offer. It seemed he wanted to move on with the transaction more than Deodin did.

* * *

The life of an adventurous *sheyaktu* came with a great number of inexplicable idiosyncrasies, most of which were annoying and tedious.

However, there were occasional perks.

Deodin stood before one of the merchants in the market and emptied the junk in his pockets onto the table. The collection included broken crystal shards, a clump of seaweed, a patch of silk cloth, and the wings from a blue butterfly. He gently cupped his hands around the pile and slid it across the table.

"A hundred and twenty curdains," the merchant said almost immediately, absently counting out the sum and handing it over. This exchange rate was impossibly favorable.

Deodin suppressed the urge to groan. *Had I known about the nonstandard currency, I would have done this first. I could have avoided the whole ordeal with the boot merchant.*

He bought a backpack and adventuring equipment from the very same vendor.

*Gather equipment for your journey:*
- ☑ *Tunic*
- ☑ *Boots*
- ☑ *Tools and equipment pack*

# Ruby (The Evertorch) – Pel

Pel realized she wasn't the only one who followed the stowaway. Whatever he had done in the market had created a reaction. As the stranger left the square, several of the merchants had followed him. Once they were out of sight from the buyers and sellers, they confronted him. Pel watched the exchange, peeking from around the corner of a nearby building.

"You lost, friend?" the boot merchant asked with a tone that was clearly an accusation.

"Is there any way for me to answer that question without you doing something stupid?" the stranger asked harshly. He was clearly irritated by the nature of this encounter.

"Ah, you know, friend. *The Maiden* just docked. Saw her crew offloading goods to the market, myself. Then you come in buying all kinds of traveling goods? At this time of night? With silver? All the while lost in the middle of Ruby? Ha.

"You'll come with us peacefully and we'll introduce you to the red mages of the Tower. If you have nothin' to answer for, they'll let you on your way." The man had explained the plan as if it were an offer, although it was clearly phrased as both demand and threat.

Pel was confused. Why had the merchants confronted the stranger at all? Even if they knew he was a stowaway, even if he had committed an egregious crime, it would make more sense for them to simply report him to the city watch. They had nothing to gain by engaging him like this. This whole scenario seemed out of character.

"Convenient that you sold me the goods and then came after me," the stranger replied with a sardonically appreciative nod. "You hope to get those goods back and keep the silver and get a reward. How enterprising."

The stowaway reached into his coin purse and withdrew a handful of coins. He played with them absently, but slowly enough to show that there was plenty of money to be shared.

"So, how about I pay you for directions to the northeast wall? Then we can part ways."

The men shared sideways glances, unwittingly and non-verbally considering the offer.

The shoemaker weighed in, clearly the most solid in his resolve. "And what'll happen when they find out we let 'im go? How much good will that money do ya?"

The men stiffened up and crept forward to surround the stranger.

# Ruby (The Evertorch) – Deodin

Deodin, meanwhile, was annoyed. Merchants and vendors often behaved strangely around him. In fact, he'd seen some of that earlier tonight. But they had never acted like this. The situation made more sense once the checklist emerged in his mind.

*Escape Ruby:*
- ☐ *Scare off the merchants*
- ☐ *Find your way to the Northern wall*

> *You know, that's not a bad way to handle this.*

The life of *sheyaktu* could easily be described as moments of peace scattered throughout a never-ending series of conflicts. When bandits, red mages, wild animals, or the monsters that roamed the world threatened Deodin's life and his goals, he responded commensurately. He had defeated a small mountain's worth of enemies throughout his escapades.

And yet, he was always justified in doing so. Certainly, if an enemy sought to kill him for all the wrong reasons, self-defense was the appropriate response. And conveniently, the Universe seemed to have made an arrangement with the local soldiers and guards: while they never thanked Deodin for killing murderers and monsters, they never complained about it either.

This encounter was different. These men were a misfit group of desperate merchants, not morally bankrupt villains.

They were victims of their circumstances, driven by fear. Deodin had no moral high ground. They posed him no real threat, so he could solve the problem without violence.

Deodin nodded, at peace with what was going to happen next. If the Universe forced this event to occur, at least the "rules" of the encounter were fair and appropriate.

# Ruby (The Evertorch) – Pel

"I'm fine with this," Pel heard the stranger say.

The stowaway delicately and deliberately set his pack on the ground, seemingly more concerned about scuffing his new equipment or breaking something in the pack than the tiny hostile mob that circled him. He turned to face his assailants with a calm that was incongruous for a man in such a situation.

His easy manner messaged that he was completely unconcerned. He stood with a relaxed posture in his shoulders, his head tilted slightly to the side to express boredom or impatience. Instead of desperately searching for an escape or trying to talk his way out of trouble, he sighed heavily. Everything about his mannerisms suggested that he didn't feel threatened.

"Gentlemen, you don't want to challenge the likes of me," he said.

A warning shout welled up in Pel's throat, but before she could intervene, the fight had started.

A brilliant radiance chased away the alley's darkness. The stranger stood at the center of it, his entire body emitting a harsh, blinding white light. The merchants shied away, reflexively turning their heads and shielding their eyes with their hands.

The light vanished abruptly. The stranger stood much as he had before, except now he held the shoemaker's knife. He gestured to the blade as if to say *I think you lost this.* The spectacle was an obvious demonstration of just how little a threat these men posed.

The shoemaker stumbled, backpedaling a few steps before finding the wherewithal to turn and flee down the alleyway, back to the relative safety of the Evertorch. The other men heeded the implicit advice and followed suit. They ran past Pel, who watched in silence.

After the assailants had dispersed, the stowaway settled his gaze on Pel.

"And you," he said with a suitably admonishing tone. His head turned slightly, redirecting his attention to her.

The next moment, he stood beside her, his shoulders squared to hers.

He had covered the thirty feet in an instant. His blue aura shone so intensely that Pel had to look away.

"Not all of this is for show, you know," the man said breathlessly.

"They do not fear your magic. They fear failing the red mages of the Tower," she retorted, her head turned. "And once the red mages learn of you, they will certainly seek you out."

The light of his aura softened, leaving the lower-intensity hue she had seen previously. He scowled with a mixture of disappointment and anger. Pel didn't feel that he was upset with her, but rather the circumstances that had surrounded him.

The stowaway sighed before continuing. "You followed me from the docks. Will you also report me to the Tower and its red mages?"

He recovered his pack and slipped into its straps. The man's narrow shoulders rose and fell and beads of sweat formed on his brow. He locked gazes with her and she stared right back, transfixed by his face.

And no, not for those reasons.

Not entirely for those reasons, at least. He was handsome enough, but the bards wouldn't describe him as a flawless specimen made of the purest skin and muscle. His jawline would not be used to measure right angles, his muscles were not comparable to jungle cats, nor did his eyes appear to shine, sparkle, or otherwise twinkle.

Underneath his tacky tunic, she could see his wiry, athletic build and dark symbols or lettering on the inside of his right arm. And his hair? His most recent barber must have blind and may have been without full use of his limbs.

Instead, she stared because his face was perfectly clear. His aura allowed her to see details she seldom enjoyed. Even from this distance, only a few yards away, she could make out the lines of his eyebrows, the creases at the corners of his eyes, the thin stubble on his face, the speckled imperfections of freckles around his neck.

The stowaway had waited long enough for Pel to respond. A magical effect welled up around his head and eyes, creating an aura with which she was intimately familiar. He observed her with a magic-detection spell of his own.

She flinched when his boredom shifted to concerned surprise.

His movement was impossibly fast: one moment he stood in front of Pel, the next, he stood behind her, locking her head in place by a rear choke hold between his left bicep and the inner part of his forearm. He grasped her right arm, supporting his hold while pinning her right hand helplessly above her head. Her world began to fade into darkness.

Had she weighed another 150 pounds, she might have been able to resist the attack. The magic that maneuvered the stranger into position had cost him. He was winded. She could feel his heavy, laboring breath on her neck, but he held her at such a disadvantage that she could not fight back.

It all happened so fast that she had no time to react.

And now, she had no breath left to scream.

# THE DISCOURSE ON MAGIC (CHAPTER 1): LIMITATIONS

*Excerpted with permission from The Discourse on Magic, by Thierren Dowdy, the noted Grand Mage of the Western Isles.*

### (From Chapter 1, Section 4: The Limitations)

Consider for a moment, the second axiom:

*The greater the scale of natural law you wish to break, the more difficult that spell is to cast.*

### Personal costs

Most spells are physically taxing to cast. Spellcasting is often paired with pain, discomfort, or another unpleasant side effect. The more powerful the spell, the more taxing and challenging it is to cast or maintain it.

Most often, these "costs" are minor inconveniences on the human body. These inconveniences can be endured. Some spells cause physical pain. The spells are limited by how much pain the caster can tolerate. Others create symptoms of dizziness, clouded vision, or nausea. Finally, most spells are physically fatiguing. It is simply exhausting to rapidly chain many difficult, powerful spells.

Therefore, the fates seemed to have placed a limit on the human capacity to master magic. Casting a single spell can be challenging, for the reasons we have discussed. For each spell that is cast, each subsequent spell will be more difficult to cast.

# DAY
# 2

# Ruby (The Evertorch) – Pel

The stranger dragged Pel away from the edge of the alleyway. It was late, the streets were empty, and she was hopelessly outmatched. No help would stumble upon them and Pel held even less hope that any would-be savior could raise a hand against her assailant.

"Let us not scream," the man said between his heavy breaths.

His grip held firm, but he relaxed her throat a little, allowing her to breathe and talk. He gasped for air himself, as the magic he had cast, along with her struggles, had winded him.

Nevertheless, his voice and demeanor remained calm, even as he wrestled Pel into the deserted alley. He moved her about in a disciplined, practiced manner.

*This is not the first time he's done this.* This realization made Pel's ordeal even more terrifying.

"No spells," he warned.

It took her a moment to conclude this was an instruction, not a statement about himself. His command seemed so misplaced that Pel briefly stopped her instinctive struggle. She held still, momentarily left indignant by his remark. She coughed with disgust.

"Spells? I'm not a mage. I detest mages," she croaked, as venomously as the circumstances would allow. His grip eased slightly.

After a pause, he asked, "And the magic around your eyes?"

"A curse from mages in the Tower," she replied. "It is a permanent magic detection spell."

"If you hate mages so much, why follow one from the docks? Why follow one into the shadows of the Evertorch? Why remain after the merchants had the sense to flee for their lives?" He jolted her by tightening his grip, reminding her of the advantage he held in their conversation.

"You are most certainly not a mage. You are *sheyaktu*," Pel rasped.

She suffered through an agonizing eternity as the man mulled this. He released her and Pel stumbled a few steps before catching her feet and composing herself. However, instead of fleeing, she turned back to face him. For reasons she couldn't explain, she felt no compulsion to run.

Perhaps she subconsciously knew the futility of the effort. She could no more escape *sheyaktu* than she could swim across the ocean. Or perhaps her curiosity overwhelmed her sense of fear. It wasn't every day she could look a god killer in the eye.

The man sighed, almost dejectedly, clearly considering their present circumstances. He was older than she would have expected. According to legend, *sheyaktu* were notoriously short-lived. The few wrinkles by his eyes and hands placed him at around thirty winters.

The stowaway took a few steps away from her and sat on a bale of hay next to one of the buildings. He stared down at the ground, his shoulders slumping heavily as if he were weary.

A moment later, he looked up at Pel.

"What am I to do with you?"

His question wasn't rhetorical. The man understood the uncompromisingly harsh truth that had played out during the past few minutes. He had every right to be deathly afraid of being in Ruby. Everything he had done tonight came from short-term desperation.

Here she stood, at the end of a forgotten, darkened alley, intimate with this knowledge. He was *sheyaktu* and she was the only person who knew it.

Despite the warm night air, her new cloak, and the heat of her recent struggles, she shivered.

# Ruby (The Burning Boar) – Garret

Garret awaited the answer. The question wasn't intended to be difficult.

"It's an ear," came Sam's eventual response. An expression of mild disgust and concern played on his face.

Sam had identified the item correctly. He sat across from Garret, who leaned forward slightly. Sam was a thin, relatively frail man with graying hair and wrinkles about the eyes. Nearly bald now, he had only a partial band of hair running from temple to temple around the back of his head.

The focus of the conversation was indeed an ear, resting quite plainly on the table in front of them. It had lost its color, leaving it a pallid, gray thing, quite out of place next to the arrangement of mugs, plates, and leftover scraps of a late dinner.

The two men sat in the primary hall of the Burning Boar, a completely standard tavern that provided all the general amenities and décor of every other tavern of its ilk. It featured simple wooden furniture arranged under the dim light of hanging candles. Its menu was predictable, its proprietor suitably gruff, and considering the time of night, the clientele was appropriately shady.

In the far corner, away from the door, Sam and his dinner companion sat at a table that matched the others; it was marred by scratches and discolored by a lifetime of spilled food and drinks, as well as blood from the occasional brawl.

The Burning Boar acted as a hub for various business interests to intersect. It was a place to share rumors, meet clients, and negotiate deals. As the night wore on, those deals would become increasingly secretive. By now, most of the conversations in the room were whispered.

"It's less about the actual ear and more about the problem it represents," replied Garret.

He had been the one to start the discussion in the first place by making the ear the centerpiece of the table and their conversation.

During his lifetime, Garret had become an expert of the Thick, serving as a guide and escort for anyone who needed to travel through it. To survive in that role for so long, Garret's list of physical attributes read like a predator's: lean, muscular, and rugged. His appearance, demeanor, and accessories fit a man who lived a life of adventure and danger.

"It's an orc ear," Sam said, finally yielding the most relevant detail.

"There you go!" Garret said with a nod, glad that things were progressing. "Now, where did it come from?"

Sam served on Ruby's city council and was always eager to hear about Garret's experiences in the Thick. But as a civil servant, Sam was unsurprisingly squeamish when presented with severed body parts.

He studied the ear with the same appalled look as before. After a few moments, he returned his attention to Garret, his expression unchanged.

"An orc," he said at last, with no hint of jest.

Garret nodded, conceding that the answer was both correct and incorrect. "An orc. Very much true. However, I was referring to the place where I found the orc. The orc itself was somewhat implied. In any case, we were near Peak's View." Garret tipped his mug as a salute. He whispered the location's name to emphasize its significance. Sam's eyes narrowed in incredulity.

"But there are no orcs in that area."

Garret turned his head sideways, maintaining eye contact.

"Yet there he was. In the wood within two hundred yards of the road. And in broad daylight." Garret finished his last comment with a flourishing gesture. He sat back in his chair and crossed his arms to allow Sam to digest his point.

The impact of Garret's story shook away any remnants of Sam's confusion. His shoulders slumped and his face relaxed, leaving the countenance of an old, weathered man who had seen much in his many years.

And his reaction was appropriate. Garret was right when he said that a single orc wasn't the problem. The concern was that the orc had been encountered so far west, so close to a major human settlement. Sam frowned. He obviously understood the ramifications of that news.

"They are rarely so bold," Sam admitted when he reached for his tankard and took a somber, quiet drink.

"Or so close," Garret added, sipping from his own mug. Sam offered a weary sigh.

"I'll tell the others. We're scheduled to meet in a day." His body language suggested that the news wouldn't be received well.

Garret replied quickly. "And?"

Sam looked as though he considered taking another drink but returned the mug to its place on the table. "You have to understand the nature of the city council, Garret." He tilted his head to emphasize the seriousness of his concern. "There are limits to its influence. To my influence."

Garret pushed back from the table. He picked up the ear and held it out in front of him, making it dance. "Oy! Orc! What brings you here?" he said in a comically squeaky voice. Then he changed his facial expression and lowered his voice to a guttural growl and continued, "Me come to kill, and rape, and eat you! In that order."

Sam watched Garret's one-act play with a flat expression. He wasn't yet angry, but his patience had clearly neared its end.

"Don't patronize me. If everything were so simple, we'd live in a paradise and men like you wouldn't need to leave the walls carrying swords and bows. I don't presume to be an expert on the Thick, with all its beasts and monsters. Don't you presume to know the politics of Ruby. I face monsters of my own, you know."

Sam's words came out as serious whispers, with no venom or malice. Garret put down the ear, but he played with it absently, spinning it around on the table. His expression softened slightly, the sarcasm having since vacated.

"You're right, Sam," he said, staring away for a few moments before looking back to the older man across the table. "Sorry about that. You get it. The people of Ruby get it."

Sam nodded.

"Good will come of this, Garret," Sam added, reaching for his purse. As he withdrew a few coins, he continued, "Stories like yours will confirm the rumors that have been swirling about the rest of the Crown. There has been concern about the safety of leaving the city walls. That concern is even more justified with your news. And ... ah ... your evidence.

People will protect themselves. Spread the word among your peers and I'll do the same at the council."

Garret nodded as Sam rose from his seat. The older man paused for a second and stretched his back. Sam laid a handful of coins on the table.

"I do not expect the Tower to take up a crusade to weed out an ambiguous orc threat. Nor, however, do I expect the good people of Ruby to watch as orcs sack their city. We can do this without the Tower's help." Sam straightened his shirt before he slipped into his cloak.

A blast of cool air rushed into the room as the front door opened. The odors of bad liquor and worse food swirled around the tavern as the two men turned to see who had entered at this late hour. It was nobody they recognized.

Garret was disappointed. Sam noticed. The older man drew a breath but held it, obviously searching for something better to express than his initial thoughts.

"You don't need to say it, Sam," Garret said.

"Why would you invite her to this place? No wonder she canceled," Sam noted, a smirk finding its way to his lips.

Without looking up from his drink, Garret responded with the crudest, most inappropriate hand gesture he could muster.

# Ruby (The Evertorch) – Pel

"You shouldn't be here," Pel said.

The stowaway tilted his head. His flat expression could only mean *no shit*. She shook her head. She wasn't sympathizing with him.

"No, you really shouldn't be here. In Ruby. Surely, you've heard of the Tower. Surely, you know of the red mages. They will come for you, once they learn what you are. They'll try to —

"I know."

"*The Maiden!* You meant to disembark at Bayhold, but they missed the port!" Pel's face lit up as she solved the puzzle that had led to this situation. After a moment of thought, she continued with a more serious, wary tone, "Let me help you."

The man smiled politely but held up his hand for her to stop.

"Thank you, but it is best for you if you simply walk away. You'd gain nothing by helping me and you'd risk everything. So, for dragging you into this intrigue, I am sorry." As if it were an afterthought, he glanced at her sideways rather sheepishly. "Also for literally dragging you here. That was rude."

She shook her head vehemently. Her heart raced. This was not negotiable. She could not allow the Tower to turn this *sheyaktu* into an instrument of their will. The only thing that prevented the red mages from completely dominating non-mages was that magic had never been fully mastered.

What if the mages of the Tower were able to overcome those limitations? The thought of those men with that type of power terrified her.

God killer or not, this man's personal well-being—and hers—was just one pressing concern. There were larger stakes. Pel raised her voice and held her ground. "You misunderstand. I am not being generous. What would become of me, and the people of Ruby, should the red mages use you for their own gain? The only way this ends well for all of us, for any of us, is if you disappear from Ruby."

The stranger paused a moment, as if considering her words.

This wasn't a debate. She continued, "I will walk away once you are safely out of the reach of the Tower and the red mages. Or when you're dead," she remarked as the thought struck her. "Obviously, the Tower couldn't build a weapon from a corpse."

He reacted with an expression of amusement. His aura fluctuated momentarily, reminding her of what he was.

"That wasn't meant to be a threat," she added hastily.

"I liked it, though. Properly menacing." He smirked.

Pel was relieved that the stranger seemed willing to cooperate with her. If anything, he was surprisingly unfazed by the severity of his situation. She felt emboldened enough to make a proposal. "Without telling me exact details, think of what you planned to do when you arrived at Bayhold. Perhaps I can help you complete those plans."

She didn't want to know the specifics. If she didn't know his goals, she couldn't betray them. And if she couldn't betray him, he would have no reason to silence her. The stranger noted the way she phrased the question, responding with an arched eyebrow.

"I've played this game before," she explained with a shrug. "I broker information."

"Let us say that the first spot is a place within the Thick," he said.

"I know someone you should meet," she replied.

# Ruby (The Mage Tower) – Mathew

*It's only a door. Just knock on it.*

Mathew found himself laughing at his inner monologue, a nervous, sardonic commentary on the absurdity of his present situation. If it were as simple as knocking on Richard's door, Mathew would have done it by now.

The man on the other side of the door, known as "Richard the Patient," was the senior mage of the Tower and its primary decision maker. Mathew had been assigned the unenviable task of bearing bad news and summoning Richard from his chambers.

In some regards, Richard's reputation for patience was legendary. As a practitioner of magic, he was among the Tower's most talented. Many even considered him the world's most accomplished magical researcher.

He had earned that reputation through scrupulous scholarship into magic that had not been mastered by human hands; his career focus was the study of the magic used by mobs. He hadn't unlocked every secret, but he had come as close as any human ever had. And with his skills and his limitless personal ambition, Richard had climbed to the top of the Tower's hierarchy.

Despite all of that, the word "patient" was also used as a sarcastic criticism, at least when whispered in confidence. In his general dealings with others, Richard was insufferable. Richard hated everyone. And similarly, everyone hated Richard.

*Fuck. Fuck. Fuck. Get it over with.*

Mathew's hand still hovered above the door. He paused, scowling.

*You know what? Fuck it. He's going to be pissed whether I summon him or not. Let him hear the news from someone else. Let some other poor bastard deal with him.* Mathew abandoned the task and headed down the corridor that led to the staircase.

He was about a third of the way down the hallway before he halted, cursed under his breath, and turned back toward Richard's chamber. He banged on the door with a closed fist.

It opened much sooner than he expected. Much to his surprise and delight, he was greeted by Mica.

She was a newer member of the Tower's servant staff, having joined their ranks during the past four weeks. She was the Tower's librarian.

He paused. And smiled. And stared.

Mica's reddish blonde hair had been tied into a neat bun to keep it out of her face. However, one or two tresses had escaped and dangled in front of her large, blue eyes that were surrounded by the tiniest, cutest array of freckles. She was almost unnaturally beautiful. She spoke with a exotic accent and had once said that she was from the East.

She made Mathew feel like a blushing teenager. He would fully admit that he stole every opportunity and excuse to interact with her.

She looked back at him with widened eyes, her head tilted sideways. Her expression could only mean one thing: *Why are you here?*

Mathew nodded to the room behind her and mouthed a single word: *Richard.*

Mica responded by silently pouring out an excited stream of gesturing that Mathew couldn't interpret. Her message was obviously important, but it was too complicated for him to understand via lipreading, facial expressions, and pantomime.

*What?* He shrugged.

She rolled her eyes. With her left hand, she made a circle with her thumb and index finger. She poked her other index finger into that hole, repeatedly and vigorously, while scowling at Mathew for being so dense. For good measure, she turned the gesture around, poking through the other side of the circle.

*Fuck…* Mathew mouthed. Delivering his message under these circumstances would be even more unpleasant.

It was quietly known that Richard's room housed a group of women who served as his harem. From Mica's demonstrative gesturing, Mathew concluded that Richard was currently occupied in their company. Those same rumors suggested that he kept them "domesticated" with drugs, magic, or a mixture of both.

Mica kicked Mathew in the shin, which relayed her message clearly enough: *Do what you need to do before you get us both in trouble.*

Mathew stepped further into Richard's chambers, which had been sectioned off into two smaller rooms, the first being the laboratory and study room in which Mathew and Mica currently stood.

The other space functioned as sleeping quarters. Centered in the room was a giant bed, several times larger than what would be considered normal or reasonable. By Richard's design, it was lavish, luxurious, and appropriate to the room's overall purpose. The four naked members of Richard's harem lay about his bed like the disposable things they were.

Richard slept in the bosom of one of them. She stared languidly at the ceiling, blinking and breathing enough to prove that she was still alive. The others displayed the same state of torpor.

The sight was unnerving. The women were eerily similar and flawlessly beautiful in a way that defied their dire situation. Mathew would have expected to see crinkles from age or blemishes on their skin, considering how Richard treated them. Instead, there were none.

Mathew stared, but not for lust. The women were ostensibly sculpted pieces of feminine beauty, seemingly crafted out of nothing more than a man's fantasies. Yet, Mathew found himself moved by their plight.

One of the women gingerly lifted her head off her pillow and turned to look at him. She shifted her bare shoulders slightly, positioning herself to get a better view. Her movement was slow and labored. Had she winced, he would have suspected she was in pain. Instead, her features betrayed no expression at all.

She noted his presence by making eye contact, uninhibited by her nudity and position. He flinched. A consciousness hid behind her lack of expression, as though she wanted to scream, or cry, or smile, or scowl—or anything. But she couldn't. Her condition locked her into a prison from which she could not escape.

A swell of emotion poured over him. Everything about this scene made him angry.

"Richard!" Mathew snarled, far louder and bolder than he had rehearsed in his mind. He tore his gaze from the woman and glared at the pig wallowing in the center of his bed and his indulgences.

Richard stirred with a start, taking a moment to gather his bearings. Once he found his wits, his face melted into an expression of anger. He sat up, coughing with rage.

"How dare you enter my—"

"There is a rogue mage in the Evertorch. The others wait on you," Mathew said sternly.

He turned around and stormed back to the antechamber where Mica stood impossibly still in the corner. He saw a streak of wetness on her cheek before she met his gaze. She blinked at him and gave him a silent nod of thanks.

Mathew stormed from Richard's quarters, too angry, too outraged, and too disgusted to share Mica's tears.

# THE DISCOURSE ON MAGIC (CHAPTER 8)

*Excerpted with permission from The Discourse on Magic, by Thierren Dowdy, the noted Grand Mage of the Western Isles.*

## (From Chapter 8, What future lies ahead)

### Research

Perhaps the most promising source of research comes from the most unexpected of places: The Monsters Born of Skycrash, otherwise known as *mobs*.

As you'll recall, by definition, mobs can bring forth magical effects without the need for conventional casting. The way mobs use this power fascinates many researchers. Mobs are living proof that magic must exist in ways beyond our understanding. That concept is exhilarating.

In fact, some researchers have advanced magical progress by merely studying the way certain mobs channel magic. Richard the Patient of the renowned Tower in Ruby has almost single-handedly pioneered the use of mobs in magical study, producing concepts that were previously well ahead of their time.

Certainly, studying mobs is not without its own perils or limitations. However, to understand how mobs use supernatural power is to solve many of the riddles that currently limit magical research.

(The same could certainly be said about *sheyaktu*, being that they can cast nearly anything without spells or consuming materials. In theory, cooperative *sheyaktu* may even be willing to be subjected to tests or experiments. However, they are so rare and so unlikely to live to adulthood, it is merely wishful thinking to hope to study one.)

# DAY

# 2

# Ruby (The Burning Boar) – Garret

Garret straightened in his seat at the sight of Pel.

She stood in the doorway of the Burning Boar, looking around the room. As she normally did, she had tucked her hands inside her cloak, regardless of the weather or temperature.

Something was atypical, however. He noted a tension about her: hair disheveled, cheeks flushed, skin glistening with a thin layer of perspiration. She scanned the room with quick, jerky movements—mannerisms more common among prey animals, not information brokers.

*She's only here on business*, Garret concluded before taking a disappointed sip from his tankard. He summoned her over to the table with a wave.

She seated herself on the bench next to him. He sat up even more stiffly. This was new. Typically, she would sit opposite him. Apparently, she didn't trust the words to travel across the pitted, filthy planks of the table. He felt her breath on his ear as she whispered and he took in the slightest hint of the fragrance she wore.

The message itself wasn't remarkable. *Some guy … the Thick … need to leave soon … don't tell anyone … don't ask questions….* It rang of the business she always brought to him, even though she delivered it with more intensity than normal.

"Right, right, right," he agreed, still stuck on the fact that she had canceled their plans and then showed up anyway because she needed to talk business.

That was inconsiderate.

"You let me down tonight, Pel," Garret blurted out.

Pel drew a breath as if she were going to speak, but held it. She took his hand, a rare gesture from her.

"I had to have dinner with Sam," Garret complained, "and he doesn't giggle at my jokes. I mean, he does, but it's just not the same."

"I know. And I'm sorry," she said. "And I will giggle at those jokes later. But right now, I need the Garret who is master of the Thick, not the one with hurt feelings."

Garret huffed. Master of the Thick, indeed.

The timing of her remark struck him more than her flattery. All of this was odd. She was never this secretive. Pel occasionally dealt with shady people but she was never this anxious.

"In the office in a few minutes. You do not want to be seen with us," she added, before sitting back at a more conventional speaking distance, taking her scent with her and replacing her hand in its resting spot under her cloak.

*That looks new. And nice,* Garret noticed.

He nodded in agreement, responding with the most serious, duty-filled expression he could muster. He raised his tankard in a toast and belched with acknowledgment.

*Not even an eye-roll or a sneer? How disappointing.*

Pel paused and frowned in puzzlement, her attention shifting to the table.

"What?" Garret asked, suddenly alarmed by the change in body language.

"What is that doing there?" She nodded pointedly to the lifeless ear resting quite harmlessly among the dishes and clutter.

"Don't worry about that one, Pel. It's … ah … ear-elevant to our business," Garret replied, dropping the shitty pun only because he knew how Pel would react to it. He waggled his eyebrows expectantly.

Pel stared at him for a moment, before reacting with a sigh and the slightest shake of her head. Garret felt a hint of satisfaction, despite himself. He enjoyed this fraction of a smile that he got from her. It was worth it.

He let out a loud "huh-huh" chuckle as Pel turned away with a sidelong look of disapproval. He laughed again. If only she were like every other girl in history, she would have reveled in the endearing charm of it all.

Instead, Pel was Pel. She held up her hand with all her fingers extended.

*Five minutes*, she mouthed.

*   *   *

Pel pulled the curtains closed after peering out the window to ensure that Garret hadn't been followed.

*Okay, this is alarming.*

Garret knew the limitations of Pel's eyesight. If she glanced out the window now, it was because she was worried or afraid, not because she had any realistic chance of seeing anything outside.

A stranger awaited him.

Garret sat down opposite the man at the heavy table in the seldom-used room above the Burning Boar. The simple, weathered furniture was arranged for a conference, with all the chairs circling the central table. The Boar's proprietor allowed the use of this room for these kinds of meetings, under the proviso that he was never informed of the dealings.

Pel did not introduce the man, so Garret's knowledge of him was limited to what he could see in the weak light of the single candle in the middle of the table. Two things came to mind immediately.

First, the man wore the eyesore of a tunic that the Trade Cabal's quartermaster had been trying to sell for months. On one hand, Garret was glad that Saul had finally been able to get rid of the thing. On the other, Garret was disappointed he had to see it again.

Equally noteworthy, or perhaps more so, was the state of the man's hair. It was a mess of different lengths and bald spots. Garret wondered if he suffered an accident or a disease.

Beyond that, the stranger featured an unremarkable, average build, thin and narrow cheeks, and attentive eyes. No blemishes, cuts, or calluses were visible on the man's hands. Whatever his trade, it didn't involve hard labor or extended periods in the sun. Nothing shed any light into who the stranger was or what he'd been doing before he arrived here.

Despite that, Garret was impressed. The stranger showed a sense of poise and confidence that didn't match the tension in the room. Nothing about his demeanor suggested he was intimidated by Garret's weapons, concerned by Pel's overly paranoid behavior, or bothered that they were conducting a clandestine meeting in the dead of night over a shitty dive called the Burning Boar. Everything about the man's body language suggested he was comfortable with this meeting.

*...even though his tunic and hair make him look like a clown. All he needs to do to complete the picture is to fart and fall face-first into a cream pie.*

Garret chuckled at the mental image, his "huh-huh" laugh loud enough to draw notice. The other man was observant enough to pick up the contextual clues that led to Garret's reaction.

"The merchant wouldn't let me buy the black one." He sighed. "If my appearance has been properly addressed, I'd like to talk business. I need passage through the Thick."

Garret resisted the urge to be catty. Because this was something important to Pel, he chose a more professional response.

"That's what I do, but do we really need to talk about this right here? Right now?"

"It's a little more complicated than usual," Pel replied. "We must get him out of the city without the Tower knowing about it. The red mages cannot know we help this man."

"That sounds a lot complicated," Garret corrected.

"There is more, and unfortunately, it applies to you both," the stranger said. He looked down at the table and paused in a way that made Garret uneasy. His hesitation did not come from shyness or a lack of confidence; the man was gathering his thoughts so he could best break bad news. "Should you accept this job, you cannot return to Ruby."

Garret remained quiet and patiently awaited the punchline because this was all clearly a bad joke.

"You seem to be taking that well," said the man with the bad hair.

Garret chuckled loudly. The absurdity of the stranger's statement deserved the absurdity of Garret's follow-up question.

"And I suppose you can pay us enough for this inconvenience? You have so much coin that we can set up in a little cottage far away from Ruby, so that the gentlemen from the Tower can never find us?" he chided with as much sarcasm as he could muster.

"Of course." The stranger shrugged off the question with a dismissive scowl and turn of his head, as if the question were ridiculous.

"R-really?"

"He's right," Pel said flatly.

Her tone caught Garret by surprise. She had spoken as if she accepted the stranger's condition. Garret stared at her with bemusement. Pel gazed off to another part of the room, her mind clearly drifting elsewhere.

"The red mages will want me. As long as I live, I will be at risk. As will anyone who might know how to find me. If you stay in Ruby, they will come for you," the stranger said, with a sympathetic, apologetic expression.

Garret had no doubt the man believed what he was saying, but that didn't make him right. Or any less crazy. "Of course," Garret said, maintaining a tight grip on the appropriate sarcasm.

Paying client or not, rich client or not, this man had delusions of grandeur to think that the Tower would give two shits about him. He looked to Pel for support, but she was still off in a distant mental place. Rather than sit through more awkward melodrama, Garret offered the only response that made sense given the circumstances.

"Then I don't take the job," he said simply. "Best of luck to you, but fuck off." He pushed back his chair, the wooden legs groaning as they scraped across the floor.

Pel turned to Garret, rebuking him with nothing more than a look.

"You have to take the job," she said, in a tone he didn't recognize — one that expressed her disappointed, unequivocal acceptance. A surrender. "*We* have to take the job."

"And why is that?" Garret asked, partly out of indignation, but also out of incredulity. The stranger's request was nearly as crazy as Pel's acceptance of it.

"He's *sheyaktu*," she said.

Garret stopped talking instantly. The weight of Pel's words hit him with more than enough force to close his mouth. The three of them sat there, exchanging glances for a few moments.

With those two words, Garret now understood what drove Pel to such a night of unusual behavior. He now understood why Pel would propose to help this man, even if it meant abandoning everything here. Similarly, he understood why the stranger would insist that they never return to Ruby. Everything about the situation suddenly made sense. No less wild, perhaps, but at least there was an explanation.

Ever the pragmatist, Garret turned to the stranger and asked the most relevant question that remained in the conversation.

"So. How rich are you? Obscenely rich, I hope?"

# THE DISCOURSE ON MAGIC (CHAPTER 6): *SHEYAKTU*

*Excerpted with permission from The Discourse on Magic, by Thierren Dowdy, the noted Grand Mage of the Western Isles.*

### Chapter 6: *Sheyaktu*

As the previous chapter illustrates, magic can be manifested by both man and monster.

- Men create an incredibly diverse array of magic through spells, after a career of study and practice
- Monsters create extremely specific magical effects, but can do so by mere instinct

There is another point to be introduced and added to that list:

- The men that are monsters and the monsters that are men: *sheyaktu*

The word *sheyaktu* describes any person who can master magic without research, study, or practice. *Sheyaktu* are like musical virtuosos who can pick up any instrument and play it better than the most experienced masters, without investing the time, effort, and cost of training, practice, and rehearsal.

### History of the Horror

It is widely understood that the first historically significant *sheyaktu* was a human male named Lyle Makee. You probably know him better by the title that eventually came to describe him: "The Horror."

A brief history of Lyle Makee is relevant to our discussions about *sheyaktu* for a variety of reasons. Makee's history before he became The Horror is as important as the history that you already know.

As far as the records can account, before he was given the name based on his reputation, Lyle Makee was simply a peasant who lived in the small town of Honeybrew, the village in the center of the triangle formed by Ruby, Tristan, and Bayhold. By our current reckoning, this was about 50 years following Skycrash.

He traveled north through the Thick and into the mountains of the Crown. Over a series of encounters, Makee used his mastery of magic to subdue and influence the orcs. If you'll remember that magic was still new to the world, you can imagine the impression he made on the primitive orc tribes. Predictably, and perhaps by design, the orcs began to revere Makee as a god.

This gave him significant leverage in their culture from that point forward. He became the grandfather of their education and their transition from oral to written traditions. He is to credit (or blame, if you prefer) for the orcs' adoption of the Common language. Orcs now speak their broken version of Common, having largely abandoned their native tongue at Makee's direction.

More impressively, Makee did the impossible. He united the otherwise disparate (and occasionally warring) tribes. No longer did they compete for resources. They began to work together as a greater culture. The orcs became more of a nation than a collection of splintered, squabbling tribes.

Finally, and horrifically, Makee gave the orcs a purpose. He used them to engineer the siege of Tristan. Fortunately, humanity rallied at Tristan and prevented a calamity that would have followed only Skycrash itself in terms of destruction.

The purpose of the Lyle Makee history lesson, as it relates to *sheyaktu*, is twofold.

First, the Encroachment at Tristan is the primary reason why there has been so much resentment of, and resistance to, the human use of magic.

Large, old wounds turn into scars that remind us of the pain of the injury. Magic was instrumental in the siege of Tristan in ways both real and imagined. Only hundreds of years later have people opened their minds to the possibility that magic can be used for anything other than violence.

The second reason relates to the first point, but also directly to the *sheyaktu*. There is no reason to think that every *sheyaktu* could and would grow up to share a fate like Lyle Makee. For reasons we may never know, Makee was a mixture of ambition, power, and magic. In an age where the supernatural had literally just begun to manifest itself in the world, Makee was its undisputed master. As history would have it, he was also its worst abuser.

Because of this, the most feared thing during the Age of Magic is not chronicled among the monsters described in Chapter 5. Even the mighty dragon, the most feared and terrible entry in the bestiary, has not been hunted, persecuted, and outright hated as much as those unlucky enough to be born *sheyaktu*.

It is no wonder that the term itself is from the orcs' ancient tongue: it describes "a thing that is both a horrible gift and a wondrous curse."

# DAY
# 2

# Ruby (The Mage Tower) – Mathew

A collective rumbling of discontent filled the library's common area. The room seldom hosted this many people and, certainly, never at this time of night. Nearly seventy mages sat at the tables arranged around the room, with another thirty standing along the walls. The whispers and hushed conversations ended as soon as Richard burst through the door. All eyes looked up at him.

*Only Richard would wear something like that. Nobody else would even own it.*

Richard was garbed in an expensive, tacky crimson robe inlaid with a shimmery, metallic thread, the hairy mane on his chest distractingly visible through the V-shaped neckline. The redness in his face nearly matched the color of his gown. Having been rushed from his quarters by the severity of Mathew's news, he had not had time to appease his vanity and address his hair. Each strand appeared to be trying to escape his scalp in every conceivable and inconceivable direction.

"One of the reds?" Richard snarled at Entorak, who stood apart from the mages sitting at the tables.

Mathew scoffed. Most late-night incidents involved the red mages.

While the red mage brotherhood had continued to seize influence and power across the Crown, they had not yet claimed total control over the Tower and its decisions. Only a few of the prominent mages, such as Mathew and Entorak, were not part of their ranks.

"All accounted for," Entorak said in a deliberate, patient cadence.

Entorak stood before the mages at the front of the room, facing Richard. He stood erect, hands held in front of him resting at the waist, his right hand wrapped around the fingers of his left hand. The posture seemed humbly servile yet elegantly authoritative.

Even from the other side of the room, Entorak was unsettling. He and Richard had both weathered more than fifty winters, yet only Entorak had aged well. He was a much finer specimen of physical health. His skin shone with a healthy tan and his clothes hung well on his tall, slender frame. Despite his age, he featured a full head of short, silvering hair.

Yet it was Entorak's manner that Mathew found so unnerving. The older mage's movement and speech were deliberately calm and patient. While most people used their mouths more than their minds, Entorak's entire persona seemed dedicated to silent, internal thought and analysis. Furthermore, Entorak expressed a cool, almost distant politeness that was neither insincere nor truly trustworthy. Mathew found it easiest to simply avoid him.

Richard looked the mages over. It was a futile endeavor: he certainly wouldn't recognize which faces should be standing at muster, for he seldom engaged with less-experienced mages.

"Not one of these ranks? Then who?" Richard asked, now more curious than angry.

Mathew also found this peculiar. Mages rarely traveled to Ruby unannounced. Visiting the Tower would be the entire purpose of a visit. There had to be a reason for an unannounced mage to cause trouble in the Evertorch district.

"Unknown," Entorak responded, with a faint hint of interest of his own. His eyebrows rose slightly. He let the comment hang in the air for a few moments, waiting for Richard as he soaked in the response. Just as Richard opened his mouth to speak, Entorak continued.

"One of the merchants of the Evertorch district sold goods to a stranger, a man who tried to pay with silver. The merchant and a band of other shopkeepers confronted him."

Richard's eyes narrowed.

"No casualties," Entorak said, answering the implicit question. "Outnumbered and confronted by several armed men, the stranger made no attempt to inflict harm. Rather, he put on a display of what can best be described as theatrics and made every effort to scare away his assailants.

"The merchants fled, fearing that they had offended someone from the Tower. Once he collected his wits and his courage, a local shoemaker came to offer his humblest and sincerest apologies."

Richard thought about this for a moment.

"Find out what this merchant knows. And assign ten of the reds to find the other merchants. Find out what they know. Find out what kind of magic this was. *Find this rogue mage.*"

Entorak said nothing, which Richard seemed to interpret as dissent. He rebuked Entorak with a scowl.

"You know what the locals think of unscheduled magic. I don't want a mob of peasants piling up at the Tower gate."

There was the classic pause as Entorak stood motionlessly.

"Very well," he said at last, displaying no emotion or opinion on the matter.

# Ruby (The Burning Boar) – Garret

Garret eyed the man on the other side of the table. The three of them—Pel, Garret, and the stranger—stared at each other in awkward silence. Garret didn't have anything significant to add to the conversation. By any legal definition, the man wasn't a true outlaw, but he would be treated as one, especially in Ruby.

*Sheyaktu.*

The word threatened to forever change his life. Or, if things went especially poorly, to end it.

*He doesn't really look like a god killer.*

Garret would have expected the man to be nine feet tall, weigh more than four hundred pounds, and cover himself in a carapace adorned with human skulls.

*Dragon skulls, actually. Dragon skulls would be better.*

Disappointingly, the stranger wasn't imposing at all. He didn't have any interesting physical characteristics and displayed no exotic features, like glowing eyes or a forked tongue. He did not look like a once-in-a-generation embodiment of power. He seemed to be a man like any other.

"We must leave at once," Pel said. "Our friend here was the center of a scene in the Evertorch that will attract attention. He will be treated as a rogue mage until the Tower learns what he truly is. We shouldn't expect that to take very long."

Garret looked at her with surprise. "They don't know he's a god killer?" He presumed that the information was already common knowledge. If it wasn't, perhaps this commotion was unnecessary; there would be no need to flee the city or fear reprisal from the Tower. Garret came to an additional point of contention. "Wait. How do *I* know he's a god killer?"

Pel blinked hard and sighed. She pointed to both of her eyes with both of her index fingers.

"Garret, there isn't time to go over all of this. The man shines like a blue sun to me and—"

Garret gestured for her to pause. He scrunched his eyes in a moment of circumspect thought while he considered the man in the seat next to him. He waved at the other side of the table. "Weren't you just sitting over there?"

The man didn't answer the question, saying instead, "She has every right to believe that the red mages will learn of me. If she … ah …" The man trailed off helplessly as he reached for her name.

"Pel," she supplied.

He nodded his thanks. "If *Pel* can determine what I am, you can be certain the red mages can. And will. She was there when the merchants tried to collect me. The red mages will come for her, and through her, they will come for you. I am sorry, but you are both in danger. Everyone in this room should leave Ruby and never come back."

Garret was still focused on the fact that he was pretty sure the man had been sitting on the far side of the table.

"I am Deodin," the man said, directing the conversation back to Pel. "I seek a place deep in the Thick, but I am not so naïve as to think I can find it without help. I had arrangements with a guide from Bayhold, not here."

There was a palpable lull as Pel chose her words.

"Was it your plan to have your guide from Bayhold retire in prosperity?" Pel's tone had changed slightly to a thinly disguised accusation. Garret recognized Pel's real question.

To his credit, Deodin also recognized her question for what it was: how could they be sure that he wouldn't just kill them after he reached his destination? That would be the safest (and cheapest) of all the solutions.

Deodin reached into a pocket and pulled out a moderately sized purse. He opened it and carefully poured some of its contents into the palm of his free hand. Garret wasn't a jeweler by any means, but he could recognize a fortune in gemstones when he saw it.

"To your question, yes. My guide and his charming wife will be disappointed, but they are resourceful enough to thrive without me. As for the fortune itself, the gems are easier to carry than the coin, but I have an abundance of both."

Garret pulled his eyes away from the pile of sparklies. "How did you come up with that? The entire Evertorch doesn't see that much in a month!"

Deodin responded with an upturned eyebrow. He waved his hands in front of his face and produced a few visible sparks of light from his fingertips. His eyes widened with dramatic flair as he mouthed a single word: *magic!*

"Huh-huh! Right. That." Garret offered an appreciative nod and an approving smirk.

Pel remained serious and stoic, enough for Garret's spirit to grow heavy. The allure of the riches fell away at the sight of her.

"Pel," Garret said, softening. He waited until she made eye contact before he continued. "We don't have to do this. He still hasn't told us where he's going. If we leave now, we could walk right up to the Tower and tell them everything we know. And it wouldn't help them or hurt him. Besides, if he's an orc-buggering god killer, he can disappear without our help. He could probably just— Actually, why *don't* you just burn down the Tower?"

"My business lies elsewhere," Deodin said with a slight touch of hesitation.

"The Tower cannot have him," Pel said to Garret with finality. "If that means that I abandon Ruby, then it must be."

The weight of her remark fell on Garret's heart. Pel clearly hadn't come to this decision lightly. Other than her run-ins with the red mages and their Tower, she loved Ruby. She had worked her entire adult life to become its master, and considering the manner of their imminent departure, she couldn't even tell anyone her destination. To protect everyone she knew, she would have to disappear and leave no clues as to where she went.

"If you must go, I will take you," Garret said, the words coming more easily than he expected.

Pel's hard mien relaxed slightly, her stoicism fading into relief. She raised her eyebrows and mouthed the words *thank you*. Garret's decision seemed so much easier now.

Garret still harbored an abundance of skepticism. Parlor tricks and potential fortunes notwithstanding, he had no reason to believe the entirety of the stranger's story. Was he really *sheyaktu* or simply a renegade running from the red mages? Were those riches genuine? Would there be treachery once they reached their destination?

These were all questions that he considered, but they were questions he asked of all his potential clients. If their association ended in conflict, it wouldn't be the first time. At worst, he would die in a grossly unfair (and hopefully) quick fight. At best, he would retire to parts unknown. The rest lay somewhere in between.

"I will gather my things," Pel said, seemingly shedding whatever sentiment had occupied her mind. Her hands returned to their usual resting spots under her cloak and the tension left her face. The decision made, it was time to move forward. She nodded to Garret and made the belated introduction to Deodin.

"He is called Garret. He is the local expert in navigating the Thick. Provided you trust his judgment, he will be able to deliver you to your destination alive and well."

Garret stood up and began collecting his belongings. Confidence in his own expertise colored the remainder of the conversation. "I'll lead you to the wall and give you directions to a meeting place. God killer or not, you should be able to find the landmark without any help."

Garret turned to Pel and spoke with an authoritative, yet sympathetic tone.

"But as for you, you come with me. A small woman with piss-shit eyesight does not travel these roads alone. I'll get him out of the city, then meet you at your place."

She nodded.

Deodin rose, hoisted his heavy pack, and slung it over his shoulder. "My thanks. And my apologies."

"Wait," Garret called out. He got up to retrieve something from the coat rack behind him. It was a simple hat, which he tossed to Deodin.

"It... What, is it that bad?" he asked, running his fingers through his hair.

"Oh gods, yes," Pel responded immediately.

Garret piled on almost simultaneously. "*Worse* than that."

# Ruby (The Mage Tower) – Mathew

*Poor bastard. Damned if he comes here to disclose everything. Damned if he doesn't.*

Mathew empathized with the shoemaker who sat across a small table in one of the Tower's lesser-used rooms. The cobbler from the Evertorch stared blankly at the far wall, his foot tapping nervously.

Located by the main gate on the ground floor, this room had been set up to accommodate the Tower's "guests." It wasn't a jail cell, in the sense that it was well furnished, comfortable, and there were no locks to prevent these guests from simply opening the door and leaving.

Fear had brought the shoemaker here and kept him planted in his seat. He feared that the consequence of leaving would be worse than whatever fate awaited him here.

Mathew reached into a cloth sack for a small wheel of cheese and a partial loaf of bread, then made several portions of both. He took a few pieces for himself and offered the others.

"Oh, thank you, sir," the man began. "Most generous of you, but I haven't an appetite."

"I understand," Mathew said. "Hungry or not, the cheese is excellent. Perhaps the best you've ever had. At least try it. If I'm wrong, I'm wrong. And if I'm right? It's the best cheese you've ever had."

The cobbler considered this for a moment before sampling both the cheese and the bread, while Mathew prepared more.

Mathew spoke.

"When they come to talk to you, they will ask you about the details of what you saw. Take your time. Try to think of how to give them what they want to know, even if you don't know the answer to the exact question."

"How am I supposed to answer a question that I don't know the answer to?" the man complained.

"It might help to think of other ways to answer their questions. When they ask how tall the stranger stood, did his head brush up against the roofing of your tent? Or was he so short that he couldn't see what was on the highest shelves? Was he ever standing next to something that can be used to estimate his height, such as an evertorch lamp or a sign?"

Mathew took another bite.

"They'll ask you about his magic. Can you remember his words? Were his hands in front of him? Or held above his waist? Or high above his head? Did he use both hands? When he cast his magic, was it a one-second count or a five-second count?"

"I don't remember any of that," the man admitted.

"I believe you," Mathew replied as he took another bite of cheese and chewed. "However, my colleagues have … *unnatural* ways to help you remember. I find those methods uncomfortable."

Color drained from the shoemaker's face. Mathew reassured the man with an outstretched hand, palm out.

"No, no, nothing will be painful. I've had the magic cast on me. I didn't hate it, but it wasn't pleasant, either. The more you can remember on your own, the more comfortable you will be."

The man burst to life as a sudden thought came to mind.

"He had a tattoo! On his arm! Some kind of mark! And ... and ... his hair was brownish and right shitty!"

Mathew smiled sincerely. He didn't care much about a rogue mage, but he had grown to resent the way the Tower dealt with the people of Ruby. The mages tended to be unnecessarily intimidating and impersonal with the public. Everything the shoemaker did tonight, right or wrong, was done because he feared the Tower, not because he felt it his duty to report an oddity in the Evertorch.

"Excellent! Those are the details you should share."

Mathew felt a sense of relief. The more information the shoemaker offered, the sooner they'd let him on his way.

Mathew and the shoemaker turned their heads at the sound of footfalls approaching the open doorway. A moment later, Entorak appeared with one of the Tower's red mages. Entorak surveyed the situation for a moment, hovering in the doorway.

"Remember what we talked about," Mathew said to the cobbler. "I'll come check on you in twenty minutes." He rose and thoughtfully brushed the crumbs off the table into the bag he had brought with him.

Entorak eyed the situation carefully, implicitly questioning Mathew's motives for being here. "I didn't think our interview interested you," he said.

"It doesn't," Mathew replied, angling his body sideways to step past Entorak through the open door.

# Ruby (Near the Northern Gate) – Deodin

Now that Deodin had met his guide, his plans had evolved.

*Escape Ruby:*
- ☑ *Scare off the merchants*
- ☐ *Speak with Garret*
- ☐ *Avoid the patrols*
- ☐ *Find your way to the Northern wall*

Ruby had not yet awakened. Deodin and his guide had time before the sun came up and brought the city to life. He and Garret had left the Burning Boar and filed through the shadows and alleyways toward the northeastern gate. They made every effort to avoid the curious eyes of Ruby's citizens.

Deodin watched Garret, quietly assessing his aptitude. The man slinked through the shadows like a predator, stepping in near perfect balance despite the cobbled streets. His movement was graceful and fluid and his mind was equally agile. He was disciplined in the sounds he made and well aware of noises caused by everything else. Even though they had yet to leave the city, Deodin was satisfied with Garret's skills.

Nevertheless, the guide was clearly distracted. When the opportunities arose, he glanced back at Deodin with inquisitive eyes. The man didn't appear accusatory or malicious, but every time they stopped, Garret had a question on his face.

Deodin recognized it for what it was: the wonderment of meeting a god killer. Whenever he shared his *sheyaktu*-ness with others, they were curious and would inevitably task him with quests and missions. This must be Garret's turn. He sighed and gestured for Garret to proceed. "Go ahead and ask, before you explode or burst into flame."

Garret squealed with delight as if his words escaped a high-pressure leak: "*Whowouldwininafight: youoradragon?*"

Deodin paused, perplexed by the question. This was not a request to deliver a message or search for a family heirloom. In fact, Deodin wasn't sure what was sillier: the question or Garret's serious, wide-eyed wonder as he awaited the answer.

"I don't know," Deodin answered truthfully. "I've never even seen a dragon, let alone fought one. I would need to see it before I had an idea of how to fight it."

Garret was noticeably disappointed by the answer. Perhaps he expected that Deodin had slain entire broods of dragons or rode one as a mount.

"I would kill it until it was dead, though," Deodin added, pleasantly surprised that the conversation had deviated from the script he had expected.

Garret chuckled. "You've seen skalgs, though, right?" he pressed Deodin. "The little lizard guys? If you came across ten of them, could you fight them all at the same time? Or twenty? Or ... or ... fifty?" he asked with as much enthusiasm as before. Apparently, these kinds of questions ran through Garret's mind frequently enough to form a queue.

"Are all your questions about hypothetical confrontations with mobs?" Deodin asked. "You aren't going to ask me to destroy something? Or someone? You don't have a historical blood feud that can only be resolved through vengeance? You have no trinkets or charms to recover? You don't need the eyeballs from an animal or a root from a mysterious plant?"

Garret scolded him with a dour expression. "Please. I am being serious. Now: have you ever strapped a live neverbat to one foot, and another live neverbat to the other foot, and flown through the air like they were winged sandals?"

Deodin laughed. "Must I astonish you with my amazing sorcery before we can move on?"

Garret replied with an excited nod, suggesting that a fantastical display really was the type of answer he had wanted all along.

Deodin drew in, near to Garret's ear, to whisper with a smile that was just slightly diabolical. "I can kill everyone. In fact—" He hesitated before continuing with a smirk. "— perhaps *you* are already dead."

Garret scrutinized him carefully, trying to judge the seriousness of the remark.

"But before it comes to that, let us leave before it gets too light outside." Deodin gestured to the other side of the street.

With Garret's attention elsewhere, Deodin used his powers to stop the passage of time just long enough for him to furtively fasten Garret's boots together. Restoring time to its normal pace, Deodin dashed across the street to the shadows of the alleyway on the other side. Garret followed.

For a half step, at least.

The poor man fell with a thump and a curse. It took a moment for him to catch his bearings and realize what had happened. From the other side of the street, Deodin snorted as he tried to suppress a laugh.

Garret wasn't angered or annoyed; his eyes were wide with awe. He stared down at his boots. The laces of his left foot were tied into the laces of his right.

*Already dead*, Deodin mouthed, his eyes wide. He waved his fingers in front of his face, arcs of color filling the air. He mouthed one final word: *magic!*

"Huh-huh!"

*Escape Ruby:*

- ☑ *Scare off the merchants*
- ☑ *Speak with Garret*
- ☐ *Avoid the patrols*
- ☐ *Find your way to the Northern wall*

# Ruby (The Mage Tower) – Entorak

After two knocks, Entorak pushed open the heavy interior door. Richard waited outside on the balcony on the far side of his chambers, through a doorway from the study portion of the room. He gazed out over Ruby, facing the perpetual twilight of the Evertorch district.

Entorak held his breath as he passed through the smell of sex and alcohol of Richard's bedroom, inhaling again once he reached the cool, refreshing air of the balcony. Thankfully, and tastefully, Richard had taken a few additional moments to change out of his nightgown.

"There is something at work here, old friend," Richard said.

Entorak weighed Richard's statement. He was not the type of person to savor a mild morning or a sunrise on a clear day. Nor was he the type to refer to anyone as an "old friend."

But there was something tangibly different about him. He seemed more alert and alive. In his years at the Tower, Richard had become bored with the day-to-day affairs. He had never truly mastered the magical arts and he started to view everything with apathy and ennui. If he were stimulated at all, nearly all his passions appeared to manifest as anger.

And here Richard stood, excited. Enthusiastic. Driven. It reminded Entorak of a much-younger Richard. That man had been ruthless and ambitious enough to carry out morally ambiguous magical experiments and claw his way to the top of the red mage hierarchy. When infatuated with sex and indulgences, Richard was merely unpleasant. When pursuing a goal and fueled by limitless ambition, Richard was dangerous. Entorak summarized what he knew.

"A tattooed mage with bad hair frightened the locals but caused no further problems. He paid for his goods with silver. He presumably stowed away on the merchant vessel that made port after sundown.

"Perhaps he was a troublemaker from Southend, stowing away to flee from the law. Or maybe someone from the Western Isles. The merchants did not mention an accent, so I don't believe him to be from the East. Regardless, if his destination is beyond the walls, I see no reason to spend time and resources on him."

Entorak assumed his usual stoic posture, hands at his waist, holding the fingers of his left hand with his right hand.

"And what of his spell casting?" Richard asked, looking over his shoulder, back at Entorak.

"The witnesses agree: theatrics," Entorak said. "His age and skill suggest that he's a practiced mage."

"Ah, but you overlook the *way* he cast those spells. And how he captured the shoemaker's knife," Richard replied, turning completely around to face Entorak. "None of the merchants could describe any hand movements. The witnesses agree that he made no gesture or incantation at all!"

The implication of Richard's remark caused Entorak's mask of disinterest to slip, if only for a moment.

"*Sheyaktu?* You wish to use Tower resources to pursue a legend?" Entorak asked without obvious intonation.

"I wish to pursue the opportunity!" Richard corrected him as he took a step closer. "Understanding *sheyaktu* is the key to understanding all of it! All of this! If I am right, if we are right, we are on the precipice of finding the master key for all magic! Within our lifetime! Why does the Tower even exist, if not for something like this?"

Richard was potentially right. If anyone could unlock the secrets of *sheyaktu* via study, it would be Richard. Entorak still believed it was much more likely that the witnesses had simply overlooked the spellcasting elements, as such details would not have been important to them.

Nevertheless...

Entorak found himself in agreement with Richard's decision. The Tower was designed to be the pinnacle of magical research. Studying *sheyaktu* could advance their discipline to levels that couldn't otherwise be achieved. That was the intended purpose of the Tower, after all.

"Very well," Entorak said, his composure fully regained. "How shall I direct the mages to conduct the search?"

"Let them sleep for the rest of the night," Richard said, with his first sincere smile in quite some time. "Come morning, we begin the search for the key to unlocking magic itself!"

# DAY
# 3

# Ruby (The Northern Gate) – Garret

Garret had to admit, for a god killer, Deodin was pretty likable. After the bit with the shoes tied together, Deodin had respectfully requested that Garret stop asking for displays of magic.

"I don't use spells and sorcery to impress people," he explained as the two of them watched the behavior of the guards at the northeastern gate.

"Impress people? Why would that matter? I would use those powers for everything, from cooking dinner to wiping my ass." Garret had intended the remark as a joke, but soon came to wonder if Deodin could, or actually did, use magic to—

"You carry that." Deodin nodded at the bow slung over Garret's shoulder. "Is that your first choice to solve your problems?"

"Not so much for ass-wiping, no," Garret conceded.

"I must be more careful than you might expect. People treat me differently when they learn what I am," Deodin explained.

"More polite? Because they are scared of you? Thank the gods, I'm not a crow. I'm not scared of you."

Deodin paused as if puzzled by this last statement. "What is a 'crow'? Are the 'Crows' a criminal group within Ruby?" Deodin asked, a look of confusion on his face.

"A crow is a big, black bird that caws. With that shirt and that hair, you look like a gods-damned scarecrow," Garret said, laughing at the punchline long before he could finish the joke.

"I can tie your arms into a knot," Deodin stated.

Garret sobered immediately. "You know what? I'll be good."

They had arrived at the edge of the city just as the sun had started peeking over the foothills on the border to the Thick. A pleasant night had turned into a mild morning, with the clear skies promising another beautiful day.

Garret suggested that they take a few minutes to watch the city guards manning the gate. He wanted to see how they interacted with people leaving the city. The guards' behavior might suggest how much they knew about Deodin, if anything.

After a few minutes, Garret noticed a trend and frowned.

The guards weren't abusive or rough, but they seemed to take far more interest in their duties than normal. They inspected the forearms of every man exiting through the gate. Their scrutiny extended to travel packs and equipment.

"What's the thing on your arm?" Garret asked.

Deodin pulled back his right sleeve to reveal a tattoo of symbols on the inside of his forearm. Garret didn't recognize the script, but it was clearly something that was unique or identifying.

"Ah. And your pack?"

Deodin turned away from Garret to present his pack. It was obvious that Deodin had equipped himself for a journey. He wore tools and gear suitable for an expedition into the Thick and carried nothing that would be appropriate for a merchant or commoner. It was also clear that the equipment was new. The leather was stiff and recently tanned.

"Did you get all of that here?" Garret asked.

"Yes, from the Evertorch last night. The merchants confronted me and tried to turn me in for being a stowaway. Any of them might be able to describe what I carry," Deodin replied.

"They know about the marking on your arm and that you carry new equipment," Garret said, disappointed. "We could split up our equipment and switch back later, but they'd still identify you because you look like you."

"Yes. I do look like me." Deodin nodded at the men at the gate. "I can make it to the other side of the wall. The grove you mentioned earlier: I can find it from the road? Even if it is dark?"

"Yes," Garret replied. "It's an obvious landmark. If you cross a bridge, you've gone too far."

Deodin nodded again, adjusting the straps as he began to move.

"Very well, I will meet you at the grove by nightfall."

"Yeah? How are you getting past the guards? Is it amazing? It's going to be amazing, isn't it?"

Deodin raised his eyebrows and inclined his head toward the guards. Garret observed them standing idly and casually talking with each other. It was the same scene they'd been watching for the past ten minutes.

"What?" Garret asked, watching for a few moments longer before turning back around.

Deodin was gone. Garret scanned the nearby area to find it empty. He scrunched up his face in a mixture of disappointment and annoyance. The god killer had performed an amazing magical feat and he'd missed it. Again.

"Scarecrow!" Garret hissed as loudly as he dared, hoping that Deodin was still within earshot.

# Ruby (Pel's Quarters) — Pel

A knock sounded at Pel's door.

She had arrived home only an hour prior and had just finished changing clothes and organizing her belongings. Pel wrapped her fingers around the door handle, hesitating before pulling it open.

*They can't know of you already.*

Pel closed her eyes. Briefly, terrifyingly, she had a vision of opening the door to see Entorak and a few anonymous, generic red mages standing behind him. She pictured him sharply dressed and bearing his unnerving, erect posture and his cryptic expression.

The knocking continued.

"Pelium Stillwater, you will open the gods-damned door before I kick it in," Garret hissed from the other side. A moment later, he continued. "Actually, I'd probably try to come in through a window. That's a pretty sturdy door."

A slight grin of relief found Pel's lips as she unfastened the latch.

It had been two hours since she had seen Garret last, but he looked different. He had changed his clothes, wore a traveling pack, and carried another. If he suffered fatigue from being awake all night, she couldn't tell. There was an energy about him that belied the circumstance. He appeared ready to go.

"Pel…" he said, softly and seriously, waiting for her to meet his eyes before he continued.

She looked at him, reminded of how utterly rugged and ravishing he was. Covered in adventuring gear and weapons, a day's worth of stubble on his face, his hair tousled just the right amount, he looked like the hero of a children's story. She had always known him as a man who conquered nature and her elements, but as he stood on her doorstep, he truly looked the part. The moment lasted precisely until he spoke.

"Move the fucking fuck out of the way." He gestured to the doorway where she still stood.

She closed the door behind Garret as he stumbled into the primary living area of her tiny home and deposited one of his traveling packs on the floor.

Pel's small, simple quarters seldom entertained visitors. Despite the imminent danger of the Tower and the intrigue of their plans to flee the city, Garret focused on the home's décor.

"Gods, Pel, these are awful," he said as he closed the cheap, shabby curtains, his sneer every bit as judgmental as his tone. "I know your eyesight is bad, but that shouldn't affect your sense of taste."

He found a pile of items that Pel had set aside for their escape. Without asking permission, he rummaged through her belongings, transferring a few items to the extra pack he'd brought with him. He assessed her clothes as closely as her furnishings.

"We're fleeing for our lives from the red mages, Pel, not visiting a relative in the Isles." Garret sighed, selecting only a fraction of the things she had collected. He paused when he found the underwear Bartlett had given her a few hours earlier. He raised the garment to make his point.

"If it doesn't help you to survive a casual stroll through the Thick, it stays here. Unless you have more things like these. These can come, even if I have to carry them."

She laughed at the absurdity, but also because of the way Garret handled himself. She didn't normally see him in his element. She saw him in hers, within the walls of Ruby, within the social and professional situations where she was the expert. Now, she saw him at his best … and for him to make time for a crude, completely inappropriate joke? Right now? Despite all this drama and intrigue? That was the quintessential Garret experience. And it was reassuring.

"Thank you," she said.

His expression softened.

"Come on, Pel. What else could you do? What could we do? We're caught between a god killer and a Tower filled with depraved mages."

"You didn't have to agree to this, though," she admitted. "You're willing to give it all up and none of this is about you."

It was the first time she had really considered his stake in this. With the excitement of *sheyaktu* and her fears of the Tower, she had put no thought into how this affected Garret. And yet, here he was.

Garret straightened and shuffled his feet. There was a change in his body language. Buried, if only for the moment, was Garret's easy-going attitude and witty confidence. He drew a heavy breath and held it as he chose his words. He looked at her with an intensity that she seldom noticed.

"Pel…"

A firm rap came at the front door, then two more.

She glanced at Garret, who was already in motion. Quietly and without being directed, he had retrieved their travel packs and moved silently toward her room.

After he had closed the bedroom door behind him, she took a deep breath and opened the front door, despite the fear and anxiety welling in her stomach. She immediately recognized the man on the other side.

Of course it was Entorak.

# Ruby (Pel's Quarters) – Entorak

*Pelium looks tired,* Entorak thought.

As always, however, Pelium radiated an almost indomitable beauty. Regardless of circumstance, Entorak had always found her pleasant to look upon. Now was no different. She wore a simple shirt and leggings, but this marked one of the few times he had seen her without her arms and shoulders buried beneath a cloak. She looked slightly worse for wear. Her hair was in disarray and she hadn't completely buttoned her shirt.

Her untidiness was, no doubt, the result of his calling on her so early in the day. Entorak sighed ever so slightly to himself before speaking, regretful that circumstances demand he be so rude.

"Pelium." He nodded slowly in a contrite gesture. "My sincerest apologies for waking you."

"Entorak," she said simply before glancing at the two red mages behind him, without quite hiding her disdain. Entorak did not hold the sentiments against her; she had every right to be annoyed.

"There was a troubling incident at the Evertorch last night. I hoped you might know of it," he said, bowing.

"*You* may come in," Pelium said, inviting him in specifically.

Entorak agreed to her invitation and gestured for the others to wait outside. She was one of the few people who could dictate such terms. Were it anyone else, Entorak might have been tempted to push the issue, using his stature to insist that his colleagues accompany him. However, considering her history, he saw no need for such incivility. She beckoned him into her small living space.

Entorak seldom had the need or opportunity to call on her, but Pelium's home looked as simple as he remembered. The curtains were ragged and the old, worn furniture was mismatched. Her livelihood as an information dealer did not allow for any scraps of modernity or luxury.

"No change in your vision?" he asked, turning his attention back to her. He suspected he knew the answer to the question, but he found himself obligated to ask whenever he saw her.

"Why would there be?" Her tone was laced with just enough venom to be noticed, but not enough to be provocative.

"Optimism. Hope. Perhaps time has allowed you to suffer less from my folly," he said simply.

Entorak's regret was genuine. He had cast the permanent detection spell on her eyes many years before. At the time, her reasons had seemed justified and her circumstance moved him. Rather than helping her, the spell had practically blinded her. He had since felt a heavy burden of guilt. She deserved no such fate.

"What of this incident?" Pelium asked.

Entorak was about to elaborate about the rogue mage but, instead, held his comments. Pelium Stillwater, of all people, didn't know about this? The notion seemed ridiculous.

"I was at the Evertorch last night," she persisted. "What incident?"

"There was a conflict with local merchants," Entorak returned, after taking a moment to decide how to best phrase it.

"When?" Pelium asked. "I was there very late, shortly after *The Maiden's Tears* came to port. I was there when her crew made delivery."

Indeed. He knew all this already, of course. He had learned that she was in the market at that time. The merchants had mentioned a woman fitting her description. And since she was there, she would likely know about this incident.

She *should* know.

"You've heard nothing of a rogue mage terrorizing the merchants?" he asked with the slightest hint of surprise. He had come here, curious to get her side of the story. Instead, he found himself increasingly wondering about her ignorance. Or perhaps, why she claimed to be ignorant.

"I was only there briefly," she replied with a shrug.

Her answer was not the issue; her tone struck him. Pelium's time was always valuable, especially at such an early hour, but she was always professional and courteous. Entorak understood her uneasiness around mages, including himself, better than most. And while she was normally cool and distant when he dealt with her, she never behaved like this. She was restless and distracted. Here she stood, in her own home, and she didn't want to be here.

This was quite an unexpected situation. He had known Pelium Stillwater for years, even before the unpleasantness that led to her decision to permanently enchant her eyes. She was a living library of knowledge of Ruby's affairs. It was impossible that she remained uninformed about something as newsworthy as last night's incident at the Evertorch.

He eyed her carefully. She shifted her weight unnaturally. Impatiently. She expressed discomfort, physically and mentally. This was exactly the behavior he had seen countless times when people had something to hide from him. She really, really wanted him to leave.

*Oh, Pelium,* he thought, unhappily realizing where this conversation was going to—

The sound of a door mechanism broke the silence. Entorak whipped his head to face the door to her bedroom, which cracked open slowly. Out walked a man.

Well, "sauntered" might be a better way to describe it.

The man's name escaped him, but Entorak recognized him as one of the local guides to the Thick. He had an athletic build, with broad shoulders and defined muscles like that of a horse or pit terrier. He squinted through half-closed eyes, as if he had recently awoken. A waft of alcohol hung in the air, drifting through the now-open door.

The man was also naked. The only stitch of fabric on his person was a small patch of black cloth balled up in his hand.

"Have you seen my shorts? I can only find yours," he said to Pel with the slightest sleepiness in his voice. He flicked his wrist slightly to unfold the black cloth in his hand. It took the shape of a racy set of women's undergarments.

An awkward silence stretched out while Entorak exchanged glances with Pelium. She could offer no reaction other than a single, nearly emotionless blink. After a moment, the naked man noticed a second person in the room.

"Have *you* seen a pair of shorts?" the naked man asked, apparently quite resolved to settle this issue.

Entorak wallowed in the awkwardness for a moment longer. Then, he released an altogether unexpected and ultimately satisfying laugh. The scene itself was comedic, but his mirth came from relief in a now-obvious realization.

"I was only there briefly," Pelium said again, this time more sheepishly. Her cheeks were noticeably and charmingly flushed. She turned away from Entorak in embarrassment, only to turn away from the naked man in even more embarrassment.

"My sincerest apologies, Pelium. I have been outrageously rude and intrusive. I'll see myself out," Entorak said, truly mortified at his manners.

Pel nodded ambiguously.

With his empty hand, the naked man gave a somewhat confused, half-hearted wave. Entorak nodded his farewell to Pelium, then offered a similar bow to the naked man.

Satisfied, Entorak turned around and left.

# Ruby (The Northern Gate) – Deodin

"OY! Adventurer!"

*Damn.*

Deodin frowned. He had hoped to leave the city without any significant interaction with the locals. The sun had just started to rise above the city walls. The longer he stayed in town, the more people would be up and about. Already, a stocky man had summoned him and waved him over. Deodin averted his eyes.

*I don't have time for this.*

The merchant had singled Deodin out among the few passersby in the street. This was the kind of interaction that found him and only him. It was another of the inexplicable burdens imposed by the Universe.

"OY! Ya fancy yourself a hero of the realms, do ya? Give me a hand, eh?" The male voice did not issue an order or a command; his tone was more pleading than authoritative.

Resigned, Deodin turned his gaze on the short, stout man standing next to a pushcart filled with breads and pastries. A coating of flour dusted the man's clothes and hair. The contextual clues implied that he was a baker who had just begun his day. He drew closer, happy to continue his dialogue even if Deodin had not yet replied.

"Are ya heading outside the walls? We're in a pinch of trouble and hoped you could help us out." He spoke with an exotic accent; unlike the rest of the merchants of the market, he dropped meaningful consonants, especially at the beginning and end of words.

"I am sorry, friend, another time," Deodin replied with a forced smile, trying to be polite enough to be unremarkable. The less this merchant remembered their conversation, the better for everyone involved.

"Thanks! Let me tell you the details," the man replied. "I need to get to the market, but I don't have all the ingredients I need to make my meat pies."

"Perhaps you'll find another to aid you. Good day."

Deodin should have been able to smile and walk on by, but he was effectively trapped, waiting for the dialogue to run its course. It was a circumstance that bound him surprisingly frequently.

"I need eight spikeboar livers to make my meat pies, but my normal supplier is three days late with his delivery!"

Deodin scowled with visible disdain.

Spikeboars were a wild species of boar that lived in the Crown, usually near the edge of the Thick. The beasts were territorial and aggressive enough to be a genuine threat to livestock and unsupervised children. They were troublesome to anyone who lived in farmlands and ranches. And while spikeboars wouldn't be regarded among the most dangerous mobs of the Crown, they were monstrous enough, equipped with an altogether hostile array of spines along their backs and shoulders, which gave them their name.

"Who eats spikeboar livers?" Deodin asked, curious. Mobs were categorically inedible. A secondary thought also came to mind: "Eight is an oddly specific number."

"Aye, people come from all around to eat my spikeboar liver pie," the merchant continued proudly. "My customers say that the pies fill their bellies and make them smarter!"

"Your spikeboar liver pie increases intelligence?" a now incredulous Deodin asked.

"Oh, aye," the baker continued without the slightest hint of jest or irony. "The Tower mages swear that it makes them better spell casters. At least temporarily."

"That makes no sense," Deodin noted.

"If you can fetch me the eight livers, I can reward you handsomely," the merchant continued, as if Deodin entertained the offer. "I can even mark their location on your map."

"I cannot help you," Deodin said, trying to remain polite. "I'd have to go all the way to the edge of the Thick just to have a chance to find them. And if you encounter one, it's a total disaster. They attack on sight, they can launch their spikes, and just when you're about to kill one of them, it runs off to summon every other spikeboar in the area to join in the fight. There's no way I'm going to try to kill eight of them."

"Well, you'd probably have to kill close to thirty of them," the merchant admitted. "You wouldn't be able to get a liver from all of them. You can get a good liver in one out of four."

"The other three-quarters do not have livers?" Deodin observed drily.

The merchant shrugged, seemingly content with his inability to answer the question.

Deodin held his hands out in front of him and gestured each point as he articulated them. "So, you're asking me to march all the way to the edge of the Thick. Survive battles with over thirty spikeboars. Harvest the livers that may or may not exist, all the while leaving a mountain of lifeless and liverless corpses to rot in the sun. And once I collect eight of these things, I'm to bring them all back here before they spoil. Finally, those livers will go into a pie that will temporarily increase my intellect?"

"Well, it sounds right fookin' crazy the way you say it," the merchant complained.

"It sounds crazy regardless of how I say it. And for what? What is my reward for all of this?"

"One of the pies. And you know what? I'll throw in the recipe for the pie itself!"

"No, thank you," Deodin said. Immediately, he felt a sensation that he had somehow disappointed the Universe.

*Help the baker:*

☒  *Collect 8 spikeboar livers*

# North of Ruby (South of the Windmill Grove) – Deodin

*Northbound from Ruby:*

- ☑ *Sneak over the Northern wall*
- ☐ *Find the Windmill Grove*

Having found his way out of the city, Deodin walked for nearly two hours. He stopped and took a moment to collect his bearings and check his notes, retrieving a few scraps of paper from his pack, including the page torn from the book in the Southend library. In one hand, he held the translated poem; in his other hand, a map of the Crown.

With all the clues now assembled, the history of the poem began to make more sense. It was believable and realistic that ancient orcs would have seen Lyle Makee as a god. It made sense that they would entomb him after his death. He could even believe that they would record the location of that tomb in a song, as part of their tradition of oral history.

So, while he believed most of the circumstances about orcs and Lyle Makee, he struggled with the notion that an orc song could be so conveniently translated into a cryptic, poetic riddle written in the Common tongue. It was an example of the Universe being lazy.

**We'll never know the god who shed the tear.**
**The god of fates, who brought them all so near?**
**The god of heart, for marching on their lands?**

106

*The god of death, the harvest in his hands?*
*The serpent's tail, the mouth that we abhor.*
*The first one of a kind they named the Horror.*

Ancient orcs spoke in metaphor. Over the years, much of the context of their poetry had been lost. Only by collecting a series of notes could Deodin interpret and understand the clues.

He had learned that the "serpent" was an expression for the Kalee River that "snaked" southwest from the mountains of the Crown down to Ruby. From what he could tell, the "tail" of that snake began somewhere in the foothills south of the mountains. The mouth was the bay near Ruby's docks.

The tear? That part of the puzzle was only recently solved. Deodin had been in Southend to visit its great library to research orc history and try to understand what the orcs meant when they described "a teardrop of a god." He was underwhelmed to learn that the teardrop was merely a giant boulder in the shape of a water droplet. It was a huge boulder, by boulder standards, but was otherwise uninteresting.

Therefore, somewhere between Netherby, Delemere, and Luton, near the Kalee River, Deodin expected to find that boulder resting on a hillside. It would be the marker for Makee's tomb. He folded the map and the poem and returned them both to a pocket in his pack.

Deodin hoped Garret was as capable as he appeared. The god killer needed to get to Netherby, escape the red mages, and find Makee's tomb. He could only hope that something in Makee's library would help him with the last stanza of the orc song, which was refreshingly transparent in its meaning:

*And once our queen awakens in her den,*
*We set out to destroy their scarlet gem.*

# Netherby – The Emissary

Tyberius Reginald Lorian, the Fourth Adept of the Lumerage Order of the Leopard, the Magistrix of Archanagia and the Emissary of the Ruby Mage Tower: Point Prominence, had been sent to Netherby as part of Richard's search for the rogue mage.

Traveling to the northwest village had taken the better part of the day. The carriage ride had been bumpy, noisy, and wholly miserable. Tyberius had just managed to enjoy enough peace to allow for a nap.

The nap ended when the carriage came to an abrupt stop. He woke and took a moment or two to come to his senses. It took a few more moments to realize that his imagination had greatly misled him.

The tiny village of Netherby had been explained to him as a simple farming and ranching community on the southern end of the mountains of the Crown. It served as a resting point for anyone traveling from the mountain fortress Delemere and the coastal town of Peak's View.

*This is Netherby?*

It wasn't a town. It wasn't a village. Instead, Tyberius could see only a single rundown structure next to the road. In front of the building, the word "Netherby" had been scratched into a plank nailed to a lonely post. The signpost itself seemed to embody Netherby's spirit by leaning heavily to one side, as if it longed to fall over and finally die.

A few small, equally dilapidated hovels and shacks dotted the hills in the background, but there was no way that this could be mistaken for an outpost of civilization. Tyberius knew the definition of "rural" and this was several orders of magnitude more rustic than even his most primitive imaginings.

*Orcs live better than this.*

At best, the inn before him was a deathtrap. The side paneling had succumbed to rot. The roof bowed inward. The walls on his right-hand side leaned enough to be noticeable and alarming. The fact that such a dwelling featured multiple floors was an affront to the laws of nature. Gravity had been absent the day this building was erected, considering how the foundational lumber seemed to hang from the boards they were intended to support.

The driver had made his way around to open the carriage door. He greeted Tyberius with a plain and altogether impatient expression.

"Hip the fookout, eh?" is what Tyberius heard, unable to understand the driver's first word.

The driver spoke with a thick accent, but Tyberius wondered if the man's enunciation was directly related to his dental state. So rotten and tangled were the man's teeth, his words must have collided with them as they escaped his mouth.

While lost in the thoughts of the lifelong conflict between the driver's tongue and teeth, Tyberius remained motionless and expressionless long enough to prompt the driver to speak again.

"Get. The FUCK. OUT," he said, this time with much better diction.

Normally, a red mage wouldn't endure such open hostility and discourtesy. However, Tyberius was more confused than angered. He climbed out of the carriage in a fugue, his mind still focused on the inn.

*People choose to sleep here? I will have to sleep here?*

Impatiently, the driver recovered the luggage from the carriage and clumsily deposited the bags on the ground. Job complete, he stood before Tyberius with an open, expectant palm. Without looking up, the red mage reached into his pocket and withdrew the sum that had been agreed upon prior to the journey.

Annoyed at the lack of a tip, but apparently glad to be rid of his passenger, the driver climbed back up to his seat. Before he even sat down, he urged his horse on with a snap of the reins, clearly eager to be gone.

Tyberius stood alone before Netherby's single "inn," kept company only by the flies that had found him. He absently waved at the insects and took a step forward, only to pause as something seemed to hold his foot in place. It was a pile of wet horse shit, like the one into which his luggage had been planted.

Tyberius stood there for a few moments more, before correctly concluding that there would be no porter to assist him with his bags. He sighed and bent over to pick up his belongings, swaying when he found that they were far heavier than he had estimated. Up to this point, others had carried his luggage for him and now he learned firsthand how cumbersome that chore had been.

He clattered through the doorway and dropped his bags on the floor immediately inside the threshold. It took a few moments for his eyes to adjust from the brilliant afternoon sun to the inn's cavelike interior. He grimaced.

A few of the customers observed him languidly for a moment before turning their attention back to whatever they were doing before. A few others ignored him entirely. He stood there even longer, expecting the staff to meet and address him properly. No greeting occurred and it became clear such a thing would not be forthcoming.

The indifference struck him as odd. He stood before them garbed in the red of Ruby's famous Tower, bearing the obvious sigils and markings of his craft, and yet nobody cared.

Then the reality of the situation hit him like a shower of ice water: these people did not know what he was. It was astonishing that people lived outside the influence of magic and those who practiced it.

Without any other obvious direction as to what to do, he found the bar and the server who stood behind it. The barkeep gazed back at him, but not out of deference, professional courtesy, or even curiosity. Instead, the lines and creases on his face merely told the story of a man who had aged more than his actual years, much of it likely spent right here.

The barkeep offered Tyberius no friendly upward nod nor a respectful downward bow. He merely stared with a flat, soulless gaze that was so unnerving, Tyberius felt compelled to look away.

The scene behind the barkeeper was no more pleasant. There was no glittering array of glass bottles and polished oak casks. Rather, behind him rested two large barrels, one of which was stacked precariously atop the other.

"Wine. Something from—" Tyberius began, his voice cracking more than he would have liked.

He had yet to even finish his request before the barkeep made an impatient, condescending gesture to the large, obviously placed sign that had, until then, escaped Tyberius's notice.

It was a simple menu, as it turned out:

Tyberius nodded absently. The bartender then retrieved a wholly unclean mug and filled it with a thick, slightly lumpy liquid from the tap on the rough keg behind him. The sound made less of a "pour" and more of a "plop" as the unfiltered beverage reluctantly escaped the spout.

Tyberius accepted the mug and brought it to his lips, nearly regurgitating at the porridgelike consistency and bitter aftertaste of weeds and tree bark. Not waiting for a review of the house ale, the barkeep extended a gnarled palm.

The payment!

Tyberius forced a weak smile at the barkeep, who glared at him expectantly. The mage wasn't quite sure how much this drink would cost, as he was more accustomed to Ruby's currency. To better ingratiate himself, he decided to overpay. He slid his hand across the filthy bar, leaving behind four shiny copper coins.

The bartender's lips drew back and his eyes widened. "What the fook, man?" he said, hooking a thumb at the bar menu behind him. The hot burn of embarrassment rolled down the back of Tyberius's neck as he re-examined the sign, this time in its entirety:

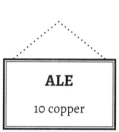

**ALE**

10 copper

Tyberius reached into his pocket and pulled out the difference, fumbling awkwardly in the process. Even after retrieving the payment, the barkeep held his expression of disgust for a few moments more. Then he shook his head and turned away to do something else.

Tyberius also turned away, to survey the room. He was here on important official business, after all. He would announce himself to the people in the tavern and see if they had encountered the rogue mage. He cleared his throat more loudly and dramatically than was necessary.

"I seek a man..." He panned his head from left to right. Tyberius had planned a short speech, but instead, he hesitated. The poor lighting prevented him from seeing whether anyone had looked up from their drink to listen.

The pause invited a reply. "I'll need a few more drinks before I fancy you," an anonymous male voice called out with a fair amount of snide.

The previously languid and apathetic patrons chuckled collectively, refueling the heated embarrassment that flooded Tyberius's face and neck. The humiliation mixed with contempt and anger into a swell of emotion.

"Just close your eyes and think of Ned," replied another, prompting another chorus of snickers and chortles. Another voice, presumably belonging to Ned, expressed outrage at the slight.

*Enough.*

The fact that he couldn't identify the specific fools in the shadows of this shithole did not matter. He heaved the mug across the room, at the silhouettes of people on the far side of the tavern. The mug was heavy and robust, surviving the impact without shattering. The liquid spilled out and splashed one or more of the peasants obscured by the darkness.

Almost immediately came the creak of wood as chairs were pushed back from their tables. A few of the more emboldened rabble rose to their feet uttering whatever local epithets came to mind.

In a civilized place, there would be a hushed pause at such an outburst. Civil folk didn't normally jump to confrontation. But such was not the case with this lot. The only thing they understood was confrontation.

*Good for them.*

The first sincere smile of the day found Tyberius's face as he gathered his hands in front of him and drew a sigil in the air. With a few choice words, he would change the complexion of Netherby for years to come.

The bright light of the explosion chased away the inn's shadows. An orange-yellow flame appeared from nowhere, centered in the group of the vengeful who had risen to their feet. The unwashed masses could claim the prize of their indiscretion in the form of a runny, slippery fire that now engulfed them.

Tyberius regarded it as a tame enchantment, at least when compared to the more horrific war spells in his arsenal. The effect was quite like being doused with alcohol and set ablaze. Fortunately for the patrons, it only affected the six or eight of them who had been at that table.

The luckier and more resourceful targets had the presence of mind to shed their burning clothing and smother the flames. The rest? Fuck them. They could wear their disfigurements as a reminder of their manners and their place.

Even though the spell had robbed him of some of his breath, adrenaline surged through Tyberius's veins. Teeth bared, he scowled at everyone with the courage to meet his gaze, menacing them with the visible ball of light he held.

"I am looking for a man!" he repeated forcefully, this time without interruption or heckle. "My height. Bad hair. New pack and boots. Tattoo or mark on the inside of his right arm. This man is a mage. Should you see him, you shall inform me. You shall do nothing else."

No response followed.

*"Get the fuck out!"* he screamed, revolted that they still dared to remain in his presence.

He didn't need to repeat the command. The rabble scuttled from their dank cave into the bright light of the outdoors, taking their filth, stupidity, and stench with them.

Still fuming at the chain of events, he stomped back to the bar and grabbed another mug of the ale that had been prepared for someone else. After a taste, a cough, and a curse, he threw that mug across the room as well. This time, it shattered with a more satisfying explosion of shards.

A motion on the far side of the room caught his eye: the tiniest flinch of a serving girl who still cowered in the room, near where the mug had landed. She had been standing there the entire time, either too timid or stupid to flee with the rest of the idiots.

"You." Tyberius singled her out with a pointed finger. "You stay here."

# North of Ruby
# (The Windmill Grove) – Pel

"You realize the gods are punishing you for canceling on me last night," Garret remarked to Pel.

The two of them sat next to each other on a fallen log in a small, remote cluster of trees Garret called the "Windmill Grove," an area far enough removed from the main road to be isolated, but obvious enough to serve as a rendezvous point to meet Deodin.

"Think about it," he continued. "We have dinner, you have a great time, you drink too much and throw yourself at me after I repeatedly ask you to keep your hands to yourself. Many hours later, the sun comes up, and life continues with the two of us being completely unaware of some god killer and his drama."

Pel smiled. The two of them had spent the day walking in the grasslands between Ruby and the Thick. The path through rolling hills outside of Ruby was smooth, easy to follow, and altogether scenic. Even with her poor vision, Pel could feel the presence of the towering mountains that dominated the northern horizon. The journey felt more like a day-long picnic than an abandonment of her life in Ruby.

Having spent the day with Garret in his element, she had found his company to be perfect. Everything about him was relaxed and confident. He seemed totally at peace with their circumstances, certainly enough to continue the joking and flirting. She enjoyed it.

"Instead," he continued, "we flee the city, camp near the largest swarm of flies in the Crown, lurking in the dark for a man who may never come. And if he does come, he may get us killed."

"Encountering a god killer was more likely than me 'throwing myself at you,'" Pel said with a note of scorn.

"You don't know that. People throw things at me all the time."

"To us, then." Pel laughed. "And the largest swarm of flies in the Crown."

She lifted an imaginary goblet for a toast. Garret replied in kind.

They had arrived at the grove two hours before. An hour after that, the sun had set. And still, Deodin had not yet arrived. Considering his head start, they had expected him to be waiting for them. Instead, they'd got there first and having nothing else to do, set up their minimalist camp.

Garret stoked the fire quietly for a moment.

"The mage that stopped by your place this morning. Which one is he?" he asked.

"Entorak," Pel replied. "He isn't the true director of the Tower, but he is one of the primary decision makers. He has his hands in nearly all of Ruby's affairs. He has a reputation for being extremely influential and persuasive."

"I can't stand him," Garret replied. "I haven't forgiven him for what he did to you."

Pel laughed humorlessly. "To be fair, he only did what I asked of him."

"Did he bugger it up on purpose, do you think? Use you as an example of what happens when the peasants try to enjoy the wonders of spellcraft?"

"No. He was shocked that it didn't work as he expected. My eyesight is the proof of magic's limitations and the human inability to master it. I am a cautionary tale."

Garret paused to search for the right words. Instead of the right words, he said, "Well, if I had thought for a second that it would have helped, I'd have kicked him in the balls or something."

"Words from the truest of friends." Pel smiled, then grew more serious. "Entorak is far more terrifying than the more spectacular mages. Most of them are reckless and impulsive. Dangerous, but predictably dangerous. He is not. He is patient, thoughtful, and deductive. If the Tower is to capture Deodin, it will be through his doing, in one way or another."

"Do you think he can escape them?" Garret said, before turning to her with a gravity she seldom saw in him. "Do you think *we* can escape them?"

Normally jovial and light-hearted, he was also self-aware enough to grasp the reality of their situation. He was a mere mortal trying to navigate an increasingly grim set of circumstances—circumstances she had brought to him. Pel brightened for a moment, reminded of the events of the morning.

"Thankfully, I don't think they'll have any questions about our involvement, thanks to that little act this morning."

"'Little,'" he echoed.

"Were it not for that, Entorak would have been suspicious, surely. Your little stunt was probably the—"

"You keep using that word," he protested, as if shocked she'd made the same mistake twice.

"Your terrifyingly enormous stunt was probably the only thing that would have satisfied Entorak's curiosity. That cleverness may have been the single most impressive thing I've ever seen from you."

Before he could object, she corrected herself.

"*Second* most impressive."

This seemed to satisfy Garret. "Assuming we survive this insanity and the god killer leaves us with a mountain of riches, what will you do?"

Pel paused to reflect on the question. She took a breath to answer but found that it was too complicated to summarize with a single sentence.

"Me too." Garret sighed. "It's not quite as simple as building a palace and being waited on by half-naked servants, is it?"

He was right, of course. Even if Deodin paid them with a king's fortune, her fate would be less certain than retirement to a life of decadence and hedonism. She would need to be careful when interacting with other people and never reveal her identity or past. A friendly, well-intentioned neighbor might inadvertently discover her secret. Even in the best of circumstances, a future of paranoia and insecurity awaited her.

"I don't know that I have the luxury to think about the problems of tomorrow," she answered. "But you know what? I'm happy to be here. Right now. With you."

"Does that mean if we survive all of this, you will finally join me for dinner? I should be able to afford something better than the Burning Boar."

She smiled. Only Garret could follow up with such a question, now, of all times. Despite mages and mobs, today's stroll had been the most rewarding experience she'd shared with anyone in years.

"I'd like that," she said. "Both surviving all of this and dinner with you—at any place other than the Boar."

# Ruby (The Mage Tower) – Entorak

"And what would you have them do, should they encounter him?" Entorak asked.

He and Richard stood over a large table in one of the Tower's study halls, poring over a large map of Ruby and the surrounding Thick. It was clearly an expensive, luxurious piece of art, no doubt the product of a great deal of time, effort, and skill. And, as was the case for most of Richard's belongings, it was nearly ruined by the way he abused it. He had littered the map with candle wax, ink, and pinpricks in cataloguing his deployment of mages across the lands. Richard clearly relished directing the pawns across the board of his game.

The red mages had been sent to the Crown's nearby villages and cities, traveling by horse and communicating by courier bird. Richard had cast a wide net. With the shady associations the red mages maintained, it seemed only inevitable that Richard would capture his quarry.

Of course, the map was also altogether unnecessary to the task. On another table, a sheet of paper featured a grid that listed the nearby communities and the names of the mages who were sent there. As they reported back, Richard added their notes to the grid. It was a far more practical and much less wasteful way of managing information than scrawling all over the map.

"They were told to keep their distance and report back," Richard explained. "I think we can find a way to entice the rogue to work with us willingly. I know that we could find an arrangement that benefits everyone."

Entorak bowed curtly, pivoted, and departed. Behind his mask of dispassion, he was concerned. The arrival of the rogue mage and Richard's quest to find him came at an inconvenient time. Entorak had plans of his own.

With the mages spread out across the Crown, Entorak would have significantly less control over who lived and who died once those plans came to pass.

# North of Ruby
# (The Windmill Grove) – Garret

Even though she had said she wouldn't, Pel threw herself at Garret.

One moment, the two of them were sitting on the log next to the fire. The next moment, she had lurched from her seat and practically tackled him. Even with her sneak attack, she was too slight to push him around; however, he was more than happy to play along.

Garret soon realized her motives were more business than pleasure. He felt a pressure on his lips, but it wasn't a kiss. Instead, the palm of her hand sealed his mouth closed, a gesture to keep him quiet. She had seen something. Her shushing him only added to the indignity of the moment.

He rolled out from under her and peered out past the tree line and into the field. They huddled in the grove, gazing into the darkness of the flat grassland that surrounded it. Garret saw nothing and a concern suddenly struck him: Pel couldn't see for shit. The only thing she could possibly detect from this far away, at this time of night, was—

"Magic," she whispered.

"Our missing god killer, then," Garret whispered back, wondering why she wouldn't have drawn that same conclusion. He knew the nature of her eyesight well enough to understand that Deodin would stand out to her, even at a great distance. Without looking away from where she was focused, she shook her head.

"No, there's more than one thing out there. I can see him. But I also see ... flying turkey lizards. I don't know if he sees them."

*Holy shit. Neverbats.*

"How many?" Garret asked.

She continued to watch the scene in the meadow with wide eyes, paralyzed by whatever she saw. Garret retrieved his weapons belt and waited for her response.

"Pelium!" He tapped her on the head urgently. She tore her attention away from the spectacle for a moment, caught his eye, then quickly looked back.

"Half a dozen or so," she said breathlessly. After watching them for what seemed an eternity, she turned back to Garret with a look that could only be one of astonishment.

"They're so fast!"

Garret hardly heard her second remark. He had already retrieved his bow and fumbled to fasten his weapons belt around his waist.

"Oh!" Pel spoke with an unusual abruptness and a hint of surprise. Her dire tone had evaporated, compelling Garret to stop what he was doing.

"He ... he must have seen them after all," she announced, now totally relaxed.

As Garret continued to fumble with his belt and weapons, he reflexively turned his head to the sound of approaching footfalls. The god killer soon emerged, illuminated by the soft, flickering orange light of the campfire. He looked much as he had when Garret had last seen him, still wearing the same circus tunic, trudging under the burden of the same heavy pack, and featuring the same clumsy haircut.

Garret groaned as he assembled the clues of what happened. "Did he just butcher half a dozen neverbats in the time it took me to put on my belt?" he asked Pel while motioning to Deodin with an open palm. Garret didn't bother to hide an expression more of annoyance than disbelief.

Still staring at Deodin with wide eyes, Pel nodded, evidently shocked.

"Did he just butcher half a dozen neverbats with an amazing display of horrible and deadly magic that I didn't get to see?" Garret blurted out, the pitch of his voice climbing.

Pel's eyes grew even wider as she nodded.

Garret clenched both his fists and his teeth, his back arching. The faintest groan of disappointed despair escaped his lungs.

# North of Ruby
# (The Windmill Grove) – Pel

"It took you longer than I expected," Pel said. The three travelers sat around the fire in the middle of the campsite.

Prior to Deodin's arrival, she and Garret had prepared the area for the god killer and his equipment. Now that he was here and she finally had a moment to simply observe him, she was fascinated. Foremost, his magical nature was unlike anything she had ever experienced. If for no other reason than his aura, he was truly interesting to admire.

However, she found herself increasingly drawn to his peculiar worldview.

"Mobs tend to find me." Deodin shrugged. The remark was neither a complaint nor a boast and the topic of conversation didn't seem important to him. If anything, it wore on his patience.

"Based on what I saw, it seems that they shouldn't, for their own best interests," Pel replied.

Deodin's laugh was humorless and sardonic.

"Mobs. Mages. Quests. Dungeons. Treasure. Adventure. Everything tends to find me, whether I want it or not, whether it makes sense or not."

"But no dragons. I already asked," Garret added.

"That seems like a dramatic way to describe it." Pel smiled. She didn't want to annoy the man, but he seemed decidedly cynical about his existence.

His expression softened. She gained the impression that he was forced into this conversation frequently enough.

"How many things, people included, have tried to kill you in the past week?" Deodin asked, looking at Pel.

She shrugged, conceding that the answer was zero.

Deodin then eyed Garret, implying the same question.

"Nothing in the past week, as far as I know. Nothing has ever successfully killed me," Garret answered.

"So, neither of you had to escape a burning building the day before yesterday? While battling a group of homicidal, suicidal, fire-hurling red mages? Or today: neither of you had to defeat a pack of wolves? And then defeat another pack of different wolves later in the afternoon?"

"Don't forget the neverbats!" Garret added happily.

"Ah yes, the neverbats. Thank you, Garret. You didn't encounter any neverbats, beyond the ones that attacked me?"

Garret cocked his head as if struck by a thought. "They must have been close enough to notice us long before they attacked you. We were certainly loud enough for them to hear us."

Deodin gestured with an open palm, as if Garret had made his point for him. "I am the Universe's favorite plaything."

Pel didn't have any reason to disbelieve Deodin's comments about mobs and maniacs, but she found herself ruminating on their subtext and his underlying ennui. He wasn't dispassionate or depressed, necessarily. He joked, laughed, frowned, and scowled when contextually appropriate. He seemed to be emotionally mature and he was entirely pleasant to be around. In fact, he and Garret seemed to have grown close, despite the newness of their relationship.

But an undertone ran beneath it all, coming off as a lack of investment in the world and its people. A lack of agency.

It was so profoundly odd that a god killer, a man who had enough power, resources, and license to do everything within his imagination, felt powerless in his own life. How did a man with no worldly concerns feel like he was at the mercy of "the Universe"?

Garret, however, did not seem to be bothered by Deodin's philosophical morass. He reveled in the opportunity to talk to him, asking questions that should have been profoundly insulting.

"What about women? Do they 'find' you more than normal? And if you attract deadly monsters, do you also attract only beautiful women, like Pel? Or do you bring out the ugly ones too?"

Deodin paused, before turning his attention to Pel. "That should be the dumbest question he's asked tonight. Yet, it's not." He chuckled.

"And you still haven't answered it," Pel prompted with a smile.

# North of Ruby
# (The Windmill Grove) – Garret

"Can we put out the fire?" Deodin asked. "The smell of smoke carries a long way."

"We didn't have enough room to carry blankets," Pel explained as she began to cover the fire with handfuls of dirt.

"Oh, no need to be cold," he replied.

A moment later, Pel reacted suddenly, almost violently. She turned her head away from the center of the campsite, closed her eyes and shielded her face with a hand. Her response was so abrupt that Garret flinched. He turned about and brought an instinctive hand to the hilt of his sword, scanning the tree line behind them.

Seeing and sensing nothing, Garret turned back to the others. Deodin apologized to Pel. Neither of them looked like they felt threatened.

"Is that too bright?" Deodin asked, brows raised.

"No, no, it's fine," Pel replied, turning her head slowly back to face him. "It's like walking outside after being indoors all day."

"What's bright?" Garret asked, even though neither of them bothered to reply. After a moment, he extended his hands to feel at the air around him. "And why is it suddenly warmer?"

Deodin replied with an amiable smile and reached out to Garret and touched his head with a delicate *doink* of his index finger. Garret's indignation transitioned to awe in an instant.

"Balls!" Garret looked around in astonishment.

"It's a detection enchantment," Deodin explained. "For the next few hours, you'll see magical auras, much like Pel does. Tell me if the effect fades. As amusing as it might be, let's not light your hair on fire."

Garret saw why Pel had flinched and shielded her eyes a few moments ago. An unnatural light bathed the campsite, emanating from a glowing ball of flame that now hovered silently above them. About the size of a human head, it flickered like a normal fire; however, it was silent and produced no smoke. It was many times brighter than any conventional light of the same size and the colors were slightly shifted toward blue.

Garret possessed a very rudimentary understanding of magic, even if it was a routine part of life in Ruby. Throughout the years, he had seen different types of mystical fire, be it in the form of artillery or the lights of the Evertorch district. The light source that hung above him was unlike any of that.

Garret began to realize just how valuable Deodin would be to the red mages. To master this kind of magic would be to change the entire world. Or, perhaps, rule it. He shivered, despite the warmth of Deodin's impossible fire.

Immediately following the amazement, Garret was struck by an intense sensation of nausea. He doubled over, crossed his legs, and winced as he caught his breath. The others looked at him with, at best, mild interest. He clarified, gesturing quite unnecessarily to his crotch.

"Balls!" he hissed, this time with scrunched eyebrows and an open mouth. With no response, he clarified his remark. "It feels like I got kicked in the balls."

Deodin laughed instead.

"The detection magic has side effects. What you feel is one of those symptoms. It should feel less intense in a few minutes."

Garret regained his composure enough to scowl at Deodin, before regarding Pel. He immediately forgot his discomfort.

Normally, Pel's face showed only limited expression. It was difficult to read her feelings or thoughts. Rarely did she express surprise or shock. And even less frequently did she grin like an idiot, as she did now. Her eyes shone in wonderment as she continued to gaze about the campsite, then across to Garret. No words were necessary.

Garret had known Pel for many years, well before she had her eyesight ruined by mages and magic. He knew her current limitations. She never got to see the world like this.

Whatever Deodin had done, he had showered the campsite in light that allowed her to faithfully see the world without the haze that clouded her vision.

"Pelium, quick: how handsome am I? Very? Exceptionally?" Garret asked, unsure of how long the light show would persist.

She turned to Deodin.

"I haven't seen this clearly in years. Thank you."

She spun around once more, slowly, soaking in the canopy of the trees above them, the outline of Garret's clothes, and finally, the texture and weathering on her hands. Garret reached out and took those hands. She gifted him with a sincere, heartfelt smile.

Pel shone in a light that he hadn't seen in so, so long. Part of it was the literal glow of the magical aura she wore about her eyes, which he could now see.

The rest wasn't.

# DAY
# 4

# Ruby (The Mage Tower) – Mathew

Mathew peered through the library's doorway. The room was empty, except for Mica in the far corner. As the Tower's librarian, she was responsible for managing its research materials. She had moved a stack of books to a table closer to the shelves and was currently putting everything away. Mathew stole a look down the hallway to ensure that they were alone before he entered the room himself. Mica looked up.

"Should I be surprised to see you? You aren't pursuing the mysterious rogue mage?"

Mathew scoffed at the notion. "Hardly."

"Did you happen to learn what he looked like?" she asked impassively, directing her attention back to the shelf and her task.

Mica seldom spoke when the other Tower residents were in earshot, but when he had her to himself, as he did now, Mathew was treated to her soft, eastern accent.

"Average size and build, a mark on his arm, brown hair that seemed to be chewed off his head by an angry beaver," Mathew replied.

Mica laughed. "Absent the mark, you describe half of the men of the Crown. Present company excluded, my good sir," she said with an insincere bow. She replaced a book, then turned to him and gave him her full attention. It was thralling and he relished the moment.

"But what of you, Mathew? Why didn't you join in the fox hunt? Why aren't you out in the remote reaches of the

Crown, chasing ghosts and whispers? Why is it that you are standing right here, when you could be the one to bring Richard his prize?"

He looked over his shoulder to ensure that they were still alone. "I don't trust Richard and his motives. Everything about this is a bad plan, executed by bad people with bad intentions. It stinks of Richard, and Entorak, and typical Tower bullshit. Nothing good can come of it."

She smiled, then gestured to the room around them with both hands.

"I meant, why are you in *here*? Now. In the library. With me," she said with a flirtatious smirk. "But I do appreciate your candor and the moral landmarks that guide you. That's endearing."

Mathew smiled at her quip. She was so pretty and so sharp. It was almost intoxicating. He took a breath. The circumstance would never be more intimate.

"Because it allows me more opportunity to be alone with you."

She clicked her teeth in disappointment.

"You should have said, 'You are the only fox I want to chase.'" She nodded at him condescendingly.

"I'd be wittier if you chose my words for me," he confessed.

"Much better. Flattering and charming. There's hope for you yet." She laughed. "And as it happens, I enjoy these opportunities, as well. Now, make yourself even more endearing and put these on the top shelf."

Mathew was delighted to help.

# North of Ruby (The Thick) – Deodin

The Universe provided Deodin with the day's objectives.

*Escort Garret and Pel through the Thick:*
- ☑ *Have breakfast*
- ☐ *Avoid the hazards of the Thick*

"Thank you for escorting us through the Thick," Pel said. "Traveling with *shey—*"

Deodin halted abruptly.

"Never say that word!" he hissed curtly. He did not intend to be hostile, but his deadly seriousness caught his traveling companions off guard.

"Of course!" Pel covered her mouth in embarrassment. "We've gotten far too casual and comfortable talking about that!"

Deodin, however, was not finished. "*Never.* And I do mean never, use the word 'escort' when you are around me," he said, emphasizing the point enough to stare at each of them in turn, ensuring that they had understood the message.

Garret and Pel shared a puzzled look that suggested that they didn't understand Deodin's remark.

"I was seventeen," Deodin began. "I met a kindly woman who had wandered from the path between two villages well east of the Crown. The entire region was peaceful and safe. She had been picking berries and had wandered off the trail. It was by random happenstance that I encountered her at all.

"She asked me to 'e-word' her back to the village. Of course I obliged. I'm a god killer, right? Naïve and young, certainly, but death and doom sprang from my fingers, right? What could go wrong?"

Pel and Garret shared another look and shrugged.

"She runs away from me. And what does she do the moment she's out of sight? Stumbles on a pack of wolves. Wolves that weren't there when I had been in that very spot, three minutes earlier. They tore her apart before I could help."

"Gods! That's awful!" Pel gasped. Garret, on the other hand, had yet to respond, opting to watch with a skeptical glint in his eyes.

Deodin continued.

"I was twenty-one. Encountered a merchant who was alone on a path. He had a pushcart that had broken an axle. It was getting late, so he asked me to 'e-word' him back to town so he could get parts and tools. The village was perhaps a mile from where we were. What's that, another twenty minutes out of my day? I say, 'Of course.' This man couldn't have been a day over thirty. In reasonable health."

Deodin waited a beat before continuing.

"It took us four hours to walk a single mile, on a well-worn path. It would have taken less time for me to lie on my face and drag myself down the path with my lips."

"I don't—" Pel began, bemused.

"Four hours!" Deodin exclaimed. "And finally, we reach the edge of town. I can see the roofs of the huts. Oops! He runs away, out of line of sight … and gets torn apart by wolves."

Deodin allowed no chance for follow-up questions as he continued to the next vignette.

"I was twenty-two. Two priestesses encounter me on the road. It was getting late and they were afraid of bandits. They asked if I would mind 'e-wording' them back to town. This time, I hesitated."

"Uh…" Garret's expression suggested that he'd started to grasp where this was going.

"But you know what? I said yes. Still *sheyaktu*. Nothing I can't handle. So, we're plodding along the path at a happily normal pace when I stop to harvest the milk from an Eolen poppy. It's a flower that has magical properties. Takes me, what, twenty seconds?"

"Deodin," Pel said.

He dismissed her with a wave of his hand.

"I stand up and look around. Priestesses gone. Both of them. 'Where'd they go?' you ask. Disappeared. Couldn't walk next to the person who said he would 'e-word' them. What happened to them, do you suppose?"

Deodin was nearly out of breath. The storytelling had been more taxing on him than the rest of the journey.

Garret ventured an answer.

"I would say 'killed by bandits,' because of the way you set it up. But I'm going to go with 'torn apart by wolves,' because that would be a better match with the other stories."

"No, you had it the first time. Bandits," Deodin said.

"Deodin," Pel repeated.

"The point is, Pel," Deodin said, motioning for her to withhold her comments. "We do not use the 'e-word' to describe any time that we're together. I can accompany you. I can join you. We can walk together. But as soon as the 'e-word' gets thrown around, someone runs off and dies. I don't ask you to understand it. I won't try to justify it. But under no circumstances shall I ever, ever, 'e-word' anyone."

Pel inhaled but remained quiet for a short while before she spoke.

"Thank you for accompanying us through the Thick."

*Accompany Garret and Pel through the Thick:*

- ☑ *Have breakfast*
- ☑ *Avoid the hazards of the Thick*

# North of Ruby
## (Doubler's Bend) – Garret

After a day of travel, the trio made camp as night drew near. This time, Garret selected a remote area he called "Doubler's Bend." The site was isolated enough that they could speak without being overheard by anyone foolish enough to travel the road at night.

Pel had slowed them down somewhat, but she held her own. The journey through the Thick was a complete departure from any walk through Ruby's streets. The undergrowth beneath the towering conifers was dense, dark, and treacherous. While Pel had no experience with such rigorous hiking, she had voiced no complaints. Whatever she lacked in physical stamina and expertise, she made up for in will. Meanwhile, Garret suspected that Deodin held back. The god killer seemed completely immune to travel fatigue.

As he had the night before, Deodin prepared a magical heat and light for the campground. He also re-cast the magic detection spell on Garret, who didn't want to put anything important, like his face, into the invisible ball of flame hovering above the center of the campsite.

For a second night, Garret spent his evening watching the aura of a mythical god killer, the human manifestation of magical things terrible and wondrous.

Pel had fallen asleep several hours before, but Garret found it difficult to find meaningful rest. He would awaken at the slightest sound, and because the Thick was a deathly quiet place at this time of night, every skittering mouse or fidgeting bird sounded like a herd of monstrous, man-eating elephants.

Then there was Deodin, by far the loudest creature in the Crown. He had risen for a second time since the group had retired for the night.

Deodin's magical aura was captivating and it still fascinated Garret to see the god killer glowing in a soft, blue light. It also intrigued him to see the god killer stumble around the campsite making enough noise to awaken everything within half a mile, including the dead. Well, everything except for Pel, who could sleep through being eaten.

Deodin proved to be a grand paradox, both amazing and mundane. Despite being the ultimate magical weapon, he tripped and cursed his way through the darkness before relieving himself, just like every other normal, mortal man—the god killer who had butchered a flock of neverbats with hardly more than a whim still had to pee in the middle of the night.

Deodin noticed Garret was awake. "Sorry to wake you," the god killer whispered.

Garret sat up, accepting their situation with a shrug. "Well. Perhaps no one should sleep too soundly out here," he said at a normal volume.

The snore from Pel came with perfect timing to highlight the irony of Garret's remark. Both men shared glances before looking to Pel, who rested far more comfortably than the circumstances should normally allow. Garret gestured to Pel with a pointed index finger. "Fleeing from the mage Tower and hiking through a mobs-infested forest patrolled by an ever-advancing population of orcs, and she can sleep like that," he remarked, unable to hide his envy.

"Still, we don't need to wake the only one who can sleep," Deodin whispered.

Garret responded with a wry expression. He picked up a small piece of dried fruit from a pouch that rested next to him and tossed it across the campsite. It glanced harmlessly off Pel's forehead, striking her mid-snore. The attack had no effect.

"Or perhaps my concern was unfounded," Deodin continued, no longer whispering.

"We all have things that keep us up at night, but for her, this isn't it." Garret gestured to the area around them and looked up to the stars.

"The red mages," Deodin said, studying Pel a moment longer before turning back to Garret. "Why does she risk her life, and yours, to defy them?"

Garret paused and reflected on the best way to answer the question. "That's really not my bit to tell...." It was Pel's business, after all.

"Very well. You, then," Deodin replied. "What were the realities that were so easy for you to abandon? Enemies? Debts? An ill-advised business relation—"

Garret decided it was easier to talk about Pel's issues than his. "Her reasons are complicated, you have to understand. She has ... ah ... a history with the Tower," he explained.

"Everyone in Ruby has a history with the Tower, it seems. I met merchants who risked their lives to deliver me to the red mages rather than defy them."

"The Tower is full of horrible men," Garret said. "The red mages rule Ruby through a fear that hangs over everyone and everything. Pel talked about it herself: what would happen if the reds were to get their hands on you? Those men, with your power? That's what she fears."

"And what of her eyesight? How is that related?"

Garret hesitated but decided the discussion of Pel's private history was justified in this context. "It was about three years ago. A red mage fancied her and tried to use influence and magic to have her. He didn't court her; he wanted to own her, like someone owns pets or livestock. It became violent.

"The harassment stopped, but the incident changed her. She became more cynical. Less trusting. Afraid. And she swore that she would never let magic surprise her again. The permanent version of that spell was her solution.

"The Tower faced unusual pressure from influential sources across the city. Pel was, and still is, loved and respected in the community. The Tower was embarrassed. As a concession, one of the mages cast a permanent detection spell on her. It was an ill-conceived, half-hearted peace offering. 'Sorry about what happened, dear, here's a magical gift.' Oops, our mistake. That 'gift' is actually a curse."

"Such magic is very difficult to make permanent," Deodin acknowledged. "There are always complications."

"Pel didn't know that, of course," Garret said. "The mage who cast the spell didn't know it, either. He was too arrogant to even consider that he might bugger it up. Now, magic shines brightly in her eyes, but she can't see for shit, otherwise. Unless it's enchanted, like you, she can hardly see anything outside ten or twelve feet."

"And what of the red mage who harmed her? Did justice find him?" Deodin asked. Garret swallowed hard. The god killer spoke in an ominous, serious tone.

"Fled, we think," Garret responded. "The Tower said that he relocated to Southend. He hasn't been seen since."

The god killer's reaction came and went before Garret could properly respond to it. Deodin's aura, which had been a modest light blue throughout the night, changed intensity. In a moment, it flashed to a brightness that was too brilliant to look upon. And hardly a moment after onset, it was gone.

While under the effects of Deodin's spell, Garret could measure magical strength with his eyes, as Pel could. And just a moment ago, he had seen Deodin's two extremes. The contrast in power and intensity was terrifying. For just that instant, Garret gained a real sense of the danger calmly sitting on a log no more than six feet from him.

Over the previous two days, Garret had briefly forgotten what Deodin was. He had forgotten the magic he wielded. It was easy to relate to a man who stumbled in the dark to take a piss. It was harder to relate to a man who literally blinded him with his power.

The god killer seemed to see and interpret Garret's reaction. "Sorry. I forgot that you could see that. I have a history with the red mages, myself. They are categorically loathsome. Your story adds another log to a fire that already burns dangerously hot."

Deodin fell silent for a bit. Then he pursued his line of thought, looking for Garret's corroboration. "And now, Pel seeks an end to the Tower and its influence."

"Of course. Everyone in Ruby would be better off if the Tower toppled over."

"And you?" Deodin returned with narrowed eyes.

"I'd be first in line to push," Garret replied without hesitation.

"Yes, but you wouldn't do it for the people of Ruby. Or even for yourself, would you?" Deodin stole a glance at Pel before refocusing on Garret.

Garret didn't look back. Both his eyebrows rose in surprise at how quickly the answer came to mind and how easily it came out. "No."

# DAY
# 5

# North of Ruby (The Thick) – Pel

"Hello," Pel said with curiosity. "What are you?"

She had found a small plant growing out from between the roots of one of the great evergreens of the Thick. It featured a striking, star-shaped pattern and glowed with magic.

"Faderoot," Garret answered. "You've seen it before, but not as a flower. In Ruby, it would be ground up and sold as a magical component. Rare and expensive."

"It's lovely," Pelium noted, commenting on its aura. "It stands out among the others. I had no idea."

Pel had only seen evidence of the supernatural in Ruby, and when she did, it usually was in the context of the Tower and its mages. It had never occurred to her that magic might exist in the natural world in the form of a flower.

Deodin knelt next to the plant. He gingerly collected its petals and placed them in a pouch on his belt.

"Skycrash infused the world with magic, including some of the wildlife. I've read that over the past few hundred years, there have been countless attempts to transplant things like faderoot, so that they can be planted as a crop. Those attempts always fail. It is believed that the supernatural power within the region keeps them alive," he said.

"Same with the mobs," Pel added. "Fortunately, every attempt to domesticate or weaponize mobs has resulted in disaster. The mages of the Tower have tried to study everything from neverbats to spikeboars, but have—"

"Spikeboars?" Garret asked, suddenly more interested. I've heard their livers—"

"—only learned that once they have been removed from their habitat, the mobs lose their magical potency. Thank the gods. The abuse of magic is bad enough as it is."

Having completed the collection of the flower, Deodin stood back up.

"Faderoot is difficult to come by. I normally combine it with the heart of a deathcrab. Together, the two can be used to craft a potion that lessens the discomfort of certain spells."

"Huh-huh," Garret laughed. "Deathcrabs."

Pel didn't know what was funny. Garret noticed her puzzlement and explained.

"You wouldn't likely be familiar with them. They are mobs that live along the coast, well to Ruby's south. I've never seen them, myself, but I know them to be horrifying." He held his hands about four feet apart, while looking to Deodin. "How big are they? I've heard they are as big as a wheelbarrow."

"Their bodies are about that long. Add their legs and the reach of their claws, maybe about eight or nine feet wide when standing up. Considering their armor, probably close to eight hundred or a thousand pounds. They are … inconvenient," Deodin replied.

"Pincers that could decapitate a horse, Pel. And this one talks about them as if they are as dangerous as puppies." Garret gestured to Deodin with his thumb.

Pel was more interested in Deodin's magical recipe than his dismissive comment about something dangerous enough to feature the word "death" in its name. "The mages of the Tower speak of potions occasionally. I understand alchemy to be a difficult skill to master, if only because the ingredients are so hard to find," she said. "The markets are not filled with merchants selling faderoot and deathcrab hearts."

"Oh, I am the punchline of a terrible joke," agreed Deodin with a frustrated scowl. "I'm all but forced to go collect the components myself. And I must travel up and down the entire world, harvesting random ingredients to progress in the skill. And a component from one region only works with a component from a different region." He pointed to the pickaxe that hung from a loop in his pack. "And this?" He scowled. "As if my time is well spent digging up an assortment of ores."

Pel brought up her hand, palm out, to gesture for quiet. All of this seemed dubious. Why would Deodin need of any of this? Why would he even care? Any magical potion would be trivial compared to what his powers already were.

"Why would you even bother? You're bloody *sheyaktu*, for the gods' sake. Why would you grind away so much time on developing your apothecary skills when a potion provides you with so little? You are already so much without it."

Deodin looked askance at her, as if her concern were ridiculous.

"But what if I find myself needing three dozen Potions of Grace? Where would I be then?"

\* \* \*

"So. About the skalgs." Garret pressed.

Normally, a trek through the Thick would be an exercise in noise discipline. From orcs to mobs, a great many threats lived in the dense forest and it was best to slip their notice.

However, Garret now had a chance to travel with a god killer in the party. Pel didn't think he deliberately set out to attract anything, but she had no doubt he would be delighted to watch Deodin fight the monsters of the Thick. It had been the only topic of conversation for the past two hours.

"Of course. They attack me all the time."

"How do you kill them? Fire magic? Lightning? I see you as a lightning kind of guy."

"I'll rip off one of its arms and then use it as a cudgel to beat it to death."

Garret's eyes lit up as if he visualized the scene. A moment later, the expression dissolved into skepticism, finally settling on disappointment. "No you don't. You're just saying that."

Pel laughed. "Garret, perhaps he wants to discuss something other than violence and savagery. It is the only thing you have brought up."

"We haven't gotten to trolls yet, though," he complained.

"I ask that we never discuss trolls. The less we think about them, the better," Deodin cautioned.

"Where is home?" Pel asked, hoping to discuss something less macabre. She smiled as she added, "But don't tell us any details if it means you'll have to kill us to keep us quiet. I'm not that curious."

"Fortunately for you, there is no home. I don't have the luxury."

His answer was odd. With his aptitude and riches, Deodin could do almost whatever he wanted. A god killer should be limited by his imagination, not by worldly concerns.

"I don't understand," she said. "Don't you have the resources to live wherever you choose? Why couldn't you buy yourself an estate? Or clear out a plot of land and live your days pursuing your personal interests?"

Deodin smiled. "People assume that I pursue adventure. That I seek it. On the contrary: adventure seeks me, whether I want it or not. Everything I touch turns to adventure."

"That seems a bit melodramatic," she said.

"Does it? Where was I supposed to go, when I stowed away on your friend's cargo ship?" He was being condescending.

"Bayhold," she said.

"And where am I now? And be specific," he pressed, gesturing to the Thick that surrounded them.

"In the Thick, fleeing for your life from red mages who would dissect you for study, while avoiding an infinite number of orcs and an endless assortment of monsters," Pel acquiesced.

"Correct. And that is ignoring the reasons why I had to get to Bayhold in the first place. I'll spare you those details, but it was the Universe that drove me to the Crown, not something I sought."

"Surely you could find a place free from all of it," Pel said. "Far enough away where 'adventure' can't find you."

Deodin smiled in a way that suggested he'd had this conversation before. It was clear that he wasn't going to try to win the argument and change Pel's mind.

"You say that as if I haven't tried." He held out his hands for her to see. Arcs of magical electricity sparked through his fingertips. "It's the cost of being *sheyaktu*. I don't get to enjoy the type of life you enjoy. I don't get to enjoy the intimate relationships that you two do."

Pel and Garret each shared a glance.

"Pel's right. Let's change the subject." Garret spoke to Deodin but was playfully smug when he looked at Pel. "Tell us more about the intimate relationship that Pel and I share."

"Oh, I just meant that following our adventure, you two can retire together to raise beautiful children. I will be pressed into another adventure."

"We should get right to that, Pel. Who are we to argue with a god killer?" Garret asked, winking at Pel as he spoke.

To avoid any further awkwardness, Pel felt it appropriate to disclose that her relationship with Garret hadn't reached that level of intimacy, but Garret was too busy enjoying himself.

"Naturally, we hope the kids have her intellect and her good looks," Garret explained, basking in Deodin's misunderstanding. "And it would be best if they had my physique. Sorry, dear, you're too short and I look better with my shirt off."

The urge to politely correct Deodin's misunderstanding of their relationship yielded to a secondary urge to stick it back at Garret.

"No, dear, you may be right," she returned. "And considering how rarely you wash your shirts, you should wear them less. Our children will probably inherit my sense of smell, being that you lack it entirely."

"The both of you: please keep your shirts on," Deodin said, clearly wanting no part of wherever this was going.

"Sense of smell? What about a sense of taste? Have you forgotten about your curtains?" Garret retorted.

She laughed, outraged that he would go there. "Taste? You eat at the Burning Boar three nights a week! The name of that place is based on how they prepare everything they cook!"

151

"Oh my gods, Pel, their food is so bad," Garret confessed, unable to keep a straight face. "I only go there to meet clients and beautiful women."

"Did you know that there are only eight types of troll caves?" Deodin asked.

Pel decided that she'd rather listen to Garret.

"Tell me more about these beautiful women."

# Ruby (The Mage Tower) – Mathew

*That door is normally closed.*

Mathew regarded the door with curiosity and suspicion. Doors were almost always closed and locked, lest one mage's work be "appropriated" by another. This door opened onto a private study in one of the lesser-used wings of Tower.

Someone was inside.

As much as he resented the Tower's games, Mathew played them well enough. He approached the door with a lighter step than normal, but loudly enough that he wouldn't be accused of trying to sneak around. As casually as he could, he peered through the doorway to see the curiosities on the other side.

Curious, indeed.

Mica stood in the room, casually rummaging through a pile of papers and books that had been laid out across a table.

She was dressed in simple, unassuming work attire. Her reddish hair was tied up out of her eyes to reveal her focused expression. The time was well past her working hours, but her face displayed an energy as she studied the works on the pile in front of her.

"It is impolite to sneak up on people," she noted, even if she didn't seem startled. With her accent, she slightly mispronounced many of her words, emphasizing the wrong syllable. It made her even more exotic. "Do you know why these are out?" she addressed Mathew.

She gestured at the items on the desk. It took a moment for Mathew to identify them. The language was in a script that pre-dated Skycrash. It was a dead language. And it wasn't human.

Orcs.

"These must be ancient. Who has been using this chamber?"

"Entorak," Mica replied. "He has been studying these papers and books for weeks. They are historical records about the attack on Tristan over three hundred years ago."

"The first Encroachment," Mathew said.

"Yes, but why would they be out? Why would it be necessary to read them now?" Mica mused.

Mathew wondered that, himself. Orcs were never an interesting subject matter in the Tower and he had no idea why Entorak would study their history.

"I'm afraid I don't know," Mathew replied. He watched Mica reflect on this, evidently unsatisfied with his answer. "Why are *you* curious about ancient orc writings and Entorak's interest with them?" he pressed. "Why would you care?"

Mica's frown softened. "Mathew, your heart is in the right place and you are not an idiot. I like that about you…."

"But…" Mathew prompted.

"But you don't notice important details. You should also get out of the Tower occasionally."

"That wasn't a very good compliment, but it wasn't much of an insult, either. I'll allow it," he said evenly.

"Consider the timing of this. Orcs have been much more active. Entorak has been studying them. A rogue mage appears the other night. Now the red mages are dispatched across the Crown to find him. Which is more likely: all of this is a coincidence, or all of it is related?"

"What recent orc activity?" Mathew asked sheepishly. Orcs had never been among his primary concerns.

Mica tilted her head and slowly blinked.

*Ah. One of the important things I didn't notice.*

"The Thick is far more active than normal," Mica explained. "The other mobs, also, all the way down to Bayhold and Tristan, and everything in the middle, including…"

Mathew didn't know what she was talking about and Mica was certainly sharp enough to notice. She eyed him narrowly.

"*Have* you ever left the Tower?"

Mathew glanced at the stack of papers on the desk, then gestured his surrender with both arms. "Orcs and mobs are active in the Thick," he acknowledged. "On top of that, Entorak has a recent, inexplicable focus on orc history."

"Welcome to the present," Mica replied. "Now, what do you think you know about the first Encroachment?"

"As I know it, the orcs unified themselves and marched on Ruby, resulting in a war."

Mica shook her head. "It shouldn't be thought of as a proper 'war.' The conflict hardly lasted a week. It was decidedly lopsided in favor of the humans. Most human casualties came in the very early days, in the villages and settlements outside the reach of the city's walls."

"Were the orcs provoked? Or were they the aggressors?"

"The texts show that the unified tribes marched on the Crown because that was the order from their master."

"Lyle Makee," Mathew said.

Mica clicked her teeth and shook her head. "'The Horror,' you mean. Human history always conflates Lyle Makee and 'the Horror.' For Lyle Makee, your understanding is that he went to the orcs, became revered as a god, and then sent them against Tristan. Is that correct?"

Mathew nodded.

"And the orc manuscripts agree, to an extent. The texts say that their *god* drove them to attack. And the orc word for that god is something that humans have translated to mean 'the Horror.' A name that became associated with Makee. So far, so good, yes?"

He nodded.

"And if you throw in colorful orc poetry, you can see how that mistake was made. They described their god wielding 'cursed magic.' And the orc word *sheyaktu* means something along those lines. However, the orcs never actually used that word to describe the god that commanded them. That little detail is always overlooked.

"Instead, the orcs described their god as 'an outsider, carved from their nightmares,' while they described Makee as 'a human, too small and weak to rival their chieftain,' and—"

She glared at him.

"By the gods, am I boring you?"

*Shit.*

He had been watching her mouth move, fixated on how pretty she was. Her teeth were flawless. He hadn't been paying attention, instead calculating the best joke or quip to make her smile.

She snapped her fingers to bring his attention back to their conversation.

"Mathew! Focus for one final point. About a third of the orcish excerpts specifically state that 'the Horror' came before Makee had ever been introduced to their history. Whatever the orcs referred to as 'the Horror,' it existed before they ever encountered Lyle Makee. This is one of those crucial details you need to remember," she stressed.

"Very well. Lyle Makee was not 'the Horror.' Why isn't this narrative more widely known?" he asked.

She replied with a flick of her eyebrow and a smirk. "That's better. Who controls the historical narrative?"

The answer was obvious. The two of them stood in the library of a Tower run by red mages. Those same red mages wrote a great number of the books on the shelves.

Mathew frowned. "The red mages. They can place the blame on *sheyaktu* and use the threat of another Lyle Makee to maintain their monopoly on magic. And the public will thank them for it." Now he was aware of another good reason to dislike the red mages. "What bastards."

"Again, your heart is in the right place," Mica replied. "And while that point is valid, remember this: 'the Horror' was a powerful entity that rallied the orcs. Lyle Makee wasn't the world's first villain; he was the world's first hero. He didn't betray humanity and lead the orcs. He defeated their master!"

Her point finally found him. Mathew momentarily forgot about her smile, her flowery fragrance, and perhaps the most amazing hair he had ever seen. "You're not worried about the orc activity in the Thick," he interpreted. "You are worried about whatever makes them active. And Entorak plays an unknown part in all this."

She smiled.

"Like I said, 'not a total idiot.'"

# DAY
# 6

# The Thick
# (Outside of Netherby) – Pel

Deodin reached out a hand, gently holding Pel back.

"Garret found something," he whispered.

Following Deodin's lead, Pel crouched and crept up next to Garret, who waited for them next to one of the enormous, red-barked trees of the Thick. He knelt quietly, until they came close enough to speak in whispers.

"Orcs," Garret said quietly, once they were close enough.

"I don't see it," Pel admitted.

"It's subtle. You have to be looking for it," Deodin said, nodding to a flower in front of Garret. "This plant has a recently broken stem. Within a few hours. And look at where it is broken. Up here, about shin high. Most animals out here wouldn't have a large enough footprint to break it here. They would be more likely to brush it aside or squash it where it came out of the ground.

"I'd think it could be a bear or mob with that heavy of a footfall. But over here, we don't see any scratches in the soil. Something that size and weight would scuff part of the topsoil with its claws. Instead, we see only slight impressions. No claws or hooves."

Deodin pointed to an area of dirt. "Not sharp enough to be a heeled boot and tread on a human-style shoe. However, this could be the footfall of a moccasin or a simple slipper. It was heavy enough to break the plant, but inconsistent with an animal, and there are no indications of a human-style boot. Therefore: orcs."

Garret finally spoke. "I have been an outdoorsman and a hunter my whole adult life and had never noticed any of the things you just pointed out. I can't tell if you're a brilliant tracker beyond my wildest imagination or if you're full of shit."

He pointed to the valley behind him. Below them, Pel could see a small group of blurry objects scuttling among the trees on the forest floor.

"Ooooooooooooooorcs!" Garret hissed as loudly as he dared.

Deodin peered over the edge, then nodded to Pel to confirm Garret's conclusion.

"Ah. There's that too."

Pel could hardly see the orcs below, so she watched Deodin's reaction. A pang of anxiety struck her in the stomach when his eyebrows narrowed with concern. Something worried the god killer. "What is it?" she asked.

"Their weapons and equipment. This is not a hunting party. They are armed for a battle."

"If they were fighting mobs of the Thick, it would be a whole lot ... screamier," Garret said. "We're not that far from Netherby itself. It's perhaps a half day to the east, if we were to take the road. But this group isn't big enough to sack Netherby."

"This must be one of the groups that has been raiding the merchants," Pel noted. She turned to Deodin to update him on recent Crown events. "The orcs have been far more aggressive in the past weeks. They've come down from the mountains and there have been skirmishes on the roads near the outer villages. There are whispers of an Encroachment."

"Yes, I know," Deodin replied.

The years of assembling contextual clues for a living led Pel to a sudden, now-obvious conclusion: *this is why he's here.* "You already knew about the orcs and their activity," she accused. "That's why you came to the Crown."

Deodin didn't answer. After several seconds he finally turned to her. "I can't tell you why I'm here."

"We're out here risking our lives for you!" she protested. *Sheyaktu* or not, they were all in this together. She and Garret were entitled to knowledge that might help them stay alive.

"All I can say is that you wouldn't understand," Deodin returned, after a hesitation. The tone was regretful, not condescending.

"Anything you can understand, Pelium Stillwater would overstand," Garret interjected.

"This is not about understanding or—" Deodin paused. "Overstand?" He looked to Garret. "You mean to say that she would understand it better than me?"

"Isn't that what I said?" Garret snapped.

This time, Deodin turned to Pel. "He makes a point out of a word he just made up, yet we all know exactly what he means."

"It is his second-most remarkable trait," she replied.

"I'm sorry to be so secretive, but I came to the Crown because I need to be here. And I will not allow you to be a part of my adventuring. You both have risked far too much already," Deodin continued.

"But we can help," Pel offered.

"And you are helping." Deodin smiled. "I wouldn't be here without you. Either of you. But just as I defer to your expertise, you must defer to mine. Unless you can bend the rules of the nature by whim and will, you don't accompany me on my quests. It's too dangerous."

Pel realized that Deodin wasn't being selfish or exclusive. "Your concern comes from previous experience."

"Previous mistakes," Deodin corrected her with a sigh. "It is an aspect of being *sheyaktu*. The Universe will bring adventure to us soon enough. The quicker we can part ways, the sooner you are free from the dangers I bring."

"This … 'Universe' knows that our relationship is really just between a service provider and a customer, right? No need to involve me in its grudge against you," Garret quipped.

"Then let us get you to your destination," Pel said. "Would it be appropriate to stop at Netherby for supplies?"

"Yes. We will part ways in Netherby. Depending on what waits for me in the area, I may need to head for Delemere or Luton. I'd still want your guidance, should it come to that."

"Of course," Pel replied.

"Until then, I will remain with you as long as I can. It would be irresponsible for me to do any less. And for the short term, let us wait and see if the orcs will move on," Deodin said.

\* \* \*

Pel had dozed off, but she awoke to the stirring of the men next to her. She couldn't see the activity in the valley below, but Garret anticipated this.

"They move," he said. "They've been lying in wait and now they are preparing for something. Something soon."

"Us?" Pel asked, fighting to overcome the fear of being unable to see what was going on.

"No, they face away from us," Deodin said. "But they ready their weapons. Bows and spears."

"Travelers. We must be closer to the road than we thought," Pel suggested.

Garret frowned as he considered her observation. "Probably. With the Thick this dense, we wouldn't see the road unless we were right on top of it. That might explain why orcs set up like that."

Pel didn't know the nuance of every merchant run in and out of Ruby, but such traffic was common, even if it was becoming more infrequent. Many of her clients traveled this route. She paused a moment longer before being struck by another, more harrowing thought. "It could also be those who would pursue us."

The god killer stirred. Quickly, and as quietly as he could, Deodin struggled to free himself from the leather straps of his pack, his gaze fixed on the orcs below.

"I'll go. This will be over before you can make your way down," he remarked.

He spoke calmly and confidently, even though he was about to descend into a conflict with orcs. There was no hesitation in his movement and nothing in his tone, expression, or body language suggested any measure of concern. Pel drew a breath to utter a protest, but the god killer preempted her comment.

"It would be ideal if the orcs ambushed the red mages," Deodin said. "The two groups could slaughter each other and I would not need to intervene. I can tell you that it is not the case, however."

"How can you possibly know that?" Garret asked, suddenly more interested. "Can you see through the trees? Can you smell the travelers from here?"

"They are merchants. The Universe wants me to save them," Deodin replied. When he spoke next, his brows rose in surprise, as if he didn't believe his own words. "...And

164

I'm supposed to do it without being seen by the merchants themselves. That's a new one."

"That's it? Your plans involve arbitrary instructions from 'the Universe'?" Pel asked, annoyed.

"No, the instructions are never arbitrary. If anything, they have unnecessarily specific conditions for success."

Deodin's odd perspective of the cosmos notwithstanding, he didn't address her concerns. Interaction with anyone came with added risk. Saving the lives of travelers would certainly be a noble act, but it would provide an easier trail for the Tower to follow. There were greater stakes. Deodin seemed to sense her apprehension.

"I need to stop the orcs from killing the merchants, Pel," Deodin said.

Pel had nothing more to say. He was right.

"Kill them extra dead," Garret advised. "The orcs, I mean. Not the merchants."

This was Garret's way of describing orc resiliency. Deodin seemed to receive the message, despite its cryptic delivery. He touched his guide with a condescending pat on the shoulder and a long, patient blink. He paused for a moment more before grabbing a handful of arrows from Garret's quiver. "Meet me down there as quickly as you can. Follow the marker, once I set it," Deodin instructed.

"And what if these heroics lead the mages to us?" Pel asked.

She could see only indistinct shapes and blurs in the valley below, but she could easily envision the carnage of a battle with *sheyaktu*. She waited a few moments for Deodin to reply before turning to hear his answer. The space he had previously occupied was vacant. That was as much of an answer as she would get.

A moment later, high above the tree line in front of them, a ball of blue light materialized. It hung above the trees, silently and ominously. And there it remained.

"Our mark," Pel said, this time for Garret's benefit.

Garret followed her gaze and frowned. His version of the magical detection spell had long since lapsed.

"Sure. Leave a marker for the blind one." He hoisted the god killer's pack. Next, he reached out and took Pel's hand to help her up.

"He doesn't want anyone else to see it," she replied. The two started their descent down the hill. "It's his way of being discreet."

Human shouts of alarm rang from the forest below. The conflict had begun. The valley filled with the sounds of battle.

"Hopefully, he's not going to melt the orcs into puddles or turn them to stone. The red mages would be sure to hear of it," Garret said.

"Likely not," Pel replied, nudging toward the marker so Garret knew which way to go. "He's being more careful than that. His plans involve the arrows he took from you. Whatever he does, it will be something that can be explained without magic. Regardless, it is still reckless."

Garret acknowledged her with a grunt while trying to hurry her along through the underbrush. He gently ducked her head under a branch that she hadn't seen. "I think you should be the one to tell him what he can and can't do." He shifted his weight to guide her around a thorny bush. "Besides, as much as you don't like it, you know he's right. What kind of bastardhole lets some poor merchant get murdered by orcs when he knows he can stop it?"

She sighed. Garret placed his hand on the small of her back and guided her to avoid the brush in front of them.

"It doesn't make me a 'bastardhole' for being concerned about the Tower finding us," she said.

She paused. The two of them were so close that she could clearly see his face.

"They can't have him, Garret," she whispered. "That is quite literally my greatest fear."

With his hand still on her back, Garret turned her toward him, to the point where they were practically in an embrace. He looked into her eyes with as serious and stoic expression as she'd ever seen from him.

"You can't continue to make every decision in your life out of your fear of the Tower."

The comment found a foothold in her mind. Was her personal fear worth the lives of the travelers on that road? It was a point that she had never considered in those terms.

Garret continued. "Besides, there are a great number of terrifying things right in front of us. The Thick could kill us. The orcs could kill us. The god killer could decide that he doesn't want to pay us and he could kill us—"

"Well, let's hope it doesn't—"

"—but he could! Easily, and gruesomely, and probably amazingly." Garret brought up a single index finger to emphasize his point. He gestured to their surroundings. "And out here, something would find us and eat our lifeless corpses before they were even cold. Our story could very easily end in being shat out by a hideous monster. Clothes and all."

The rapid reply suggested that Garret had considered such a fate before. Pel drew a breath to reply, but Garret hadn't finished yet.

"Clothes and all," he repeated. This notion was apparently worse than being eaten naked.

"Garret. That's ... not helpful."

"You are allowed to have fears, Pel. Life can be scary. But you can't allow fear to rule your life. I mean, while we're on the topic of shit—"

"We are not on that topic."

"Between you and me, I've been so scared, I haven't been able to drop one since we met the bloody god killer."

"We are still not on the topic of shit," she insisted, lamenting the direction the conversation had taken but unable to suppress a giggle.

Garret stopped talking. She met his gaze to find him positively beaming. His eyes danced with excitement and glee, as if he had just won a game or contest.

"Did you just laugh? Right now?" he pressed. His reaction caught her off guard.

*I laughed? When did I—*

"Pelium Stillwater laughed at a shit joke in the middle of the Thick, while running from red mages, and in the heat of a battle with orcs? You are in luck, my friend, because I have so much more material. Well, aside from actual shit, being plugged up, like we talked about—"

She laughed again. Her head tilting forward, her forehead coming to rest on the upper part of his chest. This time, she noticed it. This time, it was delightful.

The moment ended abruptly. With a fluid movement, Pel found herself being picked up and repositioned. Garret drew his sword and had interposed himself between her and whatever might come out of the trees in front of them.

She recognized the magic before she recognized his form. Deodin pushed aside a branch and came into view. Pel put a hand on Garret's sword arm, holding it in check.

"Deodin!" she exclaimed, shocked by his appearance.

In the space of such a short time, his appearance had changed radically. The blue light that normally surrounded him glowed weakly. His face and hair were drenched in sweat and his clothes browned with dirt and filth. It looked like he had just swum across a moat.

Garret had already returned his sword to its scabbard and taken a step closer to provide aid, but Deodin gestured for him to stand back. Pel looked away in time but could still hear the runny splatter of vomit as Deodin let it out.

Having gathered himself, he stood up straight. Of the generous handful of arrows he had taken previously, he had two left. He held them out for Garret to retrieve.

"Nobody saw me," he said with a wheeze as Garret reclaimed his ammunition.

The battle seemed to be over, but the area stirred with noise and activity. Many voices, human voices, called out from the road. Deodin had not yet recovered from the exertion of the battle, but he took a moment to address Garret.

"East of Netherby, I know there to be a series of hills," Deodin began. "They are not covered by the trees of the Thick."

Garret nodded, then continued while Deodin caught his breath. "Those hills are half a day east of Netherby, if you stay in the valleys."

"Near those hills, is there a teardrop-shaped boulder, resting on its side? Large. The size of a house."

Garret took a moment to reply. "Not really. There is a huge boulder on the northern side of the northernmost hill, but it is round on one side and flat on the other. It doesn't come to a point like you describe," Garret said. He hesitated, then amended his answer. "Maybe it *did*, though. That flat side has sharp corners. Maybe it looked like a teardrop, but the tail broke off. It's been flat as long as I've known it. If you need to go there, watch out for the... Actually, never mind. They should watch out for you."

"One week. Meet me in Netherby, in one week. Don't look for me, I'll find you," Deodin ordered between gasps. He removed a moderately sized pouch from his belt and handed it to Pel. It weighed heavily with coin.

Voices brought the conversation to an end. They were close, just on the other side of the nearby trees.

"Oy! Friend! All of them orcs are done!" An older man emerged from behind the tree, holding a spear. His simple clothes were covered in dirt, sweat, and blood. His face expressed surprise to see both Pel and Garret standing there.

The stranger relaxed, his expression transitioning from confusion to understanding. Everything about the situation in front of him suggested that Garret had saved the caravan and acted as Pel's guardian.

"Ah, yer woman is okay? Ya had to check up on her, ah?"

"That is ... exactly what happened and is happening ... right now." Garret glanced down at the two arrows he held. He displayed them as evidence and forced a smile.

Pel stole a look to where Deodin had been. He was gone. The heavy pack that should have been resting at Garret's feet had also disappeared. Whatever Deodin had done, it had saved the day without anyone knowing of his involvement. Pel turned to Garret.

"My hero." She leaned in and gave him a kiss on the cheek.

# THE DISCOURSE ON MAGIC (CHAPTER 4)

*Excerpted with permission from The Discourse on Magic, by Thierren Dowdy, the noted Grand Mage of the Western Isles.*

Taken from Chapter 4, Section 2: Spell compendium

**Influencing others**

Certainly, the obvious and overt abuse of magic is bad enough. And there are so many libraries of weapon spells that even the dimmest imaginations can comprehend their impact. Unfortunately, the more insidious abuses of magic have far subtler implications.

Such is the case when magic is misused to affect the mind. The existence of so-called "pushing" magic creates an even more chilling set of circumstances, as it describes the supernatural ability to influence the actions and decisions of others.

Let us begin by stating the obvious: pushing magic has no legitimate use. Its very existence serves as fuel for those who would seek to restrict or ban magical practice and study altogether. On the ethical and moral spectrum, pushing magic rests on the far extreme end, ranging between "terrible" and "diabolical."

(In fact, a few of my colleagues went so far as to suggest that I not include a passage on pushing magic. They would suggest I leave this discussion out of the spell compendium, simply to avoid the outcry and backlash that may come from it. Ultimately, I decided that an informed public is better off than an uninformed one. It seemed distastefully ironic to "push" such a personal, self-serving agenda onto the reader, by means of omission.)

Now, before you ruin your life with sleepless nights fraught with paranoia, forever worried about the corruption of the minds of those around you, allow me to talk about how pushing magic comes to manifest. Fortunately, like all enchantment, pushing magic obeys rules and has limits.

1. Pushing is not mental enslavement.

The caster cannot control the physical actions, movements, words, or thoughts of another. Magic cannot turn people into puppets.

2. Pushing requires an actively engaged participant.

Both the spellcaster and the "victim" of the spell must be mentally engaged. Pushing magic cannot work on a victim who is unconscious, asleep, or otherwise unable to mentally process the push.

3. Pushing magic can only affect those who want to do something but are otherwise inhibited or restricted from doing so.

This is the best analogy I've heard, regarding inhibition:

4. Inhibitions that can be washed away with wine can also be pushed aside with magic.

**Final thoughts**

Successful pushers will not affront your sensibilities. They will not challenge your beliefs, values, or worldview. They will find and test your personal boundaries and limitations. When finished, you'll find yourself agreeing to their terms and it will seem like you wanted to do it all along.

The most profound lesson about pushing is this: magic is often completely unnecessary.

# DAY
# 6

# Ruby (The Mage Tower) – Mica

Following a bright flash of orange light, Mica felt a wave of heat from the open door on the far end of the hallway. The flash was followed by a short cry of triumph. She closed the stairwell door behind her and made her way down the hall.

*Gregor?*

Only a few red mages remained in the Tower and this wasn't a room she associated with anyone else. Of the mages still on the campus, Gregor was the only one she knew who was researching a fire spell. The room erupted with another flash of heat and light. This time, it was followed by curses and angry mutterings.

She came to the door, stopped, and turned to face the person in the room. She bowed her head and held her pose for a few moments.

"Good sir, how may I serve?" she asked with what she thought was an appropriate amount of humility.

Inside was Gregor. He stood in a room that was largely empty, save for an anvil that rested in its center and a medium-sized box of potatoes on the far side.

Gregor scowled but said nothing to acknowledge Mica's existence. He retrieved another potato from the box, stomped across the room, and placed it on the anvil with the jerky, fidgety motions born of his signature impatience and ill-temper.

In her time at the Tower, Mica had learned much about the individual mages, including their personalities and the powers they researched. She had discovered that the unredeemable assholes of the Tower had conveniently color-coded themselves. Ruby's mages had done their best to earn their reputation for being self-serving and self-indulgent and the red team carried the greatest burden of that reputation. Any mage who wore an ensemble of red-on-red was a depraved prick.

Gregor, for instance, was essentially a caricature of an actual person. He was a man so warped by avarice and ambition that he could hardly be seen as anything more. He had purely selfish motives for studying magic, had zero respect for the humans with whom he interacted, and pursued interests that promised to make the world a worse place today than it was yesterday.

Gregor stepped back from the anvil and pulled a pinch of gold leaf from a jar. He then held his hands in front of his chest, moving them about in a three-dimensional pattern. Simultaneously, he uttered a guttural phrase. A flash of white-hot light engulfed the potato and the anvil beneath it. When the flash subsided, the potato was aflame and the top of the anvil glowed red.

Gregor muttered to himself. He had been trying to produce an effect that was even more potent. Mica sighed. Yet another mage toiled away on yet another fireball spell.

In her month at the Tower, she had learned a great deal about mages and their craft. It was easy enough to borrow a book from the library and read it in privacy. And while magical research wasn't part of her reasons for being here, it was an interesting, meaningful use of her free time. So many of the Tower's red mages were fascinated with the weaponization of fire spells that she'd felt compelled to read up on the subject.

Interestingly, the fireball spell had not evolved or changed in nearly a century. Of all the enchantments that had been studied since Skycrash, fire-based weapon spells had always been at the forefront of magical research. Yet, the gods seemed to have placed a cap on how destructive such spells could be. Regardless of how it was cast, deadly fire magic had reached its peak long ago. To study it anew was simply a waste of time.

That didn't stop people from trying. Nearly every mage on the red team believed that he was the single key in unlocking the "true" nature of one weapon spell or another. Creating a potion to extinguish a conventional fire that has engulfed a barn? Preposterous. Finding a magical way to warm a house through the cold months? Asinine. Discovering a weapon spell that was slightly more malicious or deadly than the scores of spells that already did the same thing? That was the dream of the red team. And based on what she saw here, it was a dream shared by Gregor.

*You should try one of the yu gestures.*

She had learned many of the names of the more common gestures used in spellcasting. She knew that *yu* was a gesture related to an amplification, a way to concentrate an effect that was already in place.

Gregor muttered to himself for a moment before saying the word *yu* out loud. His expression changed somewhat, his eyebrows narrowed in thought.

*You should hold the eee-yoht cant slightly longer and release it more abruptly.*

From what she had read, the cant would cause the effect to amplify from the *yu* gesture. Together, it would create a feedback that would allow the energy to grow.

Gregor's eyes lit up. An epiphany!

"Amplification! Of course!" he hissed. He almost skipped from the potato box to the anvil to set the next target in its place.

*You can safely handle multiple amplification effects.*

Mica felt that the nature of amplifications was an interesting read. The limitations had already been well researched: amplification effects could stack, but the timing was critical. The tolerances were too tight for most sensible practitioners to try. If you failed an amplification and were lucky, you would die quickly.

*Give it a try. You're obviously so much more skilled than literally every other mage who has ever tried it.*

Gregor turned around, filled with a renewed sense of purpose. And confidence.

Mica sidestepped out of the doorway, no longer in line of sight of the mage's experiments. A heavy stone wall separated the hallway from Gregor's spell.

She heard him cast his spell, this time adding the "eee-yoht." She thought he held it for too long. She sighed again. After all, Gregor was only human.

The flash of light was hotter and brighter than she had witnessed previously. And, much as it had before, it evaporated as quickly as it had come. When the lighting returned to normal, Mica could see the yellow-orange flickering light coming from within the room. The lighting was soft and yellow, reminding her of candles.

She returned to the doorway and peered into the test room. The entire anvil was white hot and the potato had been reduced to an ashen, ovular brick. Much as he had hoped he would, Gregor had successfully amplified the effect.

However, the success had come with a cost.

Gregor himself was the source of a small fire. His flaming, desiccated skeleton had collapsed to its knees and flickering, dying fire filled the room with smoke. A moment later, when Gregor's head became too heavy for the ashen flesh of his neck, it toppled forward, caromed off his lap, and rolled under the anvil.

Mica coughed loudly, waving her hand in front of her face in a futile attempt to clear the smoke and smell. She looked past the mage's smoldering remnants, into the rest of the room. The anvil now glowed red and the room had cooled to normal.

Satisfied that the remaining flames on Gregor's skeleton would die down by themselves and that the room wasn't likely to catch fire or collapse, she turned and continued down the hall.

# Netherby – Pel

Garret grimaced. "Just because he won't tell us why he's in the Crown won't prevent us from thinking about it. I want to know why the world's most powerful person 'needs' to be here," he remarked.

Garret and Pel had joined the merchant caravan on its way to Netherby. The merchants were so grateful for their rescue that they insisted the pair travel with them. For the rest of the afternoon, Pel and Garret sat on the back of one of the carts, enjoying the time off their feet. Separated from the merchants, they also appreciated the time alone.

Their story was a half-truth: Pel wanted to talk to Netherby's villagers to learn about the nature of the recent orc activity because it influenced business within Ruby. Garret was an obvious choice for a guide along the way. Traveling to Netherby would have been a plausible way for Pel to conduct her normal business.

And while everyone misjudged the depth of her relationship with Garret, the more time she spent with him, the more it didn't seem like a misunderstanding. He was completely forthright in his affections for her and she was becoming more honest with herself about how she felt about him.

*Had I agreed to that dinner sooner, perhaps I would have made this trip sooner.*

"I know that he hates the red mages," Garret added.

"'Hates?' He said he had a 'history' with them," Pel said.

"He and I talked the other night, after you had fallen asleep. He had given me the magic vision spell that you have. When we talked about the red mages, he lit up so brightly that it scared the shit out of me. So to speak."

Pel rolled her eyes.

Garret continued. "He's not out here to get rich. And he already knew about the increased orc activity, which is interesting in itself. Orcs are native to the Crown and aren't a threat to someplace south of the Bite, like Donkton or Southend. And we know Bartlett's ship came from Southend," Garret summarized.

"Wait. You call it 'the Bite?'" Pel asked. In her understanding, the river that separated the Crown from everything else was called the "Bayet," which everyone in Ruby pronounced like "buy it."

"You've never seen them, but the cliffs look like teeth. On both sides of the river. It looks like the upper and lower jaws of a titan. Calling it 'the Bite' would be so much better."

Pel knew of the cliffs, as they had been instrumental in allowing the Crown to survive the post-Skycrash apocalypse. Hundreds of feet high, the cliffs were jaggedly treacherous and functionally impossible to climb. During the chaotic decades following Skycrash, the Bayet River and its escarpments served as an impenetrable barrier, insulating the Crown from the mobs and the rampaging armies of the civilizations that had collapsed in the east.

"We can speculate about Deodin's intentions all we like. But to what end? What does that get us?" Pel asked.

"Pel, you're the one who knows everything. We've got big problems if you can't figure it out. I'm just here to carry your bags."

She smiled.

"Very well. You forgot to mention that he asked about the giant rock. Where is that?"

"Off the primary road, but on a trail that connects Netherby to Delemere. It sits on the side of a hill. I just use it as a landmark on the way to Delemere. I can't think of anything interesting about it."

Pel reflected on this for a few moments longer. "Well, I don't think we have enough information to guess his motives. Any discussion would be speculative. I would rather talk about his fatalistic views about 'the Universe.' I don't understand his convictions."

"What's to understand? He's an adventurer and a hero," Garret replied.

"I'm not convinced it matters to him, though. He doesn't save people because he wants to or because he values their lives. He views his acts of heroism as an obligation imposed on him by the powers that be."

"Neither of us know what it's like to be *sheyaktu*," Garret replied.

"Of course. Perhaps that's the issue. But even though he's thoughtful, and funny, and delightful to be around, I don't think any of us matter to him. The day 'the Universe' stops telling him to care about people, I'm afraid he would."

\* \* \*

It took a moment for her eyes to adjust to the dim lighting of the Netherby inn. By the time she and Garret made their way through the door and surveyed the room, she could feel an invasive set of eyes on her.

*One of the red mages from the Tower.*

The man didn't shine like Deodin, but he was draped in a faint blue aura. He sat in the far corner, facing the door. He watched Pel and Garret suspiciously.

She wouldn't have needed her augmented vision to recognize him as a mage. Only if he were bathed in a spotlight would he stand out more. Draped in his red clothing, he held his head and shoulders in a prim posture of faux nobility, a pose commonly favored and cultivated by those of the Tower.

Equally of note were the heavy bands of gold on his fingers. The precious metals were reagents for powerful spells and the jewelry served not only as a statement of fashion or wealth, but as a warning.

With his magical aura, Pel could recognize his features, even from across the room. He was an unpleasant man to look upon, with a skinny, unhealthy build, thinning hair, and a face marred with scars of both disease and indiscretion.

Equally unpleasant was the way he looked at them. He leaned back in his chair, mentally dissecting them as they stood in the doorway. He stared. At Pel. She resisted the urge to visibly shudder and directed her attention to the room itself.

The tavern told a grim story. The smell of burned wood and the sight of the charred walls and furniture suggested a recent fire. The room was completely devoid of people, including those who should be the staff. The single mage sulking at a table in the corner was the only person present.

Garret wasn't blind to the contextual clues himself. He clenched her hand tighter in a show of support.

"Have you any wine?" the mage asked, after the prolonged eye contact. The question was not meant as a casual inquiry of inventory.

"Some," Pel responded. "It is warm from the trip."

"It will suffice," he returned with an impatient sigh.

Garret understood where the conversation headed, so he started the arduous task of locating the wineskin among the other gear strapped across his back. Several heavy and muffled thumps later, he held the vessel out for Pel to retrieve.

She took it, drew her cloak around herself, and straightened the way it hung on her shoulders before approaching the man on the other side of the room. She gave the skin a few obvious shakes to show how little remained. The mage shrugged.

The exchange was curt. The man took the pouch and began to drink from it without burdening the conversation by asking for permission or offering thanks. When he was finished emptying the contents entirely, he looked up. He studied Pel for a moment before turning his attention back to Garret.

"Who are you?" the man asked. "And who is she?"

"I am Garret, a guide of the Thick. And she can speak for her herself."

*Thank you, Garret.*

"I am Pelium Stillwater of Ruby." Despite the relative heat of the afternoon, she pulled herself into her cloak. "I deal in information."

"I am Tyberius Reginald Lorian, the Fourth Adept of the Lumerage Order of the Leopard. I am the Magistrix of Archanagia and the Emissary of the Ruby Mage Tower: Point Prominence."

Garret looked at the man with wide eyes, turning his head slightly to the side. "They found a successor to the Third Adept?" he asked, apparently taken aback at the news.

Thankfully, the subtlety of Garret's sarcasm went unobserved. The mage nodded to Garret with appreciative, approving eyes, glad that someone had noticed that detail. He examined Pel more closely, his eyes lingering a little too long around her neckline.

"Why are you here?" he asked, glancing momentarily about the tavern in disgust. He obviously disliked his outing to Netherby and couldn't understand why anyone chose to be in its vicinity.

"Answers," she replied. "The merchants of Ruby, my clients, have suffered several orc attacks while traveling this road. They wish to know more about this orc threat."

"Orcs attacked again today, just outside of Netherby," Garret added.

"Attacked who?" the mage asked, his interest barely torn away from undressing Pel with his eyes.

"A merchant caravan heading north from Ruby," Pel replied.

"Not many arrows in your quiver," the mage noted, turning to Garret with a hiccup and a belch. His interest seemed to wane once the conversation turned to orcs. "You turned back this attack, then?"

Garret shrugged.

"We were—" he began, only to be interrupted by a blinding light and commotion when the inn door opened on the other end of the room. A cascade of excitement flooded the tavern as the merchants of the caravan made their way into the inn. Having put their horses to the trough and secured their wares, the merchants gravitated toward the bar.

"Where's Garret?" came a hearty, mirthful cry from one of the many who had made their way in. "So help me if he's spent a single copper in this place!" A chorus of laughs and cheers followed the comment. The merchants dragged Garret to a table and sat him down.

Pel watched the mage uneasily. Those from the caravan couldn't be expected to read the tension of the situation. Nor would she expect them to notice all the contextual clues. Fortunately, the mage seemed to be calm and, perhaps, a little bit amused. The merchants' genuine good cheer was contagious, at least to a small degree. Having been victorious in a battle against a ravaging band of orcs, they had been in a delightful mood since their rescue.

"What shall we call you, Garret? Orcslayer? Orcsbane?" one of the younger men asked, pulling up a seat next to him.

"Heartpiercer," suggested another. Quieter than his suggestion was his follow-up question, wondering aloud where the barkeep was.

"'Orcslayer,' you say," repeated the emissary, dispassionately. Oblivious to the man's dour temperament, one of the merchants continued in the merrymaking.

The man sitting next to Garret had wide eyes and was eager to tell the story.

"Aye, friend, you should have seen it! Pinned down by an orc ambush. And within a flash, the orcs start falling! Like a snake of the Thick, Garret here shot the bastards through and through! Saved the whole lot of us, eh?" he gave the mage a hearty pat on the back, to which the man responded with a silent sneer of disdain.

"All in a day's work for such a ... ah ... proficient guard, hmmm?" the mage replied, picking up the wineskin. Reminded that it was still empty, he tossed it back to the table with no small display of disappointment.

"That's just it, eh?" said the younger man. "Him and her were in the Thick by themselves. Not with us. He just appears out of the Thick and puts them orcs down by himself. True hero, he is! Had nothing to gain for himself, just savin' the likes of us for naught but a thank you!"

"And an ale!" cried another, followed by a raucous round of cheers. And again, over the din of the revelry, a few men voiced serious concern about where in the hell the barkeep was.

"Ah," the mage said, apathetically.

Pel felt an increasing twist in her stomach as she watched his expression change from unenthusiastic, unbridled boredom to one of increasing interest. Her cheeks betrayed her by coloring as she watched the mage put the pieces of information together: This man and woman were not part of the caravan? They were simply meandering through the Thick by themselves? If not traveling by the road and considering how far they had come, they must have left Ruby around the same time as the mysterious rogue mage....

Pel's palms became moist as the emissary settled his gaze back on her, not nearly as bored and disinterested as she would have wanted him to be.

"Ah," the mage said.

# DAY
# 7

# The Thick
# (South of Netherby) – Deodin

Deodin consulted his map. By his reckoning, he was south of Netherby, following a narrow trail that snaked through the Thick as he headed east. The trail had reached its end. A glorious end, in fact. An army of lumberjacks could not have done it any better.

The Universe had decided to place an impassable barrier in front of him. There could be no other explanation. A truly enormous mountain of fallen trees had been piled in front of him, blocking the path. The trees would have to have been planted on top of each other to achieve this density.

And now that they had toppled over, the fallen trees crisscrossed each other in such a way that the mass would be impossible to climb over or through. Additionally, the surrounding forest of the Thick was unusually and unrealistically dense. All the undergrowth had funneled Deodin to this specific point.

In his experience, there would be precisely one path that would lead around this obstacle and that path would feature one of two things:

1 A series of handholds, ledges, and platforms that were just within reach of his standing broad jump, or...

2 Something that wanted to kill him.

DAY 7

As Deodin approached the path, a positively massive cat emerged from between two trees in front of him.

*Find the path to Makee's tomb:*

☑  *Find the eastern path*
☐  *Defeat the panther matron*

She was a magnificent beast: wide paws, muscular shoulders, and a shining coat of black fur. She reared back up on her hind legs in a posture that demonstrated both her size and malevolence. She roared ominously, baring teeth and claws that could tear through flesh, bone, and steel, and—

"You're an ambush predator. You lose all of your advantage with that display," Deodin griped, bemoaning another preposterous turn of events.

She roared again, going through what seemed to be an unavoidable and unskippable scene. Whatever came next, he would have to wait until she was finished. During all of this, Deodin found a suitable spot to rest his pack.

With his equipment out of his way, he faced the cat, who had finally returned to all four feet. She circled toward him, her mouth open and ears pinned back. A confrontation was unavoidable.

"You're not even indigenous to this region," Deodin scolded, more annoyed with the implausibility of the encounter than this particular adversary.

It was the sixth time today that Deodin had randomly encountered something in the Thick that wanted to kill him. This cat, two bears, a spikeboar (and all its spikeboar friends that joined the fight), a giant rat, and an inexplicably mobile and carnivorous plant.

189

The cat finally pounced.

The fight itself was uninteresting and ended within a minute. With his ability to bend the laws of time and strike with a magical touch, Deodin was destined to be the victor.

The battle safely won, Deodin looked over the spoils. The cat's fur was exceptionally thick and soft, so much so that he considered it to be an inexcusable waste to leave it. And while such a pelt might fetch a hefty sum from the right buyer, it would be more valuable as raw material for equipment.

As with other things from the Thick, the mobs of the region were imbued with latent supernatural properties. Once crafted into clothing and equipment, that magic would be conferred on the wearer and—

*Hold up.*

Deodin turned to retrieve a skinning knife from his pack, only to find it was not where he left it. A moment later, something small and heavy scuttled in the underbrush, snapping branches and scraping against the ground.

Whatever it was, the thief had underestimated the weight of Deodin's backpack. The pursuit would not last long. Deodin came to a small clearing and finally saw the miscreant. It looked over its shoulder back at him, running away as fast as its little legs could go. It was the most ridiculous thing he had seen all day.

*This must be a joke.*

The perpetrator was a little forest person-critter-thing, and—dear gods—it was stupidly adorable. It appeared as if a plush doll had come to life and tried to pass itself off as a tiny, furry human. It stood about two feet tall and wore a patchwork of clothes. It stared at Deodin with big eyes that featured preposterously large pupils.

Deodin felt a modicum of relief. The creature did not seem specifically designed to kill him. It was equipped with neither fangs nor claws, wasn't draped in scales or stingers, and carried no weapons. Deodin could sense no threat or risk. In fact, the only concern was that the creature had fished out a small sack from the backpack—the purse of gemstones he had promised Pel and Garret.

"Easy, friend." Deodin gestured with open palms. Despite his circumstances, a smile found his face. As much as this little distraction had delayed him, it was also endearingly cute. This encounter was a delightful break from life-or-death confrontation. It was even refreshing to have—

"Fuck-fuck-fuck! Stay back, fuck!" the critter barked.

Deodin grinned. That it swore like one of Southend's dockhands, in a little, squeaky voice, made it even more amusing.

"Put that down." Deodin laughed. "Maybe I have a treat in the big bag that I can share with you."

The interloper proved to be significantly less charming when it tossed Deodin's purse into a hole created by the root structure of a nearby stump.

"Fuck-fuck. Work job, fuck!"

*Well. That's enough of that.*

Deodin froze time, appeared next to the little bastard, and recovered the pack with an uncontested tug. Curiously, the foul-mouthed bugger did not appear to be impressed or intimidated by Deodin's ability to cover that much distance so quickly. Likewise, the critter offered no resistance when Deodin recouped his belongings. Satisfied that his property was in hand, Deodin slipped into the pack's straps and rebuked the thief with the worst glare he could muster.

"Work job, fuck," the critter repeated, seemingly content with the way that this situation had gone down.

"You take my property and then curse at me for wanting it back?" Deodin lectured. "Rude."

He knelt by the tree where the critter had tossed the bag of gems. With the aid of a light spell, he peered into the hole, which was much wider and deeper than he had anticipated. In fact, he could detect no bottom to it. He stole a glance back at the critter, whose expression hadn't changed. Deodin began to sense what would come next.

The space under the stump was more than a crevasse formed by roots and erosion. It was an extended tunnel that was surprisingly deep and far too small for him to fit through. However, it was probably an ideal size for a forest critter thing—a thing that had suddenly become significantly less adorable.

Deodin frowned. This scenario didn't originate from bad luck. This was a set-up and a shake-down.

"Work job, fuck. Give monies back, fuck. We needs help from cave trolls that eats us all and—" the critter began.

*Dammit.* Deodin sighed.

He held up his hand in a bid for the critter to stop the exposition. The exact details were hardly important, anyway. He had been given new objectives.

*Find the path to Makee's Tomb:*
- ☑ *Find the eastern path*
- ☑ *Defeat the panther matron*
- ☐ *Help the Rashni with their troll problem*
- ☐ *Recover your gem purse*

Deodin was once again in the middle of another crisis, a problem for which he was the only solution. Whenever someone (or something) needed his help, the cause was always necessary and morally justified. The details would be only marginally different from instance to instance, occasion to occasion. Ultimately, someone needed help, and like now, Deodin would need to make time for it.

Nevertheless, Deodin pointed a rebuking finger at the forest creature and cast a sideways glance of disapproval.

"First things first: we work on your word choice."

# The Thick
# (South of Netherby) – Deodin

They called themselves Rashni, a term from their language. He could hardly understand it, but Deodin much preferred their native tongue to their profanity-laden interpretation of Common.

A race of small, unassuming creatures that carved tunnels in the roots of the great trees of the Thick, the Rashni demonstrated simple, modest values, living a life that was primitive but relatively peaceful. Their meager existence as scavengers and foragers meant they interacted minimally with nearly everything else.

However, the Thick had changed over the past six to eight months. Deodin had already known this, but his trip to the Crown shed light into the details. He was beginning to learn that the increased movement and activity of the orcs seemed to be a symptom, not the cause.

Kesh, the Rashni who held Deodin's gem purse hostage, had spoken of this change in his own colorful way. Despite the differences in language and Kesh's propensity to use vulgarities as every part of speech, Deodin learned that the balance of power across the Thick had been upset. In the case of the Rashni, they had been accosted by a clan of trolls that had moved into their area, coming to inhabit a cave system within Rashni territory.

The trolls had been displaced themselves. They were forced to move when something bigger and badder had found them. The entirety of the Thick was in discord and it created a cascade of activity.

While trolls would never have the industry to threaten the Crown itself, they were certainly clever and craven enough to feed on the local Rashni population.

Deodin stood in front of the cave that Kesh had identified as being the home of the trolls.

*Help the Rashni with their troll problem:*
☐ *Slay 10 trolls in the cave*
☐ *Return with Bonechewer's head*

Deodin frowned. The Universe had provided no conditions should the cave house fewer than ten trolls.

Subterranean troll dens were common. Deodin had encountered them everywhere he'd ever traveled, even if that region had no other natural cave formations. It was as if the caves and the trolls were integrated; one couldn't exist without the other.

He stripped out from his pack and stashed it near the cave mouth. A moment later, he entered and felt the dark, damp air on his skin and a simultaneous assault on his nose. Whether it was rotting flesh, troll shit, or something else, the smell of troll caves numbered among the most unpleasant experiences in Deodin's travels.

More importantly, the caves were simply insulting. Across his travels and a lifetime of adventuring, Deodin learned that there were exactly eight variants in the layouts of troll caves. The caves were not furnished with similar décor. They did not share floorplans.

Rather, they were identical in every way.

Whether the result of laziness or spite, the Universe had decided two things, with regard to troll caves: they would always be the same and Deodin's adventuring would periodically demand that he retrieve something from the very far end.

As expected, the closest torch was affixed to the left-hand wall, approximately eight feet above the ground, just past where the brown rock met the gray rock. He'd seen it countless times before. Deodin called this variant "The Horseshoe." It wasn't entirely shaped like a horseshoe, as there were a few branches that forked off along the way, but if viewed from the top down, it would resemble a U.

At least it was not "The Butterfly." Any cave was better than The Butterfly cave.

Deodin entered the first alcove, a recessed portion of the cave on the left-hand side. Two trolls knelt in front of the rotten carcass of a forest animal. It was a revolting pile of bone, fur, meat, and flies.

Deodin attacked first, welling a ball of magic in his hand and striking the chest of a monster twice his size. The troll hissed in pain as the magical energy exploded. Deodin had learned that it took six of these hits to slay a troll of this size. Every time.

*Why six? Why always six?* And why did every troll battle follow the same pattern, a pattern as predictable as the caves themselves?

The troll on Deodin's right attacked with an avoidable swipe of its clawed hand, a swipe from its other clawed hand, and then a lunging thrust with its jaws. The troll on his left paused for a moment and summoned a ball of glowing white light between its hands.

*Healing spell!*

Occasionally, a troll used magic. The white ball of light was a healing spell that would help a monster recover from its wounds. Deodin would need to score ten hits to slay the troll if that spell were to be cast successfully.

Reflexively, Deodin slowed time just long enough to close the distance between him and the troll spellcaster. He lashed out with a vicious front snap-kick. The attack landed squarely in the monster's crotch. A satisfying *splorch* echoed throughout the cave.

The strike wouldn't count as a "hit" for the purposes of killing the troll, but it would interrupt the spell and prevent that troll from casting that spell again, at least for a while.

Deodin returned his attention to the right-hand troll, which he attacked with a sliding strike. This time, the magic landed with an explosion that was about twice as bright as his normal attack.

Up next was another avoidable round of "claw-claw-bite." Deodin countered with a lethal blow. The troll began a death behavior by collapsing to its knees, reaching out with its clawed hands, then falling face-first to the ground with a heavy thud.

Deodin sighed. Every fallen troll would exhibit exactly one of three specific death rituals and this one was no different.

He fought through more mobs until he reached an alcove just past the pair of torches, on what he called "The Skwall." It was a row of skulls that lined the right-hand wall of The Horseshoe, past the second alcove. As he always did, he took a moment to rap his knuckles on the large human skull with a firm knock-knock, as if he were announcing himself at a door. The skull always made an amusing *cloop-cloop* sound. It was normally the highlight of his time in The Horseshoe.

Two more trolls waited within the alcove, huddled around a crude pot. They arose in unison and the fight began. He punched one of the monsters in the face, but as he did, the sensation of *déjà vu* posed a new question in his mind:

*What if there aren't different trolls in different places? What if the caves are the same because it's the same trolls, over and over again?*

In the meantime, he scorched a yellow-hided troll with a concentrated blast from both hands. The mob squealed and began its predictable and pointless claw-claw-bite attack. Deodin dodged the flurry of strikes without thinking about it.

*I manipulate time every day. Perhaps the trolls and their caves are trapped in time. That would explain why their caves and their behavior are always the same.*

Mindlessly, habitually, he returned with a counterstrike. Another hit.

What if the trolls were prisoners? And their caves were the prisons? Perhaps the trolls existed in a routine that they were doomed to repeat forever. Perhaps they were more than mere mindless, murderous monsters. Perhaps they were trapped in a nightmare of their own. Maybe they were Deodin's kindred in some special way, captives of the same twisted Universe.

He dropped out of his aggressive fighting stance and held up his outstretched palm, gesturing for the combat to halt, if only for a moment.

"If you are a prisoner trapped in time, reliving the same moment over and over again, give me a sign. Something that's not claw-claw-bite," Deodin said.

He eyed the yellow troll with narrowed, suspicious eyes and waited, daring to hope that he may have solved the riddle of the troll caves.

Instead, the troll took a swing with its right arm, then its left, then it lunged forward with its jaws. The attacks missed.

*Gods dammit.*

If the trapped-in-time hypothesis wasn't true, then there was still nothing nuanced or redeeming about the trolls' existence. And if that were the case, their stupid caves were pointless and there was still nothing to gain in all this spelunking. It made him resent the experience even more.

The yellow troll did not attempt to cast a spell, but Deodin kicked it in the crotch anyway.

\* \* \*

*Bonechewer, I presume.*

Deodin had reached the very far end of The Horseshoe cave. The last section of the cave promised to house their leader. Or patron. Or king. Or however trolls organized themselves in a hierarchy. Whatever the case, all he needed was the thing's head.

*Help the Rashni with their troll problem:*
- ☑ *Slay 10 trolls in the cave*
- ☐ *Return with Bonechewer's head*

Incidentally, Deodin didn't mind a face-off with something called "Bonechewer." At the very least, when a mob had been enough of a menace to earn a name from the locals, there was usually more to the experience than claw-claw-bite.

Sometimes, the monster at the end of the quest had something to say. This troll seemed to be waiting for him. It sat on the ground, wrapping its arms around its knees, rocking back and forth slightly.

"I smell you, human," the giant said. The massive troll turned its head toward Deodin as he entered the last alcove. Bonechewer slowly took to its feet and stood upright to its full height of more than ten feet. Its head nearly scraped the stalactites. "I smell the blood of my fallen clan. I sense a magic that I cannot hope to overcome."

"I have come for your head, troll. And I don't intend to carry the rest of you." Deodin delivered the threat while sparking magic from his fingers.

When interacting with most mobs that spoke Common, Deodin had learned that it really didn't matter what he said. The monster would make a few opening remarks, demand something unrealistic, then fight to the death when the demands were not met, all the while—

A thought struck him.

"Wait. Say that again. Something about magical hopelessness?"

"The Crown teems with magic and turmoil!" The troll took a step forward. "She has awakened and pushes us like waves to break us against your jagged shore."

*What? A troll that speaks in simile and uses words like "teems" and "turmoil?"*

Deodin stumbled backward and glanced around the rest of the cave. It was still the same alcove at the end of The Horseshoe as every other alcove at the end of every other Horseshoe. Three torches hung from the left wall, one from the right. Brown rocks on the far wall, except that gray one.

It was still the same setting, but he had never experienced this behavior from any troll.

"Please explain, uh, Mister Bonechewer. Who is 'she'?" Deodin was unsure how to politely address a troll. He wasn't even sure Bonechewer was male.

"Come, magic man!" the troll bellowed. "Let us play our parts in our tragic puppet show!"

*What in the hells is all of this? Trolls don't do this. Trolls have never done this.*

Bonechewer retrieved a towering, double-headed axe that had been leaning against the cave wall and charged.

The troll's first attack was uncharacteristically advanced. It twitched its hands and flexed its shoulders to feint a chest-high slash, but attacked with a fierce jab with the axe's handle. The blow struck Deodin solidly in the face. He reeled backward with short, shuffled steps.

Deodin's world spun with dizziness. Before he could recover, Bonechewer pressed the attack with an astonishingly fast downward chop. Were he less experienced, Deodin wouldn't have reflexively slowed time to avoid the strike. The axe struck the cave's floor with a flash of sparks, chipped stone, and dust. As the monster freed the axe from the ground, Deodin had a moment to collect his thoughts.

Beyond the ringing in his ears and his blurry, swirling vision, Deodin was numb with shock. He couldn't remember the last time an adversary had struck him so savagely. And coming from a troll? That was more stunning than the strike itself.

"This must stop," Bonechewer snarled as it changed its grip on the axe handle. "For the madness to end, you must stop!"

Deodin flinched at the way the troll emphasized the word "you." Bonechewer did not view this struggle as a random troll against a random human. The giant had some sort of personal agenda and Deodin stood in its way.

"*Me?*" Deodin asked, perplexed by nearly everything that had happened in the past twenty seconds. "I'm here to prevent the bullshit!"

He had hardly finished his sentence before Bonechewer mounted another offensive. This time, the troll swung with a neck-high swirling slash, which Deodin avoided by dilating time again and leaning back to avoid the blow. The giant had predicted the dodge and spun completely around to carry out the real attack, a downward swipe directed at Deodin's knees.

Deodin exhausted his magical reserves to bend inertial laws, giving himself just enough leverage to jump clear of harm. He tumbled to the ground and rolled away, narrowly avoiding the hissing head of the axe. *Sheyaktu* or not, the troll had nearly claimed both of Deodin's legs.

"It only ends when you stop!" Bonechewer said, shifting its grip on its axe as it planned the next move.

That pause would prove to be a fatal mistake. The troll had allowed enough time for Deodin to recover from the staggering physical blow and the shock and confusion of Bonechewer's puzzling remarks.

A moment later, Bonechewer hefted its great weapon and drove its blade downward in a ferocious sweeping arc. The strike missed and Deodin responded with a fierce, magically augmented uppercut punch that landed with a blinding flash of light. Bonechewer reeled.

"*Why* must I stop—?" Deodin began before being interrupted when the troll attacked again.

Deodin wanted to give Bonechewer every opportunity to explain itself, but the monster abandoned its axe and launched a predictable attack with its bare hands. In the span of moments, Bonechewer's unprecedented combat savvy devolved to the standard troll operating procedure.

It was infuriating.

*"Gods dammit with the claw-claw-bite!"* Deodin's frustration was aimed at the Universe behind the trolls, their caves, and the assorted bullshit along the way.

The moment was no longer novel. The situation was no longer interesting or thought-provoking. Whatever had awakened within Bonechewer had succumbed to its troll-ness and Deodin was stuck in another copy of The Horseshoe cave with another troll and nothing to gain from the encounter.

In a rage, Deodin attacked recklessly and furiously, shrugging off hits that he would normally avoid. He traded blows with the troll, knowing that he would ultimately triumph. Every strike that he suffered from Bonechewer's claw was a reminder of the pointless futility of Deodin's existence. Tears rolled down his cheeks from the pain of a lifetime of bullshit, not from physical wounds.

Red mages. Troll caves. Escort quests. Merchants and their preposterous equipment. Spikeboar livers. He hated all of it.

And right now, Bonechewer was the one to bear the brunt of Deodin's existential vexation. The rest of the conflict was ugly and brutal, but mercifully short. After being struck a killing blow, a moribund Bonechewer staggered and chose to speak in its final moments.

"For everything in the Crown, you must stop ... stop..." the troll rasped.

Then, predictably and annoyingly, Bonechewer collapsed to its knees, reached out with clawed hands, then fell face-first to the ground with a heavy thud, like one-third of all trolls that had ever died by Deodin's hand.

Deodin panted. His lungs burned. His legs ached. But more than the physical toll of the fight, he was emotionally spent. Bonechewer had awakened in a way that was unlike any troll he had ever encountered. Yet, Bonechewer was exactly like every other troll he had ever encountered. The inconsistency disgusted him.

"*Gods dammit!*" Deodin cursed with a shout.

Impulsively, he kicked Bonechewer's corpse in the ribs. The strike had no effect and the act did nothing to release any of his anger and resentment. Instead, Deodin was overcome by crushing disappointment.

As *sheyaktu*, he had always struggled with questions of "why" and "how" the world treated him differently than everyone else. Now, these questions assaulted his mind with more fury than ever before. Today, the Universe hinted at the answers to those questions, only to return to the status quo.

*It's all bullshit.*

*Sheyaktu* wasn't a gift to help him save the world. It was a curse. None of his adventuring ever mattered. Nothing changed. Today's bullshit *seemed* different from yesterday's bullshit, or tomorrow's bullshit—but it was all a different version of the same lie. Being a "god killer" did not grant him freedom. It was a condemnation. Deodin was not blessed with power and agency, only the illusion of it.

He sat down on Bonechewer's chest, half hoping that the monster would come back to life. Perhaps the troll would be able to finish its thoughts. Perhaps the troll could give

Deodin just the slightest hint as to why he should continue the questing, why he should bother with any of it.

Instead, nothing happened. Bonechewer remained dead and unhelpful.

"*Why* am I supposed to stop, Bonechewer? What does that even mean?" Deodin asked as he hoisted the troll's giant axe.

The question was never meant to be answered. It was an afterthought to a scripted encounter that forced Deodin to reconsider the nature of troll caves and the nature of his own existence. Again. With Bonechewer offering no response, Deodin set about finishing the last part of yet another meaningless quest.

After all, a dead troll wasn't going to decapitate itself.

# Ruby (The Mage Tower) – Mathew

For a moment, Mathew wondered if there had been an accident or if the Tower was under attack. After a few more strikes, he recognized the sound as the dull clang of the knocker on the Tower's primary entrance. It was rare that a visitor would reach the front door without first being met by Tower staff.

Today, the sound came as a welcome break. Documenting his magical research was not nearly as interesting as casting the spells. Mathew yawned as he rose from the library desk and made his way down the hall to the Tower's main door.

He answered the knock to find an older man waiting, dressed as handsomely as the Ruby fashion customs allowed. He was one of the few members of the general public who Mathew could recognize on sight. The man's name escaped him, but the visitor aided Ruby's council of advisers who visited the Tower.

"Greetings, Mathew." The man's eyes smiled with sincere fondness. He seemed excited to be here, pleasantly unintimidated by the task of coming to the Tower.

*I am a turd for forgetting his name.* Mathew smiled emptily as he gestured for the visitor to enter. The aide waved his free hand to decline the invitation, presenting instead a package.

"I'm not here for a meeting, just to drop off the latest version of the plans." The man's offering was a large piece of heavy paper that had been rolled into a tube.

Curiosity gnawed at Mathew as he relieved the visitor of the package. The delivery had nothing to do with him and fell well outside of his business. Nevertheless, he heard an almost deafening instruction from his mind to open it.

"Most of my counterparts are out on business," Mathew explained, meeting the aide's eyes as he untied the cord that held the parchment in its tube shape. His heart raced, but he detected no sign of protest from the visitor when he unrolled the large sheet of thick paper and looked upon its contents.

"Oh, I don't believe this to be urgent. These are merely the up-to-date revisions, reflecting the most recent changes." The aide did not appear to be bothered by Mathew's nosiness. Rather the opposite, he seemed quite eager to share the work.

It was a beautifully crafted map of Ruby. While Mathew had seen several high-quality renderings of the city layout before, each highlighting different aspects, this one was quite unique. From the deep blue that stretched far to the west to the strains of lighter blue that snaked to the north, the map focused less on Ruby and more on—

"Water?" Mathew asked.

"Yes!" the visitor said, hardly able to contain his excitement. "This is the updated plan for Ruby's reservoir. Look at the second page."

Mathew turned to the second map, which had a noticeably different patch of blue in the fields east of Ruby, west of the river.

"Reservoir?" Mathew asked, puzzled. Mica's comment about his never leaving the Tower echoed in his mind.

"We are diverting water from the river into a reservoir on the northeast side of the wall," the visitor continued.

He showed Mathew the various points on the map where the diversion and storage would be. Mathew was not an engineer, but he could see that the plan seemed sound and how the project would impact Ruby.

The council representative, proud of the fruits of his labor, carried on.

"This will give us fresh water to irrigate the farmlands during the dry season. It will be stocked with fish and will allow us to grow the summer crops that presently only grow near the river!"

Mathew was so impressed that a sincere grin of approval found his lips. He and the other mages of the Tower lived on a veritable island, largely removed from the day-to-day banality of Ruby's infrastructure management. However, this plan showed a fascinating slice of life into the people who managed Ruby's affairs.

"This is beautiful. When will the construction start?" Mathew asked, genuinely interested.

"What? The windows of your Tower extend over the walls. Do you never look out them?" The aide smiled. "The project is nearly complete! The reservoir already holds nearly all its water."

*I really should get out more.*

Mathew was pleased. Despite the challenges that Ruby's citizens faced, they had almost finished an ambitious project that could only improve the life and welfare of all the city's people. And yet, Mathew felt a true sense of shame. He lived in a Tower that avoided the responsibilities of the community yet demanded resources from those very same people.

"I am truly impressed. We should—I should—pay more attention to the affairs outside the Tower. The work of our people, your work, is truly remarkable." Mathew offered a sincere bow. He carefully rolled the maps back up and tied the package with the cord as he spoke. "I will gladly forward this on. To whom are these addressed?"

"Entorak," the visitor said, proudly.

Mathew cocked his head, surprised that he was surprised by Entorak's involvement. After all, Entorak had his hands in all kinds of things. He would be the logical point of contact for something like this. While Richard directed the Tower's influence, it was Entorak who managed everything significant.

"Very well." Mathew reached out to shake the aide's hand. "I shall leave it for him in his study and follow up with him when he returns. I am hopeful that he'll be as pleased by the pace of your work."

The aide looked askance at Mathew, as if trying to detect sarcasm in the remark. "All of this was his idea," he pointed out, before politely bowing and turning away.

Mathew lingered by himself in the Tower's doorway. While the news of the reservoir project was interesting, Mathew found himself wondering about the events that had led to its construction. Specifically, from what Mathew had just learned, Entorak played a prominent part in the reservoir's development. And yet, Mathew had reason to suspect that Entorak was involved with the threatening orc Encroachment and, perhaps, the monster that pulled the strings. It led to questions that Mathew simply couldn't answer.

*Why?* Why would Entorak bother with the reservoir if he was just going to bring an orc horde to Ruby's gate?

# DAY
# 8

# Netherby – Pel

Pel walked with her arm interlocked with Garret's. Rather than point out every trip or fall hazard, Garret had begun to lead her by the arm. She grew to look forward to it.

They had arrived in Netherby two days before. Even though they waited for Deodin to find them, Pel was in no hurry to be found. Certainly, the presence of the surly red mage soured the inn's atmosphere, but she and Garret had spent their time walking through Netherby, talking to the locals, and learning the disturbing reality about the orc activity. It had been time well spent.

This morning, yet another villager had told the same story as the rest: the orcs were increasingly active and increasingly hostile. Orcs were blamed for the loss of livestock from the more remote ranches.

The locals had provided other valuable news. The inn had not seen travelers from Delemere in weeks. In most cases, Netherby was the obvious resting stop between Ruby and Delemere. The isolated mountain stronghold had closed its gates.

The people in the outskirts grew more apprehensive as the orcs grew bolder. An unknown force strained whatever chains prevented them from raiding a place like Netherby and it seemed only inevitable that those bonds would break.

The whispers of Encroachment were no longer rumors; they were warnings based on fact. Historically, aggression on the outskirts was the greatest predictor for a larger conflict between orcs and humans.

Selfishly, Pel wanted to talk to the Netherby people for other reasons. Positive, obvious interaction with the locals seeded her alibi. Someone might ask why she and Garret were in Netherby in the first place. For an answer, it would be true to say that the information about the orc activity was valuable. And in matters of valuable information, Pel had every reason to be involved.

"Hard to say what is worse for these people—the mage in the bar or the orcs of the Thick," Garret remarked. "The orcs haven't attacked Netherby yet. The prick in the bar did that within the first ten minutes of getting here."

"I don't understand orc aggression," Pel said. "A conflict with humans is not without risk and destined to be costly. What would be so important to them?"

"It's not just the orcs, either," Garret added. "The other mobs have also been more active. More sightings. More damage. I have never known these roads to be this dangerous." He paused, thinking. "Perhaps it's not something we can understand. Maybe you have to be a mob to be affected. Or someone who is magical, like Deodin. Maybe the thing that stirs the Thick brought him here."

Pel was about to reply that such a notion was absurd, but she held her tongue. She knew decidedly little about why Deodin had come to the Crown. What if there was a relationship between it all? She had been so eager to champion his cause that she had never questioned his goals or motives.

THE NPC

"What is that?" Pel nodded at a blurry structure that stood out in the field.

"One of Timo's barns," Garret replied. "Do you want to see if anyone is there?"

Timo was a Netherby rancher, a pleasant and chatty man they had met earlier in the day. He had been all too eager to share the local news and gossip and he had invited them to talk to any of the workers on his lands.

"Yes, please," she answered.

Garret led her to the barn's large, heavy door, which was closed but not locked. The two of them called out to see if anyone was working inside. With no response, Garret suggested they go in for a short rest. Pel agreed.

They were met by a cool blast of still air as they entered. Pel slipped out of her cloak and draped it over a large bale of hay that would serve as a makeshift bench. Garret reclined on the hay, relaxing and staring up at the ceiling.

"This is familiar," Garret said. "This reminds me of Mr. and Mrs. Lattimer."

"I know the Lattimers," Pel said. "He's a prominent and successful tanner. And she is … ah … the wife of a prominent and successful tanner."

"Then you can better appreciate the story," Garret replied. "Mr. Lattimer once needed an order of leather, which was cheaper when coming from the outskirts of the Thick. He had to venture out to meet with a few of the suppliers, so he hired me to guide him for the trip. Easy job, right?"

Pel nodded.

"Now, Mr. Lattimer, was going to come out here by himself, and really, there's no reason for Mrs. Lattimer to join us.

But, when we sit down to arrange the details of the job, she meets me. Instantly says she wants to come along."

"Because of your charms, naturally," Pel added with an upturned eyebrow.

"Naturally. But we'll get to that."

"I was kidding. She really wanted to brave the Thick and come on this trip because of you?" Pel asked with playful skepticism.

He turned on his side to face her, mimicking shock. He pointed to his face with both of his index fingers. "Some women have flawless eyesight, Pelium," he said.

She laughed.

"Now, as you would know, Mr. Lattimer has done well enough for himself. He has a keen mind and savvy business instincts."

"I would agree," Pel said.

"I don't have as many compliments to pay the substantial Mrs. Lattimer," Garret admitted. "She had lived her entire adult life sleeping on down mattresses and silk sheets. She has always known the finer comforts of Ruby. And let's also say that she … ah…"

"She always makes time for a meal," Pel suggested, phrasing Garret's point far more delicately than he ever would.

"Now, I don't say all of that to suggest she looked like a spikeboar. Because she did. And I don't say that to say she ate like a spikeboar. Because she did. But I need to paint the true picture of her. As you have learned in the past week, creature comforts and fine dining are two of the things you will not experience while on a casual stroll up and down the Thick.

"Now, Mr. Lattimer didn't seem to know or care about Mrs. Lattimer's motives. Nor did he give any thought to what she would be like on such a trip. Nor did he seem bothered by the fact that I tripled his fee and took half of it up front, because Mrs. Lattimer was going to get me killed or fired."

"And here I was, thinking you would provide a discount," Pel chirped.

"Let me also set the scene and say that Mr. Lattimer was a loud and obnoxious bugger. His wife was even louder and obnoxiouser. We weren't even out of sight of Ruby's front gate before she started complaining about her feet, the heat, the insects, having nothing to eat … all of it. It was impossible to tell which was louder: her complaining or his constant nagging for her to shut up about it. The bickering went on for hours. Finally, we attract neverbats."

"Aren't neverbats nocturnal?"

"The two of them were so loud that they woke up the gods-damned neverbats, Pel. This was before noon. The mobs attacked because they wanted those two to shut the hells up, not because they were hunting. And if Mr. Lattimer wasn't paying the bills, I may have let the neverbats do the job."

She laughed. Garret put his hands out in front of him as if he were swinging weapons at imaginary foes.

"So, I fought them off. Not like the god killer, but I waved my sword around. The buggers decided it wasn't worth the effort. Big hero of the day, of course. Mrs. Lattimer was flirty and touchy before; you can imagine her spirits after I had saved her from the beasties of the Thick.

"Finally, we get to the village, and Mr. Lattimer goes off to conduct his business. Talk to the ranchers. Arrange deals. Business that will take the afternoon. Meanwhile, Mrs. Lattimer insists that there are 'monsters' in a nearby barn. Demands that I meet her there to investigate.

"I think I see where this is going," Pel said.

"No, you truly do not," Garret corrected her, "because when I get to the barn, of course she's waiting to seduce me. Of course she's fully naked. Of course she's not my… ah … *type*. And, of course, this is exactly the type of buggery that gets me fired. Have I compared her to spikeboars yet?"

"A few times." Pel smiled.

"The best part is that a skalg *was* hiding inside the barn. Mrs. Lattimer had made up an obvious excuse to get me into the barn and seduce me with her feminine charms, but that plan took a shit because there actually was something there."

"What happened?"

"Oh, nothing much left to say. I acted all menacing and scared the monster away. The skalg too. And then I got fired."

Pel laughed. When she looked back to Garret, he stared at her, waiting to lock gazes. What she saw on his face, so near to hers, could only be described as contentment, a smirky, confident grin mixed with an intensity in his eyes.

It was something she hadn't ever considered or appreciated. He wanted to be here. With her.

The two of them were drowning in the intrigue of red mages, and orcs, and *sheyaktu*, yet he seemed satisfied with it all. Buried under the mountain of fear and with a cloud of doubt looming ominously over them, Garret reclined on a pile of hay, silently messaging that this was the only place in the world he wanted to be.

Why hadn't it been this obvious the entire time? It was the same look he wore whenever he was alone with her.

She leaned in and kissed him. It was long, sensual, and far overdue.

He pulled her on top of him, the two facing each other as she straddled his lap. His movement wasn't violent, but he surprised her with both his strength and his gentleness. She awkwardly caught herself with her free hand and felt his breath on her ear.

His lips found their way to her neck, where it met her clavicle. Garret lingered at her neckline for a moment as his hands slid to her waist. She was suddenly and inexplicably short of breath.

It rushed over her. The present. This moment. This place. All this time of questing to be somewhere else, somewhere better, and she suddenly found herself in a place she wanted to be. And she shared that place with the one man in the world who wanted nothing more than to be there with her. For everything that felt so wrong in the world, this was the first thing that felt right.

All of that, and here he was, politely restraining himself by keeping his hands on her hips. She moved them for him.

# The Thick
# (South of Netherby) – Deodin

"Where is my stuff, Kesh?" Deodin asked.

"Work job, fu—" Kesh replied in his squeaky, excited voice, pausing halfway through his favorite word. "Work job, friend?"

Deodin felt a small sense of accomplishment knowing that, if nothing else, he had trained one Rashni to exchange one F-word for another.

"Did you really need the head, Kesh? It takes up a lot of space in my inventory," Deodin complained as he hoisted Bonechewer's giant head onto the stump of a fallen tree, in the clearing where Kesh could be found. The little creature examined the head for a moment to confirm that it belonged to the correct troll.

"Bonechewer friend is dead!" Kesh exclaimed, satisfied with his examination.

"Stuff, Kesh," Deodin pressed. "I have places to be."

Kesh disappeared into his stump. When he emerged a few moments later, he had his cute little hands wrapped around something fuzzy.

"Rashni make boots, friend. Walk with fast, friend! Boots make walk fast! Friend! Friend! Friend!" Kesh squealed, pantomiming a person running quickly.

The boots were made from the pelt of the giant cat that Deodin had defeated earlier in the week. That pelt had been cured and fashioned into a type of slipper or moccasin. However, the pair certainly didn't look like the type of thing an adult human would wear. Instead, they looked like cat paws with plush, decorative claws. It reminded him of costume slippers for a child.

Perhaps these shoes were the pinnacle of Rashni fashion sensibilities. Perhaps, in order to capture the essence of a cat's swiftness, it was necessary for the shoes to look like a cat's foot. Or, perhaps they had started out as normal moccasins and the "cat-ness" of the magic had physically changed their appearance. Whatever the reasons, whatever the magic abilities they conferred, they looked ridiculous.

*I'm vending these to the first merchant who'll buy them.*

"Thank you for your gift, Kesh," Deodin said. "I brought back the head. Now, where is my stuff?"

"Yes, friend, yes! Kesh like you a lot. Kesh like! But other Rashni, they not like as much."

Deodin knew where this was going.

"First, other Rashni need prayer beads from the ghosts in the temple ruins. Haunted ruins. Then you be honorary chief."

"How many beads?" Deodin asked with a defeated sigh, skipping past whatever bullshit explanation existed for what the beads were and why they were necessary. The reasons wouldn't matter. The reasons never mattered.

"Not many! Eight! And four hundred! And one thousand!" Kesh replied, as if he honestly believed that that was a small number in this context.

Deodin groaned.

*Recover your gem purse:*
- ☐ *Clear out the haunted ruins*
- ☐ *Become honorary chieftain*

Deodin was beginning to understand why the Rashni cursed so much.

# Ruby (The Mage Tower) – Mathew

Mathew tried to act casual. He had grown pleasantly accustomed to having the Tower largely to himself. Only a handful of mages remained while everyone else searched remote places for the rogue mage.

Presently, however, he shared a study room with Richard. Of all the places to be, Mathew had been unfortunate enough to be in the library when Richard had entered and started pulling books from the shelves and spreading them across the tables. The whole ordeal was inconsiderate, selfish, and quintessentially Richard.

*I was here first.*

Nevertheless, Mathew found Richard's behavior interesting. He was curious as to why Richard would be here. He had seen Richard's chambers enough to know that he had his own study area and two full walls of books. For whatever reason, the man needed access to the common library. Following nearly an hour of work, Richard had sprawled dozens of books across several tables and was thumbing through them furiously, clearly looking for something.

*Perhaps the vacant eyes of his harem made it too distracting for him to concentrate,* Mathew thought, revolted. Despite knowing better than to do it, he stared at Richard again, increasingly curious about what he was so desperate to learn.

Mathew closed his eyes and refocused. He didn't want to be noticed. He willed his attention back to his own work.

Prior to Richard's arrival, Mathew had been recording the results of several magical experiments earlier in the day. He wanted to get the report finished before moving on to something else. Anything else, as long as it happened far away from Richard. He concluded his thoughts about his research:

> ... the consistency of the stone had not changed as a result of the spell, indicating no direct or obvious effect from the ha-radeesh gesture. The testing of sample 13 yielded different results, in that the consistency of the stone had changed, leaving a chalky and brittle consistency paired with a profound yellowing color. The ra-jaheen gesture produced a destabilizing effect on the stone, quite the opposite of what had been the goal...

Mathew set aside the page to allow the ink to dry. He stretched his back as he rubbed his eyes. When he opened them, he found himself eyeballing Richard and his books.

What would Richard want from the general library? Moreover, why was it so important? It was puzzling. He had already hoarded nearly every volume that might be valuable or interesting. Considering the large, eclectic pile of materials that surrounded him, the topic of his search must have been too obscure or esoteric to take up space in his quarters.

A noise from the far end of the room compelled Mathew to turn his head. Upon recognizing the man who entered the library, Mathew quickly ducked his nose back into his work. He preferred to re-read the disinteresting discourse on the consistency of stone samples than risk eye contact with Entorak.

"Courier birds alighted today. The men in Peak's View say the road between there and Andwyn has been closed to travelers. Something to do with orcs," Richard began. "I'm more interested in the news from Netherby."

Entorak made no move or comment. He waited until Richard looked up. "Is this related to our unidentified ... friend?" Entorak asked once he had Richard's attention.

"Perhaps," Richard replied. "The message spoke of a caravan being saved at the hands of a 'heroic' ranger who happened to be in the area, on his way to Netherby. Perhaps the stories have been exaggerated by locals, but they speak of actions that were more than we can realistically expect from a mere ... human."

Entorak nodded enough to acknowledge the remark, but no more. Uncomfortable silence persisted for a few moments longer, long enough for Mathew to conscientiously resist the temptation to prompt the conversation himself.

Richard finally finished reading the passage of the book in front of him, then took a moment to stretch before speaking.

"Those of the caravan were lucky enough to run into this warden of the Thick and his charge. The message also spoke of your ... ah ... that woman you brought to the Tower all those ages ago. What was her name—? The small, dark-haired one. Pretty. The one with the permanent magesight spell."

Entorak moved his head slightly. His eyebrows arced just enough to reveal curiosity, interest, or both. The moment passed and the expression left his face.

"I have reassigned some of the mages to join you in Netherby." Richard turned his attention back to one of the books in front of him.

Entorak was unusually quick to respond. "You have further questions of Pelium Stillwater?"

Richard responded with a sigh.

"Well, that is where I seek your expertise. Perhaps she is there coincidentally. Perhaps not. I would also ask that you handle any concerns with Tyberius. There are whispers of spell-slinging in a tavern and a possible ... indiscretion or two."

Entorak yielded no emotional response in his nod.

"Do we have any more books on this? These are worthless," Richard asked as he sat back and yawned. He gestured to the tomes strewn across the tables.

"It is a subject about which few meaningful words have been written. Most of what you will read is myth or misinterpretation," Entorak countered. "But it may be worthwhile to read a few excerpts from the orcish historical traditions. They tend to offer a different perspective, at least."

"Very well," Richard returned. "You have such text?"

Entorak nodded. Richard stretched again as he rose to his feet, before ripping out an unapologetic fart that would have been inappropriate from anyone else. Entorak made no response. He turned somewhat mechanically and strode toward the door through which he'd entered. Richard followed.

A few moments passed while Mathew attempted to return to his work. He paused. He eyed the piles of books that had been the subject of Richard's study. His curiosity began to swell.

*Why is this rogue mage so important? And what does that have to do with these books? Or the writings of ancient orcs?*

Regardless of the answers, now was the time to leave and find a new place to conclude his work. If Richard did not find the information he sought among Entorak's texts, he would be more unpleasant than ever when he returned to the library. Mathew would prefer to be anywhere else.

Satisfied that the ink had dried, he collected his belongings. He took a final look around his workspace, and once he believed that he had everything, he turned to leave. It was slightly out of his way, but Mathew chose to walk by the mess that Richard had left. He wasn't foolish enough to touch anything, but he couldn't resist the opportunity to sneak a look at—

*Sheyaktu.*

It was obvious. A few of the books even had the word in the title.

*Holy shit.*

# The Thick
# (West of Netherby) – Entorak

The worst part of Ruby was the smell, Entorak decided. The stench of the city hung in the air, even far beyond the walls. A permanent rust-colored haze hung over the city, adding to the smell and occasionally shifting the color of the sunsets to an unsettling brown. Far enough inland, however, Entorak had emerged from that cloud. The atmosphere of the Thick was quite pleasant. It was free from the depressing funk of humanity and its proclivity toward waste and filth. The scent of the huge evergreen trees filled Entorak's nose. Out here, the sun seemed brighter, the sounds clearer, and the air didn't cling to his tongue or clothes.

He encouraged his horse forward with a firm squeeze on its sides.

Certainly, the Thick was a potentially dangerous place. Perhaps not as much for a skilled practitioner of magic, but it housed a great number of hazards and threats. Nevertheless, Entorak would occasionally prefer those risks in exchange for the pleasant feeling of a simple horseback ride outside the walls, free from Ruby's assault on his senses.

Finally, Entorak neared the end of the morning's journey. He had reached an encampment far north of Ruby, along the southern base of one of the famous mountains of the Crown.

He sensed the modest alarm and panic as he arrived.

The attention he received was unsettling, but he had come to anticipate the response. The sentries recognized him, yet still acted with obvious unease in his presence. There would be no need to announce his arrival—the collective and contagious hush of apprehension was announcement enough.

Entorak approached the meeting table, reflexively holding his breath. He met the elders' eyes and prepared himself to speak their language and be mindful of their customs, but their odor was distracting. He disliked their appearance and their manners, but those were nothing compared to their pervasive musk. As much as Entorak hated the smell of Ruby, these orcs smelled even worse.

# DAY
# 9

# The Thick (East of Netherby) – Deodin

*Explore Makee's Tomb:*

☐ *Find the 'Tear from a god'*

Having completed his work for the Rashni tribe and becoming an exalted member of their fold, Deodin had recovered his gem purse and continued his search for Lyle Makee's tomb. Today, Deodin had gone until almost noon before he encountered any nonsense imposed on him by the Universe.

*This must be a trap.*

The small, slender woman stood on the side of the road, next to a pack mule. She wore dark pants and a dark, hooded, long-sleeved tunic. Her head and face were covered with a religious or ceremonial wrap that only showed her eyes.

A lone merchant on the side of the road was dubious enough. A merchant wandering a narrow path in the middle of the Thick was downright unbelievable. Finally, while Deodin didn't recognize the significance of her garb, he was drawn to the one thing he could see: her eyes.

Her eyes had yellow irises and vertically slit pupils.

*Definitely a trap.*

"Come closer, traveler." She spoke with an exotic accent.

"No. You're going to attack me. Or worse yet, task me with a quest."

She laughed. "I am a simple merchant, wandering the lands and trading rare and exotic goods—"

"Oh? Do you want a pair of boots that look like cat's feet?" Deodin asked. "They are as exotic as they come."

*Gods, yes!* Deodin enjoyed a brief moment of excitement. This was his first opportunity to rid himself of Kesh's gift. He had even placed the slippers at the top of his bag, so that he could avail them to anyone who seemed interested. In a moment, he produced the cat slippers for her to inspect.

Rather than answer, the merchant pulled back her hood, reached behind her head, and loosened the wrap that covered her face. She unwrapped herself, gracefully and fluidly, to reveal a pair of pointed ears on the top of her head, cat eyes, and a face that was a cross between a cat and a human.

"What do you think?" she asked. Even though her face was catlike, her annoyance was abundantly clear.

*Chosen,* Deodin realized, astounded.

Skycrash had changed the physical landscape of the East, but it had also brought great changes to its people. In addition to the dawn of monsters, the event had given birth to entire new races.

"The Chosen" resembled cats in many of their physical features. They were famously isolationist and normally found in the East, hundreds of miles beyond Stoneheart Point. It was nearly impossible that he would encounter one here. Her presence here was nothing less than the Universe deciding to spice things up.

"That went about as awkwardly as it could have," Deodin said, still harboring the feeling that this was a trap.

"It would have been worse if you had seen my face and still made the offer," she countered.

Deodin laughed. He half expected a fight to the death, but at the moment, he was happy to banter.

"Agreed. And my apologies. I have never met a Chosen before, so forgive me if I don't know your customs."

She bowed gracefully.

"I am Dano. And as for our customs, my people value trade. I would be greatly offended if you didn't buy my most expensive wares. To walk away empty-handed would dishonor my ancestors," she said with a flourish of her arms.

Her line was total bullshit. Deodin knew it. And she knew that he knew it. It was refreshing.

"Dano, you are quickly becoming my favorite Chosen." He smiled. "I am Deodin."

"And you, Deodin, are my favorite customer. Understanding that you aren't really a customer until you buy something. Insulted ancestors and so forth," she said as she re-wrapped her head in her cloth.

"A thousand apologies to your ancestors, but I don't think I really want anythi—"

She shushed him with a wave of her hand. "Want? I have something that you desperately need. Something that you can't otherwise find or have. Something that will change you in ways you can't imagine. Ways that will make you a better man."

While he watched, she retrieved a small item from one of the boxes strapped to the mule. She displayed it in her gloved hands: a pair of scissors.

"These are the finest shears from my people, made by our master craftsmen. You can see the keen edge of each blade. You could shave with either of them. And note the fine precision of the action. Not even a hint of play between the two blades. Together, they offer cutting precision that is unmatched in human lands."

"I believe you, but I would seldom use them. They belong in the hands of someone who would use them every day," Deodin explained.

"What? No. These are not for sale. I could never replace them," she scoffed.

"You said that I needed—"

"You need a haircut. Five silver, please."

# Ruby (The Mage Tower) – Mathew

Mathew found Mica in one of the small study chambers, leaning over a table, reading a book. He closed the door behind him. She looked at him and smiled a hello, but he was too focused to be captivated by her. He led with his news.

"Richard believes the rogue mage is *sheyaktu*. That's why the red mages pursue him," he said.

Mica stiffened, alarmed. She spoke in a serious, hurried whisper. "This rogue mage: what do you know of him?"

"I overheard some of the details when the merchants were interviewed. They described his magic as minor parlor tricks. Theatrics and bluster. But I don't believe that's the whole truth. The act was to downplay his power, not overstate it. I got the impression he was far more powerful than what we were led to believe."

"Does Richard have a lead on where he may be?" she asked.

"I don't know. I know that the mages have been sent to places all along the Thick, mostly to the north. He may have said something about Netherby, but I don't know the details. Richard and Entorak are managing the hunt." He paused and gave Mica an incredulous look. "You think Richard may be right… You think *sheyaktu* actually exist."

"*Sheyaktu* exist," she said with a smile. "But more importantly, the orc texts speak of *sheyaktu* being a part of the Encroachments."

Mathew frowned. Mica's story about *sheyaktu* and Encroachments seemed even more ridiculous than Richard's fox hunt. Even though the world featured magic and the regular displacement of natural laws, Mathew had limits about what he could believe. His mind had no place for fatalism and prophecies.

"Are you going to go into some story of an ancient prophecy and the plight of the chosen one?" he asked with enough sarcasm to convey how unlikely he considered the concept.

Mica shook her head.

"I'm not talking about glimpses of the future. I'm talking about the past. The facts are here, in the library, in these very books. I've studied them myself.

"The Encroachments follow a pattern. A cycle. Once a generation, the orcs rise up and strike against Ruby or Tristan, the two largest cities in the Crown. This happens every twenty to thirty years, as far back as the first one about three hundred years ago."

Mathew flinched with surprise. He knew that there was more than one Encroachment, but he had no idea that they were so frequent or that they followed a pattern.

Mica continued. "And every historical Encroachment features a narrative involving *sheyaktu*, each of whom came to the Crown to stop the Encroachment."

It still seemed like a bullshit prophecy, but if she was right about the historical relationship between orc attacks and *sheyaktu*, and if Richard was right about the rogue mage… "I can concede that a coincidence seems less and less likely," he admitted.

"There's more to all of this, of course," Mica said. "The texts state that every orc Encroachment is driven by a great monster, a great evil that lurks in the shadows. This monster organizes and deploys the orc army.

"The orcs described these monsters. One was described as a 'dead man that walks the night and burns in the sun,' and another was said to be a 'horrific and terrifying outsider that feeds on minds.' Each Encroachment has featured a different monster, one that rules over the others. The boss monster, if you will."

Mica paused for a few heartbeats, as if to collect her thoughts, then continued in a whisper. "You remember how Entorak was studying orcs and orc history, right? And we thought that the timing was suspicious?"

"Yes," Mathew agreed.

"He's also been reading up on the lore and history of dragons."

Mathew didn't see the correlation. With a shrug, he prompted her to continue.

"The orc traditions tell of a 'dragon queen who awakens and seeks to reclaim her throne,'" Mica explained.

*Shit.*

# Netherby – Garret

"Andwyn is a total dump," Garret sneered with as much disdain as he could summon.

Pel's question had come from nowhere. One moment they were walking back to the inn. The next moment, she asked about Andwyn, the small village to the West of Netherby.

"No, I meant, how far away is it?" she clarified.

"About a day's walk if we stay on the road. Did you miss the part about it being a dump?"

"If we left tomorrow, we could be there by sundown? And if we stayed a day and walked back the next day, could we be back by the end of the week?"

Garret calculated travel time and nodded.

"We can't simply laze about the inn for four more days," she chided. Before he could make the joke she knew was coming, she added, "That would be exhausting, even for you. And more importantly, it would be suspicious.

"A trip to Andwyn explains and justifies why we are here. And it creates distance between us and you-know-who. And I'm not just saying this to make a point, but the villagers here paint a very grim picture. The orcs are coming. I need to see if the people of Andwyn sense it too."

She paused a moment to phrase her next comment. "And I quite enjoy our time together."

Her words were the highlight of his day. "As I said, Andwyn is lovely this time of year."

# The Thick
# (East of Netherby) – Deodin

"You don't have issues with Baron Iselde? I despise him. He has no redeemable qualities," Deodin said. "I can't relate to him at all."

He sat cross-legged on a patch of grass next to the side of the road, with Dano hovering behind him as she fussed over his hair. She huffed at the indignity of his comment.

"You're oversimplifying him. The baron is complex. You must consider the inner demons that compel him," she replied.

"'Demons?' His problems are the direct result of his bad life decisions. Had he not slain Haptas, he would not have had to marry Nerindor."

Dano stopped snipping his hair.

"If you hate the book so much, why did you finish it?" she asked. "You're the one making bad life decisions."

Deodin laughed. "I read the sequels, too. I felt obligated to. Everyone I meet raves about the series. I'm convinced the entire trilogy is a huge joke and I'm the punchline. I am the only person who hates the 'greatest anthology in post-Sky-crash history.'"

"Considering how you dress, might I suggest that you simply have bad taste?"

"That stabs me more deeply than a spikeboar quill."

"Spikeboar? I would pay a king's ransom for the recipe for spikeboar liver pie," Dano said.

Deodin groaned.

"Dano, may I ask you something?"

"Is it about purchasing a new wardrobe? Then, yes, please. Ask repeatedly."

"Aren't you tired of the nonsense? Don't you grow weary of this world and all its bullshit? Aren't you tired of this stupid game?"

"For personal existential crises, I reflect on the ancient wisdom of my people," Dano began.

"Dano. Please. The Chosen are only 350 years old. Nothing about your people is 'ancient.'"

"One of the wisest teachings is to be respectful of those who cut your hair, most especially *while* they are cutting your hair."

"That is truly wise," Deodin admitted with a smile. "Sorry. Please continue."

"Ask yourself, Deodin, when you complain about the world, what is the most broken thing you experience?"

"Troll ca—"

She rapped him on the head softly, just enough to interrupt him.

"I told you to ask *yourself*. It was a rhetorical question. Now, of everything that is flawed, imperfect, incomplete, or otherwise broken, what is the one thing you encounter every day and have the most power to fix?"

Deodin reflected on the question. He had the "power" to change all kinds of things. If anything, he had more power than everyone else in the world. After a few moments, Dano tapped him on the shoulder.

"That question was not rhetorical. You were supposed to answer. And the correct answer is 'you.' Deodin. You have the power to change yourself." She patted him on the shoulder. "Now, think on this. It's hard for you to experience great enlightenment if I have to spell it out for you."

"I appreciate that." Deodin chuckled. A moment later, he sighed. "It's hard to reach a Chosen level of spiritual peace when I just can't see the significance of it."

"Significance? Am I significant?" she asked.

"Of course you are, I just meant—"

"Here is where you stop talking and start consciously thinking about how significant everyone else is." She made a few more snips with the scissors.

Deodin stopped talking and consciously considered her point. After a few moments, Dano continued.

"That's better. Nothing worse than a god killer who doesn't understand his role."

Before he could question how she knew what he was, he was asleep.

*   *   *

*Gods dammit. It was a trap. I knew it.*

Deodin awoke on the side of the path with a lurch. He immediately scanned the environment to find his bearings and his property. As before, he was still on the trail east of Netherby, and surprisingly, his pack was still there, serving as a makeshift pillow.

*That was thoughtful of her.*

Deodin's instincts had told him that she had ulterior motives, but he ignored them because she was so much more interesting than every other merchant with whom he interacted.

He frantically patted down his belt. The gem purse he had promised to Pel and Garret was still there. It felt as full as he remembered it. In fact, all his property seemed to be exactly where he left it.

He was relieved. All too frequently, he'd have to embark on yet another side quest to make up time from another delay.

He reached up with his left hand to scratch his head. As he did, something fell out of his hand. A mirror. It was crude, a shard of a larger mirror that had been strapped to a makeshift handle.

Deodin glanced at himself, expecting that Dano had done something to make his hair worse than it was before. Instead, he was delighted to see that she had corrected the calamity. His hair was shorter than he usually wore it, but otherwise, it looked great. Fantastic, even. He looked less clownish than before.

Almost.

He looked down at his feet, which were now dressed in the cat-boot-slipper things that had been made by the Rashni. His other boots were nowhere to be found.

He found a note written on the back of the mirror.

*Hey handsome. The opportunity was too hilarious to pass up. I'll donate your boots to someone who needs them. Travel well. – Dano*

Deodin laughed, partially because of the joke. The opportunity was too hilarious to pass up. More importantly, however, he was grateful for the interaction.

She was right. Not just about the boots prank, but her worldview. And her comments on *his* worldview.

This wasn't the normal bullshittery. Sure, meeting a Chosen merchant in the middle of the Thick was preposterously unlikely, but this encounter was so much more meaningful and satisfying than the illogical fights and side quests. For the first time in a long time, Deodin felt a sense of gratitude to the Universe that otherwise toyed with him.

"Thanks, Dano," he said.

# DAY
# 10

# The Thick
## (The Road to Andwyn) – Pel

"I propose we retire to a place along the coast, between Ruby and Bayhold," Garret announced.

The two of them enjoyed a walk westward through the foothills between Netherby and Andwyn. At this time of the year, the road was dry and hard. They welcomed the shade from the towering evergreens of the Thick. "'We retire,'" Pel echoed, unsure what he meant.

"Right. Carve out a patch of land on the coast, build a palace that overlooks the ocean. A modest palace, of course. No more than twenty rooms."

"Of course."

"I think if we make it inaccessible by road, there's less chance of someone else finding us."

"You're off to a good start, but you have to cleanse the entire chain of the operation," Pel began. "We would hire a crew from Southend, through different middlemen. The crew should be mostly immigrants and refugees from the East. They would be harder to track down by the red mages. And construction would come in different phases by different crews.

"All of the expenses are paid in cash," she continued, "but everyone in the process believes the grounds are a legitimate retirement mansion of an obscenely wealthy oligarch from Tristan."

"You'd be a fantastic oligarch," Garret said.

"No, that's the thing. The estate must be big enough to require full-time servants. You and I will be disguised as part of the staff that maintains the grounds.

"Deliveries are accepted only by boat. For both construction and for regular supplies, deliveries are managed by the caretaker of the estate."

"Are you the caretaker?" Garret asked.

"No, the primary caretaker would need to meet with the captains and crews of the delivery vessels. This person cannot resemble you or me, because there is a chance that the captain or his crew would be looking for us," she said. "Now: here is the challenging part."

"Right. Because none of the other parts are challeng—"

"The caretaker must be ideally suited for the job. He or she is completely instrumental to all of this. We can never confide our secrets with him, but he must be totally competent and reliable in his role. And he must never have cause to think that we aren't simple servants." She scrunched her eyebrows in thought. She hadn't yet worked out all the details. "I haven't quite decided how we find and hire him. That may prove to be one of the greater problems."

"I should have clarified that I wanted to *live* in the palace and be served by the half-naked servants," Garret complained.

"As for us…" she said, disregarding his remark.

He perked up. "There is an 'us' in all of this?"

She smiled.

"We arrive at different times, hired by our mysterious benefactor. Once there, we live in separate quarters. But as time goes on, your charms begin to wear on me. We spend more hours together, each finding excuses to occupy the same space at the same time. The other staff members figure out what's going on, but don't say anything. Our tryst doesn't affect our work. Eventually, our relationship is accepted and embraced by the rest of the staff."

"Because it's so adorable," Garret added.

"Oh, and part of the reason I wanted to have separate crews and different stages of construction is because I wanted to build a place where you and I could meet in private, secreted away from the rest of the staff. If you build secret rooms, you must also keep that secret from the subsequent construction crews."

"By the gods, Pel, how long have you been planning all of this? Have you picked out the curtains yet? Because you should let me help you with that."

She hesitated. The truth was that she had been completely preoccupied with these fantasies. They had dominated her mind whenever she wasn't actively engaged in something else.

"I need to hope. I need to believe that we can survive all of this." She gestured to the Thick that surrounded them. "And I need to believe that the future is worth living through the fear and dread that hangs over me at every terrifying waking moment."

He squeezed her hand.

"You make it worth it."

It was a beautiful sentiment and one that she shared.

"You too," she replied.

The two walked together, sharing the moment. And predictably enough, Garret soon ruined it. He turned to Pel with an expression of severity. She tried to keep a straight face, knowing that one of his jokes was on its way.

"And I hope that you understand that I should probably bed one or two of the more attractive servants at the estate before I 'settle down' with you." He cocked head slightly as he gave her the bad news.

"I see," she said, playing along.

"Not because I would want to, you understand, but because it would add a certain credibility to the story. Our story."

"And what credibility would that be?" She laughed.

"Incredibility," he said with a wink.

\*　\*　\*

"Run!" Garret whispered with a sudden, terrifying urgency.

He seized Pel's hand and yanked her toward the tree line. She stumbled at first, barely catching her feet before his free hand steadied her.

She couldn't see where they were running to. She couldn't see what they were running from. She couldn't even see her footing, once Garret had dragged her into the shade of the Thick.

"Orcs!" he explained with a hurried whisper as he dragged her further into the forest.

"Where?" she demanded, tossing a futile glance over her shoulder. She could see only blurs and patches of light.

"No more talking!" he whispered tersely while he pulled her further into the trees.

For nearly a minute, they dashed through the Thick without speaking, the only noise being their footfalls in the underbrush and their heavy breaths.

Finally, Garret paused and drew his sword. He glanced behind them. Now that they had stopped, she could hear the vague, distant shouts. She couldn't make out their words, but the voices seemed guttural. Primal. Inhuman.

Garret selected a satisfactory spot, then stabbed his sword deep into the earth, driving it nearly to the hilt. He wrestled with it for a moment, wrenching it back and forth. Pel smelled fresh earth and heard the roots of the forest undergrowth ripping and tearing.

A moment later, he dropped the sword and grabbed at the flora with both hands. Instead of uprooting the bush entirely, he peeled the entire root system back as if he were pulling back a blanket away from the bed sheets.

"Get in," he said, staring back toward the road.

It took a moment for Pel to interpret his instruction, but she realized that she could climb in feet-first and bury herself completely. As she squirmed to get under the tangle of roots and vines, he finally looked at her.

"You don't move. You don't make noise. You will hear sounds. You will feel insects on your skin. You will be cold. If you have to, you piss yourself, right here."

"Garret…" she pleaded, assembling the clues to determine where this was going. The horrifying conclusion became clearer as Garret scattered the freshly dug soil to match the color of the surrounding area.

"If you must, wait all day and all night before you move again," he said, a seriousness in his face that terrified her.

"Garret! Don't leave me."

He looked back at their pursuers, toward the road. The distant voices drew nearer.

"Don't leave me!" she begged, her voice wavering.

He gently guided her head down to the ground, forcing her to lie on her back. He held her hand for a short moment before she felt the cold hilt of his dagger. He placed it in her hands and curled her fingers around it.

"I'll find you," he whispered. "I promise, but before I can, I have to lead these buggers away from you."

Before he pulled the rest of the underbrush over her, he looked at her once more. Then, he recovered his sword and arranged the last bit of brush over her head. Pel's world went dark.

She heard Garret stand up and sprint away.

*　*　*

*Breathe.*

Pel had to remind herself. Her inclination was to be as silent as possible, even if that meant she never exhaled again.

The footsteps grew louder. Nearer. The deafening sound of her heartbeat filled her ears.

Her pursuers arrived slowly and cautiously. They lingered in the area, stepping carefully around the trees and undergrowth. They whispered something to each other, much too softly for her to hear what they were saying. Closer, slower, more deliberately.

*They must have seen two people enter the area and only one leave. They must know I'm here.*

More whispers. Tense. Hurried. Footsteps. Closer ... so close.

She felt the earth move nearby, prompted by a heavy step near enough to pull on the roots that covered her. Under her blanket of brush, she couldn't see anything, but she could hear the labored breaths of the heavy orc who hovered over her. She gripped the dagger as tightly as she could with her sweaty palms and closed her eyes.

Further away in the Thick, she heard branches snap with the sounds of footsteps running away. She resisted the urge to yelp in pain as an orc stepped on her hair while pushing off in pursuit.

A few moments later, she was left in silence, the sounds of footfalls fading into the forest.

*Breathe.*

# The Thick
# (The Road to Andwyn) – Garret

The orcs had seen Garret and begun their chase. His distraction had worked.

*Shit. Now what?*

# The Thick
# (The Dragon's Lair) – Entorak

"Bold of you to come here, human. And foolish."

Even though the dragon whispered, her voice carried across the cave. The whispers of a giant were still deafening.

The cavern was dark and Entorak's eyes still hadn't adjusted from the brilliant daylight. Tychryn was somewhere on the far side of the cave, but he had no idea where. As much as this was a tactical decision, he believed that she enjoyed the position of power and dominion, especially if it created fear.

"I brought a tribute and an offer, my queen," Entorak said.

A thundering laugh filled the chamber. Entorak felt it in his ribs.

"Let us hope you offer something considerably more valuable than your life. A life that is surely forfeit unless you can provide something more … savory."

Another ominous laugh echoed off the walls.

"I offer a relic of Ruby's mage Tower." He held a scepter above his head. "The Staff of Rebirth. Should you wield the power of this artifact, your indomitable life force becomes even more fortified. The fire of your heart becomes even more impossible to extinguish."

Entorak flinched as the dragon's face suddenly emerged from the darkness, no more than ten feet from him. He could feel the heat in her breath.

The orcs had described their master, calling her "Tychryn, Queen of the Brood." They arranged this meeting with her, providing him with a map to her lair carved into one of the mountains of the Crown. He suspected they cooperated only because they didn't expect him to survive the meet.

Now, he stood before her, suddenly paralyzed by her presence. It was impossible to fully understand a dragon's size and scale until one looked you in the eye. If she opened her jaws fully, he could walk right into her mouth without crouching or even ducking his head.

Her yellow eyes were clearly reptilian. She stared at him with narrow, vertical pupils, remaining still enough for him to see the details of her face and head. Two yellowing, bony horns, each the length of a ship's mast, protruded from her forehead. The horns curved in a smooth arc over the top of her skull and ended with a modest upward curl. Another smaller horn emerged from the bridge of a snout covered in thick, black scales.

Entorak shuddered. Tychryn was more imposing than anything he could imagine. Nothing in the Crown, to include the mighty gates of Delemere's mountain fortress, could withstand her assault.

She seemed to savor the moment as Entorak swallowed hard and forced himself to exhale. A moment later, he could hear the skin of the inside of her lips dragging across her ivory teeth as she formed a morbid smile.

He stared, jaw agape. She turned her head gracefully and smoothly, yet her actions were completely silent. It seemed impossible that something so large could be so quiet and move so sinuously.

"That is an acceptable start, wizard," she hissed. "You have bought an audience with your queen. Can you now buy your safe exit?"

"I have come to barter," Entorak said.

The dragon seemed amused.

"And why would a queen haggle with her subjects? Or in this case, with her property?" She leaned in, speaking to him from the side, her tongue nearly flicking his ear.

"Because your other subjects, your *property*, seek to defy you. They covet the magic that is rightfully yours. I seek to avail those treasures for you," Entorak explained.

"How thoughtful," she quipped. "But if the treasures are rightfully mine, why wouldn't I simply claim them?"

"Your enemies will seek to hide these prizes from you. They will scatter them to the far ends of our world, burying them in the earth or sending them to the bottom of the seas. I am in a position to prevent that," Entorak said.

"And these are treasures such as the staff you have given?" she asked.

"Yes, my queen. I speak of relics that have been collected and stored at Ruby's mage Tower. Artifacts from decades of research and craftsmanship. With enough notice, I can prepare them for you. Be warned, however. I cannot deliver them. That is beyond my influence."

"You can wrap your gifts, but you cannot bestow them?" She laughed.

"Yes, my queen. I suffer from limitations that do not burden one such as you," Entorak said with a bow.

She chuckled softly.

"I sense no insincerity in you, wizard. I can smell your sweat. I can hear the beating of your tiny, tiny heart. But your heart beats with courage as much as fear. It was courage that brought you all the way here. What is it that you want?"

"Satisfaction," Entorak replied.

The dragon laughed. She moved again, positioning her giant head just in front of him.

"Humans think they are so clever with their choice of words. Always with euphemisms. Always with idioms. Always with a softer word when the true feelings are too hard to say. Always afraid to admit what they really feel. Tell me what you *really* want."

"Revenge."

# DAY
# 11

# The Thick
# (The Road to Andwyn) – Pel

Time had passed, but Pel couldn't be sure if it had been two hours or ten. The weak daylight that filtered through the forest canopy had since faded into the blackness of night.

She had been unable to sleep, too unnerved by every sound that reached her ears. Even then, she could no longer distinguish the sounds of the Thick from the exaggerated whispers of her mind.

Garret had abandoned her beneath a thin layer of roots and topsoil in a forest made of nightmares. While she had faith that he would return if he could, she was less certain he was still alive. It had been so long since she had last seen him, every second alone was another second for her mind to worry about him.

She also feared for herself. Her omnipresent terror was only partially related to orcs. She was astute enough to know, dagger or not, she was no match for anything that would seek to do her harm. To be found would be to die.

However, to be lost would also be to die. A quick, horrible death was marginally preferable to a lingering, hopeless existence of being blind, lost in the Thick, and to have no agency in her fate.

The Thick spoke. A twig snapped. A leaf crinkled. A foot scuffed as it struck the ground. Something approached. She clutched the knife in her hands, briefly wondering how to best hold it.

"Pel? Where are you?"

It was a whisper, but in an instant the insecure, doubtful voices of her mind were chased away.

"Garret!" she croaked. It had been so long since she'd spoken, her voice cracked. She started to squirm out of her earthen blanket.

"Please don't stab me," he said, close enough that she could feel his reassuring footsteps in the ground around her.

As he came into view, she gasped with equal parts relief and release.

\* \* \*

"I'm so sorry I had to bury you and run off." Garret said as they walked toward the road. It was too dark to see his face, but his tone suggested that he truly regretted the circumstances of their split. "There just wasn't enough time to explain everything."

"I know," she gasped, so relieved that he was here. "It all makes sense, now. But when you ran off, that was the single worst moment of my life. I spent the rest of the time sick with fear."

He stopped her by grabbing her shoulder and turning her toward him.

"No. Don't do that. Never do that. Courage is not the absence of fear. Courage is the confrontation of fear."

Pel smiled and took his hand. Garret was sweet and she was grateful for his support. She had calmed down enough to be introspective about her ordeal.

"Two weeks ago, I went to bed at sunset, in a bed made with soft linens and topped with down pillows. That seems like a lifetime ago," she said, the lingering pangs of terror finally ebbing.

As Garret led them back to the main road between Andwyn and Netherby, he explained why he had been gone so long.

"It took two hours just to lose them. After that, I tracked them back to the rest of their party. That took the rest of the afternoon. Once I found them, I could see they were too busy to continue their search for us, so I was able to come back here."

Pel was about to remark about Garret's skill and resourcefulness, but he hadn't finished.

"Andwyn's gone, Pel. I tracked those two buggers all the way back to the village outskirts. They joined a war party. There were about twenty of them. By the time I got there, they'd burned down everything." His voice was a forlorn whisper. "Pel, Andwyn was just a small village of farmers and ranchers. They had no chance."

A sharp ache of nausea filled Pel's chest. Her fears had been proven true. Encroachment.

# The Thick
# (East of Netherby) – Deodin

Deodin was annoyed he hadn't found this place a few days earlier. Much as it had been described, the landmark was a truly enormous boulder, larger than many buildings. And considering the ancient texts and Garret's explanation, it seemed realistic that a few hundred years ago, this could have been teardrop shaped.

Deodin awarded the Universe a passing grade for the breadcrumbs that had led him here. Considering the long chain of quests and cryptic clues, the marker was pleasantly obvious. It was prominent enough to be noticed if sought, but mundane enough to be overlooked.

*Explore Makee's tomb:*

☑ *Find the 'Tear from a god'*


Deodin scanned the surrounding area for twenty or thirty seconds. He wasn't sure what to expect, but he expected more than nothing. After a few moments of nothing, he was satisfied with nothing. It was better than bullshit, after all.

With the tomb found, he could move on with the next part of his plan. He adjusted his pack and headed west, back toward Netherby to keep his rendezvous with Pel and Garret. If all went well, he'd be rid of them by tomorrow or the day after.

# Ruby (The Mage Tower) – Mica

Richard's room made her nauseous.

Everything about it served as a reminder of what he was, what he valued, and what he was willing to do to accomplish his goals. Anyone atop the red mage brotherhood got there by being the embodiment of vice and avarice.

To kill him would do the world a favor. Several favors, even.

Fortunately for Richard, he wasn't in the vicinity to be killed. With the Tower's mages spread across the Crown on his pet project, Richard spent most of his time in the different libraries, mumbling about how best to successfully end his hunt.

Mica had learned that the best and most ironic way to avoid Richard was to spend time in his quarters, as she did now. As the librarian managing the Tower's books, including those in Richard's room, she could come and go as she needed and the other mages would never dare to intrude.

Most importantly, she could be with her sisters.

Richard had kidnapped them. He had stolen them from their home in the East and brought them to the Tower to serve as his carnal playthings. After months of suffering and sacrifice, Mica had finally tracked them here and maneuvered herself into the Tower. Now she finally stood on the precipice of their freedom. She was almost ready to execute her plan.

The scene of Richard's bedroom had not changed since her visit days before. Her sisters lay about the room, motionless and staring vacantly. Richard had a schedule to attend to their biological needs, but the rest of the time, they were unresponsive and unable to move or speak.

Richard had enslaved them with magic, and based on its effects, it was powerful. The spells were necessary to keep them docile. The instant his control failed, they would likely kill him with their bare hands.

The spell lingered in the room and affected Mica, although she hadn't been exposed long enough to be sedated in the same way. She had searched for the source of the curse, and in her time in the Tower and her visits to Richard's room, she hadn't been able to identify it.

"I may need to re-evaluate things," she said, speaking to the women. She knew she would receive no response, but she liked to think that even in their altered state, they could hear and understand her. Perhaps it would comfort them to hear her as much as it comforted her to talk.

"I have found someone in this place who I don't want to kill," she began. "I know, I know. Yes, we are still in Ruby's Tower. However, there is at least one person who doesn't deserve a death sentence. Try not to act so surprised."

She picked up one of the books on the floor and returned it to the bookshelf, straightening up Richard's personal library as she spoke.

"I don't know what to tell you, other than to say that I like him. I like the way I feel when I'm around him. I look forward to seeing him. I make excuses to bump into him. This feeling is silly, dangerous, and a distraction. Yet he occupies the front of my mind whenever I'm not thinking about you.

And no, he's not one of the red mage assholes. Give me more credit than that."

Mica knelt next to Elle and gently rolled her onto her side. Mica delicately scratched and rubbed the woman's back, careful to avoid the large scars on her shoulder blades. Satisfied that no wounds needed treatment, Mica gently returned her to her previous position.

"More importantly, I think he may be able to help, when the time comes. We will need some friends to get you home." She got up and moved to her next sister. As before, Mica gingerly repositioned her to provide some relief.

"Speaking of that, I also think that our timetable may be shorter than I had first expected. I am nearly certain that the orcs plan to attack this city. I don't yet know how we can use that distraction, but I think we'll have more opportunities for escape than without it."

A sound caught her attention. It wasn't quite a sigh, but one of her sisters changed her breathing abruptly.

"Ofri?" Mica whispered, daring to be optimistic. She darted across the room, quickly knelt by the woman's side and took her hand. It was so cold.

"Ofri? Can you hear me?" Mica brought the woman's hand to her face.

Ofri didn't answer. She never answered. None of them ever did. They just stared. And they suffered. They suffered as much as they had yesterday, and the days before, and the weeks before, and the months before. And throughout it all, Mica had been able to do nothing about it.

She gently dried Ofri's hand. It was wet with Mica's tears.

Mica was overcome by the pain, anger, and frustration of their circumstance. For weeks, she had been far from home in this miserable Tower, in this awful city, surrounded by terrible people. For months she had been trying to engineer an escape for these women. She was met only with bitter disappointment and an even greater stab of guilt for being the lucky survivor, the one who got away. She fought the urge to sob.

*You can't do this now. This is not how you help them. You help them by being here and by being stronger than this.*

Mica stood up and wiped her eyes. Her pain had transitioned to anger—a rage that she harbored for this Tower and the mages in it.

"I'm so sorry, sisters," she said. "You know how it breaks my heart to see you like this. I will free you from this prison. I will get you home."

She wanted to stay and tend to them for longer, but the better choice would be to leave. The more time she was noticed in this room, the more likely someone would associate her with these women. She gathered her things.

As she walked to the door, Mica subconsciously reached over her left shoulder with her right hand and rubbed a patch of skin next to her shoulder blade.

Much like the other women in the room, she bore the same scars. But unlike them, she had chosen to have her wings removed. It was the only way she'd be able to pass for a human.

# DAY
# 12

# Netherby – Pel

It had been two long days. Pel and Garret had walked for nearly ten hours on their journey to Andwyn. Then, following their encounter with the orcs and without much meaningful rest, they had been forced to make the reverse trip to Netherby and hope that it still stood when they arrived.

They arrived a few hours past dawn and were relieved to find the town much as it had been before. Pel was almost fatigued enough to look forward to the lumpy, uncomfortable beds the inn provided.

They had taken a shortcut through the rolling pasturelands, cutting through one of the rancher's fields on their way back to the inn. A flash of a familiar blue light burst from one of the indistinguishable structures in the distance.

"The inn will have to wait. Our friend has found us," she announced, nodding to the blurry object in the horizon.

"Dylan's western barn," Garret identified it for her.

The large structure stood alone in the field, out of sight from Dylan's house. Less than a hundred yards of cleared space separated it from a clump of trees that marked the outer edge of the Thick. The two held hands as they moved through the field.

The barn's door was unlocked and swung open with ease. A blast of cool, stale air wafted over Pel's face and neck, smelling of hay and a lingering scent of livestock. The light from the gaps between the wall boards cut into the darkness of an empty, otherwise unremarkable barn. Garret turned to bar the door behind them, but Pel stopped him by grabbing his arm and shaking her head.

"Leave it ajar. If someone were to come by, a door barred from the inside would only arouse suspicions," she advised.

"Everything we're doing in here is suspicious," Garret grumbled.

"I think the locals would be able to guess why you two sneaked away to the privacy of a barn," a familiar voice called from the loft above.

"The orcs have razed Andwyn," Pel said, turning her head to address Deodin creeping about the loft. "It can only be days before they set their sights on Peak's View or Netherby. Or both."

"We'll need to leave Netherby, but we'll also need to split up and meet outside the village," Deodin replied. "More of the mages from the Tower arrived earlier in the morning."

"Red mages?" Pel echoed.

"Several. Perhaps as many as eight. They came in at different times yesterday and this morning. They currently wait in the tavern. Aside from the bravest of the inn's staff, the people of Netherby have found somewhere else to be. They may be looking for me. Or you."

Pel eyed Garret. He seemed to share her apprehension as to why more mages had arrived at Netherby. The timing was too unlikely to be a coincidence.

"Give us a few hours to rest and we can meet you," Pel suggested. "We can avoid the inn and the red mages altogether."

Garret took her hand. He let her turn to him before he shook his head.

"We have to tell the people here about Andwyn and the orcs," he said softly. "We have to send a message, even if we run into red mages."

Pel felt a sharp sting of guilt. He was right. She had been too absorbed in her personal issues to share the life-saving news with the people who most needed to hear it.

The timber of the loft above them groaned and creaked as Deodin moved from his position at the window.

"That burden will have to fall on you two," Deodin said. "Red mages attack me on sight. They would likely destroy the village in their efforts to confront me."

Pel caught a blur of blue motion overhead. Deodin emerged from his hiding spot and jumped down the ten or twelve feet to land near them. He still wore his equipment on his back, but he landed as quietly as if he'd stepped on carpet with bare feet. The god killer glowed with magic, clearly using it to slow what otherwise would have been a crippling fall. He nodded a brief "hello" to them and adjusted the way his pack rested on his shoulders.

"You got a haircut," Pel observed when he drew near enough. "You look so much more respectable."

"No, he doesn't," Garret corrected, staring down at Deodin's cat-paw-slipper boots.

Pel ignored him. "We will warn the villagers and see if they can dispatch courier birds to the rest of the Crown. We can meet you tomorrow at dawn," she said.

"Of course," Deodin responded. "Tomorrow morning, then. Where can I find you once you excuse yourselves from Netherby?"

"Highpoint," Garret replied. "Leave the inn and head east along the road. In about an hour, you'll see a clearing to the north with a small hill that overlooks it. Highpoint is the giant boulder that rests atop that hill. It would be impossible to miss. We can be there shortly after first light."

"An hour east, along the road," Deodin confirmed, his eyes suggesting he mentally calculated the time and distance. "Take some time here. You two could use the rest."

After a nod to say farewell, Deodin disappeared in a flash of light only Pel could see.

Garret looked around blankly, keenly aware that he had missed the magic show yet again.

# Netherby – Garret

"Emissary Tyberius," Pel said with a slow, deliberate bow.

Garret briefly wondered which was more impressive, Pel's attention to social mores or how deftly she used them.

The Netherby inn stirred with more activity, but he immediately sensed a tension. The tavern's tables were occupied by men dressed in decadent red clothes and wearing more jewelry than would be otherwise reasonable. Garret counted five. The mages all stared at them expectantly, but Emissary Asshole was the only one to speak.

"Any news from Andwyn?" Tyberius asked, looking up with an unfriendly glower.

The man said only four words, yet still presented himself as being even more contemptible than before. Garret interpreted his remark as a subtle probe for them to justify their reasons for being in the area.

Pel spoke. "Andwyn has been destroyed, set to the torch by an orc raid. We believe that most of the villagers, if not all of them, were slain. We encountered part of the raiding party just short of Andwyn. We were lucky to escape. Surely, the orcs march on Netherby."

There should have been a collective gasp of disbelief and horror. The men in the tavern should have reacted to the loss of life and the greater implications for everyone in the Crown. Instead, they simply stared back, their glares just short of being blatantly accusatory.

"Orcs, you say?" Tyberius's words dripped skepticism.

Garret took umbrage at the man's demeanor. This same bugger had been here last week.

"Fucking right, 'orcs,'" Garret spat. "It hasn't been a week since the last orc attack. You were even here for it, sitting in that very seat."

"Yet you couldn't slay them as valiantly as you had before?" he replied. "Perhaps the orc threat has been exaggerated. Or your heroism."

"The more important point," Pel said, "is to warn the people of Netherby and spread the word along the Crown. We will need to send the courier birds to Ruby and Peak's View. Delemere, also, but I suspect its people may have already withdrawn into their mountain."

"The birds have been dispatched elsewhere to report other news," Tyberius said. "Your message will have to wait until one of them returns."

"Have you seen the innkeeper? He would likely know how to spread the word here." Pel scanned the room.

"The service here has its limits," Tyberius returned, looking down at his mug of ale in disappointment.

"I'll go find him," Pel said to Garret. "I'll meet you back here."

He nodded and Pel left the tavern, disappearing down the halls to another part of the inn. Garret found a seat at a table in the corner, away from everyone else.

The exchange with Tyberius had stirred the attention of two other red mages sitting at the bar. Emboldened by alcohol and hubris, the pair rose simultaneously and made their way over. The mages displayed an insincerely jovial demeanor that Garret recognized as condescension.

"Ah, the mighty 'Orcslayer of the Thick'! We heard so much about your adventures from last week," said the larger of the two, in a way that was both a belch and a yawn, yet somehow still aggressive. His singular defining feature was a full beard sodden with whatever he had been drinking. He and his colleague sat down in the two empty chairs on the far side of the table.

"Right! The skalg-buggering locals wouldn't shut up about it. So, please regale us with your adventures!" ordered the other mage, a much smaller and thinner man. His long face, huge head, and freakishly large teeth bore so much a resemblance to a horse that he must have been teased as a youth.

"Nay," replied Garret, "I wouldn't saddle you with such a dull story. Whatever you've heard is a thousand times more interesting than the truth."

"Don't be bashful, 'Orcslayer'!" the bearded mage goaded, his voice bridled with drunken impatience. He fidgeted with one of the gold rings on his finger. Absently playing with the hilt of a sword would have been as threatening. "We insist."

"Then who am I to disappoint, if the public demands it?" Garret asked.

He finished his mug with a long drink and concluded the spectacle by slamming the empty vessel down on the table. He leaned forward and locked gazes with both men in turn.

Garret spoke in a hoarse growl.

"There I was, in the Thick, near the road. I heard the cries of men. A battle! Orcs! Humans! A struggle for life and death! I ran toward that sound." He clenched his fists and furrowed his brow, inviting the others to join in the tension of the moment.

"A battle I found. Orcs, raining down arrows on the merchants, holding them fast while the spear-bearers came to the flanks. They … they were to run those men through."

Garret softened his voice to a whisper. "And then what?" He turned away from his audience to look down at his hands. "Do I simply watch them die? Could I live with that vision in my mind, for the rest of my life? Would the sounds of their screams live in my ears until my end days, ghosts to haunt me forever?"

He looked up and exchanged gazes with his audience.

"No. I would act."

He pantomimed slipping out from underneath his bow and drawing an arrow from an imaginary quiver. He nocked the arrow and drew back, then paused for a moment.

"I saw an orc. He had a bow of his own, laying fire on the merchants. He didn't know I was there, so I shot him in the back!" Garret said triumphantly.

There was a prolonged pause as his impatient audience waited for him to continue. Garret pointed over his shoulder with his thumb, mouthing the words "in the back," tacking on the gesture as if it would clear up any ambiguity about what happened. Whatever hostility had been present before dissolved into genuine disappointment.

"That's a right shitty story," the Beard observed as he straightened and turned to his colleague.

"And what about the rest of them, then?" the Horse asked. "The merchants said there were eight of them."

Garret took no pause as he widened his eyes then nodded soberly.

"Oh, they were as stubborn as mules. They continued to press the attack, firing on the merchants." Garret turned his head slightly and nodded sternly. "I shot them in the back, too. Because they didn't know I was there."

Garret and his audience suffered through ten seconds of awkward silence and eye contact.

"What about the orcs outside of Andwyn? Surely, the mighty 'Orcslayer' could have slain them as well?" the Beard asked. Everything about his body language and expression suggested he was skeptical. He may have come into this conversation with a preconceived notion of Garret and his story, but now he had second thoughts.

Garret leaned away from them and gestured for them to wait. He slowly shook his head and looked up at the Horse with wide eyes.

"Whoaaaaa. Did you miss the part where I shot the other orcs in the *back*? While they were standing still? And didn't know I was there? Orcs are much harder to shoot when they see you and are running at you and want to kill you."

The Beard and the Horse exchange bemused looks. They had clearly come to confront this "Orcslayer" on gallantry and courage. Finding zero trace of gallantry and even less courage, there was no longer any room for a confrontation. Even the way he delivered the story was too pathetic for any additional comment.

Awkwardly, the two mages grumbled their disappointed and discourteous farewells as they pushed back from the table to return to their seats at the bar.

Alone at his table, Garret turned away from the judgmental faces that continued to stare at him. Rather than make eye contact, he reached into his pack and pretended to look for something.

He had survived the moment, but his story of the orc attack on the merchants was flawed. Hopefully, Pel would return before any of the mages in this room could put any more thought into the narrative.

*　*　*

Daylight poured into the room as the front door opened. Garret glanced to see who had arrived and was immediately disappointed to watch Entorak enter the room and nod and wave to the mages of the tavern.

An orc raid was preferable to encountering Entorak. When running or fighting for your life, there was no time for panic or anxiety. When Entorak looked at him and smiled with recognition, Garret suffered through several long moments of existential dread.

At least the orcs' motives were easier to read.

"Garret, isn't it? I fear we may have never been properly introduced." Entorak seated himself across the table and sat down with a weary sigh.

"I know who you are," Garret replied.

"Yes. Well. Our reputations lead their own lives, don't they? Like yours. I suspect if your tales of heroism are repeated enough throughout the Crown, we'd have to set aside space for your statue."

Garret had several jokes in response to Entorak's comment but didn't feel jovial enough for any of them.

Entorak continued.

"At any rate, with you here in Netherby, can I hope that Pelium is nearby? In the inn or elsewhere in the village?"

"She is," Garret said. "She has news to share with the Crown. Orcs have raided and destroyed Andwyn. I saw the town's remains yesterday."

A slight gasp escaped Entorak's lips. The color in his cheeks lightened, the muscles around his eyes relaxed. He seemed genuinely moved by the news.

"Losses?" he whispered.

"Total, I think. We had to flee. We were spotted by part of the raiding party and had to escape into the Thick. During it all, I made it to Andwyn's outskirts to confirm that the village had been razed."

"When was this? As specifically as you can recall, please."

"This was late yesterday afternoon. I saw the remains of Andwyn near dusk. Whenever the orcs attacked, it was hours before we were there. In the morning or possibly the night before."

"Andwyn last night, Netherby this morning?" Entorak's face expressed a mild disbelief, apparently questioning the plausibility of their trip.

*Fuck off, mage.*

"We had been spotted by an orc party that had just slaughtered an entire village and burned it to the ground. Would *you* have stopped?" Garret jeered, hardly concealing his resentment of Entorak's tone.

"I meant to imply nothing. I merely wanted to comment on how exhausted you must be. The two of you," Entorak said, gesturing an apology with a bow. "Hopefully you can rest and return to Ruby tomorrow. Have you concluded the business that brought you to Netherby?"

Entorak was testing him, measuring his reaction to what had been posed as an innocent question.

"Yes," Garret said as innocuously as he could.

# Netherby – Entorak

"Ah, Pelium," Entorak said as she entered the tavern from the hallway to the rest of the inn. Had he not known better, Entorak might have thought her smile was sincere.

"Entorak." Pelium nodded once, the gesture serving as both a greeting and a show of respect.

She seemed surprised to see him in Netherby—she certainly did not expect to find him sitting across the table from Garret. Nevertheless, she exemplified professionalism. She withdrew into her cloak and sat next to her guide.

*And her lover*, Entorak surmised, assessing the easiness in their body language. Their partnership was more than professional, more personal than he would have expected from her. As long as he had dealt with her, she had never publicly displayed intimacy.

"Garret told me of Andwyn. How bad did it look to you?" Entorak was legitimately curious about her response. The nature of her business coincided with her presence here, and likewise, the presence of her guide was equally explicable and reasonable.

She shrugged. "I never got close enough. After we were spotted, I spent most of the afternoon buried in the ground, hiding from the orcs. Garret was the one with the courage to approach the village."

Hers was the same story as Garret's. At the very least, their accounts matched, so perhaps it was the truth. Or at least a partial truth.

"Considering the orcs, I hope you'll return to Ruby. You'll be safer there. Has your business concluded in Netherby?" Entorak asked.

Pel looked around the tavern deliberately, making an obvious point about the number of red mages in the building. She was clever enough to note how unusual their presence was.

"Our business is at an end. Is yours? What does the Tower find interesting enough to send out so many valued resources?"

Entorak smiled. He didn't quite believe her story, but he truly relished these kinds of interactions with her. He didn't view her as an adversary or rival, but she was of a very sharp mind, with a sturdy confidence to accompany it. She flipped the conversation and subtly interrogated him. It was refreshing.

But, as she avoided his questions with half-truths, he would do the same.

"If you'll forgive me for being vague, we heard some troubling rumors about some recent indiscretions from one of our order. I have been asked to look into it," Entorak said, knowing that Pel would understand this as a reference to Tyberius.

"But as for what is interesting, I must say that the news of Garret's heroism has reached Ruby," he prompted.

Pelium nodded. "We happened across a merchant caravan shortly after they were attacked, just outside of Netherby. This would be almost a week ago."

"I imagine there were some exaggerations." Entorak turned to the rugged man sitting next to her. "The villagers would have us believe you defeated a hundred orcs. But if you can forgive my macabre curiosity, how did you single-handedly turn the tide of the ambush?"

Garret perked up a little bit. He leaned in and eyed Entorak seriously. "It's easier if they don't know you're there and you shoot them in the back," he whispered. He followed up with a slow, deliberate nod, as if the battle strategy represented a profound innovation.

"I have heard that," Entorak replied. The ranger's delivery was unsatisfying, but his story had been consistent across all sources. He turned back to Pelium. "I fear an orc confrontation is inevitable. And soon. Those near the borders of the Thick are at the greatest risk."

"We will be leaving here soon enough," she confirmed.

"Safe journeys, then," Entorak said with a sincere nod and smile. She dipped her head in response, but before she and Garret could get up from the table, Entorak posed a final question.

"One last thing before I forget: have you heard anything new about Ruby's rogue mage from the other night?"

Nearly simultaneously, Entorak noted a single "knock" sound coming from the outside of the inn, like something had struck the side of the structure.

Pelium's guide noticed it, too. He turned his head toward the sound, his eyes narrowing with concern as if he recognized the sound but couldn't quite place it. Entorak awaited Pelium's response to his question.

"Nothing more than what you and I discussed," she said. "I have nothing new to add. Garret and I left that very day, to come out here. Have you anything to tell me, for when we return?"

Another knock sounded, at the same volume as the first. Pelium's guide straightened his shoulders and back, like a guard dog. Keen. Alert. Alarmed. The mages, on the other hand, had hardly taken notice. Entorak hurried to finish the conversation.

"Unfortunately, not. The most riveting news I have heard in the past week is an increasingly apocryphal tale of heroics," Entorak said, nodding to Pelium's guide.

Entorak felt a slight bit of relief, but not because she had relayed anything useful about the rogue mage. Rather, because she hadn't. Instead, she asked him about the man, because it was her business to know these kinds of things. He might have considered it suspicious had she not. Instead, she seemed to be concluding her business in Netherby. She could return to Ruby.

Entorak planned to have them followed. If they headed south, back toward Ruby, he would consider the matter closed. If not, he would need to consider other alternatives.

Two more knocks followed in rapid succession. Then several more.

Pelium's companion stood up and scanned the room. It wasn't panic in his face and posture, but he was very clearly concerned. She finally tore herself from the conversation and noticed the palpable tension of the man standing next to her.

"We need to leave," he said with an urgency that belied his calm demeanor. He didn't say the word "now," but the timetable for their departure was obvious enough.

Entorak smelled smoke.

# Netherby – Pel

Garret was acting unusual. Pel recognized his serious, attentive demeanor as he focused all his senses on the front door. Pel could almost smell his tension.

*Danger.*

He studied the rest of the room with a haste that concerned her. This apprehension became contagious, quickly sensed by everyone present. The mages rose from the tables.

She glanced at Entorak, who began to bark instructions at the mages. The orders were fast and almost unintelligible, but it seemed Entorak was splitting the mages into two groups. One was being tasked with repelling an attack while the other gathered to escort the inn staff and guests to safety.

*Attack? Escort?*

The room was suddenly awash in bright blue light as the mages adorned themselves in magical protection spells. Their auras were not blindingly bright, but each of their facial features grew distinct, even from across the room.

A strong hand grasped hers. Garret had recovered his weapons belt and made brief eye contact with Pel before directing his attention back to the tavern's din and disorder. He gently pulled her to the far corner, away from the front door, just as it exploded inward and a mass of humanity poured through. But it wasn't humanity. She shuddered.

Orcs.

They stormed in through the narrow entryway in a manner both deliberate, yet chaotic.

The first orc through the door pushed his way past the closest mage and made a desperate lunge for Entorak. The elder mage was just agile enough to knock over a nearby table and create a sliver of distance. The attacking orc tumbled to the floor. As he rolled over to regain his feet, he was only a few paces away from Pel, certainly close enough for her to see him clearly.

Pel briefly wished her eyesight was worse; what she saw was nightmarish.

The attacker was dressed in dark leather clothing that served as protection from both the elements and whatever weapons might be used against him. His hair was long and unkempt. A mottled beard covered the lower half of his face. Coarse, dark hair covered his arms and the visible parts of his upper body.

In superficial ways, the attacker resembled a human. Aside from an animalistic gait and posture, a more prominent brow, and a different shape of ear, Pel saw more similarities than differences.

Pel realized now that orcs were monsters, but not because of their looks.

Orcs thrived via savagery and violence, unburdened by civility and restraint. Neither reason nor conscience guided their actions. While humans learned to wield logic and perspective to distance themselves from their most barbaric instincts, orcs embraced these instincts.

As the attacker regained his feet, Pel stared, transfixed by the sight and paralyzed by fear. The orc's eyes opened to their fullest, with pupils so dilated that the irises appeared to be completely black. His lips parted to reveal a crooked array of sharp, yellowed teeth. Even his nostrils flared, every sensory organ working at its peak. An oppressive fist of fear grasped Pel's heart and an equally toxic pang of nausea stabbed her gut when his eyes settled on her.

The room exploded with hostility. As savage as the orcs were, the mages were equally brutal. A spell burst from the other side of the room and cut down the orc with a bright, violent arc of lightning. The orc collapsed in a flash of light and heat.

The other mages added to their counterattack quickly and with commensurate violence. Pel flinched under the bright lights of the magical hellfire that engulfed the door and nearly everything in it. Half a dozen or more orcs slumped to the floor immediately. The lucky ones lay still, scattered on both sides of the threshold. The less fortunate ones writhed and squirmed.

There was hardly a respite, however. A few of the orcs in the second wave stepped carefully to avoid their fallen brethren. Others did not. Still more attackers poured through the smoldering doorframe, each selecting a target as soon as he entered. That look of malevolent enthusiasm was shared by every orc face, every toothy smile, every pair of eyes.

At that moment, Pel came to believe that orcs could never be "domesticated." The Thick was home to a great number of monsters and the orcs must forever be counted among them.

Fortunately for her, Garret could not hear her internal, philosophical monologue about the nature of orckind. Instead, he waited for an opportunity to tug on her hand and pull her away.

He directed her down the corridor leading away from the tavern. Three doors lined each side of the hallway, aligned neatly and symmetrically past the upward-leading staircase on the left-hand side. Garret dragged Pel to the first door on the left, just past the staircase. Once inside, he slammed the door behind them and scanned the room. He didn't appear panicked, but his mind was fully engaged in solving the immediate crisis.

Pel could hear Entorak call out her name loudly and repeatedly before the heavy sound of wood grating against wood drowned out his cries. Garret had pulled a bulky cabinet from the corner and shoved it all the way across the room to barricade the door.

"The orcs must have set parts of the building on fire to flush us out," he concluded.

"Flush us out? Why in the hells would they burst through the doors of a building they set on fire?"

"Orcs," he replied, with a shrug.

"And why are *you* barricading us in a room in a building that is on fire?" she hissed frantically.

"The back door is in the kitchen, behind the bar. The kitchen should be on the other side of this wall," Garret explained.

He dragged the bed out of his way to create a small space where he knelt in the corner of the room. He retrieved the small hatchet that he wore on his belt, muttering to himself as he tapped the wall with the flat edge of the axe. Finding a sound he liked, he flipped the tool's head around and dug into the wall, using it to pry rather than chop.

The wall crumbled into a dusty, chalky cloud far more easily than Pel thought it could or should. The interior wall was made of thin slats of wood covered in dried mud plaster. The material held the partition together and allowed for small things to be mounted to it, but it was not designed to withstand desperate, axe-wielding men. It took only a few moments for Garret to create an opening large enough for them to fit through.

"Ha! No cross-members for sway control! This place is a total deathtrap!" Garret said. "Well, aside from it being on fire. And flooded with orcs and red mages. In the middle of a monster-filled forest."

He stuck his head through the hole for a moment to survey the other side. Satisfied, he slid his bow through and gently set it down. It landed with a soft clatter. He held out his hand, encouraging Pel to slip through the hole to the other side.

She peeked into the hole to see a staircase directly below her, dimly lit by the flames in the tavern. To her left, the staircase descended to a small cellar. To her right was the top of the stairs and the tavern's kitchen. As Garret predicted, she could see the inn's back door through the open doorway of the cellar's staircase. She and Garret could drop a few feet to the steps, head up the stairs, and out the back door.

She nodded as he motioned for her to go in feet first, sliding through on her stomach so she could let herself down onto the stairs below. Once she had her footing, she reached up to receive the last of Garret's gear before he squeezed through the opening himself. A moment later, he had re-equipped and rearmed himself.

He took her right hand with his left, tugging slightly to lead her up to the kitchen. Pel coughed in the dark, smoky air. As she fought through the burning in her lungs, she tried not to gag on the copper scent of blood and nauseating reek of burning flesh.

As the commotion and violence from the next room filled her ears, they crossed the kitchen to the back door. It remained barricaded by a heavy iron bar that spanned both sides of the doorframe. Garret took the bar in his hands, but before he lifted it, Pel spoke.

"Do you think they're just waiting out back for someone to open it from the inside?" she asked.

"We might survive the orcs out there. We won't survive the fire in here," he replied tersely.

A sudden blink of white light and an intense burst of heat and magic overflowed into the kitchen area. The flash was accompanied by screams of one or more of the combatants in the other room. The open hostility of the skirmish seemed to be a more fatal option than fleeing out the back door.

To complicate the decision, the back door now shuddered, as something pounded on it. Metal scraped wood under the strain of whatever was trying to break it down.

Again, Garret reacted without hesitation. He found Pel's hand and tugged at it urgently, compelling her to follow him back down the stairs into the cellar below.

They huddled in the tiny space, peering back up the stairs through the smoke-filled atmosphere and watching as the door shook every few seconds, resisting the heavy, sequential blows from the outside. The door finally collapsed inward, splintering heavily. It would not survive another strike.

Garret retrieved a handful of arrows, arranging them in his left hand so that he could loose them more rapidly. In doing so, he gently pushed Pel behind him, interposing himself between her and whatever monster would come through that door.

*This was unacceptable.*

As Garret nocked an arrow and extended the bow forward, ready to pull the string taut, Pel slid his sword out of its scabbard. It felt cold and weighed far more than she expected. And she certainly knew nothing about how to wield it. Nevertheless, she wrapped both hands around the hilt and aimed the pointy end up the staircase.

However this would go, she would stand beside him.

Pel watched in horror as the heavy iron support bar bent like a stiff piece of parchment and dropped harmlessly to the floor. The door collapsed in an impressive explosion of splinters and dust.

Garret readied his bow and almost immediately, a humanoid shape filled the doorframe. He loosed his arrow. It landed with a solid *thok* in the frame.

However, the miss was probably for the best, in both the short and long term. Deodin stood in the doorway, inches from the arrow shaft lodged deeply in the wooden frame.

"That's Deodin," Pel observed drily. "He seems disappointed that you fired at him."

Still glaring at Garret, Deodin reached behind him and ripped the arrow out of the wall with far more ease than seemed plausible. The god killer gestured that he would shove said arrow up Garret's backside if he ever did something like that again.

"I deserve that," Garret agreed.

A moment later Deodin jumped down the stairs and landed noiselessly next to them. He breathed heavily and dirt filthened his tunic and face, yet his aura shone brightly enough for Pel to shield her eyes. The god killer gestured to the kitchen's open door at the top of the stairs.

"Out the back, then to the left. All the way to the barn..." he instructed.

"What about the orcs?" Garret asked.

Still bracing against Garret's shoulder, Deodin waved dismissively with his free hand, indicating that they were not a concern.

"What about you?" Pel asked.

"I need something here first," he replied.

Pel nodded as a heavy crash from upstairs brought their perils back to the present.

"Go!" Deodin instructed.

Garret recovered his sword from Pel and helped her up the stairs, out the back door, and into the field behind the inn—a field that was currently clear of orcs. They hurried toward the barn to meet with the townsfolk rallying there.

Two of the villagers waved them over. They started speaking when Pel and Garret were close enough. "Orcs came out o' the woods and lit up the inn with flaming arrows," the taller of the two remarked.

The shorter one added, "The mages told us to gather here, while they turned 'em back by dumping fuckin' buckets of fire on their heads!"

The taller man stiffened and became suddenly more soft-spoken. "The mages ... uh ... lost one of their own, though."

Pel turned to two red mages who crouched nearby. A mixture of ash, dirt, and blood had ruined their decadent crimson garb. Both men were soiled with sweat, doubled over, and attempting to catch their breath. This marked the first occasion in Pel's lifetime that she was remotely thankful for the Tower mages.

"More mages," Pel said to Garret, nodding toward the crumbling ruin of the tavern from which they emerged. The inn was now fully engulfed in flame and billowing black clouds. Several figures straggled from the smoke.

Their auras were visible through the haze. Pel recognized Entorak's tall, poised posture as he stood up and brushed himself off in a far more dignified manner than the situation would seem to allow.

# DAY
# 13

# Netherby – Pel

Despite her exhaustion from the previous days of travel, Pel had trouble sleeping and awoke before dawn. The orcs' attack had filled her with apprehension that she could feel in her heart and stomach throughout the night. The previous two days had been a waking nightmare of repeated encounters with "monsters," both orcs and red mages.

The nightmare was not yet over. Aside from the inn, Netherby had barely survived the orc wave. It would be foolish to believe that the orcs would simply concede the village to a handful of farmers and ranchers. The only reason everyone had survived was because Deodin and the red mages were not part of the orcs' plan. Pel had to assume another attack was forthcoming and the orcs would not make the same mistakes twice.

*And should we survive the orcs, Entorak doesn't believe the entirety of our story.*

She heard soft footsteps within another part of the house. Following the attack on Netherby and the inn's destruction, the townsfolk had provided room and board for the inn's surviving guests. Pel and Garret had stayed with one of the more affluent ranchers and his family.

A gentle knock on the door came, and after a polite moment, the door opened. The rancher peered in, holding up an apologetic hand for the interruption.

"I heard you movin' about," he began. "Mr. Dylan has requested that everyone meet by his barn this morning at sunup."

Dylan did not hold an elected office but he was one of the senior statesmen for the village. Pel had spoken to him several times during the previous week.

She learned that the local community addressed their concerns through informal meetings, as the need arose. An orc attack would certainly prompt such a discussion. Unfortunately, Entorak would surely be there. Considering his influence, it was probably no coincidence that he had been invited to stay at the Dylan homestead after the fire.

Were the circumstances different, she would have helped in any way she could. However, she had a rendezvous with Deodin. Moving him out of the Tower's reach was still her highest priority.

"My apologies, but we would hope to be traveling by then," Pel explained, hoping to excuse herself from any meeting with Entorak.

"Mr. Entorak expected you to say that. He was very insistent that you stop by Mr. Dylan's barn before you leave. They'll be ready for you now." The rancher smiled. "Besides, the Dylans are cooking breakfast. You can't leave before you eat."

Pel nodded and smiled politely. Unlike some of her dealings in Ruby, there was no sinister agenda at play here. The good people of Netherby were just being generous and accommodating; the rancher knew nothing of the greater intrigue between Pel, *sheyaktu*, Entorak, and the mages.

The sun had not yet peeked over the mountains, but nearly all the Netherby villagers had assembled in front of Dylan's barn. As promised, the family was preparing breakfast for the locals and the refugees from the inn. A warm plate awaited both Pel and Garret, as well as the rancher who accompanied them. They exchanged pleasantries before Dylan and Entorak beckoned them over.

Pel drew a deep breath and squirmed underneath her cloak. Garret must have noticed, as she felt his free hand land reassuringly on the small of her back. It was his way of saying that she didn't need any help just to talk to a few old men.

"Trrr th bithcuith n bacom," he added through a mouthful.

Entorak greeted them with a bow. "Pelium. Garret." The mage stood next to Dylan, a man of approximately fifty or fifty-five winters.

Dylan's family and many of the townsfolk busied themselves in the barn. Off to the side, away from the chuckles and lightly animated discussion of the morning, sat a circle of five red mages, keeping to themselves. They dressed like the other villagers and ate their breakfast in silence. "Emissary Tyberius" was not among them.

"We lost three of our order," Entorak said stoically, correctly interpreting the implicit question on Pel's face.

She turned back to him with an inquisitive look.

"Peter fell to orc arrows while rallying the villagers during the attack. They said that he died heroically, standing between the villagers and the orcs, defending their lives with his own until the very last. Horace met his fate at the end of an orc spear in the initial attack of the inn. Even while mortally wounded, he had the skill and presence of mind to counterattack and save all of us in the inn, including the two of you. Tyberius supported our escape to the last, but did not survive the collapse of the inn."

Pel glanced to where the inn had stood. Her eyesight being as limited as it was, what should have been a blurry and indistinct two-story blob could only be described as a blurry black stain on the ground.

"I ... I am at a loss for words," Pel said, slowly. Truthfully.

Entorak bowed but held up a hand. "We can pay tribute to their sacrifices another time. With the orc attack, the villagers assemble this morning to discuss what to do in response. It is my hope that they will pack up what they can and flee to the safety within Ruby's walls."

"Mr. Entorak believes that we should pack the animals with whatever they'll carry and drive the herds south," Dylan said. "He proposes we carry and cart the rest. He said that there will be a place for us inside the walls, at least for now."

Pel digested Dylan's remark. Entorak was right. If there were to be an ideal time to abandon Netherby and relocate, it would be now.

"The reservoir project," she said. "The fields along the northeast wall should be ready soon. Your entire village should be able to ranch on that land once the orc threat has come and gone."

"Yeah, that's how Entorak described it." Dylan seemed reassured by her affirmation. "He says the land is already cleared and mostly leveled. The Tower and the people of Ruby can help us out until we can build a few fences and a place to live."

"It isn't the same expanse of land you would have here," she replied, "but you can certainly put it to good use."

"I hope to be able to leave within a day," Entorak explained to Pel. "And I hope that you would—"

A familiar voice interrupted the conversation.

"And the people of Andwyn were merely acceptable losses?"

*Deodin? Here? Now?* Pel was dumbfounded by his presence. She was even more confused when she saw him.

Everything about him was wrong. His body language screamed of anger, confrontation, and violence. He stood impatiently with clenched fists, forward shoulders, and wide, alert eyes. Unlike before, his fingers were adorned with rings of precious metal. Apart from the way he dressed, he carried himself like any and every other mage she had ever seen.

The villagers were the first to react to the hostility that Deodin had brought to their peaceful morning. A few of the more intrepid townsfolk rose to their feet, a few others took a few steps back. Meanwhile, the other mages stopped eating and were enraptured by the drama that was center stage. Throughout it all, Entorak had hardly moved, watching without any expression.

"Such a benevolent gesture from the Tower, for sure." Deodin slowly paced to the side, his shoulders still pointing toward Entorak. "Heroic mages dying to save the peasants! Grand allotments of land! I'm sure you already spun a poem for the bards."

Dylan spread his hands wide in a welcoming gesture. "Easy now, friend. The orcs are to blame for all of this, not the m—"

"How can you forget so soon?" Deodin cried. "It was within the week that one of those 'heroes' disfigured your sons and had his way with one of your daughters! And here they are, paying for their sins with promises of land and prosperity. You may have already forgotten, but the Keepers have not!"

Pel stiffened, bemused. *Keepers?*

Better known as the "Keepers of Men," the small and reasonably obscure sect lived in scattered enclaves across the

Crown. They believed that magic would be the undoing of the world, so they sought to root it out wherever it stood. They were noisy and occasionally disruptive, but they had no real influence. Apart from Pel, only the mages from the Tower would have ever heard of their order.

"I am Entorak, a representative of the Mage Tower of Ruby—" Entorak said, taking a measured step forward.

"Die, abusers of the worldtaint!" Deodin screamed.

With that, he began drawing a symbol in the air with his hands and fingers. He uttered words Pel didn't understand, and a moment later, she felt a sensation wash over her, making her feel heavy on her feet, too heavy to stand. She collapsed. Garret leapt upon her almost immediately, shielding her with his body. Screams and shouts filled the air.

The noise seemed to be getting further and further away, until it all went dark and quiet.

\* \* \*

"Ah, I'm relieved that you're awake. We all are."

Pel recognized the voice, but it wasn't the one she wanted to hear. She opened her eyes to find herself on a pile of blankets inside of Dylan's barn. Entorak and a few of the townsfolk hovered around her.

"Where is Garret?" she asked, beset by confusion and panic. Nearly everyone responded with excited responses, too many for her to understand individually. However, with all the pointing and gesturing, she understood he was sleeping on a nearby bed of hay.

"Why am I here?" she asked as she started to sit up. A dizziness overwhelmed her, compelling her to lie back down.

"There was an incident," Entorak explained. "I believe you missed most of it."

Whatever words Entorak had to say, she didn't want to hear them. She turned to Dylan, the rancher. She had only known him for a few days, but she trusted him more than she did Entorak.

"What happened?" she asked him.

Dylan seemed unprepared to speak. He took a moment to collect his thoughts.

"A madman attacked," he finally said. "He came out of the trees and started spouting nonsense about mages and magic and how they had to be punished."

"The man claimed to be—" Entorak began.

"I didn't ask you!" Pel snapped.

"The man used magic," Dylan continued, once Entorak backed out of the conversation. "He put some kinda spell on you and Garret. Then tried to attack the mages. They had magic of their own. They burned him up with fire."

Pel felt a sickening pang of dread fill her stomach.

"Help me up. Show me," she said weakly.

There was some commotion from the onlookers. They exchanged glances, silently wondering if this was all for the best. Pel wasn't going to wait for them to make up their minds. She sat up and tried to rise to her feet.

She stumbled briefly, but the villagers caught and steadied her. Still disoriented and shaky, she started to walk out of the barn. Dylan took her by the elbow and guided her outside.

"Show me," she repeated. "Where is he? The madman you described."

Dylan obliged her and led her to the road. She spotted the remains immediately, even if she couldn't see them clearly. As they approached, she could discern an arrangement of charred bones.

"Are you sure it's him?" she asked. "Can you be sure it's him?"

She looked at Dylan. He had no way to answer her question. He simply looked back at her with a helpless expression, then turned to Entorak for any kind of support.

"Can anyone be sure it's him?" Pel echoed, louder. Her voice cracked.

"His arm. The inside of his arm. The tattoos," Entorak said. He squatted next to the remains and pointed to a long, slender object. She recognized it as a forearm, the two bones of the lower arm wrapped tightly by thin, desiccated skin.

Entorak was right. She recognized the script on the forearm. It matched the markings she remembered to be on Deodin's inner arm.

# Netherby – Garret

Garret awoke in the cool shade of Dylan's barn and panicked. He didn't know how he had ended up between two blankets on top of a pile of hay. The bright light of the midday sun fought through the gaps between the planks of the barn, indicating that several hours had passed since—

He sat up with a jolt, cast aside his blanket, and rolled onto his side to get up. He was arrested by a gentle but firm hand.

"Pelium is well. You can see her there, talking to one of the townsfolk," Entorak said slowly. He sat on a stool next to Garret and pointed out the open door into the area immediately outside the barn.

Garret followed the man's gesture out the door and into the sunlight to where Pel was very much alive and well, presently talking to one of the rancher's daughters. She seemed no worse for wear and stood with her arms tucked inside her cloak, wearing the "serious business face" that meant she was working.

"She would prefer to be in here worrying over you, but she begrudgingly agreed to spend the time sharing a small slice of her knowledge of Ruby. The people of Netherby are soon to be Ruby's neighbors, so there is no one better suited to help with that transition," Entorak explained, as both he and Garret watched Pel for a few moments.

Satisfied, Garret began to get up, but Entorak interrupted with a modest gesture of restraint.

"A few answers before you are on your way, please. To help us understand what happened here this morning."

Garret relented and relaxed back into the hay. The two of them sat there for a few moments.

"Answers come after questions."

"A dialogue, then." Entorak smiled. "Please tell me the story of the man who confronted us this morning. Pelium called him Deodin."

"I'm going to stand up," Garret announced. Sensing no objection, he sat up and tried to take to his feet. The dizziness set in almost immediately. He collapsed back down into the hay. "Upon further contemplation, I am going to lie back down."

"Perhaps it is best if I begin the conversation. Pelium explained that she had encountered Deodin in Ruby nearly two weeks ago, seeing him as a stowaway on a merchant ship that docked late in the evening. She said that he had hired the two of you to take him to an undisclosed place in the Thick. Two weeks' worth of events led us to today.

"During all of this, she chose to keep this man's existence secret from the Tower. Do you know why?"

"Because you are all self-serving assholes who hoard knowledge and abuse power to pursue your own selfish goals." Garret replied, the words flowing more freely than he would have expected.

"Well. I appreciate your candor. I sense Pelium has the same sentiment, even if she phrased it more delicately. And I can see how the Tower has earned such a reputation," Entorak confessed with a regretful nod. His tone and mannerisms conveyed no venom or spite; he seemed to be more disappointed or saddened by how he was perceived. "In any case, I would really like to know why you helped him."

Garret was not an accomplished liar and was aware of every physiological response running through him. He inhaled as if to speak, but instead held his breath. Then released it. The question was harder to answer than he had anticipated. Not that he wanted to tell Entorak anything about anything, but Garret had no real reason to lie.

"Because Pel asked me to," Garret said with a sigh.

Entorak seemed almost surprised by Garret's response, as if he had expected a more complicated answer. "I can relate," he said after a few moments of thought. "About this man who hired you, do you remember his magic? Do you remember how he cast his spells?"

Garret presumed this to be a trap. Entorak was certainly trying to interrogate him about Deodin and his abilities, but as with the previous question, the truth was a better answer than any lie he could concoct.

"I know he is magical, but I only saw him cast a few spells. He created a magical campfire. He also allowed me to see the magic of the world, like Pel does. But I never saw him cast anything powerful."

"Are you certain?" Entorak pressed.

Garret shrugged. "He did some things I can't explain. Jokes and pranks. Things you might do to flirt with girls or impress children. But like I said, I never actually saw him do it."

"I see. In your travels, have you encountered or heard of a group called 'The Keepers of Men'?" Entorak asked.

Garret shook his head.

"No reason you should. They are a small order of zealots who oppose the study and use of magic. Occasionally, they resort to violence to spread their message or otherwise further their cause. As it relates to you and me, they do not have a significant presence in Ruby. The Keepers, however, do have small enclaves of support up and down the coast, including Bayhold."

The name Bayhold seemed familiar in all this intrigue, but Garret couldn't quite remember the details. Entorak nodded, seemingly sensing that Garret was trying to recall the connection.

"Your employer planned to take passage to Bayhold, if you'll recall. But his ship missed the port call and he ended up in Ruby, ultimately involving you and Pelium.

"Would it surprise you to learn that the Keepers of Men are believed to have a sect within the Thick? There is said to be a nomadic enclave where they train, east of Netherby, on the way to Luton. And your employer sought areas east of Netherby?"

Garret said nothing. Instead, he sighed again. His face must have conveyed the word "yes," as Entorak seemed to be satisfied with Garret's nonverbal response.

"One last thought, then: there were whispers that this man was a magical paragon, one who could wield magic with nothing but a force of will. I see no reason to believe any of that."

"*Sheyaktu...*" Garret said, louder than he intended.

"So they've said. But is that what you believe? Is that how you interpret everything that you have seen? Everything that you experienced?" Entorak asked.

Garret didn't have a response. Entorak's questions were more difficult to answer than he would have expected. It was the mage who spoke next.

"I think all of ... this... was more likely the result of a much more mundane set of circumstances. A rogue mage finds an ironic home with the Keepers, a few unlucky happenstances lead everyone here. The man sought vengeance for Tyberius's indiscretions, he confronted me and the other mages, et cetera, and so on.

"As for his magic, I have no reason to disbelieve what you and Pelium witnessed. But I have my own thoughts on why that magic seemed so powerful and foreign to her.

"There are different languages of men. All of those languages can describe the color of the sky or the sweetness of a cherry. Why should the language of magic be any different? If this man learned his magic from the East, perhaps he spoke magic in a different language that seemed foreign and exotic by our standards. Perhaps Pelium confused this language and wanted to believe the story of *sheyaktu.*"

Garret had sat up by now, his feet hanging over the side of the pile of hay that served as his makeshift bed. He was beset by even more questions of his own.

What was the more likely explanation for the past weeks? A man with a consuming hatred for the Tower and its mages? Mages who deserved to be hated? Or a mythical man-monster that parents used to scare their kids into eating their vegetables? Garret had never even seen any of this world-ending magic, aside from a handful of gimmicks and tricks. Tricks that didn't seem to impress someone like Entorak.

Wasn't Pel absolutely the least objective person on this particular matter? If furnished a suitable story that echoed her beliefs about the mages and their Tower, wouldn't she do anything to topple it, literally or otherwise?

When it came to Deodin, what made the most sense? A god killer, or a rogue mage who had abused his skills in a criminal or underground endeavor? If Deodin were the master of the magical arts, why would Entorak be standing here? How could *sheyaktu* even lose that fight? The fact that Entorak wasn't a smoldering pile of goo seemed to answer all these questions.

Garret stared vacantly at the far edge of the barn. A mage, a hated mage, offered a version of reality that seemed to make more sense than the one Garret knew.

"In any case, it seems likely that we will never know the entire story, considering how it all ended." Entorak turned away, indicating that the conversation was over.

"Ended?" Garret asked.

Entorak hesitated as though he sought the most socially appropriate and gentle way to speak. "Your former employer is no more. He attacked and mages of the Tower defended themselves and the innocent villagers who stood in the crossfire."

\* \* \*

Garret left the barn in a surreal haze. The events of the morning and the follow-up conversation with Entorak had shaken him. When she saw him, Pel ran over, threw her arms around him, and kissed him on the cheek. She held the embrace for a few moments longer, tightly, clearly relieved that he was up and about. He closed his eyes and breathed in, catching the scent of her hair as she tucked her head into his chest.

*Relief.* Whatever had happened, Pel was okay. And, for that matter, so was he. *Confusion.* Deodin was dead? And not a god killer? Did the past weeks make sense? *Anger.* Fuck Entorak and these mages. And actually, fuck Deodin, too.

Not that it mattered now. *If I don't like Deodin anymore, why am I so upset at the news of his death? Gratitude. Thank the gods that Pel is here, alive and well.*

Pel was also upset. He could feel the heat of her face and the warm moisture of her tears wicking through his shirt. He held her there for a moment longer before ushering her to his side. They walked with his arm over her shoulder, around the side of the barn so they could be alone.

"Are you hurt?" he asked, facing her and looking her up and down. He found no wounds or bruises to suggest she was injured during the ... the uh...

*Actually. What the hells was all of that?*

"What happened?" he asked.

The last thing Garret remembered was Deodin rambling like a madman. There were pops or explosions or something. Pel collapsed and he had jumped on top of her to protect her.

"I don't know. I fell and awoke later, after it was all over. You were still on top of me and took the brunt of whatever it was that incapacitated us. I only know what the others told me. Deodin confronted the mages, attacked them, and ... died when they returned fire."

"He's dead? What with his, you know..." Garret brought the fingertips of his hands together for a moment, before poofing them apart in a soft, silent explosion.

Pel paused before she responded with a bitter, humorless smile. Her eyes glassed as she pointed to one of the many scorch marks that littered the area in front of the barn, roughly where Garret remembered the confrontation. There wasn't anything here that answered his question. A pile of burned sticks didn't mean anything—

*Holy shit. Those were bones.*

Garret stared a while longer, conducting the mental arithmetic required to reassemble the pile of charred remains into the person who had once owned them. The fire that created that mess must have burned hotter than anything Garret had ever seen. The body hadn't been cremated to ash, but it appeared that all its moisture had boiled away almost immediately, leaving the hairless, skeleton-shaped husk covered in a burgundy film of desiccated skin.

*Actually, no.*

Garret had not fallen off the turnip wagon yesterday. The owner of those remains would be nearly impossible to identify. The hair and fat had burned away. What, of that, meant anything?

"How do we even know what that is? That could be an orc, for all we—"

Pel grimaced and inhaled sharply. She gestured as if she were writing across her arm with a pen.

It took him a second to realize that she referred to the symbol-script-tattoo thing that Deodin had on the inside of his arm.

After composing herself, Pel managed to say, "Entorak explained the mark to me. It was a phrase used by the orcs, part of their old language. For orcs, Skycrash and magic brought nothing but horror. From their point of view, Skycrash was the dawn of nightmarish monsters that now live in their territories. The symbols are an orc way of saying 'only monsters use magic.'"

"Gods," Garret remarked as he assembled the clues. In hindsight, that explanation filled in many of the pieces to the puzzle. The symbolism seemed like a perfect sentiment for a fanatical, lunatic fringe like the Keepers of Men.

"It's him," Pel said with certainty. "Everyone in the village tells the same story. He attacked, there was a brief skirmish, and the mages responded with the fire of a hundred kilns." Her voice faded to a broken whisper.

Garret found nothing to say. He wrapped himself around Pel while his thoughts drifted to the scenes of the past weeks. The sobering present was enough to make him want to close his eyes and hold her all the tighter.

# DAY
# 14

# Netherby – Pel

Pel suffered through her second night of insomnia. As before, she and Garret had been given shelter in one of the ranchers' homes. But tonight, the townsfolk had assembled an impromptu militia that patrolled the village around the clock. Garret volunteered to provide some experience on the night shift. She had lain awake for most of the night.

Pel had hoped the time alone would offset some of the sadness, melancholy, and disappointment that suffocated her. For nearly two weeks, her all-consuming concern was that the Tower would capture Deodin and find some way to use him in their studies.

Now, that would never be. Deodin had never been *sheyaktu* to begin with. Even if he was, he was dead. The events hadn't ended in victory, but nor did they result in defeat. The Tower would be no better off today than it had been a month ago. Everything would return to the way things were.

Absent, of course, an orc horde that marched against the entire region.

She sighed heavily, but the deep breath didn't clear the tension and anxiety in her ribs. Orcs might kill her tonight, in Netherby. Or tomorrow, on the way back to Ruby. Or later in the week, when the horde attacked the city itself.

Perhaps the fates would spare her life, in exchange for Garret's. Or in exchange for Ruby itself. It would be a cruel end for Ruby, to survive Skycrash only to succumb to orcs centuries later.

Pel rolled over to her other side, to face the bedroom window. The drapes were closed, but she could see the morning light through the gaps in the window coverage. It was dawn, but she couldn't remember if she had even slept.

She was exhausted, but not because of the travel, the sleepless nights, the anxiety, or the dread. Instead, the fatigue came from carrying a constant, crushing burden of knowledge. From this point forward, she knew a return to her previous life was the best possible outcome. Every other outcome promised to be worse.

That frightened her as much as everything else.

# DAY
# 16

# The Thick
# (The road to Ruby) – Garret

Garret marveled at how the Netherby villagers had responded to the orc attack.

Three days before, the orcs had attacked and razed the inn. The day after that, the villagers had assembled and voted to gather what they could and flee south to seek refuge within Ruby's walls. Yesterday had been spent in preparation for that escape.

And currently, more than seventy villagers marched southward, carrying whatever belongings they could. At their current pace, it would take another day and a half to reach Ruby.

Their decisiveness impressed Garret. The orc presence was indisputable, the threat entirely real. And rather than balk, rather than make excuses, rather than pretend that everything would be fine, the whole lot of them elected to fuck off and run away.

The "easier" decision would be to remain and fight for their homes, property, and livelihoods. And ultimately die at the end of an orc spear. Instead, here they were, walking with their possessions loaded on carts, strapped to their backs, or carried in their arms.

He and Pel were part of this flight. With Deodin having met his fate, there was no longer any reason to head into the Thick. The oncoming Encroachment was the only thing that mattered.

Curiously, Entorak harbored no resentment for their actions. Despite their attempt to smuggle Deodin out of Ruby, he considered them to be victims.

"You were kidnapped," he had explained. "Whether under direct threat or through manipulation of words, you felt you had no choice. If you had no choice, how can you be at fault? How can you be blamed?"

Even though they were alive, free from the Tower's pursuit and heading back to their homes, Garret felt hollow.

Pel noticed and squeezed his hand. They walked at the tail end of Netherby's parade of people and their property. Away from curious ears, they reflected on the recent events.

"Was it all a lie?" Garret murmured to Pel. "Not just the magic part, but the rest of him. The rest of who he was?"

"I don't know," she admitted. "Everything seemed so sincere. Genuine."

"I thought he was a good man. And a friend," Garret said. "Take away everything before the other day and what do you have? A man who single-handedly rescued a merchant caravan from marauding orcs. A man who saved us from the burning inn and a different group of marauding orcs. A man who was thoughtful enough to light the camp so that you could see the world again."

"And that's it, isn't it?" Pel asked with a sigh. "Deodin was a thoughtful man. I watched him in the Evertorch, on the first night. He was completely respectful to the merchants. And even when they turned on him and confronted him, he tried to shoo them off with a light show. With all that power, whether he was *sheyaktu* or not, I never saw him abuse it to get what he wanted. Unlike Entorak, who used magic to convince the villagers to leave Netherby."

"Really? The other day?" Garret asked.

"Yes. During their vote. He pushed the hesitant ones to vote for leaving. I didn't realize it at the time, but he's been pushing them off and on for the past few days. Look there."

She nodded to Entorak, who walked some twenty or thirty yards ahead of them, next to a young mother who rode in one of the carts. The older mage handed her a bag. She nodded, bowed, and offered a meager smile of thanks.

"He just pushed her. I can see his aura," Pel said. "He tried to offer her part of his food rations. She was being polite and refused. He pushed her into accepting." She turned to face Garret, her expression sober. "She's still nursing her child. She absolutely needs the food more than he does. And he used magic to ensure that she took it."

Garret thought about that for a moment.

"Fucking hells."

"It's the same magic I saw from him the other day. I noticed it, but I wasn't sure what it meant until I saw it a few more times."

"Changing the vote may have been the right thing to do. The ones who wanted to stay were just going to get everyone else killed," Garret said.

"Certainly. Does that make him a hero for manipulating them against their will for the greater good? Or a tyrant for taking away their right to choose?" Pel asked.

"Can it be both?" Garret returned after a moment of consideration.

"I hate it," she said. "And I hate it not because he did it, but because I find myself agreeing with him. I find myself applauding him for doing it. That woman *should* take the food he offered. The villagers *should* be fleeing from Netherby as fast as they can. And thanks to Entorak's pushing magic, they are."

She paused a short while.

"And the worst part? I wouldn't have had the courage to make that same choice, if I had the power. I'd leave them to the consequences of their decisions. I'd have just walked away from Netherby, even if that meant condemning everyone to their fate—a fate I truly believe to be doomed. How does that make me right? Or better? Or would I simply be cowardly taking the easier path?"

Garret had no reply. He simply took her hand.

"A man I have every reason to hate may be the noblest person here. And the man I had thought to be righteous and just? He tried to execute a handful of men who had been convicted of no crimes," Pel reflected.

Garret squeezed her hand. She leaned in and put her head on his chest.

"The hardest part is being wrong. Wrong about Deodin. Wrong about Entorak. The things I was so sure about, the truths that were so certain, are now all gray and blurry. Just like everything else I see in this miserable world."

She felt the tears fall down her cheeks. It was a small release of an otherwise oppressing and overwhelming sense of disappointment.

"None of us see the world perfectly, Pel," Garret said. "And, perhaps, even when we do, we perfectly see an imperfect world. All I can say now is this: whatever Entorak is, he has earned my gratitude and thanks. And whatever Deodin was, whatever he did, he has also earned my gratitude and thanks."

He drew in close enough to kiss the top of her head.

# The Thick
# (Lyle Makee's tomb) – Deodin

Once again, Deodin stood before a boulder the size of a small building, the marker for the next part of his questing.

His death near the rancher's barn in Netherby had been a ruse, of course. He created and executed the ploy to separate himself from Pel and Garret, to ensure they wouldn't risk their lives to help him in his endless questing. Throughout his life, he had lost too many friends who had wedged themselves into his adventures. Deodin had learned that the most consistent feature of the Universe was that it was faithfully merciless.

One of the fallen mages from the inn had served as his body double. Deodin had reproduced his tattoo on the man's inner forearm as part of his preparation. Once he provoked the red mages, Deodin paused time long enough to swap in the mage's remains.

Following the theatrics of the battle, Deodin lurked nearby to ensure that Pel and Garret recovered from his spell. Likewise, he wanted to ensure that they were not punished or harmed for helping him.

The rhetoric about the "Keepers of Men" seemed to work. While Pel and Garret were unconscious, the eldest mage had found the script on the inner arm of the charred remains. Later, when talking with Pel, he had gestured to the mark. Pel had done the same thing when speaking with

Garret. They had all correctly assembled and believed the clues he left for them.

Deodin assumed that Pel would be the most difficult one to convince, but she had seemed genuinely distraught by his charade. It pained him to watch her suffer, but it would pain him more to lose her and Garret entirely.

Deodin's friends and loved ones would eventually be pulled into the game. The people important to him always wanted to help, yet their desire to help would lead them into danger. A necessity of being *sheyaktu* was to drive those people away before they could be entangled in the bullshit. It was the only sensible, merciful option he had.

As much as Deodin enjoyed their company, Pel and Garret didn't belong in Makee's tomb. They certainly had no reason to be nearby when Deodin confronted "the queen." The two had earned the right to go home and live their lives. They deserved no less.

*Take that, Universe.* Deodin smiled, savoring the minor, bittersweet victory over his lifelong antagonist.

With his friends safely heading home, he could focus on the quest that had brought him to the Crown in the first place. After a day of travel to the foothills east of Netherby, he stood before an ancient landmark known as "A tear from a god."

*The name is growing on me.*

The texts had described it as a grand, magnificent monument fitting of Makee's legacy. He imagined that it would be polished and shiny, like a work of art. But he realized that if it were more prominent, it would have been long since been found by explorers and looters.

Well. *Other* explorers and looters.

So, while the landmark served as a navigational guide, it certainly didn't look like the entrance to the resting spot of Lyle Makee, the first recorded *sheyaktu*, the man who had later earned the moniker "The Horror."

*Learn the secrets of Lyle Makee's tomb:*

- ☑ *Find the entrance*
- ☐ *Find the library*

Deodin found the narrow doorway that sealed off Makee's tomb. The entrance had been built at an angle, lying flush with the hillside, half-buried in dirt and covered in brush. It took a few minutes for Deodin to remove enough debris to open the door.

Having survived an untold number of adventures, he had long since learned the rules about exploring lost tombs and ruins, the first of which being:

## Rule #1: Bring a pickaxe

The door was heavy and sealed, but after clearing away the dirt and growth, he had enough room to drive the head of the pick into the seam between the door and its frame. He levered the door ajar and was rewarded with a puff of cool air that smelled of dust, decay, and a minor bouquet of...

Berries? How nice. Most crypts smelled like decomposing feet.

He squeezed through the gap and descended the narrow steps into a cube-shaped room, about ten feet wide, long, and tall. Instead of the tomb and library of Lyle Makee, Deodin found only disappointment.

*Gods dammit.* This was his punishment for daring to be optimistic.

None of the texts or clues said anything about a giant subterranean structure. There were no mentions of vast underground catacombs. If the Universe wasn't such an ass-hole, Makee's tomb could have been a single room with no additional drama.

Instead, it was another dungeon. He sighed.

The room looked to be the entrance to something much larger. Two inexplicably lit torches hung on either side of a doorway, on the wall opposite the entrance. They cast just enough light to accent the minimalist character and charm of a stone-walled room whose wooden and leather furnishings had long since rotted away. What remained felt dusty and lifeless, with a faint breeze coming from the large, open entryway. An archway separated the entry room from a hallway that led deeper into the underground structure.

As Deodin approached the entryway, he could see that it was built from carved blocks of stone and decorated by a series of glyphs. He wasn't an expert in the ancient version of Orc, but he recognized most of the words. They expressed the sentiments one might expect to find while defiling and pillaging the tomb of the most important historical figure in the region: *Go away. Warning. Death. Land squid.*

*Land squid? Was that right?* His brow furrowed as he briefly wondered how well he remembered his Orcish vocabulary.

He turned his attention to the narrow corridor beyond the arch. Like the entrance room, sconces on the walls bore lit torches that barely illuminated the hallway's features. From there, a long, straight staircase descended for another thirty yards, ending in a closed doorway. In the soft, flickering light of the torches, Deodin saw two different lumps of rags that rested on the floor near the left-side wall.

Deodin groaned. The rags were not rags, but rather the clothing and remains of adventurers who had chosen to ignore the second rule of a dungeon expedition:

## Rule #2: The entryway is always trapped

He took a moment longer to examine the coloring of the steps, the jagged edges of the staircase, and the ominously placed holes in the walls. The layout had all the signs of a spear trap that would strike from the right side of the hall. He stepped onto the staircase, careful to stay on the top step. Satisfied that he wouldn't activate any part of the apparatus, he slid the pickaxe from his pack and buried its head into the hallway's right side wall.

He scored a solid hit, with the stone and mortar exploding in a chalky, dusty cloud. The wall gave way easily, far more easily than would appear possible. He took another swing to widen the hole. A few more strikes and he could almost pass through to the other side.

The longer he spent in dungeons, the more time Deodin spent thinking about them. The most interesting part was the construction work. Take a trapped hallway, for instance. Simple pit traps could be built after the rest of the corridor had been completed. A pit could always be added as an afterthought.

However, traps with moving parts and complicated mechanisms had to be built before the space was complete. The interior hallway wall must be added later, after the trap had been installed and tested.

Deodin took a nearby torch from its sconce and peered inside the hole he had just cut into the wall. He could see the elaborate setup of gears that were used to project and retract the spears.

While not quite as ridiculous as troll caves, dungeons taxed Deodin's suspension of disbelief. If ancient civilizations had the resources and ingenuity to make automated spear traps, why not use that cleverness to mill trees? Or carve stone into uniform bricks? There were infinitely more practical uses of that knowledge and skill, yet the Universe chose to reserve that ingenuity for dungeons and dungeons only.

Behind the façade, the gear-covered wall disappeared beyond the light of his torch. He could even see the tips of the spears that those gears would drive. The whole mechanism was uniform and had been precisely manufactured and installed.

The craftsmanship was first rate.

Nevertheless, the murderous trap stood between him and his goal. He drove the head of the pick into the space behind one of the gears, leveraged the gear out of alignment, and jammed it into the gear next to it. He tested it with his mattock. The mechanism fought back as he tried to force it to move.

Satisfied that he had locked the gearing, Deodin picked up one of the heavy flagstones that had fallen from the façade wall. With a spin, he chucked it down the hall, sending it clattering, crashing, and tumbling down the steps. The cacophony created far too much noise for him to hear the pressure plates activate, but as the rock rolled down the stairs, it set the trap in action.

The gears started and seized abruptly, filling the corridor with the sound of breaking stone. Something in the mechanism caught and snapped violently, jolting one of the gears off its moorings and fracturing another. A thin haze of dust drifted from the hole Deodin had punched into the false wall. The spears never emerged. He took a moment to slide the pickaxe back into its loop on his pack before walking down the stairs.

Deodin sighed, regretting that he'd had to destroy the machinery. The spear mechanism was over three hundred years old, constructed shortly after Makee's death. It was as much a triumph of art as it was of engineering. He stepped on a stair that clicked under his weight. Nothing else happened.

He reached the end of the hallway to the closed door. Now that he drew near, he could see that it was carved from a single block of stone and featured a series of large concentric circles, each inlaid with evenly spaced shapes and glyphs. The circles were raised above the surface of the door in a way to suggest that they could be rotated about their center. This was a puzzle-based locking mechanism. Deodin studied the door.

*What, am I supposed to arrange the circles in a specific order?*

He considered it for a few moments longer before deciding that he really didn't care what the pattern was supposed to be or how to correctly manipulate the lock.

He shrugged, seriously questioning the mindset of a person who decided to implement a door made from stone. Doors need to move. Stone was stupidly heavy. To make it strong enough to survive a serious assault, it would be too heavy to move.

Therefore, if it *could* move, it couldn't be strong enough to survive a serious assault. This was the next rule that he had learned during his adventures:

## Rule #3: Stone has limitations as a building material

He retrieved his pick again. With a heave, he drove the point into the lower corner of the door, where it would be the weakest. The strike chipped out a substantive chunk. The door would not survive more than a handful of these blows.

For this much weight, they could have built a steel-reinforced wooden door that would have taken Deodin days to hack through. He struck once more and blasted away another chunk of the door.

The trap builders would have been pissed to learn that they had created such a beautiful trap to protect such a shitty door.

*   *   *

The next chamber was so awesomely large that Deodin wondered how the tomb engineers supported the weight of the walls, the ceiling, and the hillside above it in a room with square corners and no support pillars. He concluded that they couldn't have. The Universe didn't enforce physical laws in its dungeons.

"Bullshit!" he called out.

*"Bullshit!"*

*"Bullshit!"*

The echo was satisfying.

The chamber was lit by torches along the walls and braziers hanging from the ceiling. The only door to the next part of the catacomb was on the far side of the room. The doorway was thirty feet above the ground, but there was no staircase or ladder to reach it.

There were, however, a dozen platforms arranged at different heights, sporadically placed across the room. Most of these platforms connected with horizontal grooves that ran along the walls. Finally, many of these platforms were near levers installed on the nearby walls.

Deodin approached a lever that was on the ground near the entrance and pulled it. The chamber came alive with the heavy, grinding groan of stone gears. One of the platforms about ten feet off the ground moved horizontally, which brought it closer to a platform that was five feet off the ground. A few seconds later, it moved back and returned to its starting point. The lever next to him clicked and reset itself.

He studied the locations of the platforms and the switches. Based on their layout, each platform must be controlled by a different switch. He would need to pull the correct lever at the perfect time to account for the movement of its corresponding ledge, then jump from platform to platform during the interval of their—

*Nope*, he decided.

He walked over to the far side of the room, beneath the exit, and examined the wall. It was made from hewn stone, but the stones were imperfect, and their irregularities were gapped by centuries-old mortar that had begun to fail. He retrieved a long, wooden spike from his pack and drove it into a knee-high gap between two of the stone blocks until it was snug. He climbed up on it to make sure it could support his weight.

He sighed as he climbed back down to remove the other wooden spikes from his pack. His makeshift pegboard ladder would take a few minutes to install, but it was faster, safer, and immeasurably less ridiculous than navigating the room by pulling levers and jumping from platform to platform.

As he climbed the wall to the doorway, Deodin held a debate with himself. While he wouldn't be climbing the walls if it were not for rule #3, he decided that his choice to navigate this room was a better example of the next adventuring rule:

## Rule #4: Bring your own ladder

\*  \*  \*

Deodin found himself at the end of another long corridor that opened into an enormous natural cavern. He stood on a ledge, overlooking the pit below him.

It measured fifty by fifty feet. On the far side, an open staircase ascended from the pit to a raised platform where a sarcophagus rested, surrounded by several large, wooden chests. Brilliant, white evertorches lit the area, the harsh light glinting off the golden accents. A fully populated bookshelf lined the side wall of the sepulchre. Each of these books promised to be as old as Makee himself. Beyond the arrangement of the room, Deodin could see another passageway just past the bookshelf. In his experience, that passageway was likely an exit.

Residing in the center of the pit, blocking the path to his goal, waited a gods-damned tentacled monster the size of a whale. Covered in a rubbery, purple-and-green carapace and featuring a giant, singular eyeball, the monster pulsated, a dozen or so jiggly arms protruding from its slug-like body. It featured not one, but two mouths, seemingly because a single mouth wouldn't be alien or monstrous enough. It glistened in slime and wallowed in a greenish-yellow mist that Deodin presumed to be toxic, acidic, or both.

*Land squid? It looked more like a slug-octopus.*

In his adventures, Deodin had explored dozens of crypts, ruins, caverns, and labyrinths. Each of them featured some sort of "boss monster" that stood between Deodin and the dungeon's final treasure. The horrifying and ridiculous creature below him would certainly be the dungeon's final adversary.

Of course, Deodin couldn't simply walk up to the boss monster and punch it in the face. Boss monsters were normally immune to direct, conventional attacks and could only be defeated by leveraging a feature unique to the environment. Perhaps the adversary could be weakened by nearby explosions, or tripped by roots and vines, or slowed by an icy surface.

He examined the pit itself. The walls were approximately twenty feet tall and carved into a sheer, polished rock face.

Regardless of rules 3 and 4, he didn't think he could climb out while being assailed by a many-armed monster and whatever creatures it would undoubtedly summon. After a few moments of study, he concluded there was no obvious way to escape the pit once he entered it, other than the passage on the other side, past the slugtopus thing.

"I can taste your magic. It is … different from the others … so savory…"

It took Deodin a moment to realize the voice existed as a communication in his mind, not the sound from anything's lips and lungs.

"I am not from around here," Deodin replied, briefly wondering if it was necessary to vocalize his response. He placed his hands on his hips and continued to survey the scene. The telepathic monster had more to say.

"Sooooo delicious…"

The slugtopus was clearly enticed by all of this, as its tentacles writhed in wiggly anticipation.

"Mmmm hmm…" Deodin replied, eyeing the pit layout.

Four similar pedestals surrounded the slugtopus, each object placed at opposing corners of the pit. They had tubes or pipes that all pointed toward the ceiling. Drawing imaginary lines from them, Deodin could see that they seemed to converge on a single point. And conveniently, emerging from the ceiling directly over the enormous slugtopus, hung a dagger-shaped stalactite the size of a tree. Perhaps those structures could be used to focus magical power to the giant stalactite. And if it were to fall, it would certainly impale the monster below—

Deodin groaned, annoyed by the cavern's nonsensical layout and the implicit instructions on how to slay the slugtopus. While troll caves were frustrating for their unrealistic uniformity, boss fights were infuriating because they had to be "solved" by identifying and navigating an arbitrary set of mechanics specific to the dungeon.

"I hungerrrrrrrr…" the monster complained. The mouths on the slugtopus dripped additional slime in anticipation of its next meal.

"Give it a gods-damned rest!" Deodin picked up an orange-sized rock, heaved it into the center of the pit, and hit the giant beast on its sluggy carapace.

"That was unnecessaryyyyyyyyyyyyyy," the slugtopus called out in his mind, after a short pause.

With the slugtopus momentarily quieted, Deodin surveyed the rest of the room without distraction. The cavern's ceiling featured a great deal of irregular pits and grooves, the result of years of pieces shaking free.

*Ha! Rule #4 after all! Take that, Universe!*

Deodin did not consider himself to be much of a rock climber, but he could use magic to help him navigate to the handholds on the ceiling, on his way to the stalactite. He could also use magic to wrest it free from its perch and, later, survive the fall from the height. He plotted a mental path of handholds to the giant stalactite and concluded that his plan would work.

He picked up his pack and went to the edge of the pit, where he dropped the supplies to leave himself free to maneuver. He then set out to climb the dome-shaped ceiling, toward the giant, prominent, and ridiculously placed stalactite.

The slugtopus watched, its mouths salivating, its tentacles tentacling. It waited in hungry anticipation as Deodin scaled the ceiling hand over hand. He arrived at the giant spike-shaped rock and wrapped his arms and legs around it tightly. With another spell to help manipulate his inertia and momentum, he began to push and pull on the rock by rocking and swaying. Small pieces of stone chipped away from above him, falling into the pit below.

"Uhhhh..." the monster said in Deodin's mind.

The slugtopus' giant unblinking eye focused straight up, finally interpreting the turn of events. Its tentacles changed their behavior; they now faced down as if they were trying to act as legs. However, the beast had grown far too big and heavy to be able to move by itself.

"You've lived here for how long and never saw this coming? What in the hells do you look at all day with that giant, stupid eyeball?" Deodin asked, rocking all the more. Pebbles rained into the pit.

The giant stalactite began to give way from its root in the ceiling. Suddenly, it came free. As it began to fall, Deodin pushed himself away from the rock, disengaging and magically slowing his descent.

As predicted, the stalactite sliced downward and impaled the slugtopus through its giant eye in a cacophonous crash and an explosion of dust and detritus. The eye itself erupted in a high-pressure release of multicolored goo as Deodin gently landed nearby. Shortly after the slugtopus twitched for the last time, the surrounding green-and-yellow mist dissipated.

Deodin retrieved his pack, feeling a modest measure of satisfaction. Not because he had defeated the dungeon's final guardian, but because he refused to cooperate with the Universe's absurdly orchestrated plans. He was reminded of the final rule of dungeon exploration:

## Rule #5: Boss fights are tedious and asinine

The slugtopus slain, Deodin approached the alcove carved out of the far side of the cavern. He followed the right side of the pit, up the stairs to the alcove. Deodin was seldom moved by majesty or splendor, but even he felt a sense of awe. Before him were the artifacts belonging to the most significant man in history.

The script on the sarcophagus was old, but it marked this area to be the final resting spot of Lyle Makee. It was surrounded by volumes of books on shelves, in which Deodin saw a priceless bounty of lore. He believed these works to house a great deal of Makee's personal history, his study of magic, and how his magic could be better understood.

Here awaited the secret to unlocking the answers to magic's greatest questions. And with that, Deodin hoped to find out how to stop "the queen" that threatened the Crown.

*Learn the secrets of Lyle Makee's tomb:*

☑  *Find the entrance*
☑  *Find the library*

*  *  *

On a pedestal next to Makee's coffin rested a large, purple book with silver trim. The arrangement of the book in relationship to everything else suggested it was intended to be the first thing any would-be tomb robber saw. Makee had left a message. Deodin obliged him by opening the book and turning to the first page. The first remarks alarmed him.

> *Please allow me to offer my congratulations on being born sheyaktu and living long enough to reach this point!*
>
> *And please allow me to offer my condolences, because you've gone and fucked it all up and you need to fix it.*

More alarming was that a man from three hundred years in the past seemed quite attuned to Deodin's current plight. And he got right to the point in his next paragraphs.

> *Orcs? Rampaging monsters and a malevolent force that drives them? A world that defies logic? A world that demands your constant acts of selfless heroism? A series of cryptic clues that led you here?*

> *Yes, I can explain all of that. No, you will not like that explanation.*
>
> *Nevertheless, if you are here reading this, it means you must stop whatever calamity currently threatens the world. And you need to do it now. You are one of many in the long line of poor bastards who are doomed to this fate.*
>
> *I'll explain as we go. Take this book. It was left by the poor bastard who came before you. And when you are done, you'll return the book to that same spot, as a courtesy to the next poor bastard.*
>
> *Consult the map and find the lost "Village of the Dying Moon." Once you're there, turn to the next chapter.*

Deodin sighed. Makee promised an answer to all the aggravating imperfections and inconsistencies in the world that could no longer be ignored. He promised a vision of the truth that, deep down, Deodin knew he was never really supposed to see. And in doing so, he offered him another quest. It was maddening.

He turned to the next page of the book. It showed a map that was relative to the location of the tomb itself, with a spot marked to the northeast. Deodin reckoned it was a few days' journey from Makee's tomb, toward the foothills that separated the Crown from the East.

Deodin felt the mental checklist form in his mind. The Universe was telling him something.

*Confront the Big Bad:*

☐ *Find the bullshit ruins*
☐ *Defeat the minions*
☐ *Engage in pointless dialogue*
☐ *Defeat the lieutenant*

He didn't really want to go confront a monster called the "Big Bad." He just wanted to jump ahead to the discussions about the Universe. But Makee didn't want to talk about that yet.

Deodin flipped ahead in the book's pages, with a strong suspicion of what he would find. The suspicion was immediately confirmed.

*What did I just say? Explanations come later. Off you pop.*

The rest of the pages of the purple book were blank.

# DAY 17

# Ruby (City Hall) – Mathew

It was almost painful to think about. Mathew felt a sickly anxiety as the council members read the reports from the courier birds. The experience was surreal and miserable. He wanted to be anywhere other than Ruby's city hall.

The council needed Tower representation to help navigate this crisis. With Entorak out and about and Richard too consumed with his snipe hunt to worry about Ruby and its people, Mathew had been conscripted. It was not a role he relished or chose, but he could not leave the responsibility to one of the red mages.

The orcs had attacked. The Encroachment was real. The orc threat was no longer speculation. Lives had been lost and an army marched on Ruby.

The meeting chamber was a large, poorly lit auditorium. Mathew sat among the council members at a semicircle of tables arranged at the front of the room. The few candles and evertorches on the wall cast minimal light, while the rest of the seating in the audience portion of the chamber remained empty, dark, and quiet.

The tone of the council meeting was as grim as the lighting. To begin, Avram, the council facilitator, spoke for a good ten minutes about the most recent news from Netherby. The village had been lost. Shortly after its evacuation, the orcs had put the entire town to the torch.

His report from Andwyn was worse. The village was

gone. The people could not mount an evacuation in time. A traveler had seen the carnage firsthand before he escaped and shared the news. More than fifty townsfolk had been slaughtered.

When the room fell to shocked silence, Avram continued with even more bad news.

"Delemere has closed its gates and its people have withdrawn into the mountain. They can survive for months, if need be. And the smaller towns on the other side of the Kalee report that they have moved to protect the bridges. Right now, they are on high guard, but they haven't reported any orc attacks," Avram continued with a defeated exhale. "That just means they are coming here."

*Fuuuck.* Mathew felt a dull pang of nausea. The men and women around him clearly felt the same sense of apprehension and fear. He looked back at Avram, who waited for the room's collective reaction.

Mathew had only met Avram earlier that day, but he found himself impressed by the man's poise and the way he managed the council meeting. A physically unimposing man of dark skin and hair, Avram had such a presence about him that he had successfully united the leaders of otherwise rival factions at the table. And considering the news he shared, those factions were unusually patient and cooperative.

Orcs. Orcs everywhere, it seemed. The two smallest villages on the outskirts of Ruby had been raided by orc forces over the past few days. Buildings had been destroyed. Lives had been lost. The routes through the Thick to the north were surely forfeit. And with that news, Ruby faced the reality of additional concerns. Refugees. Economic crisis. Food shortage. War. Mathew absently ran his hands through his hair. He felt sick.

With a shuffle of commotion, soft murmurs, and hushed whispers, the various members of the council reacted to the news. Their concerns were real. Could Ruby arm itself in time? Would there be enough food to outlast a siege?

Mathew felt a sensation in his mind, providing him with courage he didn't know he had. He cleared his throat once Avram came to a logical pause.

"Forgive me for being inexperienced with all of the inner workings of the council and Ruby's affairs," he began. "With the curdain being only a local currency, will the city have enough standard coin to pay for outside assistance?"

Avram looked to a man on his right, one of the bankers who operated within the Evertorch. The heavyset man scrunched his face for a moment before answering with short panting breaths. "For a short while," he explained, exchanging glances with the others in the room and choosing his words delicately. "The ... ah ... majority of the standard wealth is managed by the Tower."

The man tiptoed around the unpleasant truth that if the city were to collapse financially because of its nonstandard currency, it would be the Tower's fault.

Mathew stood up and removed the gold rings from his fingers. They felt heavy and dense as he walked over to Avram and held out his closed hand, palm down. Avram reached up to receive them and Mathew gave them away with no ceremony or hesitation. Instead, he spoke as he made his way back to his seat.

"We'll make it available," he said. "Ruby will need the aid of its neighbors. What they can't give, we will have to buy.

Understand that I don't know the limits of what the Tower can offer, and should the orcs march on us, the mages will need some of those resources to fuel the magic to defend Ruby and its people.

"But until we have conquered the challenges that we face..." Mathew said with his head down. He paused a moment before looking back up to address the others. "...we must make sacrifices."

There was no stirring round of applause or bombastic ovation, but Mathew's gesture proved to be enough. Cooperation flowed from that point, with a for-the-greater-good camaraderie among the members of the council. His offering had been enough to start the motion, which then moved by itself.

*   *   *

Hours passed. The intensity of the council session hardly waned. Amid a heated discussion about food distribution to the refugees, the council chamber doors opened loudly enough to interrupt the proceedings.

A man hastily strode down the council chamber aisle. Seeing nothing more than the man's gait and posture, Mathew could identify him. As could the others.

"Entorak!" Avram exclaimed when the mage finally entered the light of the council table. The surprise in Avram's tone matched the expressions worn by everyone seated at the tables.

*Holy shit. What a mess.*

Entorak was a disaster. His normally decadent clothes had been worn into ruined rags and stained with dirt and blood. Evidently, he hadn't changed his clothes in several days. He could look no worse if a horse had reversed the roles and rode him.

In Entorak's case, however, the clothes would never make the man. With his straight-backed posture, he sauntered to the table, helping himself to a carafe of wine and pouring its contents into an unclaimed glass.

Despite interrupting one of the most important meetings in Ruby's history, he casually dragged a chair from the audience portion of the hall and placed it front and center of the arrangement of council tables. He sat himself down, closed his eyes for just a moment, and took a drink of the wine, quite aware that he had killed all the meeting's productivity.

"We have but a few days to prepare for war," he said, opening his eyes. "We accompanied the refugees from Netherby, marching day and night to stay ahead of the orc skirmishers. Their army, or horde, or however you choose to describe it, follows a few days behind."

Entorak turned his gaze to Avram.

"We will require that the refugees—"

"The refugees' needs have been addressed," Mathew interrupted. Entorak or not, the council was not going to restart all the work that had already been done, just because he showed up late. "The men and women of the council will have Ruby prepared for the challenges we face, even if the timetable is faster than we had anticipated."

"My friend, Ruby makes its preparations," Avram said, attempting to de-escalate the tension between the mages. "We have sent orders to expect and admit refugees. We are set to launch and accept ships, for both aid and arms, to and from our brothers and sisters to the south. Ruby's soldiers are set to equip the members of the militia, as the weapons come in. The only thing we didn't know, until now, was how much time we had to prepare."

"That and the numbers," Entorak said. "Seventy-three refugees from Netherby. The orcs themselves number in the thousands. Perhaps in upwards of ten thousand."

A tide of commotion rose among the council members, all of them stirred by the notion of a siege of that size. The whispers and gasps were cut short when Avram turned to face them with angry, narrow eyes.

"This news changes nothing. And now we know how much time we have to prepare. Time that grows shorter the more we laze about here!" Avram made a large shooing gesture with his hands.

Taking the cue, the council members began to stand and collect their things.

Mathew cleared his throat. "This is the first time I've ever seen this council in session. Most of my time is spent in an ivory tower far removed from the Ruby day-to-day. And yet, I cannot express how amazed I am by the likes of this. By the likes of you. I stand humbled—so unbelievably reassured by your competence and your hearts. I have never been more honored and privileged to be a part of something so significant."

Mathew's speech elicited a collective response in the form of slow, deliberate nods of respect and appreciation. The meeting had ended and it appeared that everyone simultaneously understood their place in such a monumental event—and their place in history.

Soon enough the chamber was vacant, with only Entorak and Mathew remaining. The former was still seated and breathing deeply with his eyes closed. Mathew briefly wondered if he had fallen asleep.

Entorak spoke.

"Did you think to offer the Tower's coffers to the council, so they can do business outside the city?"

Mathew found the tone interesting. Entorak's question came as if he and Mathew had already discussed the matter and he was just following up. Mathew would have normally presumed that such an offering would be met with resistance, yet here, Entorak was double-checking to ensure that it happened.

"Yes," Mathew replied. "Under the provisions that I was neither in the position to decide how much to provide nor could I physically disburse it."

"Quite right," Entorak replied. "Allow me to address it when I get back to the Tower. There will be less conflict if I give the order."

Mathew had anticipated a confrontation, posturing, leveraging, selfishness, and other assorted Tower politicking. Instead, it seemed as if Entorak had already thought through these conditions and had expected Mathew to come to the same conclusions and execute the same decisions.

"I'm going to finish this wine and close my eyes for a bit," Entorak said. "Then I'll head to the Tower and start putting things in motion. And be sure to wake Mica on your way out. It looks as if she fell asleep."

*Mica? Here?*

Mathew scanned the dimly lit seats in the gallery portion of the room. One of the seats had a different shape than the others. Mathew ascended the chamber's wide steps to the woman curled up on one of the chairs. Mica was fast asleep.

She awoke with a start, glanced at him, then scanned the nearby area as she gained her bearings. She stiffened when she recognized Entorak resting in the center of the room. She was suddenly wide awake.

"We should leave," she whispered.

*   *   *

Mica brought Mathew out of the City Hall chambers to an empty alley that led back toward the Tower.

"You handled that very well," she said. "Ruby will be as prepared as she can be. You are a true leader, speaking for the interests of peasants like me."

*Peasant, indeed.*

The Tower's other servants would not sneak into a council meeting nor make light-hearted, self-aware commentary about their social caste. As fond as he was of her, the dealings of tonight had been too serious and grave to waste any more time with pretenses. He stopped and waited for her to turn around before he continued.

"Look. I really like you. You're brilliant and beautiful, but don't think for a moment that I believe you to be a simple servant girl from the East who stumbled into being the Tower's librarian."

The playfulness in her tone dissolved immediately. She scanned the surrounding neighborhood. It was late enough in the evening that they had the alley to themselves.

"Very well. We knew the Encroachment was inevitable. We just didn't know when. Now we do," she said.

"That's not good enough," Mathew insisted. "We've spoken of orcs. We've talked about Entorak's intentions and his plans and schemes. I understand all of that. What I don't understand is *your* role in all of this. Why did you come to the Tower?"

"I came to kill Richard," she said.

Mathew flinched in shock.

"Relax, Mathew. You asked why I *initially* came to the Tower. That plan has changed."

"Why did you want to kill Richard?" Mathew asked in disbelief. This was the first time a librarian had ever confided her murderous intentions to him.

"Well. Everyone should want to kill Richard because he is despicable, loathsome, and the world would be better without him. But to your point, Richard prevents me from freeing the women imprisoned and enslaved in his quarters.

"I could probably get them out of the Tower but he would hunt us down. He would use the red mages. He would use magic. He would vilify us, portray us as monsters, and pursue us as fugitives. I had planned to kill him, only to ensure that we could escape."

"Gods, Mica!" Mathew gasped. "I thought you were going to confess to stealing books."

"There has been some of that too."

Mathew ran his hands through his hair. One of his bosses was somehow involved with an orc horde that marched on Ruby. Now, the girl he fancied conspired to murder his other boss. Today had been quite the emotional journey.

Mica touched his hand and waited until he looked at her. She didn't beg with her eyes. There was no ploy to garner sympathy or sway him over to her cause. She was simply emotionally exhausted.

346

"They are my sisters, Mathew," she said quietly. "I was there when Richard stole them from our home. It has taken me years to find them and maneuver myself here. And when I found them, they were so drugged with magic, they didn't recognize me."

"You've been here for weeks. Why share this with me now?"

"I didn't know who I could trust. And now I need help. I can't do it all by myself."

He believed her. And he knew she was right. He had witnessed the abuses and mistreatment of the women. Freeing those women from Richard's clutches wasn't a choice for her. Nor was it a choice for him. It was a moral imperative. Luckily, her role as librarian was a perfect cover and the Encroachment would help.

"Pack up the library," he suggested. "Prepare the books to be moved. They are irreplaceable and there is a precedent to evacuate them to the Western Isles in times of trouble in Ruby. You can make your move then. The Encroachment will be the distraction you need."

She hesitated before she spoke again.

"I had said that I originally came here to kill Richard as part of my plans. And with most of the red mages spread across the Crown, I had my opportunities. Gods know, the thought occurred to me. But every time, I thought about doing it, I reminded myself of you."

"Me?"

"You wouldn't approve."

He pulled her in for an embrace and leaned forward. They shared a kiss. It was long overdue, but he kept it far shorter than he wanted.

"Back at the Tower, focus on the library. We'll use the preservation of Richard's books as an excuse to get into his room, when the time comes. Stay to the tasks expected of you, I won't always be nearby to protect you."

"'Protect me!'" She laughed. "You're adorable."

# DAY
# 18

# The Thick
# (The Crescent Temple) – Deodin

Deodin looked down from the northern slope of the foothills. The valley certainly resembled the ruins of a long-lost village.

There were clues that this village, in its time, had been prosperous and well developed. A small stone bridge had survived centuries of erosion and still connected opposite sides of a wide creek. A brick retaining wall separated the hillside from a nearby building. A wide path of short bushes and plants marked an ancient road that carved through the valley.

But the village had lost its battle with time. The structures had long since collapsed to ruins. What hadn't crumbled was covered in growth.

On the very far side of the valley, the top third of a four-sided pyramid poked out from the surrounding treetops. It matched what Makee had described in the pages of his purple book. Pages that had been blank only a few moments before.

> *A path will lead to a structure on the far side of the village, such as a temple, mausoleum, or theater. Something large and prominent and obvious. You'll know you're in the right place because it will have symbols related to the crescent moon. In that structure, you will first meet the world-ending creature, which I lovingly call "the Big Bad."*

To this point, Makee was positively prophetic, so much so that Deodin felt the need to comment on it.

"Now that's just a bit much." The tip of the pyramid featured a large, prominent crescent moon.

To be fair, however, Makee had tried to make the appropriate warnings.

> You're going to wonder how this book can have a map that will still be relevant to you, all those years in the future. And when you find the village, you're going to wonder how I was right about it. You have permission to go mad when it is all over.
>
> For now, we're not going to think about it.
>
> I'll share all of that with you after you've saved the world, found a comfortable place to read, and surrounded yourself with bottles of alcohol.

Deodin took Makee's advice and descended to the edge of the village, choosing not to second-guess Makee's ability to see the future. If the nature of troll caves had not unraveled Deodin's sanity, a self-aware book wasn't going to do it, either.

*Confront the Big Bad:*
- ☑ *Find the bullshit ruins*
- ☐ *Defeat the minions*
- ☐ *Engage in pointless dialogue*
- ☐ *Defeat the lieutenant*

In the back of his mind, Deodin hoped that the Big Bad would be interesting in and of itself. Makee explained that there was always an evil that threatened the entire region and everyone in it.

It was the Big Bad who had organized the orc army, displaced the mobs of the Thick, and spearheaded the campaign against humanity. It was the Big Bad that every poor bastard would need to defeat to save the world.

Makee had explained it in his writing:

---

*For me, "the Big Bad" was an elder god. Some sort of ancient, alien deity that slumbered throughout the course of history. Skycrash awakened it. Once it had risen, it sought to quench the light of humanity, bring about the new era of darkness, et cetera, et cetera.*

*Your Big Bad will likely be different.*

*The point is, you have to let it tell you its evil plan. You have to let it explain its motives and its goals. It will then depart to go do something terrible, leaving you to fight its thematically appropriate lieutenant. You must defeat that monster and then make your way to your city. (For me, that city was Tristan. Yours may be different.)*

*But let's not get ahead of ourselves. Go through the ruins and check the book once you have confronted your Big Bad and defeated its underlings.*

---

Deodin tucked the purple book back into his pack and surveyed the ruins. According to Makee's notes, the trip through the village would involve a number of random encounters with the boss's minions. Only at the end of it all would the Big Bad emerge, make its speech, and go about its business. And once Deodin completed this part of his journey, he would unlock the next quests in the series that Makee had lovingly called "the game of the poor bastard."

Deodin scoffed.

As prophetic as Makee was, Deodin was quite capable in his own right. A lifetime of adventuring had uncovered several valuable tips and tricks, shortcuts that Makee probably hadn't known. Deodin had no intention to fight his way through the ruins and whatever monsters infested it. That was for the filthy, casual adventurer.

Centuries of forest overgrowth and the collapse of the village structures had created a narrow, snaking route from the entrance of the village to the temple. The route promised to be densely populated by the Big Bad's bloodthirsty disciples.

Deodin ran. With his head lowered, he tore down the middle of the street, beginning at the open edge of the gauntlet and following its path toward the temple.

And predictably, as soon as he began, figures emerged from the ruins. Clad in purple-and-black hooded robes, the humanoid figures made their threatening gestures, cursed in their exotic language, and brandished their weapons. Seeing that an intruder fled deeper into the gauntlet, they pursued.

*Cultists!*

Deodin smiled to himself as he continued to run, avoiding another group of enemies that emerged from a nearby building and tried to intercept him. They couldn't cut him off, so they joined their brothers and sisters in pursuit.

Of all the enemies that he encountered during his adventures, cultists were among his favorites. First, their moral depravity was never in dispute. Not only did they want to indiscriminately murder every trespasser, they also wanted to murder the entire world by summoning their beloved master. Killing a cultist was never morally ambiguous. It was a civil service.

Furthermore, humanoid cultists usually carried money. Deodin seldom stopped to loot treasure from his fallen enemies, but when did, he much preferred coins to assorted junk carried by other mobs. Never mind that the junk could always be sold to a merchant; it was preferable to carry silver than broken carapaces, scraps of cloth, or assorted entrails.

Another pair of hooded figures emerged from the doorway of a nearby abandoned structure. Beneath their hoods, Deodin could make out large, yellow eyes with vertical, slit pupils. One cultist opened its mouth to reveal a pair of daggerlike fangs as it began to hiss mena—

*Snakemen cultists! Even better!*

In the case of snakemen, genocide itself was morally justified. No need to spare the women and children! And it was completely appropriate to destroy their eggs and younglings! As far as enemies went, Deodin had hit the jackpot.

A great and terrible roar rumbled through the valley. The birds that had not yet been disturbed by the commotion in the ruins took to the sky in unison.

*Dragon! What a day!*

Deodin had always wanted to see a dragon. They were supposed to be beautiful and awe-inspiring.

As he rounded the corner of a collapsed building, the temple came into view. He continued running, glancing over his shoulder to see that he had nearly forty or fifty cultists

354

chasing after him. Occasionally, a cultist would pause to cast a spell, but would be forced to stop once Deodin was out of range or had broken the line of sight.

Finally, he reached the temple's doorway, where he continued his run through the door, down the stairs, and into the heart of the temple.

As soon as he entered the primary chamber, the ambient sound took a more ominous tone. Time itself seemed to slow and the lighting drew attention to motion on the far side of the room.

Deodin had grown accustomed to these kinds of obvious cues. When the Universe had something to say, it often involved a dramatic, stylized set of visuals. As the lighting changed, Deodin glanced over his shoulder to ensure that his pursuers had disappeared. As he had anticipated, they were gone.

*Confront the Big Bad:*
- ☑ *Find the bullshit ruins*
- ☑ *Defeat the minions*
- ☐ *Engage in pointless dialogue*
- ☐ *Defeat the lieutenant*

Deodin chuckled. He relished every opportunity to use the Universe's flaws and inconsistencies against itself. As experienced as Deodin had become in combat, he took greatest delight in avoiding it. He had come to use his resentment as a weapon.

Years ago, he had found a flaw in the underlying mechanics of boss monster behavior (Rule #5) while exploring an ancient subterranean labyrinth. The dungeon was populated by murderous anthropomorphic insects. Throughout the cavern, on his way to their overlord, he had been forced to fight his way through several groups of insectoid defenders.

The boss itself was unremarkable—a floating disembodied head that called itself "The Tormentor of Souls," or something equally pretentious and overstated.

The most memorable part of that encounter, however, came when Deodin entered the room. While still engaged in combat with a group of guardians, he had crossed into the chamber and triggered an event. The lighting and acoustics had become more dramatic as a floating head descended from a ledge on the far side of the wall. And as evil bosses tended to do, the floating head started rambling on about how it was going to enslave humanity, or torment souls, or cripple puppies, or whatever its evil plan happened to be.

However, as soon as the floating head had begun its dialogue, the combat ceased. The insects Deodin had been fighting simply disappeared.

They didn't die. They didn't run away. They vanished.

Deodin concluded that he had uncovered another flaw in the world. When a boss monster had something important to say, any distractions that stood in the way of that message inexplicably ceased to exist. Even the minions that served the boss monster.

That exploit was worth far more than the most valuable treasure in the room. It had ended up saving him hours of his time, as it had here.

On the far side of the chamber, an indistinct mass began to move, eventually taking the shape of a winged, reptilian beast the size of a ship. The sight was breathtaking. The dragon turned its giant, triangular head to face him and uncoiled its long, twitching tail.

Ah, good. The dragon was just about ready to talk.

\* \* \*

"You are not as impressive as I would have hoped," the dragon said. Its normal speaking voice dominated the chamber.

The dragon examined Deodin's choice in footwear for a moment before spending additional time scrutinizing his tunic. The giant offered one last piece of constructive criticism: "It is difficult to decide which is more pitiful, your boots or your blouse."

Deodin hardly heard the insults. He was too captivated by the dragon's movement. Despite its size, the dragon could still control its lips and tongue with enough dexterity to speak the Common language, even if it had difficulty with the hard "t" sound.

"You look fantastic. Very impressive. Are you able to tuck your wings close to your body, or are they always fully extended like that?" Deodin was genuinely curious and sincere in his flattery.

"Silence! A queen does not suffer the clattering inanities of fools!" The dragon flapped her wings menacingly, disapproving of the clattering inanity of a fool.

"Apologies, your … ah … *majesty*. I didn't know you were royalty. And, in all honesty, I had forgotten you were female. Should I bow now, or has the moment passed?"

The dragon roared in outrage. "We'll see how clever you are when you find your world blanketed in fire and raining ash!"

*Just let her do her thing.* As much as Deodin wanted to verbally spar, he also wanted to be on his way.

"Oh, no," he said.

"Do you think the orcs pose a threat to your pitiful city?" the great dragon hissed. "Do you fear their horde as they march toward its walls?"

Deodin was unsure what the correct answer was. Ruby wasn't even really "his" city to begin with, but it seemed rude to interrupt her just to correct her on that point. He stood quietly, considering what the dragon would most want to hear.

"Silence!" the dragon roared with a scowl. "Tell me, little human, do you think you can stop me?"

Again, Deodin paused. The obvious answer was "yes," otherwise he wouldn't be here, but on the other hand, if he said no, he could—

The dragon grinned as if she found his answer amusing. With such supple control of her lips and eyes, she was very clearly smirking, as if she basked in the knowledge of some game-changing secret that only she knew. But, as was common with the bosses Deodin encountered, she was unable or unwilling to keep that secret to herself.

"The fool wizard Entorak thinks he can manipulate me? I shall destroy Ruby's precious Tower and all its mages! And my elite assassins shall stab him through the heart! Such a fitting end to mankind's greatest traitor, don't you think?"

"Sounds good," Deodin agreed.

"Fool!" she bellowed. "I shall plunder the Tower of its treasures! Weapons to outfit my army, spells to char the flesh from bones, power to control the world itself! And without the Tower to stop me, my army shall swarm the Crown, erasing the blight of humanity forever! Your entire world put to the flame, removed from existence and finding the fate your kind so richly deserves!"

A towering, lumbering figure emerged from a passageway on the far side of the chamber. It was huge, standing approximately twelve feet tall as it walked on two legs. Towering above its shoulders was a large set of dragon wings. As it came into the light, Deodin could see that it was scaled and possessed giant, clawed hands. It looked to be a half-human, half-dragon monstrosity.

While the half-dragon was enormous and menacing, Deodin's eyes fell upon the large, double-edged weapon it twirled menacingly. It was as if a blacksmith had fashioned two identical double-edged longswords and attached them at their hilts by a two-foot steel bar. The half-dragon was clearly practiced with the weapon, spinning and twirling it in a dramatic flourish.

"Lord Apo'stra'phii!" bellowed the dragon.

"Yes, Queen Tychryn!" replied the half-dragon monster.

"Slay this intruder!"

"With pleasure, my queen!"

Despite the explicit instruction to kill him, Deodin found himself transfixed on the half-dragon's weapon, not the monster himself.

*How idiotic.* The more aggressively the monster attacked with one end, the more likely he was to strike himself with the other. A simple spear would be a hundred times more deadly and a thousand times safer to wield. Plus, the dragon man could still do all the impressive spinny-twirly shit.

Her instructions given, the great Tychryn readied her wings, crouched, and leapt into the air. As she launched upward, she stirred up a choking, stinging cloud of dust and debris until she burst through the temple's ceiling, freeing tons of stone and mortar as she took to the sky.

Once the dust settled, the sun peered through the giant hole torn in the roof. Standing in the spotlight, Deodin faced off against a giant man-dragon and his preposterous weapon.

*Confront the Big Bad:*
- ☑ *Find the bullshit ruins*
- ☑ *Defeat the minions*
- ☑ *Engage in pointless dialogue*
- ☐ *Defeat the lieutenant*

\* \* \*

The duel with the man-dragon had lasted nearly twenty minutes, but not because the battle itself was a true test of Deodin's skills and mettle. He spent the entire fight maneuvering and goading his enemy into impaling himself on his ill-conceived double-edged, double sword thing.

*Totally worth it,* Deodin concluded as he watched the half-dragon run himself through with the killing blow.

While Deodin's eyesight and hearing were more acute than normal, his sharpest sense was irony.

# Ruby (The Docks) – Pel

A nervous energy infused the docks. As the refugees from the surrounding villages made their way through Ruby's gates, the buzz of the approaching orc horde infected the city. Normal business had ended, with all able-bodied citizens assisting in the preparations.

Now, just the morning after they had returned from Netherby, Pel found herself in the middle of their efforts. The messenger birds had been sent across the Crown, the call for assistance shouted across the region.

Encroachment at Ruby.

She and Garret came to the docks before sunrise. With Pel's knowledge of and experience with the gears of Ruby's machinery, she played a vital role in introducing people and helping to calm the tempers of competitors, rivals, and enemies. If they were lucky, there would be opportunity for self-serving interests and intrigue once all of this was over.

While Pel served Ruby with her mind, Garret had opted to take off his shirt and help with his hands. He wasn't particularly fond of the docks and was downright terrified of the sea, but he refused to leave Pel's side. Until his expertise was needed, he helped in whatever ways he could. She smiled, glad he was here.

Pel couldn't see him clearly, but judging by the way Garret carried his shoulders, he was winded. Offloading *The Maiden's Tears* was tireless work in the best of circumstances. Today was different, with the pace greatly accelerated. Once they had off-loaded *The Maiden's* goods, two other ships awaited their turn.

"Look at that one, will ya? Fit and rugged like a stallion. You've outdone yourself," a familiar voice called out.

She turned her attention from Garret and the dockhands and looked over her left shoulder to find Bartlett standing behind her. He jutted his chin in Garret's direction while eating from a bag of seeds and nuts. He nodded in approval.

"The first words out of your mouth are an assessment of my personal life?" Pel asked. "Amid the greatest crisis of our life-time, it's important enough to judge Garret on his physique?"

"Let's not be daft. I plan to judge him on everything. I'm simply starting with his physique," Bartlett confessed.

He had come ashore about an hour prior, but Pel had not yet had the opportunity to talk to him. His crew needed their captain just as the community at large needed her. The two of them both managed different sides of the expedited delivery of his goods. Now that he was clear of his obligations, he could make time to talk to her.

He directed his attention to Pel. They were standing close enough that she could detect a seriousness to him that she seldom saw.

"Now. Would you rather us chat up about your shirtless friend or the skalg-buggering orc Encroachment? Those are the two main topics of the morning."

"The orcs. Let's hope we can talk about Garret and me another time." She sighed. Talking about Garret was a short-lived distraction from their reality.

The two of them turned to survey the busy dock. Members of the militia had arrived with empty carts to retrieve the weapons Bartlett had brought with him.

"I wish you'd been wrong about this," Bartlett said softly. "I fear this won't be enough."

"When you are done here, are you off to make another run to Bayhold, or up to Peak's View?"

"I don't know, my dear," Bartlett replied with a sigh. "I bought out everyone's steel and arrows. More ships are on their way, bringing whatever aid they can. Other than an army, what else would Ruby need? And if I knew, could I even get it? Would anyone be able to sell? Or willing? Encroachment or not, the cities of the coast have their limits."

"What about the inland cities? Have you heard anything from Tristan or Donkton? Can we hope for aid?" Pel asked, even though she could anticipate the answer.

Tristan was the Crown's easternmost city, on the border of the Bayet river that separated the Crown from the rest of the world. However, if the orcs threatened Ruby, Tristan would likely be their next target. The people of Tristan would most likely be preparing for their own needs.

Donkton was a large, isolated city about eighty miles inland from the coast and on the other side of the Bayet, outside the Crown. Encroachment or not, it had a great deal of local problems. In many ways, Donkton was more dangerous than the Thick, with systemic crime, a culture of deadly political intrigue, and subversive, monstrous influences from the East. Ruby's circumstances would have to be worse for Donkton to offer meaningful aid. And even then, the people of Ruby would be wise to refuse that aid.

"I think Ruby is on its own," Bartlett said.

A fist of anxiety grasped Pel's stomach and chest. During the orc attack in Netherby, she'd had no time for dread. Those few minutes had been terrifying, but that feeling was offset by adrenaline, panic, and desperation. In the days following the destruction of Netherby, that pang of fear and uncertainty had grown from a faint discomfort to a sensation that dominated nearly every waking moment.

Two figures draped in faint magical auras approached from the heart of the city. One of them was Entorak.

"Captain. Pelium," he called.

Pel had become familiar with his voice over the past few days. Entorak had cleaned himself up since the last time she had seen him. Shaved. Rested. A change of clothes. He had returned to his normally poised, polished persona. He stood nearly motionless, holding his left hand in his right.

She didn't recognize the other man. Twenty or twenty-five years younger than Entorak, the man was unlike the other mages she had met. Handsome. Dressed casually and practically, in brown britches and a cream-colored shirt. He wore no jewelry or reagent pouches to suggest he was a mage.

"Captain Bartlett, Pelium," Entorak said, "This is Mathew, one of the more astute mages of his generation and one who promises to be a prominent and respected leader of tomorrow."

Pel nodded.

"Much of all of this," Entorak gestured with both hands at the docks' hustle and bustle, "is the result of Mathew's direction, when he represented the Tower at the most recent city council meeting."

Pel eyed Mathew carefully before glancing back to Entorak, who betrayed no further insight.

"Then we owe you and the Tower another debt, for your generosity and thoughtfulness," Pel said with enough of a nod to be noticed, but not enough to be interpreted as insincere.

Mathew scoffed with enough venom to cause Pel's heart rate to spike. She made it her business to tread delicately around mages, yet Mathew reacted as if he were offended.

"Pelium Stillwater," he began, "the Tower has enjoyed years of prosperity, largely on the backs of the people of Ruby. At best, the Tower has a history of being apathetic and slow to react to Ruby's needs. At worst, the mages of the Tower are responsible for serious crimes. The Tower has a multitude of sins for which it must atone. So, thank you for your kind words, but I believe we both know who owes whom."

Pel looked back to Entorak to see what kind of reaction he would offer, if any. This young mage had just made an outright criticism of Tower policies. He resented many of the same things about the Tower that Pel did. Entorak simply let the moment hang in the air.

"What brings you to the docks, then?" Bartlett said.

"To speak with you." Mathew nodded to the ships in the port. "And the other captains. We hope to arrange your next cargo."

"Ah." Bartlett glanced at the waterfront before turning back. "Me an' Pel were discussing just that. Not so sure of what more I can bring back to Ruby. Only so much to go around. Only so much the other cities have, regardless of what you're willing to pay."

"It is a matter of what you can take to other places," Entorak said.

"We hope for a way to evacuate the Tower's support staff to the Western Isles. They are the guardians of the research conducted in the Tower. Much of that work is irreplaceable and we would like it housed elsewhere," Mathew added.

"Why me? Why my ship?" Bartlett asked.

"Because of your relationship with Pelium and the urgency of the situation," Entorak replied, hardly changing his posture. His apparent indifference was in complete contrast with the seriousness of his remark.

Mathew looked askance at Bartlett, as if he struggled to understand why there was a need for this discussion. His face lightened.

"You must not know! The orcs have assembled just south of the Thick, across from the fields of the northern gate. We expect an attack at nightfall, or at the latest, tomorrow morning."

The nausea in Pel's chest gripped her tighter. She found it hard to swallow.

# The Thick
# (The Crescent Temple) – Deodin

Deodin consulted the purple book. Pages that had previously been blank now featured more of Makee's messages.

> *Finally. We have some time now. The Big Bad will visit your city tonight, just as the orcs make their attack on the city walls.*

Deodin flinched. Ruby was several days' journey from here. Even on horseback, he'd have no way to reach them in time—

> *Relax. The travel to your city is the least of your concerns. You don't face the Big Bad there tonight anyway. It is much more important that you learn the truth than it is for you to try to get involved with the orcs at your city.*
>
> *One of the reasons you came here was for answers, right?*

Deodin peeked at the purple book's remaining pages. Makee had more to say now, but the final pages were still blank. Whatever happened next wasn't the end.

*Let me start by saying that I don't have an explanation for all of it. All I can do is see it and relay that information to you. When confronted with questions of how and why, I have no good answer. I want you to be armed with this knowledge so that you can be prepared for it. So that you can understand the choices that you'll be required to make when the time comes.*

*As best as I can tell, we poor bastards are simply different from everyone else. And I don't mean in the obvious sense, with the mastery of magic. The best way that I can phrase it is "the world treats us differently."*

*You've surely noticed it. How is it that monsters always seem to find you? Why do random strangers either task you with quests or try to kill you? Why are the merchants always so willing to buy the random junk from your bag? And do I need to even mention troll caves?*

*Now ask yourself: Do those same monsters find anyone else? Does anyone else get tasked with those dangerous quests? Is there any realistic way that those merchants can stay in business? And again: TROLL CAVES.*

*I could go on, but you've been there yourself. You know this.*

*What makes us different is what makes us cursed. We can experience the flaws of our world. Everyone else cannot. Regardless of how often you explain it, how well you point it out, how diligently you document it, nothing will change. Other people cannot be made to understand, or even recognize, the realities of this world. It's as if they had been born without noses. They can never be made to understand how badly everything stinks.*

*And that's not the worst part. The greatest tragedy comes at the expense of everyone else.*

*The people we encounter are real in every meaningful way. They live their lives. They love. They laugh. They look forward to holidays and a good sandwich.*

*These people also experience fear and pain and misery. They can suffer. And the longer they are around you, the more you continue your adventuring, the more likely you bring that suffering to them.*

*You must never forget this, in all your adventuring. Because the harshest reality is that you are not merely an observer of this altered, calamitous reality.*

*You are its source.*

# Ruby (The Mage Tower) – Pel

Pel closed her eyes and forced herself to draw a deep breath. Every time she thought of Garret, she felt a pit in her stomach. She had grown accustomed enough to the familiar, heart-pounding blood rush of fear; she was new to the caustic, sickening toxicity of anxiety and worry for someone else.

*He's going to be fine.*

She opened her eyes. Her reality was no more reassuring. While Garret defended the city walls with the rest of the militia, she stood in the heart of the Tower in one of the many rooms dedicated to the Encroachment crisis. Among those who circled her were Richard and other red mages.

"I'll have it easier," Garret had smirked, before he kissed her goodbye to join the city's defenders. "All I have to do is stand on top of a wall and shoot arrows. You're the one who has to face monsters."

It had been a conscious, difficult decision for Pel to cross the bridge to the Tower earlier that day, a decision she had not made for herself. The inhabitants needed her. Ruby needed her. During the city's greatest crisis in several decades, they needed the counsel of the person who had the greatest understanding of all of Ruby's moving parts. She was likely the only resource that couldn't be found elsewhere.

She wasn't alone in the room, even if she still felt isolated. She knew nearly everyone on hand: her many business partners had clamored for her presence as an intermediary for the fiercer rivalries, because she could be entrusted to manage interests and conflicts without bias.

Other faces were present, like Garret's friend on the city council. Sam was a valuable expert on orc behavior and history. Likewise, Mathew was a welcome addition to the meetings, if only because he seemed to be a mage who was unlike the others.

Entorak continued handing out assignments, fielding questions, and resolving issues that came up during the process.

"Captain, I have a list," Entorak said to the leader of the militia.

Entorak rubbed his eyes with his free hand as the captain reached for the paper. The activity of the past week had taken its toll.

"These mages will join your defense by assisting your warriors on the wall. This is Ruby, after all. The orcs have no understanding of what type of defenses they face, should they come within spell range. You'll find these men most capable."

It was Richard who seized the list and read it over. He sneered with incredulity as he went further and further down the names.

"Why these? Barnard alone can shoot more death from his cock than the ones on this list. The red mages excel at dealing death."

"Indeed," Entorak agreed. "They will stay here to protect the Tower itself. As should you." Entorak briefly flashed with a magical aura, then it subsided completely. Richard seemed deep in thought for a moment, before nodding in consent. He handed the list back to Entorak, who passed it to the captain.

*Fucking hells.*

Pelium consciously forced her expression to remain dead-pan despite her surprise. Entorak had just pushed Richard into agreeing with his recommendation!

Entorak shot her a glance, clearly aware that Pel would be the only one who could interpret what had just happened. He seemed satisfied with her lack of response.

"Mathew," he said, turning to the mage. "Continue with the evacuation of the remaining personnel and Tower property, please. Ensure that everyone and everything gets to a ship and see to it that they are well accommodated by the ship captains."

"No," Pel said, drawing the eyes of everyone in the room. This was the first time she had taken ownership of the conversation. Both Richard and Entorak stiffened at her dissent. But before they could take issue, she continued.

"With respect, I would be best suited for that. I have a much better relationship with the captains and those at the docks. The ship captains have already agreed to help, but it will be more complicated than that. The dockhands and sailors are only human. In all candor, they resent the Tower and its influences. The evacuation of the Tower comes off as a mission of mercy if I oversee it. It comes off as an abuse of power if overseen by any of you."

Richard rolled his eyes. "Fu-cking peasants—"

Entorak raised his hand to quiet him. "I understand. Will you see to these arrangements?" Entorak handed Pel a list of evacuees he had already prepared.

She reviewed the list. The instructions seemed as simple as Entorak had summarized a few moments before. She nodded and placed the list into a pocket in her cloak.

"As for Mathew…" She leaned over the map and pointed to Ruby's water reservoir. Pel was intimately familiar with the project. Nearly every part of its construction had gone through one or more of her contacts. In her dealings, she had helped to build it.

"Perhaps he can sail up the Kalee, to the reservoir. With its western gates wide open, the reservoir will drain into the fields northeast of the wall. We flood the fields as the orcs advance." She traced her finger up the river and tapped it on the western edge of the reservoir.

"How you gonna make sure the water goes whur ya want it?" asked Nils, one of the council members, his voice sounding like the earth echoing from the collapse of a distant mountain. Nils was a giant man with red hair and a full beard who stood a head taller than every other man in the room. His manner of speaking was as overwhelming as his physical size.

Nils represented the interests of the laborer unions and guilds, such as the stonecutters, masons, and carpenters. Pel had met him a few times and remembered each occasion in vivid detail. He commanded such a presence that she always visualized the spelling of his name in big, bold, capital letters. The man was huge and loud and difficult to understand, but he served Ruby well with his sharp mind for construction and craftsmanship.

He continued.

"And without fookin' up everythin' else?"

Pel restrained a grin. "The mages will help with that. Much of Mathew's magical research has been a study of how to manipulate stone and earth," she replied.

Mathew shot her a look of both curiosity and concern. The two had never discussed his research.

"I asked about you," she explained.

Satisfied, Mathew answered Nils's question. "I can marginally reinforce the strength of earth and stone. I've also stumbled across many ways to weaken it. Even if it's not a straight downhill shot, I can manipulate the soil so the water goes in the right direction."

The militia captain looked up to Nils for his opinion on the viability of the plan. The big man consulted the map for a moment and agreed with an approving nod. Satisfied that the engineering was sound, the captain explained the value of the proposal.

"The orcs would be forced to advance while knee-deep in mud, out in that open ground. That should push them to the north. That would create a choke point where we can rain down missiles from the ramparts. We can concentrate more of our forces to that side," the captain said, using his finger to circle an area immediately outside the northern wall.

"That bunches them up for the death magic," added Richard with macabre enthusiasm.

Richard's optimistic bloodthirst aside, murmurs circulated among the various decision makers at the table. Pel's plan was sound and could significantly alter the outcome of the confrontation. In only a few moments, the proposal was confirmed.

"I'm comin wit' you, then," pronounced Nils. "Ya want ta to slow the orcs wit' mud, not divert the whole fookin' river through tha main gate."

Mathew and the giant redbeard shared nods, then the two of them swam through the others and out the door. Pel watched them leave, then turned back to the rest of the meeting. Entorak was waiting, his gaze already locked on her.

"You should also go. Lives may depend on it." He focused on her a bit longer until he had her full attention. "And Pelium: leave the Tower by sundown and do not return."

He flashed in magic briefly. She nodded in assent.

She had been hoping for the opportunity to excuse herself from the Tower. With her role seemingly satisfied, she happily accepted the opportunity to leave. But Entorak was right. Now that she had an assignment, she needed to get started.

She passed through the doorway to see Mathew and one of the female servants at the far end of the hallway. They were talking excitedly and seriously, evidently concluding a hurried, important conversation. The woman reached out and grabbed both of Mathew's hands, leaning in to whisper in his ear. Both nodded.

Pel politely looked away as they shared a kiss. For a few seconds, they stood there and held each other's hands in silence. Then the servant broke free and jogged down the hall toward Pel. Mathew watched her go before turning and heading the other direction. The servant did not wait for pleasantries and polite customs.

"May I see your list?" the woman asked, her voice touched with a subtle accent Pel could not place.

More than her speech, Pel was struck by the woman's demeanor. She was impatient, but not quite rude. She moved with a confidence not shared by any servant Pel had ever met. Rather than wait for Pel to answer the question, the woman merely stood there with her hand out, expectantly.

"I was told it is a list of names of the Tower staff to be evacuated." Pel retrieved the list and handed it over. The servant scanned the names before she glanced at the other side of the paper. She returned the page to Pel.

"It is incomplete," the servant said. "Let us gather these first, then return for the others." She stepped to the side, gestured for Pel to accompany her, then paused, as if suddenly remembering her role as a servant. She faced Pel and bowed with the half-assiest of half-assed curtsies.

"Forgiveness, m'lady. I am Mica."

# The Thick
# (The Crescent Temple) – Deodin

As it turned out, Makee had made quite the claim.

> *The magic that grants you the powers of the poor bastard is the same that drives the calamity in your world. It is what draws the monsters to you, what leads people to expect you to solve their problems, and what compels you to help them. It is the same thing that makes that merchant buy the three hundred iron daggers that you crafted in sequence, just so you could get better at crafting daggers.*
>
> *We poor bastards exist only to play our part in this game. You only exist to play your part. And the more you do it, the more of a game it becomes.*
>
> *Do you remember when you first began your adventuring life? Do you recall how comparatively unskilled you were? How unpracticed? How you commanded so much less of your power than you do now? Do you remember when you first helped that person who needed your help?*
>
> *It was a simple task, I'm sure. Gather a mineral or herb. Slay the pesky critter to protect the crops. Deliver the item or message to someone else. Something along those lines, yes?*

Deodin thought back on this. It had been a long time, but yes, Makee's statement held true.

> *And now, you can deal death from your fingertips. But have you ever noticed that your skills and abilities have increased at the same rate as your adversaries'? You have come to command so much magic, so much power, yet it still takes nine blows to defeat a cave troll?*

Deodin scoffed. Nine blows? Makee was an amateur, by comparison.

> *And what about the stakes of your heroic deeds? You were a hero from wherever you started, having ended the threat to your village or local community. And then, your adventuring led you to something larger. A bigger community, such as a small city, fort, or colonial outpost.*
>
> *And following your victory there, you were drawn here, to the Crown. To the Big Bad. To something that threatens the entire region. You've gone from butchering rats for a kindly old lady to fighting the monster that wants to drown tens of thousands of people in fire (or ice, or shadow magic, or poison, or whatever flavor is appropriate for your Big Bad).*
>
> *As time goes on, as your power increases, so do the powers of your enemies. The more power you obtain, the more powerful your enemies become. The more powerful the enemies become, the more powerful you become in order to defeat them.*

*Have you noticed the cyclical nature of all of this yet?*

*Worse still, there is a single commonality across all of this. Something that spans every villain and monster, every item of treasure, every person, village, or region threatened by the perils of this world.*

*You.*

# Ruby (The Northern Wall) – Garret

Garret's perch atop the Ruby ramparts afforded him two views, each of which were impressive in different ways. In one direction, a horizon of light pierced the dark night. In the other, an ocean of people flowed through the streets.

There, behind him, the good citizens of Ruby had accomplished more in the past few days than he thought possible. Men and women moved purposefully below him, each person carrying out one role or another, all relating to defense from the impending Encroachment.

Garret himself was one of the thousands of able-bodied men who had volunteered (or had been conscripted) for the archery corps. Because of his experience, the equipment he already owned, and the relationships he had groomed over the years, Garret seized the opportunity to sit atop the city walls. Most of the archers were being organized behind him, preparing to loose volleys over the walls and into the fields on the other side.

More impressive than the force of arms, however, was the personal commitment behind it all. A surge of newfound pride and awe shoved aside Garret's cynicism. He was astonished that a place like Ruby could unite so quickly under a common cause, temporarily setting aside the histories, differences, and conflicts, many of which he'd seen firsthand. Being a part of something larger than himself gave him hope—a hope that he needed to feel when he looked out the other side of the wall, across the northern fields to the edge of the Thick.

The dark horizon was ablaze with what looked like a wildfire. The lights from the orc horde danced and swayed next to the tree line, the slowly approaching tide of hostility drawing closer to Ruby. Each pinpoint of light in the distance represented a single torch carried by an orc. The sum of that torchlight, with its promise of sharp, pointy things and ill intent, made Garret shudder.

# The Thick
# (The Crescent Temple) – Deodin

Makee's journal had left Deodin in an awkward state of incompleteness, as if Makee had been interrupted while writing his final thoughts. The remaining pages were blank.

The gap made sense when Deodin felt a familiar, compelling sensation emerge in his mind. The Universe was ready to move things along.

*Encroachment*

☐ *Return to Ruby*
☐ *Find and defeat the orc infiltration unit*
☐ *Confront Entorak*

As he watched, more pages in the journal filled with Makee's handwriting. Only the final pages remained blank.

> *We'll finish the discussion of your existential crisis next time, I promise. Right now, the world needs you at your best. And you can't be at your best if you're in the fetal position, cursing the gods and wondering what the point of it is.*

*The easy part is, now that you've reached this stage of the poor bastard saga, our game has seen fit to waste less of your time. Under normal circumstances, how long would it take for you to get to your city? Several days? A week?*

*Not anymore!*

*Look around the ruins here. You'll find something that acts as a doorway to a few of the places you've already visited. One of the selections will be the front gate of your city. Walk through that doorway and via one impossible way or another, you'll arrive at your destination.*

*The portal itself will vary from instance to instance. It may be a glowing, circular hole in reality, but I've also seen them as mirrors or glowing door frames. Regardless, look around these chambers and you will find such a thing.*

*And, as normal, you may have to pull switches, press buttons, or solve an asinine puzzle. The standard dungeon rules still apply.*

Deodin scowled. Makee's notes had taken a decidedly ominous turn with no real hint that things would get better.

A moment later, one last line appeared on the page.

*Go! Go! Go! We're almost there! Isn't this exciting?*

# The Encroachment on Ruby – Pel

A yellow-brown haze lingered in the Ruby skyline. The city's defenders had lit fires along the outside of the walls to deny cover and concealment to the opposing horde. The smoke darkened the skies and signaled the beginning of war.

As Pel and Mica made their way from the docks back to the Tower, what had started as a background noise grew louder. It sounded like a cheering throng of spectators, even though every scream or shout could mean that someone had fallen to an orc arrow or spear. It was surreal. And nauseating.

*Garret.*

Pel could hardly concentrate. Mica led her through Ruby's deserted streets after dropping off the last group of Tower refugees at the docks. Or, more specifically, the penultimate group. Mica insisted that there were more people to evacuate, beyond the ones Entorak had listed.

Finally, they arrived back at the Tower. Pel had spent more time here in the past few days than she had during the previous eight years. And really, considering the circumstances, the Tower should have been far less imposing, with all but a handful of its people and contents elsewhere. She silently chided herself for still regarding it with the same degree of dread.

Pel really, really didn't want to be here. She especially wanted to be elsewhere come sundown, because ... because ...

*Actually...* She thought about it for a moment.

"Bastard," she said, coming to the realization that Entorak had magically pushed her out of the Tower when he told her to be out by sundown.

She knew enough about pushing magic to know it wouldn't prevent her from returning, but it certainly could make her especially sensitive to the fears and insecurities she already had.

Mica, meanwhile, didn't seem to notice. She had been altogether quiet and pensive when she and Pel led the Tower staff to the docks. Once that primary business was done, Mica had become exceptionally focused and driven. She had all but dragged Pel back to the Tower to complete another objective.

In the few hours they had spent together, Pel concluded that Mica was not a librarian. The young woman's demeanor was not nearly, well, *subservient* enough for her to be the Tower's hired help. The ruse may have been successful to this point, but for whatever reasons, she no longer played that character.

Mica made no pause at the foot of the bridge, striding as quickly and with as much intent as before. However, Pel stopped. Entorak's magic or not, the Tower still terrified her. Mica noticed immediately and turned to challenge her.

"We don't have the time for this!"

But Pel hesitated, drawing herself into her cloak. "I ... have other places to be," she countered weakly. Technically, the statement was true, because when compared to the Tower, every other place was an improvement.

"Pelium Stillwater, your story is well known throughout the Tower. Your 'gift' is the envy of half the men who live there. It is only Entorak's will that keeps the mages from seeing the world through your eyes."

"They know nothing of my 'gift'—" Pel spat, indignant.

Mica rebuked her with a glare before Pel could finish her thought.

"You *dare* to think that you have suffered the most at the hands of those in the Tower?" Mica fumed. Her eyes widened, shoulders came forward, weight shifting to the balls of her feet, hands at the ready. Pel flinched. It was the same type of posture Garret took when preparing for a fight.

Briefly, Mica flashed with magic, before shuddering and willing it away. Her aura differed from those worn by the mages or even Deodin. It seemed monstrous, like the never-bats Pel had seen in the Thick.

Mica closed her eyes for a second before calming herself. Her stance eased. Having regained control of her emotions and whatever magic she wielded, she composed herself enough to speak through clenched teeth.

"You, of all people—you should want to help me. You, more than anyone else, should know what it's like to be victimized by the mages of the Tower. And I wouldn't ask your help if I didn't need it. If *they* didn't need it." Mica pointed to the Tower that dominated the skyline. She was on the verge of angry, hateful tears.

Pel shrank at Mica's remark. Pel was worldly enough to know that she couldn't be the only victim in the history of the Tower's misdeeds, but she had been too uncomfortable—too selfish—to dwell on that notion. She had never considered that there were others, who had it worse, right now. And they needed help. Someone's help. Anyone's help. Her help.

*You can help them,* called the voice in her mind.

Softly, at first. But as the message repeated itself, the voice became increasingly less timid, less meek. Louder. More frequent. More demanding. The voice became angry, impatient, and disappointed. The message itself morphed from a theoretical noncommittal concept to an overwhelming and personalized command.

*You must help them.*

"What do you need of me?" Pel asked, her voice barely a whisper. Surely Mica knew Pel was neither warrior nor witch. What assistance could she possibly provide, deep within the heart of the Tower?

"Right now?" Mica asked, before nodding to the ominous building behind her. "Courage."

# The Encroachment on Ruby – Mathew

Nils and Mathew interlocked their hands at each other's wrists. The great man reached down to help Mathew up to the control deck of the west side of Ruby's reservoir. Mathew looked up to make sure his partner was ready.

"Gently!" Mathew cautioned. "Don't rip my hand off at the wrist!"

Nils smirked. "More likely I'd tear ya' arm off at the shoulder," he explained, as if he spoke from experience. A moment later, Nils hoisted the mage onto the platform and helped him to his feet.

"Ya did good," Nils continued, surveying the tract of land that Mathew had prepared. "Tha' water'll run to the fields. Ya' didn't fook it up."

Mathew stood up and faced the field. Their trap was ready. The chalky, brittle soil would yield to the onrushing water and flood to the north, well away from Ruby's outer perimeter and into the orcs' advance.

"Ya dunno shit about nothin' else, but ya did good with tha' magic."

Mathew concluded the remark was the apex of a Nils compliment. After an afternoon of exhausting labor, Mathew was glad to have the giant's approval.

Nils was like no one Mathew had ever met in the Tower. A lifetime in the trades had granted him vast expertise about the world. The man was a magician in his own right. As they prepared their trap, Nils explained the critical details about flood plains, culverts, and water management. Certainly, he was loud, crude, and inarticulate—but he was also more an expert in his field than Mathew was in his.

During the time he'd worked with him, Mathew had learned that Nils's size and strength were his least impressive assets.

"Let's go, mage. Here's your chance to save the day." Nils gestured to the valve that controlled the reservoir's water level. The last part of the plan was to open the valve and send the water on its way. Now that the orcs had moved into the heart of the field, about to engage Ruby's northern walls, it was time to execute the plan.

Mathew grabbed the sluice control with both hands and heaved. The wheel that operated the valve refused to move.

"Fucking hells," Mathew snarled. "The valve is stuck!"

Mathew reached down again, grabbed the wheel, and pulled with as much force as he could muster. The flesh on his fingers yielded first. He yelped in a combination of pain, disgust, and disappointment.

He cursed again. This venture could save an untold number of lives and he couldn't open the gods-damned valve.

Naturally, Nils found the whole spectacle amusing. He laughed and laughed at Mathew until he was good and ready to do something to positively contribute.

"Get the fook out the way!" Nils bellowed between guffaws.

Mathew backed up instinctively. He did not want any of Nils's power to find its way to his face, should he lose his grip or rip the valve from its mount. Mathew watched in awed anticipation as Nils stood there for a moment, rolling his shoulders in preparation...

Then the giant man reached down to pull up the six-foot iron bar that was conveniently housed next to the valve. He slid the rod into a fitted slot and used the added leverage to easily open the gate. He returned the bar to its resting place and opened the gate by turning the valve conventionally.

Mathew had never noticed the rod, nor its mounting slot. They were two important details that Mathew had missed. Nils found this hilarious.

"Ya should rilly git out of the Tower once—"

"Yes, yes, I know," Mathew interrupted, tired of hearing it.

# The Encroachment on Ruby – Garret

Garret wouldn't consider himself much of an aficionado of the arts, but the sounds that surrounded him were almost musical.

Behind him, the commander of the archer regiment barked out orders in a slow, deliberate cadence. He called out in a strident scream that was immediately followed by a deafening, booming response of the archers themselves. There was a rhythmic timing to it all, with each command and response sounding like coordinated parts in a grim orchestra.

"HARCHARS READAAAAY!"

"HOOO!"

"HARCHAAAAARS ... FAAAAH"

"HAAAA!"

Per volley, thousands of arrows whistled and hissed over Garret's head, over the wall, and into the field on the other side. It was a spectacle that was simply astounding. And terrible.

From his position at the top of the wall, Garret could see only the indirect results of their efforts, but that view was still surreal. As the thousands of torch lights came closer, dozens of those torches would tumble to the ground whenever one of those volleys landed. And Garret was only watching one portion of this scene. Regiments of archers were scattered across the northern wall. He could only imagine that the view was the same from each rampart.

Then came the magic. Holy shit, the magic.

Because Ruby boasted so many mages and their Tower, the local citizens were accustomed to occasional displays of magical lights and explosions. During holiday events and feasts, the mages would conjure displays of lights and sound, casting spells that created colorful airborne explosions of shapes and patterns. Now, instead of those explosions occurring harmlessly hundreds of feet above the ground, weaponized versions of those same spells found their way to the oncoming attackers.

Once the orcs were in range, the mages began their assault. Dozens of magical explosions split the darkness in the fields beyond the northern wall. A few of these spells were simply to provide light to the battlefield: balls of harsh, white light hung in the air, blinding the assailants and making them visible as they made their way to Ruby's walls. The rest of the magic targeted the orcs themselves.

Garret did not consider himself squeamish. Nor would he harbor sympathy for a horde of attackers, orcs or otherwise. Regardless, he had never seen imagery so horrific in its savagery and scale.

With the sorcery bathing the field with light, he had a clear, macabre picture of what was going on. Under the scorching magical daylight, he could see that the attackers were knee-deep in mud and altogether helpless to escape the onslaught that befell them.

No wonder their advance stalled the way it had, where it had. It must have been exhausting to cover all that open ground in the best of conditions. However, with all the mud, missiles, and magic, that endeavor transitioned from "challenging" to "outright suicidal." The orcs were completely spent, trapped in open ground, and subjected to warfare on a seemingly limitless scale that rained down on them.

"HAAAAAAAAA!"

The boom of the archers called out, just as another volley ripped through the night to land in the heart of the squirming, screaming mass of attacking forces. A moment later, that same area erupted in a magical explosion. The sound of the carnage proved to be far worse than the sight.

Garret looked away. The queasiness in his stomach was no longer the result of the anxiety and fear of battle, but of its reality.

# The Encroachment on Ruby – Deodin

*Magical bullshit.*

Deodin had found something that looked like a puddle of molten silver hanging on the wall of the temple. It rippled when he touched it, feeling almost metallic on his fingertips. He had never seen such a thing before, but it seemed obvious that it was a view of another place in the Crown. He recognized the destination as an area on the outside of Ruby's northern wall.

He took a breath and stepped into the puddle. The sensation was disconcerting. Once he stepped in and put his weight on his forward foot, the portal did the rest and squeezed him through to the other side. It felt as if he had been shat out of the bum of a metal giant.

Once he was entirely through, the image of the temple rippled and ultimately disappeared. Deodin felt like he needed a bath.

*Encroachment*

☑ *Return to Ruby*
☐ *Find and defeat the orc infiltration unit*
☐ *Confront Entorak*

The temple's portal had deposited Deodin onto the middle of the Encroachment, amid a roil of commotion and

394

violence. Under the flashing lighting of magical artillery, a volley of arrows soared over Ruby's northern wall, over his head, and into the field behind him.

In front of him, mages and archers defended the city from the wall's parapet. They were actively firing at something—

A scuttling behind him demanded his attention. He turned in time to see a mud-covered orc charge him with a spear. It was a crude, clumsy attack that Deodin avoided with a slight time dilation, returning to full speed with a charged blast of magical power that he delivered to the orc's chest.

A great explosion of white magical light split the darkness as Deodin's blow hit. The orc fell over, instantly slain by the blast.

This gave Deodin pause. Orcs did not normally fall so easily. The power of his magical strike must have grown since his last real battle. This power gain was a sensation he would feel occasionally, as one or more of his abilities reached a new tier of force and effectiveness.

Considering what Makee had written, the feeling of might was more concerning than exciting. If Makee was right, it merely meant that his adversaries had grown in power as well.

# The Encroachment on Ruby – Pel

Pel had never visited this part of the Tower. From what she understood of the mage hierarchy, the more senior mages coveted the upper flights. She and Mica paused in a doorway, high atop the Tower's prominent spire.

Mica slipped a key into the lock and wrenched open the door with a harsh metallic clang. She strode in swiftly and disappeared from Pel's line of sight. Pel followed, only to be completely taken aback by what she discovered inside.

The room was clearly someone's quarters and that someone was undoubtedly a mage. Blue magical light permeated every corner, allowing her to see clearly. Even from across the room, she could read the titles of the books on the shelves, make out the detail in the molding and tapestries, detect the stains in the seams between the stone tiles of the floor. It was beautiful and marvelous.

However, as soon as she came to notice these details, her wonderment ceased. *Gods. This must be Richard's room.* Pel scowled in disgust and confusion when she saw his art collection.

*Cocks. Richard. More cocks. More Richard. What the hells is wrong with this guy?*

Her disgust became grave concern as she entered the bedchamber, where four naked women in a state of torpor lazed about on the bed as though nothing were going on outside.

Mica knelt next to one of them and tried to rouse her into action.

"Come on, Sophie! You need to wake up," Mica pleaded, lovingly holding the woman's head. There was no response. Mica cursed in a foreign language before she turned a desperate face to Pel.

"This is why I need you. Why *they* need you. It's somewhere in this room."

"Mica, I don't understand," Pel said helplessly. By the gods she wanted to help, but what—

"It's magical. It inhibits them. It must be one of the trinkets in this room," she said in a terse, hurried whisper. "If I knew what it was, I would have long since destroyed it!"

Pel scanned the room. Magical auras were everywhere. In most cases, she could interpret the function of a spell or magic item by reading its aura. Only a few of the items had unfamiliar enchantments. She dumped a nearby basket onto the floor and used it to collect anything with a strange or an unfamiliar aura. She hurried over to present them to Mica.

"These all have a magic I don't recognize," Pel explained. "What you seek is probably in here."

Mica didn't have to search for long before she found a relic she didn't like. The color faded from her face as she nodded to one of the many, many cock replicas that Richard had lying around the place. This one was inscribed with a language Pel didn't recognize, but based on Mica's reaction, the text meant something to her. And now that Pel thought about it, the aura looked sickly and toxic. It reminded her of Richard.

"Bastard," Mica said weakly, as if she choked back the urge to retch. "Gods, Stillwater, hurry and destroy that thing. I can't touch it."

Pel retrieved a heavy candelabra from a nearby shelf, set the magical phallus on the tile floor, and brought the base of the candelabra down as hard as she could. And again. And again.

She reduced the trinket to small shards of rubble, with no fragment larger than a grape. The aura faded almost immediately. She glanced back at Mica, who attended to the women.

They looked much better already. Their color had begun to return, they blinked and breathed at a more normal, healthy rate. One of the women even moved her arms.

"Water, Pel. Please," Mica instructed, gently helping one of the women in her efforts to sit upright.

With her free hand, Mica directed Pel to the pitcher and matching cups on a nearby shelf. Pel filled a cup for each hand, gave one to Mica and kept one for herself. Together, they helped the women upright and let them sip from the cups.

One of the women had regained enough of her voice to speak. She rasped something in a language Pel didn't recognize. Mica responded in turn. Pel couldn't understand the conversation, but she was reassured by Mica's tenderness.

The woman next to Pel had recovered enough strength to roll over to her hands and knees, as she readied herself to stand up. Heavy scarring was visible on the inside of her shoulder blades, forming two fist-sized marks on either side of her spine. There was a similar, smaller mark above her buttocks, centered on her back.

Pel was confused. There was a symmetry in the scarring that did not seem consistent with an incidental wound or injury. She noticed that each of the other women shared the same scars.

One by one, they slowly rose, increasingly in control of their limbs. By the time they had stood up completely, they began to shine with a mild magical glow.

Their auras vaguely resembled the aura worn by Entorak and his pushing magic. It would be difficult for Pel to describe to someone who didn't see the world as she did, but she saw a more ... *pure* form of his magic? Perhaps a more concentrated version? The aura wasn't brilliant, like Deodin's, but it was very precise and specific. Like, say, a neverbat or another mob of the Thick—

Of course.

Pel swallowed hard. Her confusion quickly transitioned to fear when she remembered where she had seen that magic before.

It was the same aura she had seen flash in Mica.

# The Encroachment on Ruby – Deodin

Expectedly, the debris and landscape of the battlefield outside of Ruby's northern wall had created a singular path for Deodin to follow. The Universe commonly provided predetermined routes that kept him within the confines of wherever he was supposed to be.

Formed of burning debris, entrenchments, and phalanxes, the route he followed ran parallel to Ruby's primary wall. The path came to an end where Deodin found one of Ruby's guards slumped against the wall.

Deodin rushed to the man to provide aid, only to discover that the man was gravely wounded. Above the fallen soldier, was a series of climbing spikes driven into the stone. The contextual clues suggested that orc attackers had ascended this wall and that the human had fallen or was thrown from the parapet.

"O-o-orc assassins," the soldier stammered. "Six of them, wearing black and purple. You have to stop them."

There was no plausible way this man would know that Deodin would be able to stop the orc assassins. Normally, mortally wounded men would seek help or perhaps ask to deliver a message to a loved one.

Instead, this man had tasked a perfectly random stranger with a quest that a perfectly random stranger would never be able to carry out.

But Deodin was never a perfectly random stranger. He was always the right person at the right time.

Yet, for the first time in a long while, Deodin didn't complain about the nonsense of it; he didn't roll his eyes and begrudgingly comply with a seemingly arbitrary list of tasks brought forth by the inexplicably flawed, annoying world.

Everything he had grown to resent no longer felt like bullshit.

It didn't matter if Deodin saw the blemishes in the fabric of reality. It didn't matter if he followed rules that were different for everyone else. The bullshit of it all changed nothing about the Encroachment, Tychryn, or the fate of the Crown—nor would it change anything for this man. Deodin grasped his hand, looked him in the eye, and nodded.

Deodin chose to accept the quest. He chose to honor the dying man in front of him by avenging his death and saving the Crown from the orcs and their dragon overlord. Deodin chose to fight for Pel and Garret, and Dano and Kesh, and every other person or creature he had encountered along his journeys.

None of this was bullshit to them.

Deodin decided to stop hating the Universe for its flaws and idiosyncrasies. Perhaps he should be thankful, because being *sheyaktu* gave him a purpose that only he could have. Perhaps he shouldn't bemoan his time spent in this silly game.

Perhaps he should cherish it.

"I shall, my friend," Deodin said. "For the Crown."

"For the Crown," the man rasped before closing his eyes.

# The Encroachment on Ruby – Garret

*Would it be in poor taste to leave now?*

Perhaps twenty minutes had passed from the point when Garret had turned away from the "battle" to sit down, his back against the rampart wall. He wasn't quite sulking or pouting, but he certainly didn't want to participate anymore.

He had not loosed a single arrow. The orc charge had been such a catastrophic, suicidal failure that Garret felt no need to participate in it. Instead, he spent his time debating how to best steal away without facing unnecessary social criticism and stigma.

Leaving couldn't be any more cowardly or disrespectful than sitting against this wall, doing nothing. In conversing with himself, Garret had to admit that Garret had a point. What would "they" do? Belittle him for not participating in the massacre? Insult his manhood for not succumbing to the bloodlust of battle? Shit, he had already earned the "Orcslayer" achievement, back when it was hard and meant something.

So, Garret sat on the rampart and debated the most socially appropriate way to skip out on the most historically important event of his generation.

While he stewed, something large and heavy passed overhead. Underlit by the magical hellfire of the battle below, a giant winged thing briefly filled his field of view before disappearing as quickly as it had come.

Had he not heard the dull hiss of the air splitting as it soared overhead, he would have dismissed the vision outright. Instead, he stood up and peered back over his shoulder, toward the path the object seemed to take, toward the heart of Ruby.

With the Evertorch district on the other side of town, there was not enough ambient light to see anything in the sky. Most of Ruby's torches and lanterns remained intentionally unlit, so that there would be no advantage for the attacking orcs.

Only the mage Tower remained bathed in light, a magical shine that persisted throughout the night. It stood out as a prominent, unmistakable beacon in Ruby's darkness.

A moment later, a huge shadow seemed to swallow the tip of that tower. No, not a shadow. It was certainly a thing. A moving thing. The shape was unfamiliar and mysterious.

# The Encroachment on Ruby – Pel

The Tower was home to other dangerous things. Mica reacted so quickly that it seemed she could read Pel's mind. Or at least, she could read Pel's face.

"Relax, Stillwater. Meet my sisters," Mica said, amused that Pel had finally assembled all the contextual clues in front of her.

Pel would not relax, frozen as she was by the realization that these women glowed with magic and shared the same scarring because they were not really women. Not human women, at least. She now had a label for Mica's aura.

*Succubus.*

Mica and her sisters were monsters from the East, widely hated and hunted across the world. The scars on their backs had resulted from the removal of their wings and tails.

Succubi were supposed to be evil, self-serving, and depraved. Yet nothing that she had seen in Mica supported that belief. From what Pel had witnessed, the most evil, self-serving, and depraved monster in the Tower was Richard.

Mica spoke to the women briefly in her native language. The discussion was clearly about Pel, as they all turned to look at her during Mica's address.

The woman next to Pel stepped closer. Still naked, still flawless but for the scars, still bathed in magic, she reached out and slowly wrapped her arms around Pel, who stood in a state of paralysis, completely unsure of what she should do. She could feel her heart throb as the woman drew close enough for their faces to touch. It was an embrace.

"Thank you," she said with a thick accent.

"Yes. Thank you," Mica said, her voice thick with emotion.

Mica had lost control of the magic she normally suppressed. She was moved to the point of tears. However, the job was not yet complete. Mica composed herself and tore through Richard's wardrobe, tossing handfuls of mismatched clothes for her sisters to wear.

"We need to go. There will be—"

The deafening crack of splitting stone cut Mica short.

The Tower trembled suddenly. Loudly. Violently. So severe was the jolt, Pel briefly thought the floor might collapse underneath her. Books and trinkets fell off the shelves.

The crash was followed immediately by different noise from another part of the Tower. Shouting. Then screaming. Then silence.

# The Encroachment on Ruby – Deodin

Perhaps one of Makee's journals would explain why he taught the orcs the Common tongue. Regardless of Makee's intentions or plans, Deodin was thankful for his efforts. It made eavesdropping much easier.

And so much more entertaining.

Having tracked down and defeated four of the elite orcs, Deodin had found the final two orc assassins huddled at the edge of a building on the west side of the Tower. They crouched in the alleyway, planning the best way to reach the Tower's bridge on the eastern side. Deodin sneaked up behind them as they spoke. This was the first time he'd ever had the opportunity to hear them speak to each other. Deodin was astounded by the orcs' accent. Their use of Common was comical and they had filthier mouths than the Rashni.

"That mage facka's gonna be inside, by the door," said the thicker of the two orcs. Like his partner, he carried two large, nasty-looking daggers.

"Wouldn't that facka be on the top?"

"The fackin drygan said he'd be by the fackin door. Ya gonna argya with ha'?"

"Is 'e by tha door t' keep us out?

"Nah. That facka's keepin them otha fackas from layven." The orc laughed to himself for a moment. "Heh. That facka might even let us in. 'E prally still thinks we're friends."

The smaller of the orcs found this amusing. He performed a short, one-act play inspired by his plan for the evening.

"Oy! Facka! Let us in!" he pretended to wait for the imaginary door to open before stepping inside and making repeated jabbing gestures. "Stab! Stab! Stab! Hahahaha!"

The other orc found this equally amusing.

"Yeh! Let us in, an' we promise that we a' dayfnetly not gonna stab ya!"

The larger orc made a sincere face as he waited for his imaginary victim to open the imaginary door. He made a circling gesture with his left hand, silently instructing his would-be victim to turn around. "Stab! Stab! Stab! Hahahaha!"

Deodin was going to let the orcs conclude their performances. Their antics mixed with their accents made for downright hilarious theater. However, his plans changed as soon as Tychryn landed on the Tower with the force of an earthquake. He no longer had the time to listen to the two idiots in front of him.

The bodies of the two remaining assassins had hardly come to rest before Deodin was on his way to the far side, to the Tower's bridge.

*Encroachment*

☑ *Return to Ruby*
☑ *Find and defeat the orc infiltration unit*
☐ *Confront Entorak*

# The Encroachment on Ruby – Garret

Garret was no longer confused by the thing on the tower.

The shadowy shape was suddenly backlit by a piercing bright, orange-and-white light. With enough illumination to provide context, Garret had a much better understanding of what he saw.

The orange-white light was fire. Conventional fire that spewed out of the mouth of a large creature at the top of the Tower. This creature had a pointy, triangular head, wings, and a tail, and was about the size of Bartlett's ship. Garret was no expert on the matter, but it sure looked like the various artist renderings he had seen on the subject.

*Dragon.*

He felt confident that he watched a gods-damned fucking *dragon* wrap itself around the pinnacle of the Tower. Furthermore, the monster actively tore the structure to rubble, ripping at it with its claws.

As a man who took pride in his knowledge of the ways of nature, Garret felt satisfied in how the dragon attacked like a cat, latching on with its front limbs while using its more powerful back legs to kick and claw at the structure. The cat comparison ended, however, when the beast opened its mouth and released a breath of a syrupy fire into the hole it had just created.

The best part? It was not as if the dragon tore into an orphanage for crippled children. The best part of the whole spectacle was that the dragon had serious issues with the Tower and the assholes in it. Oh, and speaking of them, they fought back and the dragon was hardly inconvenienced. It was glorious.

He laughed to himself. The spectacle of a real dragon was amazing and surreal. He wondered if the thing glowed in magic so Pel could see—

Garret jerked upright. He picked up his bow and frantically dashed to the closest stairs down the rampart, toward the heart of town, toward the Tower, and toward the dragon.

Toward Pel.

# The Encroachment on Ruby – Pel

Cursed with her poor eyesight, Pel had learned to be more attuned to her other senses. With the assault on the Tower, her senses were overwhelmed. More screaming. More shaking. She felt the deep rumble of crushing and crumbling stone. The smell of smoke and burning flesh filled the air. Whatever had happened to the Tower was still happening and showed no signs of slowing.

Mica led them all down the staircase that spiraled to the ground floor. The Tower had been almost entirely evacuated; they had not encountered anyone prior to finding Mica's sisters.

However, the Tower wasn't completely empty. Descending the stairs as quickly as they could manage, they encountered one of the red mages as he ran up the stairs, toward the screaming and shouting. Pel didn't recognize the man, but he glowed in magic, wore plenty of precious metals, and dressed in red like the other mages.

Mica moved with an inhuman fluidity. Hardly breaking a stride, she ran up the outside wall of the stairwell. She flashed in a bright magical light as she introduced the man's head to her elbow.

She connected with a solid blow. The man had barely enough time to bring his hands up in front of his face. The defensive gesture did nothing to protect him. He fell over backward, then landed awkwardly and clumsily on his arm as he tried to brace his fall. He fell with a gruesome crunching and a yelp.

Mica maneuvered herself to land almost perfectly on top of him, lending her weight to an already catastrophic impact. If this man were to survive his injuries, he would certainly never walk again. He wheezed with obvious difficulty.

Pel paused by the man, even though the others passed him as if he wasn't there.

Mica noticed this and held up, if only for a moment. "I have served the people in this Tower for weeks, Stillwater. The red mages deserve neither your pity nor your help. This one especially," she hissed as she motioned for Pel to continue down the stairs.

They descended without pause for another ten seconds, to the third floor. The main exit would be at the bottom of the staircase, at the far end of a long hallway. Mica led everyone to the hallway, but paused immediately once she had made her way in.

Pel hardly recognized this place. Debris littered the floor. The chandelier of evertorches had been wrested from its mount on the ceiling. Now fallen, it scattered its lights across the floor and dimly backlit a haze of dust.

Mica stood at the head of the pack, fixated on something on the far side of the hall. Pel followed Mica's gaze to the lone figure between them and the doorway. Even in the shadowy light, Pel could read the aura of the only other person in the room.

Richard.

Mica whispered something urgent and terse to the others in their language. The other women moved slowly and deliberately, spreading themselves out. Their movements reminded Pel of wolves as they cornered their prey.

# The Encroachment on Ruby – Deodin

Deodin enjoyed a slight break to admire Tychryn as she attacked the Tower. It was satisfying to watch her chew through the Tower's defenses. The red mages had been his mortal enemies for as long as he could remember. He felt no sympathy as they received their karmic justice in the form of teeth and a sticky, liquid fire. By Deodin's accounting, the Universe owed him dozens of favors and apologies. He would consider this spectacle as repayment of a fraction of that debt.

In the meantime, the dragon queen seemed destined to win the fight. Deodin's greatest concern were the spoils of that victory. She had promised to seize enchanted relics and artifacts from the Tower—prizes that Entorak had provided.

Deodin considered Entorak's part in all of this. Their face-to-face interaction had been exceedingly limited. They had only met out in front of the rancher's barn in Netherby, when Deodin had staged his death. He knew nothing of the man, other than that he seemed to oversee the red mages.

Yet, he wasn't a red mage himself. Deodin seemed destined to talk to him, not fight him. Why was he so important that Tychryn would bother to have him killed?

Deodin heard more cries and shouts as another batch of red mages baked in Tychryn's fiery jaws. He resumed his journey to the Tower, deciding that he had better find Entorak before the dragon did.

# The Encroachment on Ruby – Pel

The magic in this room was as hostile as anything Pel had ever seen.

On the far side of the hallway, Richard stood, his shoulders square to Mica and her sisters. He was draped in several spells, his aura nearly toxic and sickening. Through the glow of magic, his face carried a sneer of pure contempt.

*Hatred.* It was probably the only emotion he properly understood.

"You have nowhere to go," he said. "You are only safe with me."

His aura radiated brightly with pushing magic. Pel wasn't being targeted by the spell, so she could analyze its effects in real time. He was trying to control Mica. Dominate her.

Pel had no idea how Mica would react to this. She wasn't human, but that didn't make her immune to magic. Mica was also desperate and had already displayed an aptitude for violence. Had the women regained enough of their strength to be able to resist Richard?

Mica said something in her native language. The other women remained silent, but they stopped their advance.

"We'd certainly be safer with you," she agreed, but her statement was not because she had fallen victim to the spell. She glowed with a pushing magic of her own.

Mica was pushing back! And judging by her aura, she was significantly better at it. Pel watched from the back corner of the hallway, afraid to get in the middle of a magical duel.

"But can we be safe as long as there is a big, terrifying dragon up on the top floors?" Mica continued. Richard seemed to consider this, but Mica had more to say.

"Richard the Patient is the master of the monsters of the Thick. Richard the Patient has unlocked the mystery of every mob he has ever seen. And now, he can go conquer the mightiest monster of them all."

"The dragon," he said, nodding as he considered what it would take to tame the mightiest mob in the world.

"The dragon," Mica agreed. "But only *you* could ever hope to master that much power. Nobody else could do it. Nobody else would even dare. But you can. And you will. And then, you can imagine what people would think about you. Richard the Patient? How about Richard the Immortal?"

"Richard the Immortal," he echoed with a sincere grin. Richard was as happy as anyone Pel had ever seen. He was nearly gleeful.

"Go. Make the Tower safe for us. Subdue the dragon. Rule everyone else. The Tower. Ruby. The Crown. Only once everyone truly loves you, will you be satisfied."

Mica gestured to the staircase.

"They *will* love me. Everyone will love me," Richard said contentedly, clearly delighted by this plan.

He ran right past the women, through the door, and up the stairs.

# The Encroachment on Ruby – Tychryn

The fool ran straight into the chamber. The dismembered remains and smoldering corpses of his colleagues had not served as a proper warning for what awaited anyone who dared enter.

"You have come here to seek power," the cretin began. "And power, you have found! I am Richard the—"

She snatched the loudmouthed buffoon in her jaws, feeling most of his bones snap with a satisfying crunch. Nearly instantly, however, she spat him out across the room. He landed with a thump and a wide smear of blood on the floor. The attack hadn't killed him, but so much of his head had been crushed that he no longer had the capacity to wonder what went wrong.

Tychryn didn't enjoy the experience either.

She roared in disappointment and lunged to bite the next fool who dared enter the room. Hopefully, that one would taste better.

# The Encroachment on Ruby – Pel

Mica led Pel and the others down the hall and the remaining flights of stairs to the Tower's entry foyer.

The dragon's attack had shaken nearly everything to the floor. Whatever had been mounted to the walls, from shelves to evertorches, rested on the ground under chunks of plaster and a fine blanket of dust.

Near the door, a man stood watch. He was draped in a weak but familiar magical aura.

"Pelium! Mica!" Entorak croaked in surprise. He shifted his weight to move toward them, but his strength failed him. He collapsed to a knee. "By the gods, you have to get out of here!"

Pel's heart raced but not because of all the stairs she had just descended. Mica had already demonstrated that no one would prevent her sisters' rescue.

"I'm not here to stop you," Entorak explained.

Pel puzzled a moment as she interpreted his remark.

He was the gatekeeper! The Tower was about to collapse on itself and he was down at the front door, ensuring that nobody entered.

Or escaped.

This is why he wanted everyone out of the building— and why he had pushed her out earlier in the day. It was the reason he had selected Richard and the red mages to remain.

The Tower shook again. More particles of plaster broke free from the walls and ceiling.

"Every atrocity in this Tower happened with your knowledge," Mica hissed. "Perhaps you should go upstairs and discuss your sins with the dragon."

Mica glowed with magic. She hadn't pushed Entorak yet, but it seemed almost certain that she would. Surely, he would suffer the same fate as Richard if Mica willed it. Pel reached out to grab Mica's arm to stop her but one of her sisters had beaten her to it.

A brief exchange followed between Mica and the women she rescued. Their voices were hurried and urgent. Mica scowled at first, but her anger transitioned to surprise, shock, and then disbelief. She glanced at Entorak. Whatever her sisters had said, it was enough to place doubt in her mind. She addressed the man at the door.

"She... They say that you tried to free them. Both earlier today and a few times in the past few months. But you couldn't wake them and you couldn't disable the magic in Richard's room."

Mica was dumbfounded, as if she didn't believe the words coming out of her mouth. She simply stared at Entorak.

"You must leave," Entorak said. "You are not meant to be here."

Pel could sense a finality about him—a resignation to his fate. He looked truly disappointed, but not out of concern for himself. He did not plead for his life; he pleaded for theirs. And they didn't listen.

Despite his fatigue, Entorak's magical aura was still strong. It reminded Pel of how he had pushed her out the door earlier in the day. This would be the absolute best time for Entorak to use magic to convince them to leave. With a few words, they would all be delighted to run out the front door as fast as their legs could carry them. Instead, there was no magic flash as he spoke. Perhaps he didn't have the strength.

Or perhaps he gave them the choice.

Pel chose. She stepped in front of Mica and her sisters, interposing herself between them and Entorak. She reached out to grab Entorak's arm. She pulled on him, compelling him to stand. Curiously, he recoiled from her and shook his head.

"My work here is not yet done," he said, panting. "Yours is."

The Tower trembled heavily again, a reminder that whatever their decision, they had better make it soon. Pel released Entorak's arm and instead took a firm grip of the latch on the Tower door. She pressed down on the handle and shoved open the heavy door, allowing the air and noise of the outside world to flood in. Pel stepped through the doorway, turned to look at Entorak one last time, and gave him a slow, respectful nod.

The gesture was a sincere display of esteem and thanks, even if she didn't really know why she felt compelled to do it. For years, she had believed Entorak to be at the heart of the Tower and all its evils.

Yet, over the past week, she had witnessed him being so much more complicated than she ever could have imagined. Like most everyone else, he had clearly lived across the moral spectrum. And even if she had every right to hate him, she had an even greater obligation to thank him.

Entorak nodded back and turned to Mica, who glowered at him for a moment, before looking again at Pel for an opinion on the matter.

*Let's go*, Pel mouthed, gesturing to the relative safety of the outside.

Mica seemed to think on this for a moment longer before cursing sharply under her breath. She and the others left Entorak to whatever fate awaited him.

# The Encroachment on Ruby – Garret

*Nobody runs toward a dragon*, Garret realized while doing just that. After several agonizing minutes of running from the outer wall, he had nearly reached the bridge to the Tower.

And interestingly enough, he noted, nobody ran away from a dragon, either.

Instead, people on the streets stood with mouths agape, watching a giant flying lizard monster go to work on what remained of the Tower's pinnacle. The Ruby townsfolk didn't quite cheer for the dragon as it laid down carnage and soaked up whatever resistance came its way, but they weren't upset by the prospect, either. In a fight to the death between evil red mages and a legendary monster, Ruby's people stood to win.

The throng gasped in unison, prompting Garret to look up. He caught a view of a large pile of rubble splashing down into the body of murky water that served as the Tower's moat.

The structure had been torn to hell. The top three or four floors had been knocked cleanly off its bulk. Many of the lower floors were ablaze, with a weak, flickering light visible in the interior through a thick pillar of smoke.

Garret reached the last corner, finally close enough to see the bridge and the Tower's ground floor. Under the backdrop of the flames, he found great relief in seeing who ran toward him across the bridge.

*Pel!*

Without words, she jumped into his arms. The two of them shared a moment of peace amid the avalanche of noise and smoke and fire and dragon and smoldering Tower ruins.

Pel's safety confirmed, Garret noticed that she had been accompanied by, perhaps, the five most beautiful women he had ever seen. But their beauty was not the most remarkable thing about the way they looked. Four of them were dressed like red mages, wearing red pants and tunics that were obviously sized for other people.

Garret sensed a threat. The redhead looked like she wanted to kick someone's ass. Her eyes were wide and alert, her shoulders tense, as if to strike. It was the same body language he saw in people right before a bar fight.

Why was Pel even with them? She was supposed to be out of the Tower hours before—

The dragon in the background roared, reminding everyone that it hadn't finished its visit to Ruby. In fact, it had finally pulled ahead in its struggle against the Tower and its occupants.

The beast seemed far too graceful for its size. Garret watched the way it traversed the Tower's crumbling face.

Its hind legs had torn an opening in the wall, and almost immediately, it had inverted itself to bury its head into the hole. Its shoulders ducked in and out, as if it were a bird digging out grubs from a rotted log.

A flash of fire followed. A moment later, its movement changed again. Rather than the excited pecking of earlier, there was a much more delicate, deliberate motion. Whatever it did, the dragon chose to be more careful than it had before.

The dragon's head emerged briefly, with something long and spindly in its mouth. The monster flicked its head and spat out whatever it held. The object soared across the moat, sprawling and tumbling before it landed with a sickening *splat* on one of Ruby's cobblestone streets. The monster was emptying the Tower of any occupants who were unfortunate enough to remain.

The dragon continued to rid the Tower of another six or eight defenders. Finally, it ducked its head back inside, emerging one last time with a large, rectangular shape held gingerly in its mouth.

Apparently satisfied with its efforts and its prize, the dragon crouched over its haunches and leapt from the Tower, toppling several heavy stones into the moat below. It flapped its heavy, broad wings a few times, climbing just enough to barely miss the tops of the Ruby buildings, but close enough to knock down loose shingles and anything that wasn't securely fastened.

And a moment later, it was gone.

The whole ordeal must have radiated in magic, because Pel's pale, terrified face matched the horror roiling in Garret's stomach. He grasped her hand. She squeezed back.

# The Encroachment on Ruby – Pel

Garret was observant. His years in the Thick had cultivated his instincts.

The dragon had left and Garret still had a mind to identify the greatest dangers in Ruby. He had subtly placed himself between Pel and her female entourage. Had she not seen it before, Pel might not have noticed the way he folded his arms to leave his right hand closer to the hilt of his sword.

Garret had never met Mica or her sisters, but he regarded them with the same caution given to the mysteries of the Thick. And knowing nothing else, he could see they had just come from the Tower. Never mind the fact that they were unarmed, barefoot, and their clothes suggested they were escapees or refugees. By every measure, they should have been completely unthreatening, yet his instincts prevailed.

Considering their plight, however, Pel knew they were far more likely to be the victims of violence than its perpetrators. She clenched Garret's hand until she got his attention. With a shake of her head, she indicated that these women were no threat.

"What next?" Pel asked, addressing Mica.

"We will buy, smuggle, or influence our way aboard any ship heading south," said Mica. She glanced at Garret before dismissing him as a concern.

"Find Bartlett, instead," Pel replied. "You met him earlier. He's the big, loud man with the large beard. He and his crew will allow no harm to come to you, even if they were to learn of what you are."

"What you are…" Garret echoed casually.

"From the pages of the 'monster compendium.' The *Succubus* entry, specifically," Mica said with a curtsy.

Garret's eyes nearly launched from his skull.

"That would explain why the lot of you are so incredibly beautiful!" he squealed. Almost as an afterthought, he added, "Please don't eat me."

Mica inhaled and held it for a moment. Rather than rebuke Garret, she addressed Pel.

"You know that it was Richard who wrote that compendium, yes? We have him to thank for how we are perceived and all the atrocities we suffer."

She turned back to Garret.

"Whatever it is you think you know, you are misinformed."

"I get that a lot." Garret sighed, the look on his face confirming that he got that a lot.

Pel reached across Garret's body and untied the coin purse that Deodin had given them in Netherby. It contained the standard gold and silver currency that could be used throughout the Crown. The contents would certainly be enough to ensure passage home for Mica's sisters, wherever home happened to be. She handed the purse to Mica.

"Take this, too," Pel added, slipping out from underneath her cloak.

There was a brief interchange between Mica and the other women, presumably as Mica updated them on the current situation. Pel didn't speak their language, but she noticed a change in the tone of the conversation. Instead of her sisters listening to instructions, they were talkative. Animated. Adamant. Mica seemed to be losing an argument.

"What is the concern?" Pel asked.

"They…" Mica replied slowly, as if she were conflicted. "They said they can make it back without me. If Bartlett can get them to the south, they can return home by themselves. But they want me to stay here."

"Why?" Pel prompted. "What do *you* want?"

"After I am confident that they are safely on their way, I want to meet Mathew at the docks when his ship returns," Mica said.

Pel flinched. She had grown rather fond of Mathew. He was a candle of decency in the darkness of the Tower.

"What do you want of Mathew?" Pel asked, concerned.

"Mathew," Mica said pointedly.

*Oh.* The second entendre caught up to Pel and a rush of blood flushed her cheeks. Garret chuckled. The tension of the moment defused, Pel directed them away before *The Maiden* could depart.

"Go. Tell Bartlett that he will not be invited to my wedding if anything happens to your sisters," she instructed. Mica nodded her thanks and led the women off to the docks.

Once they were left alone, Garret turned to face Pel. He looked at her with suspicion.

"What was that part about a wedding?"

# The Encroachment on Ruby – Garret

Garret finally had time to catch his breath. However, he was more overwhelmed by the moment than fatigued by his run from the northern wall.

A marauding horde of orcs. A rampaging dragon. The collapse of the Tower. The decimation of the red mages. A flock of succubi. He had lived an entire lifetime and never encountered any of those things. It had been an unforgettable night and dawn was still a few hours away.

"Are you hurt? And what happened to the orcs?" Pel grasped Garret's shoulder. He reached in to embrace her, but she held him at arm's length so she could look him over in the weak light of the burning Tower.

"I'm fine. The orcs were routed from the very start. They had no chance, even before our people opened the reservoir and flooded the northeast field. After that, though, the orcs may have suffered total losses."

"I arranged that flood," Pel said, astonished. "I didn't expect it to work."

"Really? Gods, Pel, you may have saved hundreds of lives. Or thousands. You funneled the attack into our deadliest defenses," Garret said.

Pel seemed disheartened by the news. He decided to try to cheer her up by putting things in perspective.

"If there are any orcs left to write songs, they'll write one

427

about how you ended their kind under an endless rain of arrows and a nightmarish display of death magic."

"I hope the slaughter of the orcs doesn't become my greatest legacy," she said flatly.

"Your turn," Garret prompted. "What happened in the Tower? Why were you there? Why was the dragon there? Did it glow with the magic? Did the succubi? And why didn't they have wings and tails? Because they're supposed to."

"I went back to help one of the women free her sisters from one of the red mages. He had been using them as slaves for his pleasure. Then the dragon attacked, but I don't know why," she said.

Another voice answered Pel's implicit question. Garret recognized the voice immediately. Deodin.

"The dragon attacked because Entorak promised her something in return for destroying the Tower," the god killer explained, emerging from behind one of the bridge's support pillars.

Well, if he *was* a god killer. Garret was undecided on the matter. He slipped the bow from his shoulder and nocked an arrow. Deodin's status as friend or foe was subject to debate.

Deodin frowned, clearly annoyed by Garret's reaction.

"Garret. Please. We both know you're right shitty with that thing. You're more likely to hit someone on the other side of town."

The god killer looked mostly as Garret remembered, even if he wore fuzzy kitten slippers and his tunic was now ridiculous *and* filthy. He no longer bore any markings on the inside of his forearm, nor did he look like a burned pile of bones.

"You are not as dead as I remember," Garret observed, his bow still drawn.

Deodin acknowledged the comment with a single, upturned eyebrow, a message that Garret was testing his patience. The god killer glanced over to Pel and his expression softened immediately.

"Pel. I'm so sorry." Deodin grimaced as he approached her. "It was the only way for them to move on. And for you to move on. Everyone had to believe it, most of all you."

By the time he had finished his apology, he was only an arm's length away. Pel fought back an angry, disappointed tear as Deodin gathered her in an embrace. A moment later, she pushed him back hard and swung at him clumsily, striking him near his shoulder. He made no move to defend himself.

"You could have told me! You should have told me! About the Keepers and your plan … all of it!"

Garret stepped in and offered an embrace that Pel accepted.

"You're a dick," he said over his shoulder. Garret wanted to comfort Pel, but he also felt his own storm of disappointment, resentment, and relief. All the while, the god killer (or perhaps not) stood looking lame and helpless. Garret continued.

"Wait. Why are you even here? The orcs? The dragon? Red mages? Flightless succubi? The Keepers of Men?"

Pel pulled herself out of Garret's arms and wiped off her cheeks with her forearm. "He's not a member of the Keepers of Men," she began thoughtfully. "That was just a way to tie up the loose ends. He needed a way to convince the mages to stop their pursuit. And to convince us to leave him alone for whatever he had to do. He planned something like that from the very beginning."

"That symbol—" he pointed to his bare arm "—is easy to produce and remove. One of the fallen mages served as my body double," Deodin said.

Garret nodded. The god killer's story was the obvious conclusion. Garret then realized that both Pel and Deodin had explained it all exclusively for his benefit.

"Well, now I'm offended," he complained.

Pel approached Deodin, this time with open arms. He returned the embrace, whispering another apology into her ear.

"It hurt, you know," she said with a sniffle, her head held sideways against his chest. "To lose you like that. But it was worse to second-guess who and what you were. I hated myself for being wrong about you."

"I'm sorry. It hurt to do it," he admitted. "It hurts now."

"And you were right, of course," she said, stepping back and wiping her eyes. "Entorak would have seen through it all, had you told us."

"Is he here? I expected to find him in the Tower." Deodin regarded the remaining half of the structure. After surveying it for a moment, he continued. "Tychryn tore that thing apart, didn't she?"

Garret flinched at Deodin's comment.

"The dragon? That thing has a name? And you know his name? And *he* is a *she?*"

"Tychryn is the mastermind behind all of this," Deodin explained. "She's the driving force behind the Encroachment. But the attack on the Tower is different. It makes this whole saga with the orcs, the Tower, and Entorak all the more interesting."

"What 'saga?'" Pel asked. "And yes, Entorak was in the entry foyer a few moments ago. He may still be there, if he's still alive."

"Oh, I'm sure the Universe saw fit to spare his life. I'm supposed to confront him," he replied. Deodin turned to face them. "I spoke with Tychryn, the dragon queen who ordered the orc attack. She explained that Entorak wanted her to attack the Tower. The orc Encroachment was going to happen regardless, but Entorak used it as an opportunity to destroy the Tower, something he could never have done by himself. Tychryn tried to kill him for it, which is why I want to talk to him."

"What?" Pel scoffed. "The idea of Entorak destroying the Tower makes as much sense as a captain sinking his own ship."

"Does that mean you don't want to come?" Deodin gestured to the other side of the bridge.

Garret glanced at the crumbling remains.

"Would that be safe?"

Deodin shrugged. "Would it be more dangerous than thousands of orcs, a dragon, red mages, and … did you say 'flightless succubi?' As in 'more than one?'"

Garret shrugged in return. Safety was a relative concept in the Crown tonight.

"Good talk, then," Deodin said.

Garret turned to walk across the bridge—and fell clumsily. It was a familiar sensation. He glanced at his feet to see that his boots had been fastened to each other.

# The Encroachment on Ruby – Pel

Pel had seen a great deal of magic since being granted her augmented eyesight. She had witnessed spellcasting and she grasped the principles as well as any non-mage could. But even with all of that, she could not explain Deodin's new aura.

There was no question: he was more powerful than before. Whatever he had done, wherever he had been, he had discovered or unlocked something new. Pel could hardly distinguish where the man ended and the magic began.

His aura swelled as he approached the front of the Tower. The door before them had been built as the primary entry to the most important building in the region. As such, it stood as several hundred pounds of wood and iron, all bound together and hanging on heavy hinges sunk into the stone frame.

A moment later, the door was no longer on those hinges as it scraped and crunched its way across the floor to the other side of the room. The various pieces of furniture that had previously occupied the space between that door and the far wall were now broken, scattered across the rest of the room, or both.

Deodin hadn't punched it with his fists. He hadn't thrown his shoulder into it. He had collected up a concentration of magic in his hands and applied it to the door in a smooth, graceful stroke. He had performed yet another feat of magic that had previously been impossible.

Pel was shocked. The level of destructive power would rival that of the dragon that had ravaged the Tower just a few minutes ago.

"Gods, man! You could bring down entire buildings."

"You'd think that. The Universe only lets me do things like this on certain color-coded doors, usually after the completion of a critical event. I'm only as powerful as the Universe wants me to be." He said this without rancor.

Pel and Garret looked at him, waiting for more explanation.

Deodin responded with a humorless, close-lipped smile and a slow nod.

"You know what? We're not going to talk about it. I'll see you inside." Before anyone could protest, he was gone.

Pel looked over to Garret, who stared through the vacant door frame with a wide-eyed, jaw-dropped expression that quickly morphed into an altogether childish, charming smile of wonder.

"Huh-huh."

A moment later, Deodin called for them to enter. Pel and Garret exchanged glances, both reluctant to go inside the precarious structure, even with a friendly god killer protecting them.

Pel hesitated, but Garret pleaded with his eyes. He wanted to go in.

She felt it too. The intense, burning curiosity of it all.

*How? Why?*

Those answers awaited within. They entered.

The room was reduced to near ruin. Whatever was not bolted down had been shaken to the floor. Cracks in the foundation snaked up the interior walls. The few remaining evertorches, now scattered recklessly across the floor, provided only meager light through the heavy dust lingering in the air.

Deodin stood out in all of this, his aura highlighting him from across the room, staring at something at his feet. Pel followed his gaze to a man curled up on his side, covered in chalky mortar and debris. He glowed in a faint, familiar magical aura.

Entorak.

Deodin's chest rose and fell visibly as he inhaled deep, intense breaths. He towered over Entorak, shoulders forward, fists clenched. He looked pissed.

Entorak lay on the floor, slumped against the wall of the Tower, near the desk where Pel had left him. He appeared conscious and breathing, but he wore little magic about him. He looked exhausted.

"What of the orcs?" Entorak asked, ignoring Deodin and directing the question to Garret.

"Slaughtered. Few, if any, ever made it to the wall," Garret returned.

"And Mica and the others?" Entorak asked, this time directing the question to Pel.

"Gone. You don't need to know the details," Pel replied.

Entorak's chuckle became a cough and he struggled to catch his breath.

"I understand," he said, "but, I am gladdened they are free."

Seemingly satisfied with his immediate concerns, he looked at Deodin. Entorak was a brilliant man, so he required neither time nor explanation to piece together what Deodin was and how he came to be standing in front of him.

"And you: I apologize for your, ah, death. Your ruse was convincing. Were circumstances different, I would so very much like to talk to you about magic," Entorak said, seemingly unthreatened by the way Deodin stood over him. If anything, he seemed to relish the ability to look a god killer in the eye. "As for Tyberius, your body double from the inn: at least he offered value in death."

"Why?" Deodin finally asked. His tone sounded like parental disappointment, as if he'd expected more, as if he expected better. When the mage didn't answer right away, he raised his voice and repeated, "*Why?*"

"It is a complicated story." Entorak strained to sit upright.

"I can make time," Deodin replied.

Entorak chuckled and smiled weakly.

"It seems you can do just that."

Now Pel vented her frustration. "You've avoided his question. Why? Why all of this?" She gestured to the ruin that surrounded them.

Entorak sighed.

"The red mages who overtook this Tower were a disease," he explained. "They were the worst of humanity, yet they came to dominate everything about this place.

"It wouldn't be enough to just leave it behind. I would have been just as guilty. I am just as guilty. The whole place had to fall. The literal Tower, yes, but also the red mages within. Our future world cannot live under the shadow of a place such as this."

Pel noticed the way he held his left hand in his right, as he often did, but for the first time she noticed the subtle movement of his right hand as it rubbed his left ring finger.

*He fidgets with a wedding ring that he no longer wears.*

Entorak noticed her expression and offered her a regretful smile.

"I didn't know what this place was, *what I was*, until after she died. My wife. It took that loss, that pain, to force me to see the truth of this place. For me to see the truth of myself. And to build enough resolve to do something about it."

The emotional fuel that drove Entorak was finally exhausted. Tears ran down his face.

"This had to end," he explained in a broken voice, gesturing to the Tower ruins. He required a few moments before he could compose himself enough to continue. "Tychryn was simply the means to make it happen. As the Thick began to swell toward an Encroachment, I saw the opportunity. An Encroachment was perhaps the one justification to arrange what—and who—was to be in the Tower when she came."

"How did you convince her to be a part of this?" Deodin asked. "She's not to be trusted, you know."

"I promised her a stash of enchanted items in exchange for destroying the Tower and mages inside. Ideally, those items would have been destroyed. But she would have razed Ruby had I not delivered them. My hope was that the world is better off having those relics stashed away in a dragon's lair, away from the red mages."

A quiet fell over the room. Pel's mind swirled with Entorak's account and how it played into the night's events. Garret and Deodin had yet to react, the two silenced by the weight of a ruined tower, a fallen horde, a mighty dragon, and an earth-shattering betrayal.

Pel chuckled sardonically.

She realized that she was the first of them to find Entorak's story believable. In fact, it was the only explanation that fit the facts as she knew them. From his arrival in Netherby to his involvement in the preparations for the Encroachment, everything Entorak had done was designed to bring about this exact set of circumstances. Tonight's series of calamities was a triumph. A testament to his resourcefulness and guile. A victory despite it all.

"You're not the villain," she said, astonished.

She wasn't speaking to him, or even Garret or Deodin. It was an admission to herself. Here she was, an expert in analysis, yet her own biases had prevented her from seeing any of this before. And now that she did, she was amazed.

Garret wasn't convinced.

"Isn't he a traitor somewhere in all of this? Conspiring with orcs and a dragon to attack Ruby and its people? Aren't we some of Ruby's people?"

Pel scoffed. "Who did he betray? An orc horde? A dragon? A Tower full of murderous red mages? In all of those cases, history will thank him. Furthermore, he bought us time and brought the dragon's threat into the light. The Crown can now prepare."

As the facts were revealed and she began to unwrap the clues of the previous weeks, she began to see how the Encroachment and Tychryn's attack would unfold. She started to understand the complexity of their situation. Tonight was not the end of the saga; the next pages of their story focused on what would come tomorrow.

Deodin narrowed his eyes. "You may be right. Had he done nothing, the Encroachment would still have happened. Ruby would have fallen and Tychryn would have seized the rest of the Crown. And beyond."

"Instead," Pel said, "the victory came at the cost of a handful of lives *and* he freed Ruby from the tyranny of the mage Tower. The only reason we are all alive and in a position to complain about it is because it worked! Because he did it," she pronounced, marveling at the delicate parts that led to this nearly impossible conclusion.

"So, then what?" Garret asked. "When the people of Ruby learn of this, do they crowd up to watch a victory parade or a trip to the gallows?"

They were all silent for a moment.

"If nobody knew your story, if nobody knew the truth, how would history remember tonight?" Pel asked Entorak quietly.

"An Encroachment. An opportunistic attack by a dragon," he replied, almost as if he had rehearsed it.

"Of course," she said. "And the people of Ruby? They united and rallied to bring about one of the most lopsided battles in history. And the red mages? They fought along with Ruby's citizens. They died defending Ruby from a dragon. History will remember tonight as a human triumph in the face of orcs and dragons. Congratulations and commendations all around."

Then she drew closer to Entorak and stared at him with severity.

"So, then. How will history remember *tomorrow*?"

The void of silence nearly sucked the life out of the room. Entorak didn't respond. When it was clear that he had no answer, Pel scowled. She felt annoyed.

"Tomorrow, or next week, or next month, Tychryn and her *real* army march on the Crown, since you helped her to topple the one institution that could hold her in check," she scolded.

"That's why she sent the assassins to kill you," Deodin said. "You're the only human who knows where to find her lair. With you dead, she would be free to finish her plans without being stopped by the likes of us."

Garret gave him a sideways look.

"By the likes of me," Deodin corrected.

"Tychryn's mobs will march on the Crown armed with the weapons *you* provided," Pel said venomously. "Tomorrow, Ruby faces a fresh economic and civil crisis, now that its power structure has collapsed. Ruby may be in greater peril than ever. Have your plans accounted for all of that? For *any* of that?"

Entorak slumped his shoulders, silent.

Clearly not. Pel was amazed and conflicted by all of it. Entorak and his story proved to be far more complex than she had conceived. He had brought ruin to the mage Tower, a fantasy she had harbored for years, but in doing so, he had armed an enemy that might prove to be even more threatening. She couldn't decide if he was a devil or a savior, a genius or a cretin. Had he saved Ruby? Or destroyed it?

Either way, she saw only one way out of the crisis. Ruby did not need anger or vengeance. Ruby needed solutions.

She stepped next to Entorak and helped him stand. As he gathered his feet beneath him, she brusquely straightened his clothes, dusted him off, and brushed aside the dust and debris that covered him. "You sought to atone, yes? Your goal was to right the wrongs of your past and free yourself from the guilt of your complacency?"

Entorak nodded meekly.

"You did none of that tonight," Pel lectured. "You will start on that path tomorrow."

# DAY
# 19

# Ruby (The Ruins of the Tower) – Deodin

Deodin didn't hate Pel's idea. The man who had engineered Tychryn's attack might be best suited to undo its effects.

History might still judge Entorak. Ruby might still find him guilty of crimes. For the moment, however, Ruby would need its most capable people to survive the aftermath of the Encroachment. Two of those people stood in this room. And Garret too.

*Encroachment*

- ☑ *Return to Ruby*
- ☑ *Find and defeat the orc infiltration unit*
- ☑ *Confront Entorak*

Tension filled the air as Entorak mulled over his fate. Garret had remained quiet for the entire duration, which meant that he was overdue to say something both silly and profound.

And poor Pel simply looked exhausted. The fatigue in her eyes reminded Deodin that she and the others did not enjoy the benefits of his stamina.

*Time to put the kids to bed.*

"Yes, yes, all of this is a total outrage. Please. Sit. Everyone." Deodin took charge, gesturing at the dusty remnants of the remaining serviceable furniture.

Once they realized he wasn't going to continue until everyone had taken their seats, Entorak, Pel, and Garret begrudgingly acquiesced. Entorak seated himself on a debris-covered plush chair while Garret and Pel found a nearby couch.

Once they had settled, Deodin cast a sleep spell, much like the one he'd used in Netherby. Entorak slumped over immediately, far too weak to be able to resist its effect. Pel slumped over as well, her head falling gently into Garret's lap. Garret fought against the magic but was impaired by its effects. He stirred slowly, a look of confused anger falling on his face.

"What the fuuuuu—" he slurred.

Deodin laughed. "Gods, Garret. Go to sleep. You need it. You all need it."

Normally, Garret's fighting spirit served him well. Right now, however, he and the others were all exhausted and needed to be fresh for tomorrow. This was not a polite suggestion. Deodin cast the spell again. Garret closed his eyes and relaxed. Pel started to snore.

As for Deodin, he seldom bothered to sleep. It was one of the perks of being *sheyaktu*, one of the occasional inconsistencies of the world that worked out in his favor. He sat down on a nearby footstool to share the night with them and ensure that no harm would come to them.

He sighed. The attack on Ruby had failed. The orcs had been routed. And yet the game had not come to an end. He felt saddened when a new set of imperatives came to his mind:

*The weight of the Crown*

☐  *Meet with the new caretakers of Ruby*

Considering Makee's knack for timing, Deodin decided to consult the purple book. He retrieved it from his pack and reviewed it in the weak light of the evertorches strewn about the floor. As he had anticipated, Makee had more to say.

---

*Here we are, nearing the end of your journey.*

*And no, not because you die. Our game sees fit to bend its rules for the poor bastards. Your story doesn't end in the jaws of the Big Bad. You will confront and slay him (or her). But you already suspected as much, didn't you?*

*Instead, there is a different, painful end to this game. When you heed my advice, and you are honorable and sensible enough to do exactly that, you'll realize that this end is bittersweet. The pain will come from the fact that you won't want it to end like this. But it must.*

*Go and talk with your new friends. You know, the ones who have woven themselves into the fabric of your life throughout this journey. The ones you have saved on more than one occasion. The ones who have, in turn, supported you. These people have made you realize that, despite the nonsense and flaws of this world, you must continue to play this silly game, if only for them.*

*It is my somber duty to tell you that you have one last act of selflessness. You have one more duty to them. One more duty to the world.*

*One last obligation of a poor bastard.*

---

# Outside of Ruby (The Harbor) – Mathew

One night. It had begun and ended in one night. Rather than a sense of triumph or relief, Mathew felt only anxiety, tension, and doubt.

Throughout the night, Mathew and Nils had watched the "battle" unfold from their perch atop the reservoir control gate. They had seen the torches progress toward the wall, only to be cut short as they came within a few hundred yards. They had seen bright explosions of light as the mages had illuminated the front lines. The unlucky attackers who survived the hailstorm of arrows had faced a worse fate, once they came within spell range. Mathew recognized the destructive war spells as they poured onto the battlefield.

The archers. The mages. The mud. The orc charge and their subsequent inability (or refusal) to withdraw. It culminated in what could rightly be regarded as nothing less than a total victory. Once the sun had fully emerged from the mountains, Mathew could comprehend the carnage that sprawled from the city wall and into the fields south of the Thick. So many orc bodies, but so little movement among them.

And then there was the Tower. Something had taken place there, as it seemed to explode at a few points in the night. However, with too little light, Mathew and Nils had no context to help them understand what had happened. When daylight finally arrived, the picture was more catastrophic than expected.

The top several flights of the tower seemed to have been scraped off, leaving crumbling, jagged edges that had once been sturdy, solid walls. Smoke still billowed from the structure. The once-pristine white façade was now charred by ash.

*Mica.*

She could take care of herself and Entorak had assigned her to Pelium Stillwater. She was in good hands. Furthermore, their instructions had been well defined: Mica should have been well clear of the Tower by the time it was attacked. Nevertheless, her plan to free her sisters was dangerous. Something might have happened to her along the way and Mica was precisely the type of person to disregard her own safety to accomplish her goals.

They had said their goodbye. They had shared their moment. She had explained that she would escape Richard and the red mages. If it took the rest of her life, she'd vowed that she would find him.

In truth, though, he hadn't been sure that either of them would survive the night.

"Think of it this way: it takes an army of orcs to separate us," were her last words to Mathew. He remembered her smile and fragrance.

It should have been a glorious sunrise over a triumphant Ruby. Instead, the aftermath of the battle was depressing. The only thing he took away from the previous night was melancholy.

He sighed, these thoughts whirling in his mind during a free moment shipboard. With their task completed and the battle over, Mathew, Nils, and the rest of the crew had sailed back downriver so that they could return to Ruby and assist in whatever relief efforts were necessary. Despite the overwhelming victory, there was little mirth on the decks.

The battle with the orcs seemed decisive, but there were still so many unanswered questions. Everyone on board had loved ones within Ruby's walls, any of whom could have fallen victim to a stray arrow or spear. A large creature had assaulted and nearly destroyed the mage Tower. As much as everything seemed to have been an overwhelming success, lingering pangs of doubt and concern hung in the air.

The mood changed as the ship emerged from the river into Ruby's bay. The tension and anxiety yielded to startled amazement—enough to force a collective gasp as they sailed into the harbor.

More sails dotted the bay than seemed possible. It teemed with vessels. One could almost walk from one end of the cove to the other, simply by stepping from ship deck to ship deck. So busy was the sea, Mathew and the others would have to wait another hour for harbor traffic to clear for them to dock.

The port also crawled with activity. As Mathew's ship awaited its turn, thousands of Ruby's people were in action, offloading and loading cargo or moving carts between ships and shore. It wasn't business as usual; it was business beyond anything approaching usual. Twelve hours before, an orc horde had beset the city. Now, it flowed with more life than Mathew had ever seen or even conceived.

And despite all that movement, the one thing he noticed, the thing that mattered most, had hardly moved at all.

She must have been standing at the edge of the docks long before Mathew's transport had come into view. There she was, a single point of stillness against a backdrop of endless activity. As the ships came and went through the commotion of harbor traffic, she had hardly moved.

Mathew and Mica were finally close enough to make eye contact.

*By the gods!* She looked more magnificent than his most lucid and lurid imaginations. Her hair shone in the morning sun, her eyes sparkled, and she waited with such a sincere smile—a smile meant for him—that it wiped away his fears and anxieties. It was impossible to worry about the concerns of tomorrow. She was the only thing that occupied his mind.

"Fookin' hells, man," Nils whispered, admiring the picturesque woman on the docks.

*Nils*, of all people. Nils had actually whispered.

The giant of a man tapped Mathew playfully with the back of his hand, nearly sending him off his feet. "She here fer you?"

"Yeah," Mathew replied, returning Mica's smile with one of equal sincerity and sparkle.

Nils threw his head back and laughed.

# DAY
## 20

# Ruby (City Hall) – Mica

Mica had grown to respect Pelium Stillwater. The woman had faced her fears and ventured into the Tower, even when she had the chance to escape. She had found the item that magically bound Mica's sisters. For a human, Pel was as trustworthy and competent as Mica had ever seen. And in the two days following the attack, Pel had become a primary leader in Ruby's recovery.

*But that doesn't automatically make her right.*

Yes, Richard had found his fate in the jaws of the dragon. Yes, the Tower was all but destroyed. Yes, the red mages were no more.

But that didn't mean that Ruby was free from their influence. Pel had not spent those agonizing weeks in the Tower. Pel had not seen the sins of red mages. Pel had not watched them abuse their power. The attack against the Tower was meaningless if the remaining mages simply re-established control over Ruby's affairs. Mica would judge for herself and act, if necessary.

She observed from the balcony of the council chambers. The city leaders were trying to steer Ruby toward recovery. The threat of the orcs having passed, their legitimate worries about the city's future remained. When the Encroachment had shone light on the Crown's immediate threat, they saw the other dangers lurking in the shadows, awaiting their turn.

*There he is.* Mica watched Entorak enter the room, accompanied by Mathew. The council had requested a representative from the mages. Two had come.

As Mathew had explained it to her, the red mages were no more. The other mages—those who had been positioned along the Tower's walls during the orc attack—had survived. But, without the Tower and the infrastructure it controlled, they were directionless and without any leadership.

*We'll see about that.* Regardless of everything that she had seen and everything she had been told, Mica fully expected Entorak to influence himself back into a position of power.

"Welcome back," Avram greeted the two mages warmly. "You're just in time. We were about to discuss how the mages planned to rebuild the Tower and what resources they would need."

"Well-timed indeed." Entorak took his seat at the table. "I have something to say."

*Ha!*

Mica briefly entertained how she would prevent Entorak from reassuming control over Ruby's affairs. Assassination seemed a bit much, but she wasn't above pushing any dissenting voices into taking a stand—

"I am here to announce the surrender of my day-to-day duties and responsibilities as a member of the council and a representative of the mages of Ruby," Entorak announced.

*Well. Shit.*

Mica's surprise was vocalized by those below on the council floor. Before they could bury him in questions, Entorak continued.

"The Tower weighed on me heavily. And now, I am free of that burden. It is time for Ruby's past to yield to Ruby's future," Entorak explained with a sigh.

With that, he made a two-handed gesture, pointing to Mathew as if he were presenting or introducing him.

"If I were indulged in a final act as a representative, I would nominate Mathew to serve as primary liaison to the mages of Ruby."

The announcement hung in the air until Mathew broke the silence.

"I am flattered, but I do not want a position of that sort," he said.

"All the more reason you should hold it. Too many others would seek it for the power it represents," Entorak replied.

*How appropriately pompous of him to say something like that.* Mica still expected a change of course in this conversation.

"The collapse of the Tower and its leadership created a hole that only you can fill. None of us have the tools," Pel said to Mathew with a smile. She was practically gushing with support. Her sentiments were obviously sincere.

Mica chuckled. Pel had praised Mathew as much as Entorak had. Yet, it sounded so much better when she said it.

"And don't be so modest," Avram added. "We haven't forgotten how much you united Ruby under the Encroachment. We are less interested in what you seek and more interested in what you provide. Ruby needs leadership. And you have demonstrated it."

The council members put it to an official vote, with nearly every representative raising their hand to confirm the nomination. Present but distracted, Nils missed the chance to vote because he was too busy pouring an enormous tankard of ale down his throat during the brief election.

Mathew seemed dazed as his fellow council members took their turns with congratulatory handshakes. He was gracious and sincere in expressing his gratitude. Mica smiled. He was a very capable human, even if he was occasionally naïve. His reaction to all of this was cute and endearing.

When the council moved on to other business, Mathew looked across the room to her with an accusatory glower. He was fully aware of her magical pushing skills and her history of ethical flexibility. She smirked and shook her head, informing him that she had done nothing to make his appointment happen.

He rolled his eyes with a shrug and a sigh, apparently accepting his fate.

She could have pushed them, of course. She would have certainly considered it in the past. Recently, however, she had grown to value Mathew's moral guidance. In this case, she let the humans decide their own fate.

They had chosen well.

# DAY
# 21

# Ruby (City Hall) – Pel

Pel yawned.

It was late, and the day had been spent in a long meeting with Ruby's most prominent decision makers. She glanced at Mathew. Appointed only yesterday, he had taken ownership of his role as the city's leading mage. The role suited him, and after years of the red mages, the city deserved him.

As news from the Encroachment trickled in, these representatives offered proposals on how to proceed, to address both the immediate needs and plan for the long-term future. Despite their different values and goals, the work was productive. It was meaningful. Pel felt a sensation she had nearly forgotten: hope.

The day wound down. Only the council members remained, including Mathew, Avram, and a few representatives of the trade guilds and commerce unions.

With the day's work at an end, Pel closed her eyes and gave an exhausted but satisfied sigh.

Tomorrow's Ruby promised to be greatly different from yesterday's. It promised to be better. She opened her eyes to find herself surrounded by the council members.

"Gods, what did I do?" Pel asked.

"Congratulations!" said Avram with no hint of sarcasm or insincerity. "The council has decided to create and fund a new position. You've been elected to serve as Ruby's prime minister."

"Elected by whom?" she replied, shocked.

"The likes of us." Avram smiled and gestured to their compatriots. "Ruby needs someone to settle disputes, mediate conflicts, and be an objective party to our various interests. Rather than argue every minute detail among ourselves, the only thing we could agree on is that you would be ideally suited for that role."

"Ruby is a delicate machine made up of an untold number of moving parts. You are the only person who understands that machine," Sam explained.

"I—I am flattered," Pel stammered. "But I could never accept such a position."

"Ha!" Mathew exclaimed, playfully indignant. "When they conscripted me into the counsel, your exact words were, 'This is a hole that no one else can fill. We simply don't have the tools.' That applies tenfold to you."

Avram reassured her with his calm demeanor and a genuine smile. "We wouldn't ask it of you if it were beyond your skills. And if any of us could do it, we would. The list of viable candidates had only one name."

She studied the faces of the counsel to see if there was any way out of their decision. The role they described seemed to be far too much for someone like her. That type of power was suited for other people. More important people.

"Oy! Go get the ale and wine for the celebration. And cups. Until then, leave her be," Garret called out.

He forced his way to the front of the crowd, squeezed himself between Avram and Sam, and pushed each of them out of the way. He stopped pushing when he stood next to Nils. Conventional wisdom would demand that Garret keep his hands to himself.

He looked up. "You too. Please? Sir?"

Nils paused for a moment before responding with a toothy grin through his beard.

"Ya heard 'em! Fookin' clear out! And bring me another ale. A big one." He stomped off and threw himself down in a chair to wait.

Rather than argue against Nils or his demands, the crowd dispersed, leaving with well-wishes and congratulations. Soon, only Garret remained near Pel. He pulled up a chair and sat across the desk from her.

"Minister," he smirked.

"Gods, Garret, don't you start on me too." Pel held her hands up defensively.

Garret picked at the calluses on his hands absently as he spoke.

"Where did you think this would go, Pel? The red mages and their Tower are no more. Their influence is gone. Who would you rather see making the difficult decisions about Ruby's future? Who is better equipped? Tell me his name and I'll do my best to give him the job."

"I'm not important enough. I'm not significant enough," she protested.

"Your vote would have made the tally twenty-one to two, then. Not enough to change the outcome," Garret smiled.

"Oh? Who else voted against me?" she asked, suddenly curious.

"Fucking Saul from the Trade Cabal. He nominated and voted for himself, the self-serving bastard," Garret scoffed.

"I'm not ready for something like this," Pel whispered.

She believed it. She was confident within her professional space, but that didn't mean that she could shoulder the burden of responsibility of being Ruby's most pivotal caretaker. She was comfortable working in the cast, not the lead role.

Garret stopped fidgeting and regarded her. "As we fled Netherby, we were talking about Entorak and how he pushed the villagers into fleeing. Do you remember?"

"Of course," she replied.

"You said you didn't think that you would've had the courage to make the decision he did. You would have left them to their fate. A fate you knew to be doomed. You would have sacrificed over seventy lives rather than make that decision."

"I remember."

She recalled their conversation, but more importantly, she remembered how that discussion had made her feel. She remembered how much she disliked herself for being so timid and passive, too afraid to make such a difficult decision.

"And now: if you had Entorak's magical pushing powers, and if a similar circumstance came up again, what would you do?"

"I would push the whole bloody lot of them out of Netherby as soon as I could," she admitted.

"Then you are ready to lead, Pel," he said quietly.

Garret was right. The council was right.

Ruby's factions would splinter and become violent without someone managing their conflicting interests. A civil war was possible. Beyond that, the threat of Tychryn still hung over the city.

Too much was at stake to let her fears and insecurities about herself stand in the way of what she needed to do and who she needed to be. She straightened in her chair and smoothed out the wrinkles in her shirt.

"*Madam* Minister," she corrected.

# DAY
# 24

# Ruby (City Hall) – Pel

In the three days since her appointment to minister, Pel lost her sense of time. Today, she had spent the entire morning at her desk, navigating a stack of tasks and challenges related to the city's multiple crises. By the time she looked up, it was late afternoon and time for another meeting.

Throughout it, she thrived.

The council had made no mistake when electing Pelium Stillwater to her position. While she was new to budgeting and resource management, she was completely knowledge-able about every person, organization, and entity that was best suited to address nearly any given problem.

However, her vast, intimate knowledge of these people made some decisions more difficult. Especially if the decision were to come at the expense of someone she had grown to respect. Like her upcoming appointment.

Pel's aide announced her visitor before excusing himself with a modest bow. Entorak waited for her on the other side of her desk. His aura had diminished so much it was hardly noticeable. He had not been using magic recently.

"Madam Minister," he said with a gracious nod.

His gesture was authentic. And in hindsight, she real-ized that he had always been sincere. She had assumed his mannerisms were the result of a cultivated persona, a veneer that misdirected who he really was. But during the past few weeks, in her dealings with him, she realized something was wrong with how she saw the world. And how she saw him.

She gestured for him to sit. He obliged.

"The irony comes in the fact that your shitty spell clouded my judgment in addition to my eyes," Pel said.

Entorak squirmed slightly in his chair. "That is a curious way to begin a conversation."

She smiled wryly. "I'm not afforded time for pleasantries. The days are spent addressing the problems of the people. They all have an equal right to my attention. Forgive me if I have to get right to it."

Entorak nodded and gestured for her to continue.

"I hated the Tower. I hated the mages. I hated you. Every time I looked at the Tower, I was filled with dread, anxiety, and resentment. And then this happened."

She gestured to her surroundings, referring to the series of events that led them here. "Despite my vision, I've had to re-learn that everything is not so black and white. The world. Our involvement in it. Your involvement in it. There is gradient and texture that I didn't see at the time. I can only see it now."

She slid a small stack of paper across the table. Entorak collected it and began to review the pages. She summarized the content for him.

"This is how the history books will remember this Encroachment. The substance of it speaks to the ills of the Tower and how the red mages used fear and intimidation to dictate policy and influence decisions. It speaks of the abuses at the hands of people like Richard and Tyberius. It speaks of crimes that went unpunished and the justice that was never served.

"And then it speaks to your involvement. How you manipulated a gods-damned dragon to come in and bring an end to the Tower's reign. It speaks to the night of ten thousand deaths, with only a handful of them being the good people of the Crown. It speaks of Entorak, who shall be forever known as 'The Mastermind.'"

She paused, softening slightly.

"The name was Garret's touch, I'll confess. With all of our landmarks and historical figures bearing a pithy nickname, he wanted to continue the tradition when referring to you."

Entorak sat still for a moment, clearly taking it all in. "My nickname, however, is subject to interpretation. Am I a hero or a villain? A sinner or a savior?"

She slid another page across the table to him. It was the next page of the history lesson.

"You're both. History will also remember you as the man who risked the lives of the Crown for his personal agenda of revenge. As much as 'The Mastermind' freed Ruby and its people from the oppression of the red mages, he did it for all the wrong reasons and in all the wrong ways. You're welcome to read it, but I think it is a fair and accurate assessment."

She reached across her desk and pulled a pen from its ink well. She began to sign another paper. He looked at her with curiosity but said nothing.

"Therefore, with this order, the minister of Ruby will exile Entorak of Ruby, also known as 'The Mastermind,' from the Crown. History will remember that he was banned from the region and fled to the south. There, he died alone, destitute, and miserable. A fitting end to the man who came within a breath of destroying Ruby under a dragon's fire."

She reached into a drawer and pulled out a moderately sized sack, which she tossed on the desk in front of him. It clinked like a bag of coins and sounded heavy.

"Interestingly and unrelatedly, history will also record that a bald, bearded man arrived in the burned remnants of Andwyn with the ambitions of rebuilding the village. He anonymously invested heavily in the town and its people, financing much of its rebuilding efforts.

"The man lived his life as a recluse and was seldom seen by anyone travelling through Andwyn. Instead, he spent his time as the village's teacher, sharing his wisdom with the children and teaching them how to best use their minds. Interestingly, this man knew so little about magic that he could hardly pronounce the word, let alone practice the craft. Years later, he died peacefully and was missed by everyone who was touched by his life." She allowed a corner of her mouth to turn upward.

Entorak sat silently for a few moments. His eyes were moist as he struggled to maintain composure. He spoke softly.

"Thank you. Truly. And I am confident that Ruby will fare so much better under your guidance. But as for Andwyn, I don't believe I deserve that fate."

Pel scoffed.

"Now you are the one seeing the world in black and white. You deserve both fates."

\* \* \*

A day of meetings had concluded with Ruby's prominent decision makers.

The *other* prominent decision makers, Pel reminded herself. She still had difficulty accepting that she had become someone with meaningful influence.

With the meeting over, the council chamber was left largely vacant. Under the soft light of the candles on the far side of the table, Mathew sat before a ledger and documented the day's promises and plans.

As Pel picked up one of the empty wine carafes, Deodin appeared right next to her, seemingly from nowhere.

"Gods, man! Don't do that!" she squeaked.

"No, do it again!" Garret complained. His back had been turned when the god killer made his entrance and he had missed what Pel had found so alarming.

"It seems as if the city is in good hands, Madam Minister," Deodin noted.

Nearly a week had passed since the orc attack. This was the first time that she had seen Deodin. She had presumed he'd turn up sooner or later, once his *sheyaktu* business had reached its conclusion.

They shared a brief embrace. In the previous days, Deodin had been able to finally replace the haggard clothes that he had worn throughout his journeys. He was dressed in a sleek green-and-black outfit with matching breeches and tunic. The ensemble was sharp enough to pass as formalwear, yet practical enough for proper adventuring. He looked like a god killer.

"How long have you been here?" Pel asked, before continuing to clear the meeting's clutter. "How much of all of that did you see?"

"Enough to be impressed. By the city leaders and representatives. By you." He smiled.

Pel wanted to catch up with him but was distracted by the way Deodin shifted his weight. Hesitation, reluctance, uncertainty. He was to be the bearer of bad news.

"What?" she asked as a swell of anxious concern overcame her.

"Tychryn will soon equip her army with prizes she claimed from the Tower," he said. "She will return with more mobs armed with those treasures. She wants no less than to burn Ruby to the ground, then do the same to Tristan."

After a pause, he added his analysis to the situation.

"Her army falls apart without their general."

She considered Deodin's news. The red mages had been unable to withstand her attack and they were the most lethal of Ruby's magical defenses. The mages who remained would be no match. Likewise, Ruby's archer corps were suited for volley fire over the wall, but they would be a perfect target for a dragon's fire breath if they were to line up in a similar battery. A dragon was simply too much for Ruby. A dragon was simply too much everything in the Crown.

Everything except a god killer. Pel looked to Deodin with a profound feeling of guilt. Ruby needed to ask the unthinkable of him.

*She* needed to ask the unthinkable of him.

# Ruby (City Hall) – Deodin

*The weight of the Crown*

☑ *Meet with the new caretakers of Ruby*

Deodin recognized the look on Pel's face. It was certainly not the first time that someone had contemplated how to send him on a suicidal quest.

But this was her first time.

Up until this point, she had walked in the periphery of his adventuring and hadn't been an active piece in the game. But following the changes to Ruby and her rise to a position of responsibility, she had a greater duty than to her friendship with him. The duty weighed on her.

"You can ask, Pel," Deodin said softly.

She swallowed hard. The words did not come easily. But to her credit, when she finally composed herself enough to speak, her voice did not waver.

"You must defeat her before she can make her attack. You are the only one who can prevent the total destruction of Ruby and the people of the Crown."

He raised his hand for her stop. He wanted to skip to the end of this conversation rather than watch her struggle to maintain her composure. It was hard for her.

And it was equally difficult for him.

"For the Crown," he said with a sincere bow.

"For the Crown." She returned his bow.

*The final conflict*
- ☐  *Journey to Tychryn's lair*
- ☐  *Defeat Tychryn*
- ☐  *Return to Ruby*

# Ruby (City Hall) – Pel

Until now, Garret had been reclining on one of the chairs, out of everyone's way. He had remained silent until Pel assigned their friend to a suicide mission. "You want to send him to confront a dragon? In her lair? Deep in the heart of the Thick? By himself?"

Before he could continue, she cut him off. "Garret…"

He dismissed her with a shake of his head and exhaled sharply through his nose in frustration. He looked to Deodin. "Can you do it?"

Garret's words stabbed Pel's heart. His question came with none of the childlike enthusiasm he had displayed every other time he had asked a similar question. This was no longer a silly, speculative game of "who-would-win."

This was Garret asking if he would ever see his friend again.

"'God killer,' remember? A dragon should be no match," Deodin said, minus any of the charm or warmth that should accompany such a quip. There was no smile, no chuckle, no reaction that would make this conversation any better. Any easier.

Mathew took a step forward to inject himself into the conversation.

"Come to my office when you are ready. Entorak left a map for you. And there may be other mage resources at your disposal."

Mathew nodded goodbye, then bowed as a way of excusing himself. After collecting his belongings, he made his way to the aisle that led out of the chamber. A few moments later, the door's heavy latch clanged loudly, echoing through the still, tense air that filled the room.

A weight of melancholy fell over Pel. Her shoulders sagged as she returned to the table and organized her belongings. She felt the burden of responsibility and duty that she now carried. She also felt the heavy weight of the personal costs of that responsibility.

"It seems I have become a pawn of this game you play with the Universe," she said with a defeated sigh. "I didn't believe it when you first said it, but when adventures and perils don't find you by themselves, people like me assign them to you."

"And it means so much more for it to come from you," Deodin assured her. "Besides, with your new position, you have the riches of Ruby to help fund my reward. I still want the black tunic from the merchant in the Evertorch district. Without having to complete a dozen side quests along the way."

She looked back at him. Aside from the clothing and hairstyle improvements, he looked much like he had on the night she first met him—calm, confident, and capable.

"I don't know why I'm worried. There is precisely one being in this world powerful enough to punch a dragon in the face," Pel said. "I just wish it didn't have to be you."

"If you're going to punch a dragon anywhere, you should punch him in the balls," Garret said, his eyebrows raised as if discovering a profound battle strategy.

Both Deodin and Pel replied instantly, reminding Garret that the dragon in question was female.

Garret amended his statement. "In the hoo-haa, then."

"I don't have a good way to explain this, but I will win the fight. I expect a battle with fiery explosions, a collapsing ceiling, and other assorted bullshit, but I will defeat her and whatever minions come to her aid."

Pel sighed, this time with a measure of contentment. Somewhere, considering everything that she had witnessed and everything that she had experienced, she knew he was right.

"I should hope so. You can stop time, after all," she said.

"Wait, you can stop time?" Garret nearly exploded in shock. He seemed prepared to carry on about that detail, but he wound down nearly as quickly as he had gotten spun up. "That explains pretty much everything, actually."

Deodin laughed. The hard lines in Pel's brow relaxed to a resting state. This situation was absurd. Her solution was absurd. Their entire world was absurd. Garret's remarks just served to remind them of it.

Deodin reached into his pocket and pulled out a leather pouch the size of a large potato. It was full and wrapped tightly in a long leather strap. He tossed it over to Garret, who caught it delicately. It crunched as if it were a pouch of beans or rice.

"This is our goodbye, at least for now," Deodin said with a sigh.

Pel forced herself to smile as Garret untied the pouch and peered inside.

"Are these ... uh ... real?" he asked. After a moment of thought, he added a second question in a whisper. "Are they stolen?"

Garret pulled out a gem to show to Pel. The contents of that purse would amount to a true fortune, much as Deodin had originally promised.

"Plundered from the many ruins and tombs of the Thick and the East. As for them being stolen: if their rightful owners return from the dead to claim them, you have a larger set of problems," Deodin replied.

Garret responded with a "huh-huh" and a childish grin. The smile faded. "You say that as if it were a possibility."

Deodin offered no other answer to Garret's concern.

"As for you," Deodin said, turning to Pel. He produced another pouch. "Open this, please. I don't like touching it."

She obliged him and withdrew a grey, polished rock set to a clasp, connected to a fine chain. A necklace. Considering the pouch that he had just presented to Garret, this seemed odd. The rock was simple. About the size of a flattened, irregular grape, it was completely unremarkable—

No, it *is* remarkable.

Her hands had changed. Color! The blue tint had vanished. She stared down at the pendant in puzzlement, oblivious to the silent instruction that Deodin had panto-mimed to Garret: *Help her put it on.*

Garret delicately took it out of her hands by the chain, finding its clasp. Pel pulled her hair out of the way while Garret gingerly draped it around her neck. She looked at him in curiosity for a moment, before gasping suddenly and reflexively covering her mouth with her hand.

Garret's eyes were brown.

She knew this, of course, but she hadn't seen their true color in many years. And not just his eyes! She could see the color in everything else. The lighter tone of a small scar on his face. The green-and-brown combination of his clothes. A few of the hairs on his head and face had started to gray.

She turned to Deodin, who no longer shed a magical aura. He stood there as plainly as any other person. And like Garret, she did not see him in her dreary, monochromatic world. This rush of color came with a visual clarity that she had all but forgotten. She had not yet reclaimed her voice from the shock of it all, so Deodin preemptively answered her questions.

"That stone is worth more than everything in that other pouch," the god killer explained. "Skycrash brought magic to the world, but also things that refuse magic. It is called a 'null-stone.' It exists in a field that prevents magic. This includes your ability to see it, if the stone is close enough to your eyes. Whether you consider your eyesight a gift or a curse, you can be free from it for as long as you wear the necklace."

"I don't know what to say," Pel whispered, fully appreciative of the magnitude of the gesture. She slid the nullstone around so that it hung on her back, draped her arms around Deodin and buried her head in his chest.

She had so much to say, but she found herself overcome by such profound emotion that it choked her throat and flooded her eyes.

Her life had changed when she met Deodin. He had been at the center of those changes, whether it was her newfound relationship with Garret, the dramatic shift in the dynamics of Ruby, or this incredible gift.

And more importantly, Pel herself had evolved. At the end of it all, following the drama, intrigue, and calamity, she liked who she had become. And now, he was leaving? Possibly never to return? Could words express a fraction of that emotion, let alone all of it?

She pushed back and shooed him away for a moment. Tears trickled down her cheeks. There was simply no room in her throat for words to escape.

"Thank you," Garret said. "For everything."

Pel turned to him to see that he spoke for both of them. His eyes were also teary, moved by both Deodin's gift and the effect it would have on Pel. He was also aware of the significance of Deodin's goodbye.

Her laugh was a burst of emotional release from everything that presently overwhelmed her. Deodin reached out to shake Garret's hand, but Garret would have none of it. The two shared a farewell embrace.

"Try not to die," Garret said.

"Right in the hoo-haa," Deodin replied, making an uppercut gesture with his fist.

Pel smiled but no longer felt like laughing. The moment was far more bitter than it was sweet.

And suddenly, Deodin was gone. Pel and Garret stood alone in the council chamber. It took a moment for her to realize what had happened.

"Gods, is that what it's like when he does that?" she asked with a sniffle. She wiped her eyes. "That's unnerving."

Garret looked down to his feet. She followed his gaze. His boots were fastened together.

# DAY
# 31

# The Thick (Tychryn's Lair) – Deodin

It had taken a week to reach Tychryn's lair, despite Entorak's map. Predictably, Deodin had been delayed by countless mobs and a few unavoidable side quests. Finally, he was near the end of his journey. The great dragon seemed to expect him; he could see her stirring at the far side of the cavern as soon as he passed through the lair's entrance.

"Do you want to send out your minions now or during the fight?" Deodin asked as he set down his pack.

*The final conflict*

- ☑ *Journey to Tychryn's lair*
- ☐ *Defeat Tychryn*
- ☐ *Return to Ruby*

Tychryn moved with snakelike fluidity as she took to her feet and spread her tremendous wings. She arched her back to demonstrate her fearsome size and eyed him with glaring, narrow eyes. Her lips parted to bare a sadistic, hateful sneer.

"FOOL! Your flesh will be the first to burn!"

"Mmm-hmm," Deodin agreed absently as he looked over the chamber. For being a giant, world-ending monster, Tychryn had an eye for décor and interior design. She had carved out her lair on the eastern side of the mountain, behind a roaring waterfall. Light refracted through the stream, glinting off the piles of treasure and creating an eerie, flickering lighting effect. Three sections of the large cave were bathed in direct sunlight. They formed a triangle, with Tychryn at the center.

Deodin sighed. The contextual clues suggested that the rest of the floor would crumble away, leaving only those three spots. Certainly, he was expected to jump from platform to platform, dodging the fire, striking at the dragon, fighting minions—

*Bullshit*, he complained, reminded of Rule #5.

"Oh! Does this strike fear in you, by the way? I found the 'Dragon Spear of … of …'" Deodin hoisted an enormous polearm over his head to show her. However, he drew a blank on the weapon's proper name.

A slight burn of embarrassment flooded his face and neck. Here he was, threatening the ultimate boss, and he had forgotten the name of the artifact infused with special dragon-killing bullshittery.

He had seized it from yet another dungeon on his way to Tychryn's lair. It was a truly legendary halberd, larger and more ornate and elaborate than every other weapon of its type. Considering how difficult it was to obtain, it was a weapon he would wield for a great while. Yet, its name escaped him.

*Shit.*

"…The Dragon Spear of stabbing you to death!" he proclaimed, holding it proudly above his head, having decided it was better to say something asinine than nothing at all.

Tychryn made another remark about him being a fool but seemed otherwise unconcerned with anything Deodin said or did.

Deodin retrieved the pickaxe from his pack (Rule #1) and rested the dragon-slaying artifact on the stone floor (Rule #3).

As he had anticipated, the lighting and atmosphere changed as Tychryn began to posture and speak. He would have a moment to himself as she started her monologue.

"So, you chose to die here today? You don't want to savor the few remaining days and perish with the rest of humankind?" She spread her magnificent wings in an intimidating display, then continued with a self-indulgent speech about death and terror and fire and all the things that appealed to her values and sensibilities. The boss monologue was always more for their benefit than his.

As she spoke, Deodin used the pick to dig out a deep and narrow hole. It was just wider than the shaft of the polearm. Satisfied, he drove the hilt of his halberd into the hole, lodging it so firmly he would need to dig it back out again.

When the work was complete, the spear jutted out of the ground at a modest angle, the blade standing at about the height of Deodin's head. Satisfied, he stood in front of the weapon, between its blade and the dragon before him. Tychryn had not yet finished, though she had moved on from talking about herself, focusing now on the doom that would befall the Crown, then the rest of the world.

"—as my army marches towards your pitiful—"

Deodin picked up a fist-sized rock and flung it as hard as he could. "I'm ready," he said as he heaved.

The rock struck her in the head, mid-prattle. For the first time, she seemed to notice. Not because the attack caused any damage, but because the gesture had been so unexpected, so unprecedented, and so breathtakingly rude. Her eyes widened in absolute shock and legitimate outrage.

"Such … such…" she stammered, clearly never having been so insulted or offended.

"Insolence? Impudence? That's what someone like you would normally say," Deodin suggested. He threw another rock, to ensure that he exceeded all insolence and impudence tolerances. It connected with her forehead with a satisfying *thok*.

This time, her eyes widened with rage. She didn't berate or insult him. She reacted with the impulsive, barbaric violence of an enraged dragon. Following a roar, she lowered her head and charged, using her wings to provide additional power in her acceleration.

When she got close enough, Deodin dilated time and sidestepped her lunge. She ran into the halberd that he had buried into the ground. Her own momentum drove its blade deep into her heart.

She should have died right there. The blow was certainly fatal and considering the magical power of—

*FuryThunder? No, that's something else. I suffered through such a long and tedious questline to get it, too.*

—the artifact, she should have died painfully, awfully, and instantly. Instead, she took to the sky, flew a gratuitous lap around the top of the chamber, then crashed into the middle of the room. Following a spasm and one last curse, she slumped over dead. The lighting in the cavern returned to normal.

*Such bullshit.*

*The final conflict*
- ☑ *Journey to Tychryn's lair*
- ☑ *Defeat Tychryn*
- ☐ *Return to Ruby*

\* \* \*

Makee's purple book had a few final words. Deodin had an idea of what they would be, but he wanted to read them anyway.

---

*Be sure to loot the chamber of the Big Bad. That obscene pile of gold in the corner will inexplicably fit in your bag. And you'll want a mountain of riches, even if you've never wanted such a thing before.*

*Because after you return this book to where you found it, you're done. No more adventuring. No more questing. No more heroics. Following the defeat of the Big Bad, the last act for the poor bastard is to return to your home city and meet with your friends. And after a few months of peace, another Big Bad will emerge and threaten the Crown, the world, or the entire cosmos, or whatever.*

*The pattern will never end. We both know that given enough time, all your friends and loved ones will be lost to your adventuring.*

*Therefore, you cannot return to your city and complete that final quest. To complete the quest is to set the next one in motion. For this cycle to stop, you must stop. The only way to win the game is to stop playing it.*

*And that is why you are a poor bastard.*

*Your final act of heroism will be to abandon those friends without even saying goodbye.*

---

Deodin closed the book. He had already concluded what Makee had explained. He already knew that to leave the current quest unfinished was the only way to prevent another quest.

Yet Deodin found himself smiling as he scooped piles of treasure into his bag. As brilliant and helpful as Makee had been, he was only the first generation of god-killing heroes, the first of the poor bastards.

Makee had never considered that any of his successors might be better at playing the Universe's ridiculous game.

Makee had never considered that someone could win.

# EPILOGUE
## MONTHS LATER

# The Western Isles – Deodin

"I fuckin' hate the sea," Garret cried out.

He looked pallid. The stains on the side of *The Maiden's Tears* suggested that he and his stomach had disagreed about what to do with his lunch. He held his right hand to his gut and directed his left hand to offer Deodin a rude gesture.

Meanwhile, Pel was beaming.

"Why would you pay to bring the entire wedding party, the guests, and the bloody caterers to the Western Isles?" Pel called out from the deck, cupping her hands over her mouth to amplify her voice. She stood next to Bartlett and Garret, with a great number of people behind her.

The dockhands hustled to moor *The Maiden* and help the passengers disembark. While they waited to come ashore, Pel pointed to landmarks and sights in the distance, tugging on Garret's arm. She was radiant, so happy and excited on the eve of their wedding.

She called out to Deodin again. "It would have made so much more sense for you to simply come to Ruby!"

*The final conflict*

☑ *Journey to Tychryn's lair*
☑ *Defeat Tychryn*
☐ *Return to Ruby*